...pher Fowler's
... May mysteries

'Quirky and original . . . the relationship between
Bryant and May is done brilliantly'
Mark Billingham

'Imagine the *X-Files* with Holmes and Watson in the place of
Mulder and Scully, and the books written by P. G. Wodehouse,
and you have some idea of the idiosyncratic and distinctly
British flavour of the Bryant & May novels'
Black Static

'What Christopher Fowler does so well is to
merge the old values with the new . . . he's giving
us two for the price of one'
Lee Child

'Fowler, like his crime-solvers, is deadpan, sly,
and always unexpectedly inventive'
Entertainment Weekly

'I love the wit and playfulness of the Bryant & May books'
Ann Cleeves

'Invests the traditions of the Golden Age of detective fiction
with a tongue-in-cheek post-modernism'
Evening Standard

'One of the quirkiest and most ingenious pleasures
to be found in the genre: atmospheric, sardonically
funny and craftily suspenseful'
Barry Forshaw

'Witty, sinuous and darkly comedic storytelling
from a Machiavellian jokester'

BRYANT & MAY
The Lonely Hour

CHRISTOPHER FOWLER

BANTAM BOOKS

TRANSWORLD PUBLISHERS
61–63 Uxbridge Road, London W5 5SA
www.penguin.co.uk

Transworld is part of the Penguin Random House group of companies
whose addresses can be found at global.penguinrandomhouse.com

Penguin
Random House
UK

First published in Great Britain in 2019 by Doubleday
an imprint of Transworld Publishers
Bantam edition published 2020

A CIP catalogue record for this book
is available from the British Library.

ISBN
9780857504081

Typeset in 10.23/12.12pt Sabon by Jouve (UK), Milton Keynes.
Printed and bound in Great Britain by Clays Ltd, Elcograf S.p.A.

Penguin Random House is committed to a sustainable
future for our business, our readers and our planet. This book
is made from Forest Stewardship Council® certified paper.

MIX
Paper from
responsible sources
FSC® C018179

1 3 5 7 9 10 8 6 4 2

For Darrell and Lesley, bon vivants

There are two places in the world where men can most effectively disappear – the city of London and the South Seas.

HERMAN MELVILLE

All the wonders lie within a stone's throw of King's Cross Station.

ARTHUR MACHEN

1

BATS

Script extract from Arthur Bryant's 'Peculiar London' walking tour guide (Hampstead Heath, 2 hrs, sturdy shoes)

At night London is a sea of crimson eyes.

Look – you can see them everywhere. They peer down from the starless sky, clustered as tightly as pins on a map of the constellations. They mark the tops of the cranes that drift on the night currents and stalk the city like metal mantises, always with one red eye open to watch over the streets.

The cranes are a sure sign that whatever you've read or heard to the contrary, London is booming. London is always booming, because of where it is and what it was and what it has become, the sprawling home to nearly nine million people.

Ladies and gentlemen, my name is Mr Arthur Bryant and I will be your guide to the metropolis at night. Seen from up here on Hampstead Heath, London's thoroughfares are as tangled as veins. Over there is the city's heart, Piccadilly Circus, an electric sunburst that erases the diurnal cycle, its diodes banishing shadows and driving away miscreants. Who would have thought that the Piccadilly Commandos, those good-time girls who lurked by the arches on the north side of the circus, would be driven out by illuminated advertisements for hamburgers?

But look, a short distance away are patches as dark as lost pages of history. Hyde, Green, Regent's, Battersea, the parks at night are absent from London's map of light. We stand to the north of these, in the largest, darkest blank of all: Hampstead Heath.

The heath was once densely forested, the home to boar-hunting prehistoric tribes. The Romans drove a road through it, and those fearing the Black Death hid on it. In 1584 a great beacon was built to warn us if the Spanish Armada landed. An elm tree grew so huge here that inside it were forty-two steps leading to a viewing platform that held twenty observers. Whenever the end of the world was predicted, Londoners came to the heath. The Gordon Rioters headed here, but were diverted with free beer at the Spaniards Inn. Literary clubs met, duellists fought and a court of law was transferred here under canvas during the Great Plague, creating 'Judges' Walk'. To this day, the heath still hosts bank holiday fairs, and 'Hampsteads' are still rhyming slang for teeth.

The Ladies of the Night usually met at dusk on the paths into the heath. They came armed with infra-red cameras, motion detectors, glow sticks, notepads and hip-flasks of tea. In the winter they only met once a month because of reduced nocturnal activity. Tonight they were gathering at an unusually late hour because there was to be a cloudless sky and a full moon, and Pamela's shift at the hospital didn't finish until 2.00 a.m.

Matilda was the first there because she was early for everything. She volunteered for the local wildlife rescue service, which meant being willing to drive a hedgehog to an animal hospital at midnight, so this sort of activity seemed perfectly normal to her. Sparrow had yet to appear but could be heard crashing through the undergrowth from a hundred yards away. Pamela arrived with a sports bag on her back and an LED torch on her headband. She was their self-appointed leader because she was the oldest and the most experienced. She had lately become officious because life had started to disappoint her. Sparrow had a pretty face but nothing seemed to keep her weight off. Matilda meant well. All three wore black and kept their voices low, like secret agents on a night mission.

'That must be Sparrow,' said Pamela, listening to the crackle of dead branches heading their way. 'She's as blind as a you-know-what and not exactly light on her feet.'

'Is it just the three of us?' Matilda asked. 'Where are the others? What happened to that woman with the alarming nose?'

'No sense of commitment.' Pamela set down her bag. 'I don't know why people sign up for things if they're not going to see them through. Mrs Hardwick stopped coming without so much as a by-your-leave.'

'She went into hospital,' said Matilda.

'She could have told me.'

'She didn't come out.'

'Oh.' Pamela was taken aback. 'I didn't know she was ill.'

'She wasn't. She took a beetroot salad in for a friend and got septicaemia from a trolley.'

Sparrow appeared beside them in a cascade of broken twigs. 'Are we the only ones? I suppose it's too late for most. They've

3

no way of getting home.' She brushed bits of bark from her bosom. 'I came up that hill on my bike. I've got calves like concrete.'

'What's that funny smell?' asked Pamela.

'It's probably me.' Sparrow checked her bag. 'I've got a veggie carbonara in a Tupperware but the lid's loose.'

'If we want to find a winter roost we should come at dusk,' said Matilda. 'It's better when the colony is active.'

'We already know where the colony is,' Pamela explained. 'We need to map out the roost sites. I know it's late but you both said you didn't mind coming along at any time of night. Sparrow, you couldn't make more noise if you arrived in a JCB.'

Sparrow carded holly leaves from her hair. 'I couldn't help it. New contacts. I've got drops in. I lost the path.'

'You didn't have to create a new one. We're not meant to disturb anything.' Pamela shook her head. Ungainly and eager to please, Sparrow was less like a tiny bird than a Labrador that had been kept in a small flat for too long.

Pamela turned back to Matilda. 'We have to submit our biodiversity action plan before the end of the week or we won't be eligible for funding. The LBG will get it all.'

The London Bat Group worked tirelessly to protect the capital's population of noctules, pipistrelles, serotines, Natterer's and Daubenton's bats, but there were many other rogue groups, of which the Ladies of the Night were one.

At least nine further organizations were scattered across Greater London from Osterley Park to Oxleas Wood, and their members could be extremely territorial. This group had started out as an excuse to get away from husbands, partners and children, but had evolved into charity work that included the organization of midnight walks, fun runs, swimathons and bat studies. Pamela was tireless, which made her exhausting.

'It's ever so late.' Matilda looked in her backpack for

something to drink. 'I'm not normally up at this time. Don't you miss your sleep?'

'I've got insomnia.' Sparrow made it sound like something you catch.

'Do you know what Alfie told me this morning?' said Pamela. ' "The government should round up all the poor people and put them in camps." I don't know where he gets it from. He's eleven and has the makings of a serial killer.'

'He does have something of the night about him, doesn't he?' said Matilda unhelpfully. 'I hope for your sake it's just a phase. He'll calm down once he's learned to masturbate.' She peered at her notes. 'Tell me we're not doing pipistrelles again.' Pipistrelles were happy roosting in urban areas, under eaves and soffit boards, so they could be found in every part of the city, which somehow made them less interesting.

'Do you never read your emails?' Pamela swung her head-lamp over.

'There's not much point in being out at this time of year at all,' said Sparrow.

'Why not?' Matilda asked.

'Hibernation. They spend six months asleep. We might as well be hunting tortoises.'

'Tortoises don't live in trees,' said Matilda, confused.

'Matilda, you know what I told you about thinking,' Pamela reminded her. 'We've got a Brandt's bat. Tiny and very rare. There's a clump of ash trees just this side of the water. We think it must be in there, but we don't know for sure.'

'Just the one?' asked Matilda.

Pamela rolled her eyes. 'How do I know? There was a sighting of a Brandt in the woodlands just before the ponds, and that's why we've volunteered to search for its little home.'

Matilda persevered. 'If it's a single tiny bat how are we sup-posed to find its roost?'

'They're very distinctive. The whole point of coming this

late is to ensure that we don't disturb its flight pattern,' Pamela explained as laboriously as possible. 'I have a diagram.' She unfolded a sheet of paper with an unedifying sketch at its centre showing a very big tree and a very small hole.

Matilda could remember when there were fifteen women in the group, ambling about in the golden summer dusk, but the bats were fewer now and the volunteer spotters felt they had better things to do than catalogue flying mice.

'Have you noticed that when you drive to the seaside you don't get insects all over your windscreen any more?' she remarked. 'That's why the bats are disappearing. How do we even know it's a Brandt's?'

'Somebody found a dead one,' Pamela explained. 'It was very old.'

'So what?'

'Brandt's bats live longer than any other species, so there are a lot of interesting and useful things we can learn from them.' Pamela had the ennui of a teacher explaining the appeal of a dead language. 'What, Sparrow? You don't have to raise your hand.'

'Is it true that bats have sex upside down?'

'Yes, and they can eat three thousand times a night, just like my husband.' The others stared at her with incomprehension. Pamela wondered why she bothered. Faithful, hopeless Matilda understood nothing, Sparrow had the timidity of a recently assaulted cat, and neither of them got her jokes. 'Come on, let's spread out. Sparrow, I want you down near the lake. We'll be finished before four.'

Sparrow stopped for a moment and released a heavy sigh. 'You know, sometimes I think it's marvellous that we're helping to protect the urban biosphere but other times I think, you know, *bats*.'

The Ladies made their way along a ribbon of earth that cut between rowans and maples. The Brandt's putative flight path had been marked on Pamela's map. As soon as the three of them located the central woodland track they split up and staked out their territory. They passed other bat roosts in woodpecker holes and patches of rot. The Ladies' mission involved jotting down any likely locations and matching them to flight paths. They could just as easily have done it by day, but Pamela was keen for them to present themselves on Instagram as the bad girls of the bat world. In some obscure way it made up for the timidity of her marriage.

After agreeing on a meeting time, the Ladies split up and headed in different directions.

Sparrow kept her torch low, watching out for molehills and rabbit holes. It was the new year, and she felt dyspeptic and exhausted. Christmas with her parents had weighed heavily upon her. The usual arguments had arrived with the familiarity of buses: why could she not settle in one job, why didn't she try dieting again and, with grim inevitability, why had she not met somebody nice?

Unfortunately her last 'somebody nice' lived in Newcastle and would only see her if she went all the way up there every time. The relationship lasted until she told him she wasn't paying another fortune to sit on a replacement bus service somewhere outside Darlington. He hadn't seemed that bothered.

She dropped down on the stump of a diseased oak and watched the distant glistening pond. Clouds drifted apart like separating ice floes, revealing a moon the size of a dinner plate. Light washed across the grass, turning the slope into a luminous tide, as if the landscape was lit from within.

Something rustled through the long grass. An owl dropped from a lofty branch. There was a shrill squeak and a scrabble, and it flapped away with its furry prize.

Sparrow pulled the zip of her jacket higher. The air had a damp chill that could coat your bones. It smelled of loam, fungus and wet clay, a peculiar odour that always made her think of London bricks. Her grandmother had told her that the suburbs were once teeming with wildlife: stag beetles, juniper bugs, moles, grass snakes, hedgehogs and tortoise-shell butterflies, slowly killed off by cars and concrete. It felt right to do something that would help restore the natural balance, even just a little bit.

It was the kind of activity in which she had tried to involve her older brother. James was so bored by the world that nothing suited him. Friendless, jobless and finally homeless, he had returned from Goa to stay with her once again. She couldn't manage many more late nights sitting on the floor with a bottle of cheap wine, listening to him explain what was wrong with the world while he made his art, which invariably consisted of obscenities scrawled across collages assembled from pornographic magazines. She had always been a night owl, but made a point of getting to bed before he unwrapped the little leather pouch that was never far from his side. There was no point in telling him to stop. He was a natural addict, and took to drugs like a duck to water. Lately he had started carelessly leaving evidence around the flat. The stuff was dangerous. She had to get him out, but where could he go?

She knew there was a Toblerone in her bag, and snapped off one piece after another until it was gone. She tried to identify the leaves picked out by her torchlight and failed. There was phantom rain in the trees, not quite dry, not truly wet, but every now and again the branches bent and released a fall of water. A temperate climate, her mother always said, that was why the Romans chose it. *Family,* she thought, *they tell you anything just to make you stay where you are.*

The light breeze was enough to make the trees whisper secrets. Her thoughts drifted. She went to a place she had never been, a hot, bright seashore with palms and turtles. She suspected she was snoring.

A holly bush rattled. Something shrieked and fell silent. She awoke with a start and checked her phone. A quarter to three. There was no sound from either Pamela or Matilda. They were both older, with dismissive husbands and difficult children. For them these expeditions were lifelines to sanity. Sparrow was an insomniac because she suffered from sleep apnoea, and the night hours weighed heavily on her without something to do.

She took out her field glasses and tried to identify the trees, but the night and the drizzle obscured everything. Pamela had marked out some possible roosting sites. By the light of the torch she drew a number of flight paths over the ponds, leading around a series of overgrown redbrick arches where moths, gnats and beetles could be found. Re-capping her pen, she left her notebook on top of the bag and poured a tea from her Thermos.

There was a new noise now. Something larger than a badger or even a deer. She dug out the carbonara and tried to get the lid off the Tupperware quietly. She couldn't remember packing a fork. Another rustle. She set the container down. Perhaps it would be better to find the others and remain with them. The blanket of the dark removed contours. It was impossible to tell where things ended and began.

She was trying to decide her best course of action when she looked up and saw someone staring at her. The man was just as startled to see her and dropped out of sight, vanishing into a thicket of wet gorse.

Before Sparrow had time to close her mouth he popped up again and stumbled towards her. He was now no more than ten feet away. There was a thrash of foliage as he fell once more.

If he's looking for bats he's not going about it very professionally, she thought.

The man reappeared directly in front of her, through

9

clumps of reedy grass, making her jump. He had an incredibly thin skull-like face and huge eyes. He climbed painfully to his feet. He was skeletal, young and Indian, with a neatly trimmed beard and a look of startlement.

A second figure divorced itself from the penumbral gloom of the nearby bushes. It blundered into some low branches and swore. Sparrow wondered how many others were here. The young Indian yelled something unintelligible but easily understood. He needed help.

'Are you all right?' she asked. She had no idea what he said in reply – it sounded like a mixture of English and Hindi – but he was clearly terrified.

Before he could speak again there was a crunch of sticks and leaves and he disappeared from sight once more. From the noise of torn bracken and the movement of the ferns she could tell he was being dragged backwards. The thing that was pulling him (she had difficulty imagining it was human) slowly unfurled itself in a patch of moonlight and glowered down at her. It wore a long black coat and looked like a pig. In one hand it held a silver spear.

This demonic vision was simply too exotic for Sparrow. With a wail rising in her throat she rose, snatched up her bag and ran, climbing up through the grasses and bushes, the spikes of winter branches snatching at her clothes. She scrambled over hillocks and across ditches, no thought in her head but to get as far away as possible from whatever these people were doing.

She did not stay to see the pig-thing drop on to his victim's back and loop a cord around his neck as if roping a steer, yanking it tight as he lifted the helpless young man from the ground by his neck.

It wasn't until she had reached the main road that she realized she had left behind her notebook. When she finally managed to locate Pamela and Matilda, they seemed less concerned about her hallucinatory encounter than the fact that she had lost the bat journal. Pamela told her primly that imagination could be triggered by too much food.

Upset, Sparrow left the others and rode her bicycle home. The nocturnal sojourn of the Brandt's bat was destined to remain unglimpsed and unrecorded. The journal would prove to be of no interest to non-bat lovers, but it did contain Sparrow's name and address, a fact which was noted by the pig-man, whose name was Hugo Blake.

Sophie Ward didn't know it, but she was approaching the spot where Sparrow had confronted unexpected night-time activity on the heath four hours earlier.

Her journey here had been undertaken because of a drunken resolution on New Year's Eve, when her husband had thoughtfully given her tips on looking better in front of his friends. This would be the year she got fit and showed him who was boss. She had decided to start with an early-morning regime, and to this end had purchased a fitness wristband, a pair of hi-vis lemon Lycra shorts, a sports bra, trainers, a micro-weave sweat-top and a gym bag. Then she thought about what kind of exercise she should try. Running had seemed a good idea because you could stop whenever you wanted without being judged, and didn't have to shower in front of other people. She had carefully planned out her route.

Less than twenty minutes into her first run things had started to go wrong. First she snagged her top on a branch and slipped over on a patch of mud, and now she was hopelessly lost.

It was not quite light, and at 7.55 a.m. the woods had a fairy-tale quality. Patches of milky vapour cocooned the bases of the trees, parting and closing behind her as she trotted through them.

The heath was notoriously tricky to negotiate in half-light. Pitted paths plunged across each other and doubled back in tangled loops, leading to clumps of foliage so identical they might have been purchased by a model-railway enthusiast to furnish a track layout. There was more likelihood of breaking an ankle on a half-submerged root than getting fit.

As Sophie pounded past a lethal-looking holly bush that she felt sure she had seen several times before, she was halted by a pathway that split and twisted into three different routes, all going downhill.

Although her sense of direction was poor, she was fairly certain that she needed to start heading upwards towards her car. After all, it was only her first day. She was out of breath and feeling unnerved. Her husband had suggested that she should start out by jogging through the backstreets, but it seemed such a waste of nature. The heath, London's vast hilltop common land, had survived for more than a millennium. Here you could walk for a day without redoubling your tracks, but it was clearly not a jogging circuit for beginners.

Sophie turned about, trying to regain her bearings. She had never been good with nature. Trees all looked the same, although she was fairly certain that the one beside her now was a willow. Its fine branches were bent over like whips, making natural curtains dense enough to conceal . . .

. . . a body.

It was hanging upside down inside the willow like a human bat. Its ankles were tied with blue nylon cord, the backs of its hands brushing the ground. The other end of the nylon rope had been knotted around the trunk of the tree. The hanging man was skinny, young and Indian, dressed in a pale blue work shirt and rather old-fashioned navy trousers.

Sophie looked down at her feet. Her new Nikes now sported a plimsoll line of blood. She was standing in a dark pool of it.

She thought about helping him down until she saw the hole in his bony throat. The coagulated gore had leaked from it.

The puncture looked deep. Sophie gingerly stepped out of the blood pool and felt for her phone. As a nurse at the nearby Royal Free Hospital she was inured to deathly visitation, although it normally came to her attention in a neat white bed, not dangling by its feet from a tree.

Afterwards she admitted that although it had crossed her mind that the attacker might still be nearby, curiosity had got the better of her. She tried to see if there were signs of life left in the hanging body.

Light had begun to show through the trees. Her first attempt at visual diagnosis ruled out any kind of stupid accident and went for suicide, quickly revised to murder when she realized that it would have been impossible for the poor man to kill himself in such a manner.

There was no knife lying in the cropped grass beneath him, but there were plenty of other strange items lying around. Her right heel disturbed something round and hard – a red church candle, half buried in the mulch of leaves. When she looked about, she saw that nearly a dozen candles had been arranged in a circle before the hanging man. Two of them were still burning beside a pile of headless dolls, a couple of inverted crucifixes and a snakeskin.

There was no point in calling for an ambulance. She rang the police instead, and as it was early on a Sunday morning she was put on hold. The music sounded suspiciously like Morrissey's 'First of the Gang to Die'.

While she waited, she took a pace back and looked up at the body. He had been hoisted high enough to bring his throat to eye level. His eyes were wide and surprised. Some kind of small fluttering insect, a bug or even a tiny bat, flew out of his open mouth.

Sophie Ward finally became unnerved upon considering these strange details, because what she had stumbled upon was not just a scene of violence, but an act of madness.

2

REPORT

Raymond Land sat staring at the white sand beach fringed with tall coconut palms. The sun was rising in a crisp azure sky, promising another hot day, with only a single small cloud on the sea's horizon. He was in Mexico, on the Yucatán Peninsula, an ecologically protected coast that was home to miles of pristine shoreline, exotic tropical birds and one of the world's great cuisines.

He was thinking about what to have for lunch, and had narrowed it down to red snapper or octopus, when he noticed that the small grey cloud had grown much bigger. A dark shadow had started to stain the sand. When he looked up again he was shocked to see that it had taken over the whole of the sky.

As he stared into the dense charcoal-coloured mass he began to see a face in it. The face was chubby and wrinkled and had innocent blue eyes, a striped scarf (partially unravelled) and a squashed trilby hat. There was a roll of thunder and it began to rain.

Land awoke with a start and found himself still staring at the deserted beach on his laptop's screensaver. He turned about in his chair and groggily looked out of his office window in King's Cross, London. Stumpy the one-legged pigeon stared through the rain-spattered glass at him with a malevolent orange eye. With a deep, world-weary sigh Land returned to the keyboard and began to type.

PECULIAR CRIMES UNIT
A specialized London police division with a remit to prevent or cause to cease any acts of public affright or violent disorder committed in the municipal or communal areas of the city.

The Old Warehouse
231 Caledonian Road
London N1 9RB

STAFF ROSTER SUNDAY 6 JANUARY

Raymond Land, Unit Chief
Arthur Bryant, Detective Chief Inspector
John May, Detective Chief Inspector
Janice Longbright, Operations Director
Jack Renfield, Operations Director
Dan Banbury, Crime Scene/Forensics
Meera Mangeshkar, Detective Sergeant
Colin Bimsley, Detective Sergeant
Giles Kershaw, Forensic Pathologist (off-site)
Crippen, staff cat

PRIVATE & CONFIDENTIAL MEMO
FROM: RAYMOND LAND
TO: ALL PCU STAFF

This wasn't my idea, coming in on a Sunday. Even God took the day off. He wouldn't have been able to if he'd been working for the Home Office, though, as they're determined to make us try flexible working hours. Perhaps they can also convince criminals to work from home.

I trust you all had an enjoyable Christmas. Thank you for your cards and gifts. Whoever bought me the aftershave can have it back. Apart from the fact that it smells like burnt oranges, Aqua Manda was discontinued in 1973 so I'm assuming it was a regift from Mr Bryant. He might have taken the price off, especially as it was in shillings and pence.

While you were off gorging yourselves with loved ones I was in temporary accommodation on Cable Street with Crippen and her intestinal parasites for company. You know there's something seriously wrong with your life when the high point of your Christmas Day is worming a cat, but, as Mr Bryant likes to remind me, anyone seeking dignity will find it in the dictionary just after 'Death', so let's move on.

This week's roster includes two newly promoted job titles. The unit's most senior detectives have finally accepted official status as Detective Chief Inspectors in order to ratify their pay grades with the Met's homicide division. This does not entitle them to Luncheon Vouchers, first dibs on the Friday cake or any kind of special treatment. Mr Bryant has promised me that his new status won't change him at all, which is a pity. The change will move you all up a peg, so everyone gets a Crackerjack pencil except me.

In the accompanying spreadsheet you'll find the latest bulletin from the School of the Bleeding Obvious, aka the annual Metropolitan Police crime stats for Central London. Of course we're not technically part of the Serious Crimes Division but their problems affect us, so give it a shufti. That chattering noise you hear is officers' teeth; there's a cold wind blowing through the Home Office right now. The Met is so stretched that CPS cases are repeatedly collapsing due to incomplete evidence.

Knowing the length of your attention spans I can summarize for you: officers on the street are down 32 per cent, violent crime is up 29 per cent, gun and knife crime up 46 per cent, anti-social behaviour, hate crimes, rape and assault are all soaring.

'No wonder London is ranked fifty-third in terms of liveable cities,' said John May as he read the memo back to his partner.

'Yes, but what's in the top ten?' asked Bryant, patting pockets for his pipe. 'If you want to go and live off-world in the empty corners of the Mercator map, good luck to you. I want to be where something outrageous is happening.'

Domestics and violence with fatal injuries are up, so-called 'honour killings' are up, daylight drug deals are everywhere and we have the reappearance of a charming form of gang violence indigenous to the East End; chucking sulphuric acid in someone's face is something I associate with *The Phantom of the Opera*, not a spotty nonce with a Sideshow Bob haircut who thinks somebody nicked his bird or disrespected his trainers.

The policy of reducing the service in favour of electronic surveillance has been dealt a swift kick up the jacksie by the latest stats, which show that its new national facial recognition system is 95 per cent inaccurate. At least it explains why Mr Bryant is able to confound our own state-of-the-art system by wearing his scarf the wrong way round.

The national picture isn't looking good. Knife-crime figures are skewed by gang attacks within specific communities, especially rural ones, which increase in direct proportion to cutbacks, the so-called 'debt and threat' trap. There are now some thirty thousand children in criminal gangs. If you're poor, schooldays are definitely not the happiest days of your life.

Only 40 per cent of all calls made to the Met last year were about crime; they're still picking up the pieces from the galloping retreat of State instead of catching criminals. There were the usual time-wasters, including people calling to complain that the KFC was shut and one old dear who rang the emergency services because she couldn't get the lid off her biscuit tin. In between dealing with toilet-seat-related incidents and members of the psychopaths' union who think they're being sent alien messages through their toasters, they did manage to put away a few career crims causing social unrest. Unfortunately they also lost over forty London police stations in the last twelve months, which means that the most vulnerable and disadvantaged members of society have been left without support. It seems they no longer come forward and we no longer have the resources to go looking for them.

On a lighter note, there were over seven hundred thousand mobile phones snatched last year, so many that the Met no longer regard it as an actionable crime. Quite right too. You can't count every little Stone-Island-wearing street-slug on a moped waiting round the corner for the coast to clear before pouncing on a pissed-up City boy pestering his coke dealer, that's just social Darwinism.

'He's a bit minty this morning,' said Bryant.
'He's been cooped up with the cat,' said May.

Which brings me to the statistics for the Home Office's outsourced special units, of which, you may be amazed to learn, you are still one, even after Mr Bryant got the building quarantined and nearly managed to burn us down again. How did we do last year? Percentage of crimes we solved: 72 per cent. Number of important officials we upset during the course of our investigations: 165 per cent.

'How could dissatisfaction be above a hundred per cent?' asked Arthur Bryant. 'I assume the American consul was happy that we found his missing son.'

'Buried in our basement,' May reminded him. 'I would not say "happy".'

Let's look at our own data. Four murderers apprehended, one London regatta disrupted, one capital-wide riot provoked, one siege staged in our own unit and a near-fatal strangulation in that well-known hotbed of violence, the British Library. I know you sometimes have to break a few laws to get results but must you always break them so publicly? The next time you feel the need to trash a national institution or pull a Sweeney through the backstreets could you at least wait until everyone important is in bed? I don't like opening my copy of the *Metro* and seeing your faces leering out at me before I've had a coffee and one of my tablets.

Despite the fact that most murder investigation teams would kill for your strike rate, we still have plenty of enemies out there who would like to see us taken down. Historically speaking, we know what happens to units that attract public attention. Clue: nothing good. The government had Alan Turing chemically castrated. Let that be a caution.

I'm not pretending this year is going to be easy. A few weeks ago, the body of the son of the US consul was found in the cellar of these premises and was removed to a secure military facility somewhere outside of Chicago, Illinois, for independent analysis. The consulate is now actively pursuing a case against us.

In addition, we have the usual problems to contend with: funding restrictions, limited resources and an ageing – in some cases, extremely ageing – workforce. The public surgery will continue to be held each Monday morning from nine to twelve, and everyone will be taking their turn in the barrel. Janice will handle this week's gathering of nutters. I'm not putting Mr Bryant on the roster because he's too old to be punched.

Now, house business. Our Christmas children's weekend was meant to allay fears about meeting the police. Instead, several parents complained that you traumatized a group of under-sevens by locking them in a cell and misplacing the keys. I think you owe Janice an apology for leaving her with the mopping up.

This week's inter-unit football match has been cancelled due to a complete and utter lack of interest in any kind of sporting activity from everyone except Colin, who'll have to find someone his own size to knock unconscious.

The PCU Saturday Night Film Club screening will be *This Happy Breed*, and was of course chosen by Mr Bryant, who says he missed it in cinemas, probably because it was made in 1944. Perhaps he was washing his hair that night.

I've asked the two Daves to stay on and repair the fire damage on the first floor. It would be cheaper to put them on the payroll, except that I'm loath to take advice on the policing of the capital from a pair of Turkish builders. They'll repartition the open-plan arrangement and turn part of it back into separate offices, seeing as you don't seem capable of sharing a workspace without turning it into some kind of Goth student squat. We're keeping the operations room but could whoever brought in the Emmanuelle chair, the goat's head table lamp and the portable barbecue please take them away again?

Speaking of our workmen, the two Daves would like to offer everyone a glass of something they nicked from the evidence room to celebrate the second anniversary of their arrival here at the PCU for what was intended to be a three-week residency, when they set about transforming a respectable old King's Cross warehouse into the macabre, infested deathtrap it is today. Perhaps this year we could

forgo buying them presents, partly because I still only have
half an office and because Mr Bryant's gift of an ant farm
last year caused the kind of chaos we all expected.

'I don't know what the fuss is about,' said Bryant. 'I bought
a snake to get rid of them.'
'Yes,' May agreed, 'but you lost the snake.'

Speaking of our most senior detective, I understand that Mr
Bryant is now fully recovered from the mystery illness that
prevented him from turning up to work on time or showing
anyone an ounce of politeness, decency or respect. He says
he's finished his medication and has stopped hallucinating,
although it's hard to tell. I know several of you regard him
as a mentor so can I say this? Don't. He is not a shining
example of metropolitan policing. He is Fagin with a badge.

This was meant to be my annual pep talk, thanking you
for all your hard work and hoping we'll have many more
successes in the coming year, but if you could just get
through it without placing us in another hostage situation
or causing the entire Metropolitan Police Force to treat us
like a leper colony I'd be most grateful.

So, here we go again. Remember to think on, look sharp
and if you encounter any problems my door is always open,
mainly because I still don't have one. We're another year
closer to total police surveillance technology and the mer-
ciful release that obsolescence will bring. Get on with your
work and don't – just don't.

Your Commander-in-Chief,

Raymond Land

PS I've gone back to sending this out as a printed memo
because somebody remixed my last recorded message and
posted it online over footage of a dancing cat. Try doing
that with a sheet of A4.

3

GUN

The explosion made everyone else jump.

While she was making phone calls Janice Longbright painted her nails Strawberry Blush, a colour that hit the peak of its popularity in 1956. She capped the brush and admired her handiwork.

Another detonation resounded through the office. A framed photograph of the PCU staff on an annual outing to Brighton in 1982 fell off the wall.

With the receiver nestled under her right ear Janice peered at her hand more closely. The varnish on her right thumb would need another coat. She waved her fingers back and forth and blew on them.

A third boom followed. Some plaster dust pattered across her desk. Her pencil mug landed on the floor. She was not entirely sure that her forefinger was dry before having to insert it in her left ear. 'No,' she said, 'go on, it was just a gunshot. You were about to say—'

She moved the phone away and waited a moment before continuing. The blasts were coming at regular intervals. *Bang*.

She moved the earpiece back. 'So when was this? If Giles Kershaw is already in receipt of the deceased I can make arrangements directly with him. Leave it with me.' Replacing the receiver, she gingerly picked up her paperwork and rose from her desk.

In the hallway she collided with Raymond Land, who had the habit of appearing before his staff with the suddenness of a cricket ball coming through a window. 'What the bloody hell was that?' he bellowed. The unit chief was coming down with another winter cold and not in the mood for mischief. He caught sight of himself in the hall mirror, saw that his comb-over had sprung up like a trapdoor and hastily smoothed it back into place.

'Mr Bryant says you gave him permission to conduct a ballistics test,' Janice explained.

'Yes, but on the range over in Clerkenwell, not here in the bloody building.'

Land tentatively pushed at the door to the detectives' office and stepped inside, then leaped back as sand cascaded around his shoes. It was pouring from a punctured sack that hung on the wall. A photograph of his own face was attached to the top of it.

Arthur Bryant raised his pilot's goggles and peered through the settling dust. 'Raymondo, is that you? I'm awfully sorry, I didn't mean to disturb you.'

'What are you talking about, not disturbing me? You're firing a gun, for God's sake!'

'You shouldn't come in, I'm firing a gun,' Bryant shouted back. 'Hang on.' He set the rifle down and removed his earplugs. 'I thought the sandbag would help keep the noise down.'

'I've told you before about this sort of thing,' Land admonished. 'You nearly gave me a heart attack.'

'Nearly doesn't count. Still, no harm done, eh?'

'No harm done? It went right through my wall!'

'Really?' Bryant's cornflower-blue eyes widened. 'It shouldn't have. I ran projections based on velocity, energy, bullet weight and sectional density. I'll speak to the Daves about the poor quality of their partitions.'

'It's not the partitions, it's you. You could have killed me! You *cannot* discharge loaded firearms in here. Why are you firing that thing at all?'

Bryant perked up. He liked being asked to recall murders. 'You remember the Richmond Park Sniper? I had a brain-wave about those sightlines not matching up. His gun and shells were still in the evidence room. The chap was using the St Paul's sightlines but he had a squint. That's why his aim was off.'

'I don't need to remind you what happened the last time you fired a gun in an enclosed space . . .' The state of the detectives' room caught Land's eye. It looked like a cross between a bombed-out library and the basement of the Cairo Museum. 'Look at this place – bits of paper, pencils, bullets, books and ink everywhere. And what's that?' He pointed to a badly painted statuette of a shepherd strangling a goat.

'A gift from an admirer,' Bryant explained airily. 'It hasn't quite found its place yet.'

'Why can't you be paperless like the others?'

'It seems wrong to abandon something that's been with us since AD 105. You knew what we were like when you first came here. The clue's in the name.' Bryant held up his hands, creating a frame. 'Peculiar. Crimes. Unit. We're free to experiment.'

'Only if it doesn't involve murdering members of staff.'

'It's technically manslaughter but I take your point, my little dandiprat. I hope I didn't disturb your fudgelling. Do we know where the body is yet?'

'I thought *you* knew,' replied Land. 'I got a call from Colin.

It's meant to be a day of rest. I'd have had a lie-in if I still had my house.'

'Mr Bryant, John's bringing the car around for you now.' Janice was sensible enough to remain outside the door until the rifle had been stowed away.

'I'm sure the Met only passed this to us because it's Sunday morning and they're all hungover,' Land moaned. 'I never get asked to join them.'

Bryant lightly tapped his cheek. 'Ray, my drop of golden sun, we'll happily invite you to the pub. You came to the Scottish Stores with us before Christmas.'

'Yes. You stuck me with the bill, and while I was there a tramp set fire to the unit.'

'I must speak to old Harry about that. He trousered our petty-cash box. You have to understand the nature of this job, Raymondo. We're detectives. We detect.' He wiggled his forefingers before Land's eyes. 'You're a manager. You – manage. That's all you have to do. Your job is to be like one of those people who mind buildings at night. Put your feet up, read a young adult novel, leave the heavy lifting to us. Division of labour. We're highly trained professionals who can draw together all the strands of the investigation.' He kneaded the air with his fingers. 'You're more like one of those people they drop into a seat at the Oscars when a star has to go to the toilet. Useful but mostly for show. Have a sherbet fountain.' He handed Land a yellow tube with a liquorice pipe sticking out of the top.

Despite his unworldly and somewhat disdainful attitude to policing, Arthur Bryant commanded unswerving loyalty from his staff, who were prepared to follow him anywhere, if only out of curiosity. They tolerated him much as teachers might beam benignly upon a smart but scampish schoolboy. When Bryant's home-made cherry brandy, distilled and bottled for his own label, *Dangereux à Boire*, gave the staff mild symptoms of cyanide poisoning they laughed it off. 'Mr Bryant's performing one of his experiments again,' they said, rolling their eyes and nudging each other, 'what a card.' It deeply annoyed Raymond Land, who tried every trick in the book to gain the respect of his employees and thus singularly failed to do so.

'I know old men turn back into babies,' muttered Land as he joined Longbright in the corridor, 'but they're not meant to be carrying loaded guns. Why does he have to be so offensive all the time?'

'He's just having a bit of fun,' said Longbright.

'By insulting his superiors.'

'Well, that depends on how you define—'

'And what's *fudgelling*?'

'It's an eighteenth-century term meaning to pretend to work when you're not actually doing anything,' Longbright replied crisply. She had seen the bookmarked volumes of old English slang lying open on Bryant's desk, and knew that her boss would also be wondering about Bryant's use of the term *dandiprat*. It was probably best not to tell him it was a sixteenth-century word describing someone physically and socially insignificant.

'I'm not putting up with it any more. I've had enough of their tomfoolery.' Land stared at the liquorice pipe. 'What am I supposed to do with this?'

'Suck it, sir,' said Longbright, heading off along the corridor.

4

RITUAL

John May sat behind the wheel and glanced at the dashboard clock. There was a formula for working out exactly how late his partner would be. You just deducted the imaginary time Bryant reckoned it was from the actual time, then added another ten minutes. Sure enough, there was that face looming at the passenger window, looking as rosy and wrinkled as an aged apple. He knocked on the glass with unnecessary force. May leaned over and opened the door.

'What on earth is this?' asked Bryant. 'It looks like an Uber. Do you want me to sit in the back?'

'It's a Kia,' muttered May. 'Get in. We could have taken yours if you'd got it fixed.'

Bryant had managed to knock both wing mirrors off Victor, his yellow Mini-Minor, after following his phone's GPS directions into a branch of Primark. He made a theatrical fuss about squeezing into the Kia's passenger seat with his battered brown briefcase, walking stick and umbrella. 'Not much room, is there?' he complained. 'Where's the BMW?'

'It failed its MOT again. It's costing me a fortune to run.

This is leased to the unit.' He pressed the starter while his partner fidgeted about looking for the end of the seatbelt.

'You start it with a button?' Bryant suppressed a laugh.

'It's against my better judgement, but I'm to give you a remote for it.' He handed over a keycard.

'Janice said we're going to Hampstead. We could have taken the tube.'

'No,' said May patiently, 'because the murder site is past the Vale of Health and that's a long walk uphill from the station with your knees, plus you hate the Northern Line on a Sunday.'

'Yes, but only generically, in the way everyone hates folk dancing. Janice said the circumstances are unusual.'

'They're always unusual,' May replied. 'If they weren't the case would go to the Met's MIT. A murder on the heath.'

'You already know it's a murder?' Bryant dug himself down into the seat and tore open a brown paper bag filled with sherbet lemons, sending them all over the floor.

'The victim was found hanging by his ankles with a cut throat, so it would have to have been a very determined suicide,' May pointed out.

'Perhaps the Russians got to him, like that GCHQ codebreaker they found inside a sports bag.'

May indicated and pulled into Caledonian Road. 'The Met decided that Gareth Williams's death was accidental.'

'Yes, he folded himself inside a bag in his narrow bath, padlocked it from the outside, wiped away all fingerprints and somehow placed the clean key of the now-locked bag under his own body,' said Bryant. 'Do you know how many fixers and spies the FSB has assassinated in Britain? They get stabbed in the night and poisoned with rare toxins, they turn radioactive, fall under trains and out of windows. Their deaths read like chapters taken from cheap spy novels.' He peered out at the closed Sunday shops and offices of Euston

Road. 'Remember all those supposed GCHQ suicides we investigated a few years back? This could be another one.'

'You wish. You'd like to get stuck into a good international conspiracy, wouldn't you?'

'Presumably someone's already there at the site.' Bryant crunched a sherbet lemon. 'Do we have an ID?'

'Nothing yet. The body's still *in situ*. Dan's gone on ahead. Hampstead Met took one look and turned it over to us.'

'I wonder why they did that. I hope it's not a political matter. Murderers can be held culpable but diplomatic departments have the resources to blur every fact and remove every shred of evidence. Our little unit isn't equipped to deal with something like that.'

'Let's wait and see what we've got first, shall we?' May suggested.

'Good idea. Don't worry about the cow going blind.'

'I think it's a horse.'

'Where?'

'Going blind. Not a cow.'

'I have no idea, John, I live in Zone One. Did I already ask you if you wanted a sherbet lemon?' He waved the torn bag enticingly. 'Be careful, I think there are a couple stuck under your brake pedal.'

They passed through Camden Town, which still looked like a battlefield the morning after another wild Saturday night. Haverstock Hill took them up through Belsize Park, tree-lined, discreetly wealthy and deserted except for a Japanese family, as still as statues, dressed in black and beige, silently waiting beside a closed Starbucks. Sunday morning was the quietest time of the week.

May leaned forward and studied the sky. 'It's going to rain around ten.'

'Then you'd better put your foot down. Don't you have one of those magnetic blue lights you can clamp on the roof?'

'No,' said May, 'this isn't *Hawaii Five-O*. We don't even have a parking permit for the car yet, so I'll be needing some change for the meter.'

'On a Sunday?'

'It's Hampstead. The artists have all gone. There are only bankers left up here now. Funny how the poor always occupy the lowlands and the rich live above them.'

'Not strictly true, old bean.' Bryant dug candy from his dentures. 'Belgravia and St James's are lowlands, but I take your point. There's a simple explanation, of course. Hilltops are enriched by breezes. Flood plains are cheap to live in because they're damp. The slums on the Isle of Dogs were always flooding. In 1928 many lost their lives trapped in basements, but back then poor families were regarded as barely human. Their local vicar, one Father Lawless, described his own congregation as "incarnate mushrooms".'

May shook his head in wonder. 'I don't know how you remember all this.'

'I could hardly forget, John. Our family lived through it.'

They passed Hampstead tube station and turned right on to Heath Street, winding between the pastel *bijouteries* primped with winsome hand-painted names. The crest of the hill brought an opening-out of the city. At Spaniard's Road the buildings fell away in a moment, leaving dense evergreen foliage on either side of the narrow route through the heath. 'I still bring my tourist groups up here in the summer,' said Bryant. 'They always look so surprised. There's no mention of the place in their brochures.'

'Perhaps it's better left that way.' May checked the location marker Banbury had sent him. 'We should be here,' he said, pulling over. 'Dan said it was a bit of a walk. I hope you're wearing boots.' Bryant was unsteady at the best of times, but today would probably involve muddy trails.

Bryant climbed out, stretched, broke wind and looked

about. 'I don't like it up here,' he complained. 'Too many trees. Fresh air gives me the creeps.'

There remained about Bryant something twinkling and primal, a light burning in the ignorant darkness that might guide you home safely or set everything ablaze. Even his partner was never quite sure which way things would go.

John May got out and locked the car. Of him gentler things were spoken: that he was a little younger, more charming, empathetic and humane. He understood a fundamental truth, that decency makes one a little dull, and was peacefully resigned to his role. He was the straight man in a music hall duo, the foil who made the comic palatable. A complementary pair of opposites, then; one destined to be loved, the other to be remembered, but always coupled together like the names of old-fashioned department stores or the ingredients in pies.

Bryant stepped back to let an elderly lady pass. She was being pulled towards the heathlands by a gasping terrier. The detectives stepped over the grassy bank beside the road and headed down through a sepulchral gap in the trees.

Bryant glanced back unsurely. 'Do you know where we're going?'

May held up his phone. 'You have one. You should try it occasionally.'

'No, the last time I used the Google map thing it said I was in Edinburgh.'

'Where were you?'

'Well, Edinburgh, but I didn't want anyone to know. My location went out to the entire police network. I suppose you want me to avoid upsetting Dan.'

'He's a little less cavalier about the dead than you, Arthur. He doesn't appreciate your jokes.' May pushed back a clawlike branch so that his partner could pass. 'Your sense of humour is an acquired taste.'

Bryant was indignant. 'I know regular jokes. I heard one quite recently, as a matter of fact. Do you want to hear it?' He thrashed his Malacca walking stick at a holly bush. 'This fish – well, he wasn't a fish, he was a shellfish, a lobster I think, they change colour when you boil them, I know that much. It's quite easy to get muddled because the smaller ones have other names in different countries, like scampi, crayfish, *camarones*, but they're basically all forms of sea-lice. So one night the lobster goes to a nightclub, an underwater one obviously, probably in a rock pool or something, a disco, so he's in this underwater disco looking for, I don't know, a lady lobster, although how they can tell each other apart is a mystery, it must lead to a lot of confusion, but instead he picks up a crab. No, wait, he pulls a mussel. That's it.'

May stopped and gave him an old-fashioned look.

'I'm probably not the best person to write my own memoirs,' Bryant admitted.

'I'll lead the way from here, shall I?' May suggested, forging ahead.

Bryant stayed close behind his partner as they followed Banbury's yellow markers to the murder site. The crime scene manager heard the querulous banter of elderly men approaching through the trees and called out. 'Don't step inside the circle, I haven't finished the—'

Bryant wandered through the cord Banbury had painstakingly attached to a series of pins around the site, snapping it with a ping.

'—photography yet,' Banbury concluded, rocking back on his heels in annoyance.

'Sorry, old sausage, I didn't see you there.' Bryant tipped back his hat as he peered inside the branches of the willow. 'My word.'

John May followed his line of vision. The young man dangling upside down from the willow bough had a strand of wooden beads loosely tied around his neck from which coagulated blood hung in crimson stalactites.

'Not a suicide, then,' said Bryant. 'I suppose if you managed to hang yourself upside down there's a chance you could stab yourself in the throat, but it wouldn't be intuitive.'

'Thank you, Sherlock Holmes.' Banbury pointed down with his tweezers. 'There's some rigor but it's not fixed yet. From the hypostasis and the fact that there's no blood spray below the neck I'd say he was hung up alive and stabbed by someone reaching up, although I'm no expert on such things. A few bits and pieces fell out of his pockets. Take a look at the ground. I have to log them, so don't touch anything.'

May saw a black leather folding wallet, keys on a ring, some coins. 'No phone?'

'Apparently not.'

'Did you examine him?'

'Not my job. Giles will do that.'

'He didn't go up there without a fight. The ground is disturbed all around.' Bryant came closer and eased himself down on to his haunches. He ran a forefinger across some dead leaves and licked it.

'Mr Bryant, please, that's unhygienic and I'm trying to keep this area ...' Banbury gave up. 'Can't you at least put on bootees?'

'No, Dan, they're undignified and I hate baby blue. Can you see what I'm seeing?'

'I hope not, with your eyesight,' said Banbury testily. 'What are you seeing?'

'Here, and here. You have to imagine the ground before his boots churned it all up. It's salt.' Bryant indicated traces at several points beneath the body. 'An arrangement of rock salt and candles, one for every point and junction of a pentangle.'

'I can't see that at all,' Banbury admitted.

'You have to mentally put the leaves back where they were

before the scuffle started. Oh, there are fetish items too.' Ignoring the CSM's protestations, Bryant snapped off a twig and had a poke about. 'What have we got? Necklaces, plastic beads, a doll with its hair burned off and limbs missing, a pair of small, brightly coloured socks and a bracelet.' He hooked it on the end of the twig and lifted it high. 'John, I've not got the right glasses with me, can you see what that says?'

May examined the etched plate on the bracelet's chain. ' "Some men are born great, some achieve greatness." '

'*Twelfth Night*, isn't it? A fight over a lady, perhaps? *Cherchez la femme*. But all of this other stuff . . . The only thing that's missing is – oh.'

It took a lot to shut Bryant up. Banbury rose and followed his gaze. Half buried by the leaves that had accumulated beside a tree stump was a goat's head, with tidy little horns and white whiskers.

'You have got to be kidding,' said Banbury, rubbing at his neck.

'What did you see, boy?' Bryant asked softly.

'Mr B, you're talking to a goat's head.' Banbury raised his hands. 'I'm just saying.'

May stared at the evidence lying scattered across the leafbed. 'Don't tell me this is some kind of satanic ritual. Who would go to all the effort? It's a fair walk down here. Did he come all this way with a duffel bag containing a severed goat's head?'

'Apparently so. We had one of these before,' said Bryant.

'You mean the business in St Bride's Church,' Banbury recalled. 'This looks like someone's gone the full Dennis Wheatley.'

'He's Indian; it could be a hate crime,' said May. 'All this mumbo-jumbo could be a way of disguising racial motivation.'

'I don't know,' said Bryant. 'These things tend to come in cycles.'

'What do you mean?'

Bryant was helped to his feet by May but his knees still cracked alarmingly. He dusted himself down and stretched. 'The last big revival of occultism in London was back in the 1970s. A rash of desecrated cemeteries, mutilated animals and ritualized killings. Much of it was centred within walking distance from here, down at Highgate Cemetery. It went on for a couple of years. Uncertain times renew old beliefs. Whenever there's political upheaval remarkable things happen.'

'*Remarkable*?' The word displeased Banbury. 'Tying some poor little sod up by his feet and hacking into his throat? How is this different from feral kids hurling acid over each other?'

'Oh, Dan, Dan . . . you have to learn to separate these things out.' Bryant patted him on the shoulder. 'The use of acid came about because of the crackdown on knife crime. A knife attack is attempted murder whereas acid is GBH, and it's not illegal to carry a bottle of bleach around with you. What's more, the attacks occur almost exclusively in deprived areas. We're in one of the richest and most exclusive parts of London. Even getting here is hard work. That's what keeps it exclusive.' He pointed at the forest floor. 'This is something . . . very different.'

'How hard would it have been to get him up there?' May wondered, peering into the foliage. 'The branches are pretty springy.'

'He's small and light,' Bryant pointed out. 'Look at him, John, he's a bag of bones.'

'There's a team on its way to cut him down.' Banbury began to pack away his equipment. 'I'll seal up all of this and get it back. No wonder the Met's MIT left us alone. Usually there'd be a dozen officers tramping around here by now.'

'They knew it wouldn't be their case,' said May. 'It happened in a public space, which places it under our remit.'

'He was left upside down in a tree, John. God help us when this one gets out.' Banbury disentangled a pair of scorched doll legs and bagged them. 'Mr B, can you please stop doing that?' Bryant was pressing the tip of his boot into the bloody ground beneath the corpse. 'Apart from anything else, what you're doing is unhygienic. Cadavers leak. You have no way of knowing what excretions you're standing in.'

Bryant chose not to hear him. 'Take a look around for a weapon. It's very sharply tipped, with a long handle.'

Banbury waited for something more forthcoming.

'Well, it's obviously not an ordinary knife. Look.' Bryant reached across to the body. 'To go that deep he had to hold the victim by the back of the neck with his left hand and push forward with his right. He should have used a cut-throat razor. You get a wound as clean and deep as a surgeon's scalpel.' He mimed slashing a face. 'This is something with a tubular end but just as sharp. You can see the fellow's trachea. There's over a gallon of blood soaked into the ground. The only reason to hang him up is to drain the body. He's some kind of sacrifice.'

May threw his partner a look of deep scepticism. 'So the killer leads his victim here, knocks him out, ties him by his ankles, hoists him up, assembles a pile of childhood objects beneath him and opens his throat, covering the ground in blood. That's a satanic ritual, is it? A bit rubbish, if you ask me. What's it going to invoke?'

'That depends on the incantations spoken,' said Bryant. 'He might have used Anton LaVey's Satanic Bible, or he could have opted for the Book of Leviathan. I have a grimoire of satanic invocations back at the office.'

'This would be your office in the seventeenth century, I assume,' said Banbury. 'Would you two listen to yourselves? We don't have occult murders here any more.'

'If not here, where?' Bryant countered. 'Occult, Latin, from *occulere*, to hide. London was always considered to be the secret centre of the magical world. Perhaps it's come out of hiding.'

'So we're turning the clock back to the bad old days of ignorance.' Banbury placed a handful of burnt doll's heads into compartments in his bag. 'My father used to read the *News of the World*. It always ran photographs of witches, inverted commas, dancing naked in the woods.'

'Dan, can you check the nearest car park and all the kerbs along the main road?' May asked. 'There's a lot of mud up there. See if there are any fresh tracks, or any vehicles that have been left overnight.'

'How do we know they came by car?' Banbury asked.

'We don't, but the tube is a fair walk away. There's a night service to Hampstead at the weekend. I'll speak to Anjam Dutta at the King's Cross Surveillance Centre and get him on to it. We can check CCTV for buses and vehicles, but the cameras up here are designed to read licence plates, not look inside vehicles. If we can identify the cars we can work back to the drivers.'

'A nice job for someone.' Banbury snapped his forensic case shut. 'Not me, I hope.'

'Hand it over to one of the Met's central surveillance teams,' Bryant muttered, studying the ground.

'They won't be happy about that.'

'I don't care. I need your mind on higher things.'

'You think this is a higher thing, do you?' Banbury looked up at the body, which had started to rotate a little in the rising wind.

'Well, it's not a random act of violence, is it?' Bryant watched the turning body, fascinated. 'It's premeditated. Somebody brought along a backpack full of equipment and either arranged to meet the victim here or dragged him from somewhere else. As for the ritualistic paraphernalia, it's either there to satisfy a personal obsession, or to send a signal.'

'What kind of signal?'

'Whoever did this knows the details will get out. Somebody wants to be seen as a very bad man.'

'In that case,' said May, 'we'd better make sure that nobody finds out about the ritualized element. Let's contain it in the unit.'

Bryant picked up one of the candles and examined the wick. He dabbed his finger and sniffed it. 'Rosemary oil. Let's find out where these came from.'

'What did I tell you not to do?' the CSM growled in exasperation.

'It doesn't matter,' said May. 'I don't imagine they're admissible evidence.'

'Let's find out,' said Bryant. 'I'll send someone to see Mrs Brandy first thing in the morning.'

As the breeze picked up, leaves spoke and the willow tree creaked. The corpse had turned to face them, its blank brown eyes staring.

5

TEMPEST

When the lights went up, Sparrow Martin realized that she was one of the only people in the audience not wiping away a tear. She never believed film romances because the barriers to love could always be overcome with a last-minute change of heart and a dash to an airport. In her experience, nobody ran into each other's arms. Women were coerced into falling for monsters.

She eased her way out of the Curzon Cinema and walked down through the lower half of Bloomsbury, crossing into the crowded streets of Covent Garden. It had started snowing – the first fall of winter – and was just cold enough to settle. The whitening pavements reversed the polarity of London's light, reflecting it upwards into the yellow night sky. The buildings of Long Acre were outlined with twinkling LEDs and the market was guarded by giant silver reindeer, reminding her (as if it could be forgotten for a second) that Christmas seemed to last for ever in London.

As she walked, she phoned her mother and explained that she would not be travelling up to Suffolk for her birthday celebration next weekend because she had to carry out the post-Christmas stock-take at the Belsize Park Bookshop, which was only the palest of lies.

'Is this about you becoming a vegetarian?' her mother asked. 'Because I'm sure we can find you something to eat. Can you manage chicken? After all, if you eat eggs I don't see how—'

Sparrow made an excuse and rang off. Tonight Covent Garden was proof that human beings were only available in pairs. It seemed as if every laughing, kissing couple in the country had come out on Sunday evening to be planted in her way. She had never felt quite so alone before.

She had always told herself she liked her own company, just not all the time. Without thinking about where she was going, she found herself walking down to the roads sloping from the Strand to the river. Some were narrow alleyways that had to be reached by steeply descending staircases. Within these ginnels time was stopped. There was nothing of the modern age to be seen in them.

The pub stood at the end of a railway tunnel. It was brightly burnished in red and gold, and looked inviting. A few smokers were standing outside even though it was snowing. She enjoyed drinking alone, and went in.

Twenty minutes later she was still there, sketching in another notebook, feeling warm and calm again. Savouring the last mouthful of her brandy, she rose from her place at the tiny circular table and began to gather her belongings. At first she thought she must have left her scarf in the cinema, but then she saw it around the neck of a man who looked as if he was about to leave.

In this situation the first words out of a Londoner's mouth usually constitute an apology. 'I'm sorry,' she began, 'I think you have my scarf.'

When he turned, she was alarmed by his appearance. He

was stoutly built and sharp-eyed, around the middle of his years, with a beard of three days' dark growth and a pugnacious, scowling countenance. He wore a new-looking red baseball cap, and at his neck, quite unmistakeably, her black woollen scarf. He looked down at it now and was about to protest when he saw his own, lying on the floor beneath her stool.

With a gruff noise of apology he set about untangling the one around his throat, passing it back to her with a sheepish shrug. When she stooped to collect his scarf from the floor she lifted the table a little, which knocked her brandy tumbler on its side and caught the edge of his bag so that an electrical screwdriver, a roll of tape and a bristling ring of keys fell out. In the jumble of rearrangement that is always required before venturing back into the cold they laughed a little at the idea of two adults unable to perform such a simple task as exchanging an item of clothing.

As she handed back his belongings she caught sight of something else in his bag, a mortise lock and a door handle. He saw her looking and explained that he worked for a security company. He had been called out to change a lock on the way home.

Now he had decided not to leave after all, and flopped on to his stool, pushing everything back into his holdall. 'It's not easy, is it?' he said. 'Lately everything I do goes like this,' and she agreed. When she looked up she saw that the snow flurries had become a blizzard, and suddenly she felt like staying in the pub for the rest of the night.

He must have caught the look on her face because he said, 'Can I buy you a replacement?'

'It was very nearly empty,' she said and he hesitated, but she added, 'Yes, you can.'

When he returned with the drinks he introduced himself. 'I'm Hugo.'

'I'm Sparrow,' she replied, hastily adding with some embarrassment, 'I know I don't look like one, I like my food too much, I just prefer it to my actual name – Candice. I don't know what my mum was thinking.' The nickname had stuck during early childhood and had stayed around to mock her.

'The same with me,' he said. 'My grandfather used to call me Hugo. My real name belongs to an earlier life. Where were you tonight?'

'How do you know I was anywhere?'

He smiled. 'It's late.'

'I went to hear a talk about *The Tempest* at the National,' she said quickly. She had actually gone the week before. There was no reason to lie, but it suddenly felt important that he should not know everything about her, and should definitely not know that she had sat alone in a cinema watching an absurd romantic comedy.

'I can identify with Prospero.' Hugo rubbed at his nose, thinking. 'He loses his kingdom, then everybody hates him or wants to kill him except his daughter and Alonso.'

Sparrow tried not to look surprised. She reminded herself not to judge people on appearances. He was drinking Guinness, and wiped away a white moustache after his first draught. There was a roughness in his voice that suggested a hard life. When he removed his cap and workman's jacket she could see that he was corded with muscles. His thick tattooed arms hung away from his sides. He looked more like Caliban than Prospero.

'But Prospero wants to control everything and he can't,' said Sparrow. 'Nobody can because people don't behave as you'd expect. They're too human, too messy.'

'I certainly am.' He laughed, wiping Guinness foam from his jeans. 'Sorry, my body's too big for me sometimes.'

And now she laughed because he looked so gentle and awkward. 'I like the National,' he said. 'I didn't think they did shows on Sundays.'

'They don't. It was more like a lecture.'

'Did you go by yourself?'

'Well, yes, but I bumped into some friends there.'

'Funny, because there's a good bar at the National, and yet you crossed the river to come here alone.' He gave her a look of such intense scrutiny that it felt as if he had just asked her to turn out her pockets. She became cooler towards him, but the moment passed and he made a terrible joke, and she found herself laughing, and in the easy swing of the conversation the moment was forgotten.

'I thought for a moment you might be a burglar when I saw what was in your bag,' she said.

'And I thought you must be a writer. Careful you don't lose it.' He tapped the little leather notebook she had left on the table.

When the time came to leave they stood in the rain and stared into their respective phones as he gave her his number. Just before they parted he reached forward as if to shake her hand, then pulled her near to give her the shyest of pecks on the cheek. It was such a childlike gesture that she could not take offence.

'Call me whenever you like,' he said, 'early, late, in ten minutes' time – I don't mind. I'm hardly ever asleep.'

When she reached home Sparrow decided to ring the number. He was twelve years older than her, not wearing well and entirely unsuitable. Her mother would be appalled. Sparrow imagined walking through the city with him, stopping in pubs to listen and disagree and tell white lies. There was something closed off about him – she liked that. He was the opposite of most men she met, who told her too much and vanished without warning.

Sparrow Martin, who instinctively felt that she would pass an unshared life, who always showed such determination and independence, who denied herself any sentiment or sympathy, realized very early on (a few minutes after they had first met, if truth be told) that although she had never in her twenty-three years fallen for anyone, if she were to care for someone now it would be in this way, with this awkward, unsuitable, childlike, rough-handed man.

6

COURT

There were currently twenty-four murder investigation teams within the Met, and the fact that the Peculiar Crimes Unit only handled homicides infuriated every one of them.

Stories of the unit's unprofessional approach to policing had reached the status of legends. Outwardly the detectives appeared to have a reckless disregard for the sanctity of human life. They failed to follow even the most basic rules of procedure, creating nightmares for the Crown Prosecution Service, who had to find plausible ways of dealing with lost evidence, compromised crime scenes, inadmissible statements and flagrantly broken laws. What their critics misunderstood was the reason for this behaviour; it was caused by the unit's founding principle: to seek new ways of dealing with criminality and to ensure that these experimental methods found purchase within the legal system, creating precedence.

There was a pint-sized unsung hero in all this, the person who stood between the unit and the Old Bailey. Her name was Margot Brandy and, as she crossed the flagstone court-yards between London's four Inns of Court, Gray's Inn,

Lincoln's Inn and the Inner and Middle Temples, she was over-looked by the bustling barristers who flapped past in their gowns, lost in abstruse arguments with their colleagues. She cut a pleasing maternal figure but looked out of place, like a lost tourist or a lady delivering packed lunches to the legal profession. No one, if they stopped to consider her, would realize that she was one of the nation's most essential conduits between crime and the courts.

The detectives referred to Mrs Brandy as a court officer, the title given to those who prepare the courtroom before a case, working with the clerks of court, but because she advised on the admissibility of evidence she was more like a CPS lawyer. The unit's consistent success rate meant nothing without the means to prosecute, and Mrs Brandy found ways through the byzantine crown court system that ensured the detectives' efforts were not in vain.

Her colleagues did not pass by in complete obliviousness. Some quietly ridiculed her, for when Mrs Brandy opened her mouth they heard in her nasal cadences and rounded vowels the sounds of an East End market. Her diction was redolent of smoky streets and blackened buildings, fish porters and tea stalls. The passing lawyers heard her on the phone and winced. In short they misjudged her, and by doing so betrayed their professional impartiality. To Mrs Brandy's mind, under-estimation was a weapon that backfired upon the user. She loved watching their faces alter as they realized she was a more than worthy opponent, and so played upon her image, adding glottal stops and cockney neologisms that any decent stage director would have blue-pencilled.

Now she was heading across Lincoln's Inn, her patent-leather heels clicking on stone, with Janice Longbright at her side. 'You're asking me to get involved a bit too early on, lovey,' she said, turning sharply into an arched alley. 'They've only just taken receipt of a body, haven't they?'

'That's the point, Margot, they want to pre-empt any obstruction due to the nature of the death. You know what Mr Bryant will do; he'll be off talking to Satanists before Giles has even completed a preliminary examination of the victim. I want to avoid problems before they start piling up. I need to know how we stand legally.'

'You could have just phoned me for that, sweetheart. Sensational murder – the press will be on it like blowflies. Bury the details. Turn left here, I'm running late, not that it'll make any difference this morning. The prosecutor has ignored my advice and is wrecking the case. Months of careful work to get the defendant to court, all for nothing. You're lucky you're not at the Met any more. I bet you can't remember the last time you had to give evidence.' She swung into an even narrower alley, forcing Longbright to walk behind her. 'I've been meaning to ask, where do you get your hair done?'

'Maison Maurice in the Balls Pond Road,' said Longbright absently.

'Blimey, is he still around? He's got to be ninety. It must be the bleach keeping him alive. We're all getting on. My bathroom cabinet has completely filled up with expensive little pots. That's a bad sign.' Her own hair was a bronze meringue with a rivulet of gold meandering through the waves that made Longbright's blonde Ruth Ellis curls appear almost tame.

'This could be very harmful to us, Margot. Black magic – it sounds like a perfect fit for the unit but not at this time, not after the year we've had. Nobody will take us seriously.'

'You say that, but look around – these courts are steeped in blood and magic.' They had arrived at a cobbled square of unassuming redbrick houses, their doorways framed by small, neatly clipped bay trees. Holborn's mid-morning traffic could only be a few dozen yards away but here it was completely silent.

Mrs Brandy pointed to a bare corner occupied by a single

bedraggled crow. 'In 1586, right at that spot, a nobleman called Anthony Babington was cut into quarters while he was still alive. He made such a racket that Good Queen Bess demanded more humane treatment for his fellow traitors.'

She tapped out a cigarette and lit up as she walked. 'Elizabeth trusted the occultist John Dee. His works were written in hieroglyphs without a code key, but we think he may have translated them using an encryption process called Trithemian steganography. He was sending secret reports from here to Queen Elizabeth. Politics, magic and the law, see, all neatly knotted together. You can't unpick them, love. The circumstances of the death will only create a problem if you use them to prove culpability. Do you see what I'm saying? Don't admit it and it won't become inadmissible. What have you got so far?'

They stopped but could not sit as the only bench was wet. Longbright opened her bag and checked her notebook. 'The victim is a twenty-four-year-old third-generation Indian identified as Dhruv Cheema. He worked in the family's fashion business in Whitechapel, no criminal record, two brothers and two sisters, probably the last person in the world you'd associate with a satanic ritual.' She handed over a slender fold of brown cardboard. 'There's not much in it yet but I'm sure there's already more in your inbox. Look at the last two photographs.'

Mrs Brandy waved smoke from her face and peered at the shots. 'OK, you have some candles and what looks like burnt personal belongings found at the scene. That doesn't make it an occult killing.'

Longbright wasn't so sure. 'Isn't modern occultism mainly about ethnic belief systems? That African boy whose torso was found in the Thames had been ritualistically dismembered, and no one was ever arrested.'

'There hasn't been a successful occult prosecution in the

UK since 1944. You'll have to keep the black magic trappings off the board. They're legally irrelevant.'

'I'll do my best, but John and I have no control over Mr Bryant, you know that.'

'He can investigate whatever he wants, darling, you don't have to enter it in the log. I've got to go.' She ground out her Superking on a Victorian drainpipe. 'Keep me updated, will you?'

Longbright watched Mrs Brandy clatter off across the cobbles on golden heels. Then she raised her collar and headed back into the traffic on High Holborn.

On this most dismal of Monday mornings, number 231 Caledonian Road was incandescent with light, a sure sign that the investigation into the death of Dhruv Cheema was officially under way.

Officers like Colin Bimsley were the backbone of the force: dependable, unfazed, stubborn and infuriatingly patient. He blinked a little, sipped his tea and watched as a pair of hands, then arms, slowly appeared. He was waiting for the large-format printer to deliver a shot of Cheema's body *in situ*. John May had asked for it to be pinned up at the head of the operations room, where everyone could study it and be reminded of what had occurred.

This morning he had been left alone with Jack Renfield, which always made him uneasy. He felt sure that Renfield had not forgiven anyone for making him the butt of their jokes when he was still a desk sergeant at Albany Street nick, and was looking for an opportunity to get back at them. He had only recently rejoined the unit after walking out, and an attitude of bad faith hung over him.

While he was waiting, Colin crossed over to the whiteboard and added incoming data. 'Conflicting stories,' Renfield told him. 'The mother says her son was home all night, but one of the sisters reckons she heard him go out at ten p.m. There are four of them still living at home in Whitechapel: mum, the two brothers and one sister. The father passed away and the other sister left to run a shoe business in Bradford. There are loads more relatives knocking about: kids, grandparents, friends staying over, cousins, aunts and uncles who aren't actually related; it's a complicated picture. The interviews will be a pain in the arse. Buckets of really sweet chai from the mum and everyone contradicting each other.'

Bimsley looked over at Renfield's notes. 'How is she, the mother?'

'Devastated, anxious to help and in the way. They have three stores called Krishna Sarees. They live above the main shop and in the house next door. They're well known around Whitechapel, which probably means a few villains know them too.' Renfield looked about. 'When's Janice due back?'

Colin raised a hand. 'Can you just stop it, Jack?'

'What?'

'You check your watch every five minutes when she's out.'

'Do I? I don't think I do, mate.'

'I think you need to give her a bit of space.'

'That's what you think, is it?'

'She's not going to take you back.'

Renfield smoothed his hair as he studied the board, keen to appear unconcerned. 'Has she told you something?'

'She doesn't need to. You left her. She only gives men one chance.'

'Wait, has she been seeing someone?'

'Not since you. Not to my knowledge.'

Renfield snorted.

'What does that mean?' Colin asked.

'Your knowledge. What, of women? How long has it taken you to get Meera on your side?'

'It wasn't for lack of trying. I knew what I wanted. You didn't.'

Renfield stepped a little too close. 'You don't know what you're talking about, pal.'

'I know that Janice is too good for you.'

Renfield moved so swiftly that Colin was caught by surprise. The hand that pinned him to the whiteboard tightened around his throat. 'You've been a few rounds in a boxing ring. So have I, but not with my mates. Only with people I don't like. Are you still falling down a lot? I checked that out, did I tell you? Irlen Syndrome, isn't that what it's called? You'd better mind your own business, Colin. You might fall down a long flight of stairs soon.'

Meera saw everything from the doorway. She had always had her doubts about Renfield. His insecurities found their outlet in a volatile streak. Stopping the confrontation would have made matters worse. She stepped back into the corridor and silently watched as Bimsley pulled himself free.

'From now on I'm looking for you,' Renfield warned. 'I know you and Janice get on well. You're protective. That's OK, that's expected. You can carry on as you are. But if you do anything to get in the way of us, I will take you down. Are we clear on that?'

Bimsley did not trust himself to answer, and stared back in mute anger. Renfield suddenly reached forward and Bimsley flinched. Renfield patted him daintily on the shoulder. 'I'm glad we had this little talk.'

Meera instinctively knew that for now it was best to keep counsel. She drew a deep breath and walked into the room.

7

RITE

In the operations room, the staff reorganized themselves into natural pairings and continued tracing witnesses and filing reports until the online London magazine *Hard News* updated its site at 5.00 p.m.

Janice Longbright knew they were in trouble when she saw the red on-screen band: *Breaking News: Police Hunt Hampstead Heath Black Magic Murderer.*

Everyone gathered around the monitor. The victim had not been named and the unit was not cited, but basic details about the death were present and correct. The article was by one Vincent Dillard, who had tracked down Sophie Ward, the nurse who had discovered the body. She had chosen not to heed John May's warning about talking to the press, and had granted the magazine an extensive interview.

'He must have paid her,' said Longbright. 'Do you want me to close her down?'

'No,' said May, 'the damage is done.' He looked back at the whiteboards. They resembled a large hand-drawn jigsaw with most of the key pieces missing. 'There are way too many gaps here. What don't we know?'

He picked up a red Sharpie and wrote on the board. '*Why he went there.* Dhruv Cheema had few friends outside his immediate circle in the East End, and none in North London. It's not his manor.' He wrote again. '*How he got there.* His Oyster card wasn't used on the Hammersmith & City or Northern lines between Whitechapel and Hampstead. We know he was using a burner, but GSM phones have an IMEI code that the carrier can see, so we can geolocate it to Hampstead at one fifteen a.m. The problem with data like this is that it tells us nothing new.'

He carried on down the board. '*Who he was with.* Was he mugged and taken there, or did he arrange to meet someone? The dark covers up a lot of bad behaviour. His family say he wasn't one for socializing and no obvious names come to mind. *What he was doing there.* Mid-point between Saturday night and Sunday morning, an odd time and place to arrange a hook-up. The most obvious question: Was it sex? Hampstead police tell us the area is still popular with closeted males at that time of the morning. Was there anyone else around who saw something? *Who he met.* No witnesses, no descriptions. So far we haven't found anyone who saw him on Heath Street, so we need to look further afield. *When he went there.* The brother and sister can't even agree on whether he stayed home or went out. Meera, you spoke to the family – what did you make of them?'

'They didn't strike me as dodgy, if that's what you mean.' Meera scanned her notes. 'The mother's just like my mum, protective and argumentative. I asked her about Cheema's dating status and got the "he hasn't met the right girl yet" speech, so for now it's open to conjecture. I also talked to the shop owners next door to Krishna Sarees. The Cheemas are hard-working and well liked. There's a question mark over the other brother – he hangs out in the Blind Beggar with a bit of a sketchy crowd – but we've never had cause to feel his collar. At this moment anyway, the Cheemas are pretty clean.'

'Good for the family, lousy for us.' May looked around. 'I want some clear answers, so let's start by resolving the question of Cheema's whereabouts earlier on Saturday night. Put some pressure on the family, check out his local, dig up some friends. Has anyone seen Arthur?'

'He's upstairs with that crazy woman,' said Meera.

'Which one? Narrow it down.'

Meera rolled her eyes. 'You know, Madame Arcati, the one who blessed the building when we moved in.'

May knew only too well. Maggie Armitage had sprinkled consecrated oil throughout the place to banish evil spirits. Unfortunately the oil consisted of herbs mixed with WD40, and was so slippery that everyone had to hang on to the bannisters to get upstairs. Colin solved the problem by pouring sand on the floors, but it had turned the crossing of the first-floor landing into a vaudeville routine.

May's eyes narrowed in annoyance. 'What is that woman doing here?'

'I think someone invited her across the threshold,' said Meera.

'I do not want Maggie Armitage anywhere near this investigation. If Raymond catches sight of her he'll go through the roof. Didn't Mrs Brandy warn against introducing sensational elements into the investigation?'

'She said they'd damage the credibility of our case,' Janice confirmed without looking up from her laptop. 'The occult paraphernalia would be ruled inadmissible because it doesn't add proof of intent to harm.'

'Then let's play it by the book for now. Stay away from questionable outside sources, all of you. I'll get Arthur to do the same.'

'Good luck with that,' muttered Renfield.

May looked up at the ceiling. He dreaded to imagine what his partner and the white witch might be discussing.

'The ageing process,' said Bryant, pausing at the top of the stairs. 'It's killing me. Hang on a minute, I have to get my breath back. You know the things I hate most about getting old? Kneeling down and wondering if I'll ever get back up again. Never leaving the house without having to pee first. Old people tell me about their illnesses and assume I care. Your lungs turn into deflated balloons, your feet hurt all the time. Look at me – I look like a bald bat. And your ears get huge. Did you ever see Noel Coward in later life? He looked like a taxi with its doors open.'

Bryant ushered his old friend into the musty attic-turned-evidence room. Half a dozen red steel IKEA storage racks had been set up beneath the eaves. There was a dead pigeon on the cross-beam of the vaulted ceiling. Something brown and viscous was pooling beneath a bin bag full of unidentified evidence that no one had been brave enough to move.

He tried the light switch. Nothing happened. The room remained as stubbornly shadowy as a forensics laboratory on a TV show. Much of the evidence held by the Peculiar Crimes Unit existed in limbo. Having not been presented by the prosecution, it could be retained indefinitely. Often the defendant failed to claim back seized items. There were pieces here that went back to the founding of the unit, including a Victorian chamber pot, a scythe and a wooden ventriloquist's dummy that would have given Jack the Ripper the creeps. Other more exotic items had gone missing during Christmas parties.

'Why did you want to see me?' asked Maggie. The little white witch had made a game attempt to dress fashionably but still looked like a beloved old pet dressed up by children. Having forgone wintry shades, she had opted for rainbow leggings, a purple Indian smock covered in poorly rendered tigers and a vintage nurse's cape. There was still a scallywag air about her, from her upturned nose to her bitten emerald fingernails.

'I tried a few people at short notice and didn't know who else to ask, so I ended up with you,' Bryant explained.

'How thoughtful.' Maggie was used to being the last resort. 'It smells of death in here.'

'That'll be Colin's socks. It's the only humidity-controlled room in the building so he leaves his gym kit up here.' He led her to a shelf stacked with bulky Ziploc bags. 'Evidence from yesterday. I want you to take a look.'

'Can I take them out and handle them?'

Bryant surveyed the plastic sacks on the shelf. 'We'd better not. Dan will kill me. You can peep inside them, though.' He opened the top of one and showed it to her.

'A black candle.' Maggie sniffed the air. 'Rosemary. It increases cognizance, so it's used in occult rituals for protection and purification. It's used in exorcism rites too.'

She peered along the metal rack, opening the other Ziplocs that contained candles, sniffing each one in turn. 'Goodness, that's overwhelming. You need a snort of fresh coffee beans between each one to clear the senses. Valerian, mugwort, fleabane, pennyroyal and honeysuckle.'

Bryant was amazed. 'You can tell all those from just one sniff?'

'They're labelled.' She turned over one bag and showed him. 'Waitrose. Each of these contains a herb used in ritual magic. Either somebody knows what they're doing or there was a BOGOF.'

'What *are* they doing?' Bryant wondered.

As a Grand Order Grade IV White Witch of the Coven of St James the Elder, Kentish Town, Maggie was rather over-qualified to answer. 'Well, he – I'm assuming it's a he?'

'Cheema is a small chap, young, fit, probably under ten stone, but someone still managed to haul him high on a rope, so let's say yes.'

'I don't think he's trying to do the most obvious thing.'

'Which is what?'

'Perform a sacrificial rite to summon the Devil.'

'Good to know. I'd have had trouble selling that in. There was some rock-salt left around, roughly in the shape of a pentangle.'

'Are you sure it was a pentangle? Rock salt is preferred for purging and filtering rituals, but the pentangle goes against its use. The two don't fit together.'

Bryant searched among the bags. 'There's something else here. You'd better put gloves on.' He tore plastics from the roll on the shelf and handed them over. 'Try to get all your fingers in this time.'

He passed her the doll parts. Maggie pressed them to her breast theatrically and closed her eyes. 'Occult crime, animal mutilations and suchlike are usually the work of bored teenagers. They don't sacrifice adults in satanic circles.'

'Why not?'

'The genuine rituals take forever and are incredibly boring, mainly because the liturgical texts are cobbled together from books published anywhere between 1487, when the *Malleus Maleficarum* appeared, to the late 1930s, when there was another revival of interest in sorcery. Most of it consisted of unreadable doggerel churned out by ill-informed amateurs and sensationalized by the tabloids. What else did you find?'

'Dan hasn't had a chance to sort these out yet.' Bryant tipped the contents of a clear plastic bag on to a table top. He waited while Maggie went through the pile of leaves, blackened necklaces, clothing and pebbles.

'Thirteen stones, sprigs of holly, laurel and willow, burnt effigies, all of the terrible old clichés present and correct.'

'What do you mean?'

'The trouble with ceremonial rites is that they're copied from a handful of original liturgical texts and then embellished – personalized, if you like – by the practitioner. If you need followers, the best way to create loyalty is by giving them something unique to do.'

'Are you saying the fellow has acolytes?' Bryant asked, fishing out a piece of singed blue nylon, possibly from a bed-jacket. 'This looks like it belongs to a woman.'

'You know, before the Enlightenment the Catholic Church was entirely to blame for demonology. The Witchcraft Act of 1735 wasn't repealed until 1951, when the courts realized that "occult" crimes mainly consisted of fraudulent claims made by fake mediums.'

'You're quite sceptical for a believer,' Bryant pointed out.

She patted his hand. 'I have to be, darling. There are real sensitives, of course, people like me who are adept at reading others, but cheesecloth ectoplasm and spirit photography vanished with the arrival of decent camera lenses. But people who become fascinated by sacrifice and ritual can be highly irrational, dangerous even. Drugs are often used to heighten the split from rationality.'

'Can you get anything else from this lot?'

'I'll make a list of the items then whip through my arcana, see what we can come up with. My spiritualist friend Kiskaya Mandeville is popping over later in the week. We could summon Squadron Leader Smethwick.'

Bryant was surprised. 'I thought you could only get hold of your familiar through that stuffed Abyssinian cat her mother owned.'

'Kiskaya located another conduit to the afterlife through a ginger tom called Arbuthnot who got himself run over. She's only on week three of her taxidermy course. He's got his smile back but he's still a bit flat.'

'By all means summon some spirits,' said Bryant, humouring her. 'If you think it will help.'

'Well, no, I don't,' said Maggie. 'That's the point. Squadron Leader Smethwick is C of E, so he'll be hopeless. This is not Christian black magic.'

'How can you be sure of that?'

'May I?' She emptied another plastic bag on to the table. 'These herbs and wooden beads are associated with Santeria, a Spanish–Caribbean religion connected to the worship of saints. The candles and the pentacle are familiar from images of the black mass. The effigies are *djabs* allied to Cuban Vodou, and the rest has been culled from old Hammer horror films.' She held the remains of a scorched bat. 'He could have been conducting a cleansing rite, and came up with all this to fit some personal theory about the victim.'

'But for what purpose?' asked Bryant, confused.

'To strike fear into his enemies and gain respect from his peers. A gang initiation, perhaps. In America students have been known to die in college hazing ceremonies.'

'Maggie, I think it's more likely that the perpetrator is suffering from some kind of undiagnosed psychosis,' said Bryant. 'Enough to drive him out on to the night streets and find demons inside people. There are at least a dozen different kinds of psychotic behaviour exacerbated by drugs and alcohol. If he went to the heath looking for a victim, he could do it again.'

Maggie carefully swept the remains back into bags. 'You can start by finding out where all these items came from, but I'll tell you now, it's all mass-produced. You need to get hold of something more personal. It doesn't take a white witch to tell you this.' She hesitated. 'How was the victim stabbed?'

'He was hung upside down and jabbed in the throat. Why?'

'I was thinking of medieval witch trials, the ones designed so that they couldn't be won. You know, if you cry out or bleed it means you're guilty, that sort of thing. The witch-finders used metal skewers.'

'You think this chap was tortured for information?'

'Or to implicate someone else. That was what usually happened.'

'It's worth looking into. I'd better get back to the operations room and make it look like we're running a normal investigation.'

'I thought you had John to do that for you.'

Bryant dropped to a conspiratorial tone. 'He can be quite unorthodox in his methods if you don't watch him.'

'You've worked together a long time, haven't you?' Maggie reached out and gave Bryant's houndstooth waistcoat a stroke. 'Give me your right hand. Oh dear, bad circulation.' She rubbed his fingers between her own. 'I have to tell you, Arthur. I wasn't going to see you today. There's something coming. Something very harmful.'

'How do you know?'

'There's been a gathering of signs around both you and John. And there are portents everywhere. This morning my bedroom was full of moths, and last night there were four cats in the garden all with the same genetic background. They're sending me messages.'

'R-i-ght,' said Bryant very slowly.

'I know, this is my psychosis, but I believe I have the curse of true sight. We're not supposed to warn people in case they try to change the course of fate, but you need to know.'

This was not something Bryant wished to hear, but Maggie's instincts rarely failed her. The hardest part was understanding her predictions, which never arrived clearly labelled. 'What's going to happen?' he asked.

'You and John.' She was struggling to shield him from pain. 'You've always relied so much on each other, but I think that's coming to an end.' She patted his hand before letting it go. 'I see a fracture. You may have to learn to rely on yourself from now on.'

'What do you mean?'

'I'm so sorry. I wish there was something I could do but it's forewritten.'

'What's forewritten, you second-rate Cassandra? You can't just not tell me.'

'I'm not *allowed* to tell you.'

'Who says so? Zeus? Satan? Buddha? Your washing machine?'

'Forget I spoke, Arthur.'

'I wish I could.' He stuffed the last of the evidence back into its bag and replaced it on the shelf.

'You brought me here for advice about the case.' Maggie seemed anxious to change the subject. 'There are some people you could meet who might be able to give you more accurate information but I have no way of contacting them.'

'Why not?'

'They're being followed.' This was a not entirely unfamiliar conversational route for Maggie to take. Her mind was like a railway carriage that rolled on to branch lines and frequently ended up in a siding.

'I'll let you know if I need them,' said Bryant. 'Let me get you an Uber. You were here on police business so the unit can pay for it.'

She stayed his hand on the phone. 'No, I won't use them. They sent me a most bizarre and offensive message.'

'What are you talking about? Show me.'

She separated the tissues stuck to her ancient pink sparkly Nokia and unlocked it. Bryant read through her incoming texts. 'It's an automated response,' he said. 'Even I know that. They're asking you to rate your driver.'

'Oh.' She took the phone back and squinted at it. 'I misread that. So sorry. I'm afraid I've really been no help at all.'

He sent Maggie ahead while he locked the door. He knew

she was a little touched, but still did not wish to look into her eyes, which sometimes saw too far. If she told him there was a gathering of signs it was because she believed in such a thing with all her heart. She had never told him how these insights first gained access, but he knew they had started in the difficult years after her divorce. She had once told him, 'We English are such appalling hypocrites. We say success is vulgar but secretly crave it, treasure our privacy but hate to be alone, and constantly complain about the Continent until we can afford to live there. I say what I feel to be true, and I'm only taken seriously if they think I'm a witch. Nothing has changed in half a millennium.'

He caught up with her on the stairs and slipped a twenty-pound note into her jacket pocket. 'I'm sorry I called you a second-rate Cassandra. Where can I get more advice about the ritualized elements of the attack?'

'Do you have a few minutes? I can introduce you to Percy. I'm heading that way myself.'

He hesitated for a moment. 'Is this fellow in any way connected with your coven?'

'Don't worry, he's perfectly normal even though he runs a bookshop,' Maggie assured him. 'I'll walk there with you.'

8

HARUSPEX

'Atlantis, Watkins, Treadwell's and Mysteries would have been my first choices but then I remembered Percy,' said Maggie, knotting her sunshine-yellow rain-hat. It had started to pelt down so she huddled under Bryant's umbrella as they crossed Euston Road, which was steaming with angry vehicles. 'The owners are all knowledgeable and happy to share information, but there's a new shop nearby, Merlin's Prophecy in Woburn Walk. The owner is Percy Pinner, not much of a believer.'

'Then why is he running an occult bookshop?' Bryant threatened a taxi with his walking stick much as a tamer would send a lion back. 'And how old is he to have a name like Percy?'

'He's unfeasibly young, took his grandfather's name. He's a follower of Charles Fort, opened the shop as "a forum for the incurably curious".'

'Are there still such people?' He allowed Maggie to lure him deeper into the backstreets.

'There must be,' Maggie replied. 'They're helping to fund

the Coven of St James the Elder. In return we teach them spiritual enlightenment and upholstery repair.'

'I wouldn't have thought of those as a natural fit.'

'Oh yes. There comes a point in your life when you find you can transcend to a higher plane more easily in an armchair. Here we are.'

They had turned into one of London's barely noticed time capsules. Woburn Walk had been its first pedestrian shopping street, and although it was now a couple of hundred years old, the cobbled lane was still filled with low, bow-fronted shops. Here, beside the house where the poet Yeats had lived, stood a newcomer. Maggie pushed back the door and set off an electronic chime.

'Penderel's Oak!' Bryant clapped his hands excitedly. 'What a treasure trove! First editions of Raleigh's *Science of Alchemy* and Sprague's *Spirit Obsession*. I was beginning to doubt their existence.'

If any shop could have been explicitly designed to excite the senses of an elderly esoteric it was this one. Every corner of its limited space was crammed with out-of-print editions that drew the eye like jewels in the Cheapside Hoard. There was no Disneyfied magic here to entice passing trade. The dense, virtually incomprehensible texts on display were more demanding than a long kneel in a cold church. There was a scent of amber and clove in the air, with top notes of disinfectant. In a city of T-shirt stores and coffee chains an emporium of curiosities felt ephemeral and doomed.

'I say, an old issue of *Mephiticus*.' Bryant picked up a copy of the least popular esoteric magazine ever produced by an embittered Bloomsbury academic. 'William Blake. What a misery guts. He knew London at night, though.'

The owner appeared through a pair of burgundy velvet curtains. 'Sorry,' he said. 'Sometimes I get so absorbed I don't hear the bell.'

He stopped to take in his visitor. Lumpy brown overcoat, mismatched belt, trousers belonging to a very old suit, the benign features of a Cabbage Patch doll that had seen better days. A fairly typical customer.

'No doubt you were lost in some exquisite volume of arcana,' said Bryant happily.

'No, playing *Call of Duty*. It gives me a break.' Pinner had a laugh like somebody rubbing a mark off a window. He was in his mid-twenties but had the pudgy, unformed features of a man who would become defined when he hit forty, much as Bryant himself had done.

'I like your door chime,' said Bryant, 'Da-*daa*-de-da-daa-de-dah-*dah*, very amusing.'

'Ah yes, Gilbert and Sullivan's *The Sorcerer*. "My name is John Wellington Wells, I'm a dealer in magic and spells." You're the first person to get it. Excuse me.' He sneezed violently. 'When I'm cataloguing in here the dust gets so thick I need my inhaler. We've had new stock in. Another dead collector, always welcome.' He turned to the white witch. 'Maggie, you're always bringing me customers.'

'This time I'm bringing you a copper,' said Maggie. 'Arthur Bryant.'

Bryant shook the proprietor's hand. 'I didn't think anyone was still interested in this kind of thing any more. Especially a man of your age.'

'Well, I'm not a man of my age, that's the trouble. I go to the Bloomsbury Esoteric Book Fair and there's just me and a dozen elderly men with carrier bags full of yellowed paper. I thought Harry Potter might have brought in some fresh blood, but his fans are more interested in wands. I'm afraid we're literally a dying breed. At least we're free to pursue our heretical enthusiasms. In times past we'd have been burned alive.'

'So, what is it?' Bryant asked.

Pinner looked puzzled. 'What is what?'

'Merlin's prophecy. If you're going to open a shop with that name it's a good idea to have an answer.'

'Oh, *that*. Merlin's an amalgam, of course. He's many different figures squashed into one by Geoffrey of Monmouth in his *Historia Regum Britanniae*. He's a cambion.'

'That's French for lorry, isn't it?' asked Maggie.

'No, you silly woman, that's *camion*,' said Bryant. 'A cambion is born of a mortal woman and an incubus.'

'Oh, well done, you know your stuff.' Pinner was delighted. 'Merlin prophesied that a great tree would grow at the Tower of London with just three branches, yet it would overshadow England. The North Wind would destroy one branch, the second would overgrow the third and the remaining branch would shelter many foreign birds, which would promptly lose the power of flight.'

'That's a bit obscure even for me,' said Bryant.

'But that's the point,' Pinner replied. 'It can be read in so many ways. The Hanoverians thought it was a comment on the German royal family occupying the British throne. Now it could be seen as an argument against Brexit. Look around you. What's the common thread that connects these books? It's humankind seeking answers. We seek to beg gifts from gods and prophesy the future.'

'You know what they say. When the king seeks advice from the seer, the empire is in trouble,' said Bryant.

Pinner was suffused with passion. 'And you know why? Because whenever we lose our way we turn to prognostications and auguries. Once the nation stops believing it is the master of its fate, when it no longer chooses intelligence over emotion and starts divining truths from signs, it's pretty much *arrivederci, baby*.'

'And yet here you are,' said Bryant, 'a haruspex offering to look through the entrails of a sacrifice.'

'Many of us are lost and looking for signs, Mr Bryant.' He poked himself in the waistcoat. 'What we find is ourselves, but we need something to validate our opinions.'

'He's got a satanic murder he wants you to have a look at,' Maggie blurted out. 'It's got all the signs—'

Bryant hated someone stealing his thunder. 'A homicide on Hampstead Heath,' he said over her. 'You may have already read about it, unfortunately.'

'No. I've been bogged down in the new Philip Pullman. Sometimes real life feels less authentic than what you read.'

'I have some photographic evidence from the scene here.' Digging into his satchel, Bryant pulled out a dog-eared folder and spread some photographs before the startled bookshop owner.

'Hang on, are you supposed to let me see this sort of thing?'

'No, of course not, but I can let you have a butcher's at the paraphernalia.'

Percy pulled up a pew and studied them carefully. 'Well, this is interesting. I don't see how I can help.'

'Just tell us what comes to mind,' Bryant suggested.

Percy perused the pages. 'An occult ceremony. But not, I fear, a very realistic one.'

'Why not?'

'There's a rule of thumb you can apply to magic. Anything that is worth doing has already been done with great frequency. Anything that remains out of reach should be given a wide berth.'

'A cynical reading of your stock-in-trade, surely,' said Bryant.

'Mr Bryant, this is intended to look like a ritual because it contains all of the elements which are most familiar to us.' He pulled a large volume from the shelf behind him and compared photographs. 'Some of these items belong to rituals of so-called "offensive" magic, invoking curses so that "nothing may prosper nor go forward". They're usually conducted around the lunar cycle. What was Sunday, a full moon? That could be significant. Were there any numerals or words found carved into trees in the area?'

'We didn't look specifically,' said Bryant, 'but I'm not aware of any being found.'

'No other disturbances? Just two sets of footprints?'

'It's a muddy wood. There was some disruption of foliage. No cast-aside vestments or blood-filled chalices, nothing Crowleyish.'

'Oh, *Crowley*,' said Pinner dismissively. 'A boring old sex addict with rich parents who ended up on the cover of the *Sergeant Pepper* album. I think it's pretty obvious what you've got here.' He began to reassemble the photographs into a neat pile and replace them in the folder.

'What's your conclusion?' asked Bryant.

'It's not an occult ritual at all. That's what you want to know, isn't it?'

'But the dolls, the candles, the pentagram . . .'

'The trappings are all wrong. For example, the candles. They're either used for divination – you drip the wax and study the patterns – or to request something.'

'How do you do that?'

'You make a wish and write it on a piece of paper, then fold it up and burn it. The magical power is supposedly contained in the flame. But here you've got black candles, used to sow discord and protect the user from retribution, and red ones, which are a symbol of courage and love. They negate each other. Whoever did this copied them from lousy horror films and novels, a bit of image-magic here, an invocation there, a few creepy-looking bits and bobs. It's just thrown-together rubbish.'

Maggie gave Bryant a look that said *I told you so*.

'Real rituals are highly complex and evolve over several

long and very boring hours of incantations. The ceremonies are designed to prove the faith of the participants.'

'I have a full inventory of items here.' Bryant handed him a list.

The bookseller checked through it. 'No witch bottles, runes or magic squares, just stuff you'd find in a teenager's bedroom.'

'Then why bother to assemble it at all?'

'He's either Neolithically dim or off his head on drugs,' said Pinner cheerily.

'So much for the expert opinion.' Bryant snatched the folder back.

Pinner reached out and laid a hand on his arm. 'I'm not saying there isn't a purpose, Mr Bryant. Crowley wanted women to believe he was a mystic. This man just wants to scare someone.'

9

RESCUE

The crane lights shone down like dying red stars, marking mountain ranges through the West End, tracing a financial graph over the Square Mile, swinging like ships' masts along the Thames. They turned the city into a desolate place at night.

The oil-dark surface of the Thames mirrored the crane lights and fractured them as a breeze brushed the reaches of the river.

Few boats moved across the water at this time of night. A solitary black cab drifted over the bridge and along the Embankment, following a bright, empty night bus. At this time the streets were no busier than they had been a century earlier. A hundred years ago some workers would have been on their way to factories. Now a handful were heading home from clubs.

Hugo Blake studied the panorama before him. The wide grey terrace of Somerset House was behind, on his left. The cubist concrete blocks of the National Theatre squatted on the other side of the river. It was an oddly comforting structure that reminded him of the decks of a container ship. A green dot-matrix message still ran across the façade as if to announce a departing flight: *The Tempest by William Shakespeare*. He could smell the musk of Thames silt, filtrated through the oxygen that daily bloomed from the embankment trees. The elements were all around, the dank wind on his neck, moisture dampening his jacket, settling in droplets on his upturned cheek.

There was no traffic at all on Waterloo Bridge. One southbound lane was shut for roadworks; perhaps drivers had diverted to Blackfriars or Westminster. The wind was raising goose pimples on his bare arms. He wore a loose-fitting black T-shirt, a denim jacket, black jeans and rubber-soled work boots. He walked to the bridge rail and swung one leg over the top, then the other, nimbly shifting his weight to the edge of the bar.

Balancing on the white steel pole, he pressed his heels against the concrete lip of the bridge. It was a long way down. He could feel the wind drawing through the arches beneath him. Somewhere below in the darkness a barge moved swiftly and silently between the starlings.

As Blake checked his watch, he heard someone approaching.

Luke Dickinson was heading home from a birthday celebration that had turned drunk and messy. Why did every bad party end with a girl crying in the bathroom? The taxi he'd ordered had got lost somewhere along the Strand so he'd cancelled it and decided to walk. He needed the air anyway. When he ran a hand through his hair he found it slick with sweat. That was the weird thing about London: you could be cold one minute and overheated the next, even in the middle of winter. His grey suit jacket felt hot and damp on his back. The occluded sky could not decide between rain or snow, and settled for neither.

As he walked on to the bridge heading to the south side, he saw a broad-shouldered man in a red baseball cap balancing on the white steel pole of the balustrade. He knew at once that he was about to see someone jump. The man was sitting on the wrong side of the guard rail, facing out over the water, bracing himself, ready to push away.

The river was as high as he had ever seen it, turbulent and fatal, rushing and dark as liquid night. Anyone plunging in there now would be unlikely to surface.

As Dickinson approached he slowed down. He was quite drunk, and concentrated on walking in a straight line. He wanted the jumper to see that he meant no harm. Below them the shining black water slapped and sucked at the foreshore.

'Hey, pal – hey, mate – that's a long drop,' Dickinson called, raising a hand, trying to sound friendly. 'Do you want to get on this side of the railing?'

Blake inclined his head slightly, not really seeing, listening to the water. 'It's full of secrets, the river,' he said.

'Maybe, mate, but you wouldn't want to see 'em up close. If you fall in you won't come back out. There's a really strong downstream current. The tide's going out. The river bed's uneven and the undertow can pull you down in seconds.'

Dickinson knew it was important to keep talking, to stop him from thinking about jumping. As he got closer he tried to recall what else he knew about the river. 'Even if you survived the fall and didn't lose consciousness the cold would hit you with a gasp reflex, and you don't want that. Because it was raining last night, and there'll be plenty of sewage overspill in there. If you survived they'd have to pump your stomach and, mate, I had that once after taking some duff gak and it was bloody horrible.' He was close now, almost close enough to grab the guy, who looked completely out of it. *Keep talking,* he told himself.

'I mean, even if you swam straight to the bank you might not make it to the other side. It's impossible to swim across in a straight line. Who knows where you'd end up. Dartford, maybe. Or Southend. Who wants to go to Southend? You ever met anyone from there? Me neither.'

He was lightly touching the older man's shoulder now, but felt him flinch and tense up. He was surprised to feel solid muscle beneath his palm. 'Hey, things can't be that bad, can they? Really?' He didn't know what else to say.

Blake turned and looked up at him, seeing him properly for the first time. His eyes were in shadow. 'The river was here before us, and it'll be here after us,' he said.

'Fair point. Come on, let me get you back on to the right side of the barrier.' He held out his arms and the man finally, tentatively, took his wrists. 'That's it. Lean on me, I'll get you over. Just lift your leg . . .'

The man had a surprisingly strong grip. He was stocky but appeared to be in unusually good shape. His left hand dug into Dickinson's arms. The balance of weight shifted between them. Dickinson steadied himself to haul Blake back over the guard rail, but was quickly dragged forward. He braced his left leg on the pavement and pulled harder.

For a moment they grappled silently. 'You have to work with me—' Dickinson began, before the older man suddenly pulled down hard on Dickinson's arm.

Dickinson yelped and tried to break free.

Blake brought his face close. 'Tell me what you did.'

'Mate, you've got the wrong guy—' Dickinson tried to back away but the man rose up in front of him and carefully explained what he wanted.

Blake waited for an answer.

Understanding dawned on Dickinson's face. He tried to say that it was all a stupid mistake. For a moment he thought he was about to be released. Then in one smooth movement his throat was pierced with something that stung like ice.

Yanking his rescuer past him, Blake sent him over the rail.

Dickinson tumbled out but did not fall. Reaching up, he clutched at his attacker's jacket until it tore. One hand kept him attached to the railing, the other was held at the gushing wound in his throat. His left foot remained on the concrete ledge below. He tried to cry out but blood muffled the sound.

Dickinson hung from the bridge, his grip on the steel railing incrementally loosening. His foot slid off the ledge. A beard of blood hung from him, blackening his clothes. The older man raised a boot and kicked out at his upturned face.

Dickinson tried to cry out as his fingers fought for purchase. He slipped out into the oblivion of the river. A flailing cry, a distant splash, then a barge passed over the surface of the water and all was silent once more.

Blake stepped nimbly back on to the pavement. He pulled his jacket straight and pocketed the mobile he had lifted from Dickinson. His jacket had a large patch of blood on the front. He emptied the pockets and dropped the jacket over the side of the bridge.

His watch gave him one minute past four. He knew he should have allowed several days to pass after the first death, but opportunity was not a lengthy visitor. His hands had stopped shaking. He hurried off across Waterloo Bridge, the burden of his task already easing.

He walked on through the city, following the line of the Thames but staying several streets back. He knew instinctively when to turn, tracing the river's treacherous folds so that his direction remained steadfast. He passed no one. Even the churches were bolted shut. There was no sanctuary left in London now.

In the backstreets hybrid commuter cars stood before their owners' houses like funfair carriages waiting to be filled. Nobody seemed to drive much any more. The only vehicles he saw on the road were guided by hollow-eyed Uber employees, who stared at their electronic maps and barely noticed the avenues of houses through which they passed. In the backstreets there were no cameras to catch the antics of late-night revellers. Monday was transforming itself into Tuesday, and the houses were dark with sleepers storing up energy for the rest of the working week.

He moved on to a main thoroughfare. No sun arrived to herald dawn. Lights tinked on in high-street stores, the first workers appeared and the darkness slowly lifted, from indigo to a hundred hues of grey, as if the sky was made of wet cement. London in its long winter was leached of colour and enclosed in cloud, as if the city had rejected all offers of natural light.

In Rotherhithe an over-bright café sat in a row of darkened one-storey shops. They were a unique London feature that even lifelong residents failed to notice; the once-elegant Victorian houses had been constructed with spacious front lawns, but while the rich retained their gardens, in the poorer areas these had been built upon, so that their social inferiors found themselves living above shops. And so London continued to stratify its population.

The café was clean and utilitarian. Across the window were laminated aerial shots of breakfasts, photographed like studies of skin diseases. Blake checked his fingers. The nails of his right hand were rimed with blood. It looked odd that he was outside in January without a jacket. He entered and ordered a Full English at the counter, carrying a mug of tea back to a table. In the corner a pair of young African men were arguing softly, fiercely, one stabbing at a piece of paper. Blake was invisible to them, invisible to everyone because he knew how to withdraw and become unobtrusive. He tried to clear his head and think about his next step.

When Blake closed his eyes he saw Cheema dangling from the tree, attempting to grab him, blood cascading from the hole in his throat. He saw Dickinson bleary and confused, struggling to keep his balance on the edge of the bridge. He tried to read his own feelings. Could they have been innocent? Did he have any regrets, feel any shame or sympathy? He remembered what his mates had told him: if you can't be sure, burn them all.

He had failed twice now. Things would be even more difficult from this point. If it went badly again he would have to
rethink everything. He needed to be practical. He told himself to repeat the rules:

Keep moving whenever you're outside.
Only pass through areas where there are no cameras.
Never use buses or tubes after midnight because the
*   journeys are traceable.*
Don't allow yourself to be noticed or remembered by
*   anyone.*
You're less visible if you look poor.
Rely on no one but yourself.

Breakfast arrived, a mass of orange, brown and red. He
folded a rubbery square of white toast in half, soaked it in his
tea and munched it slowly.

You have to treat this as a military exercise, he told himself. *Use fear, the way you were trained. Let them know
you're on their heels. Leave clues. Send messages. Anything
that will prepare them to expect the worst.*

An exhausted, overweight man with bruised patches for
eyes came in and ordered liver and bacon, a brave choice at
this time of the day. Blake studied the man's security guard
uniform. *Poor bastard,* he thought, *paid to sit in an empty
building all night long.* Offices were better protected than
people. He felt a kinship with the guard. They had both been
shut out and denied a daylight existence.

After finishing his tea he headed out into the misted dawn
streets, where the houses were coming to life. Above him the
crimson eyes of the cranes winked out one by one.

His phone lit up. He answered it.

'Oh God, I didn't wake you, did I?' asked Sparrow Martin.

10

WINDMILL

On Tuesday morning Niven, the owner of the Ladykillers Café, King's Cross, watched in revulsion as Colin Bimsley folded a fried egg over half a sausage and pushed the whole lot into his mouth with his thumb.

'Is it safe to assume you never went to a Swiss finishing school?' he asked, thumping the grounds out of his Gaggia. 'You'll put my other customers off.'

'You haven't got any other customers.' Colin loaded up another forkful.

'I'm not bloody surprised. They look through the window and see the Chamber of Horrors. Do you need jam on that?' He pointed to the immense slab of loaf on Colin's plate.

'Yeah, the lime and tequila marmalade.'

Niven was bald and short and very loud. He had to stand on a box to reach the jam shelf. At this time of the morning the café was still quiet and he could chat to customers. 'We've got gin and lavender.'

'Not with sausages.' Colin took another great bite, then realized that perhaps it was too great. He looked like a python attempting to swallow its first goat. He chewed, chugged tea for lubrication, swallowed and managed to speak again. 'Don't worry, I'll burn this lot off by lunchtime.'

'You're not my responsibility, love. What you do with your aorta is your business.' Niven wiped the dust from his Peppered Banana Surprise, not the most popular jam in his arsenal. 'Something's up. Out with it.'

'It's nothing. Trouble at work.' He looked for somewhere to dump his napkins. Niven took them from him as if clearing up after a child.

'You're on a new case, then,' Niven guessed. 'I don't suppose you can say what it is.'

'The problem's not something, it's someone. We have to be able to trust each other and I can't trust him. I'd like to tell you but I can't.'

'Understood. When I was in the music business we all had to sign NDAs. Our performers were very demanding. Herbal teas, extra cushions, wind chimes, bath salts. It's easier to deal with rock stars if you think of them as batty old ladies. I guess you must see some pretty unusual sights.'

Colin thought about his encounters of late: lying witnesses, corrupt officials, corpses, explosions, riots and murders. 'You wouldn't believe me if I told you,' he said, checking his watch. 'We only get the cases nobody in their right mind would believe. Can I have a toasted cheese and mustard pickle to go? It's for Mr Bryant.'

'He's a funny little chap, your Mr Bryant, isn't he?' Niven took out a knife as long as his forearm and started slicing cheddar. 'Not quite with it. He keeps asking me for things nobody makes any more. Last week he wanted a packet of Fruit Spangles and some beef dripping. I said, "Where have you been for the past fifty years?" And he said, "Right here, while you were out with Snow White and your six brothers." Which is rude, frankly. The other one's nice. Mr May. Proper old school, lovely speaking voice. They're your bosses, aren't they?'

'They're more like my uncles.' Colin wiped his mouth and dug for his wallet.

'You can have the next one on me,' said Niven. 'You look like you've lost a shilling and found sixpence.'

'Cheers, Niv, you're a gent.' He dropped the package into his backpack and made his way across to 231 Caledonian Road. The yellow-brick Victorian corner building had rain-stained plasterwork, filthy windows, rotted sills, cracked chimney pots, missing tiles, leaky gutters, overflowing drains and detritus from the nearby McDonald's flapping wetly against its entrance door. January in London robbed every-thing of grace.

He tried the facial recognition system at the unit's entrance. As usual the screen fuzzed and settled into what appeared to be a scene from an old film, so he rang the bell instead.

'Come up to the operations room,' said Longbright. 'You're late. We're about to be briefed.'

Bimsley entered and felt a tingle of energy in the corridors. First he headed for the detectives' office, where Bryant was waiting for him. 'The security monitor is showing *Carry On Screaming* again,' he said.

'It wasn't me, I barely touched it.' Bryant peered into the proffered sandwich bag, dug into his pocket and pressed some coins into Bimsley's palm.

Colin checked his hand. The coins felt as large as dinner plates. 'This is old money, Mr B. Twelve and six.'

'That's just over sixty-two pee.'

'The sandwich was three pounds fifty. This isn't legal tender.'

'So it's probably worth more. You could clean up. Do you have the number of a good numismatist?'

Raymond Land swept into the room with an air of cunicular

panic. 'Giles Kershaw says he's taken receipt of a suicide and we're to handle it,' he told anyone within earshot.

'A suicide?' Bryant repeated. 'Why is it coming here?'

Land rattled a sheet of paper importantly. He still printed out certain emails and filed them because it gave him something to do. 'Some paralytic whelk decided to swim home by jumping off Waterloo Bridge in the middle of the night. The Thames River Police pulled him out of the muck first thing this morning. They said they'd normally deal with it themselves. Can you put that weapon away? Of all the people who shouldn't be allowed near firearms . . .'

Bryant had forgotten that the Heckler & Koch rifle was still on his desk. He stood it in the corner. 'So why do we get a jumper?'

'Do you ever bother to read my memos? If the Met doesn't want to touch it, it comes to us. Do you have any idea how stretched their services are right now? They've been stripped to the bloody bone. The SCD can't afford to take on any more cases that might collapse before they get to court. They won't handle soft work like this because it's all – I mean they can't—' He fell over his own words.

'Dear Raymondo,' said Bryant kindly. 'Try not to think before you speak or we'll be here all day.'

'We're getting the case because of an anomaly,' Land managed.

'What kind of anomaly?'

'There's an idea going around that he cut his throat before jumping. Anjam Dutta is sending over some surveillance footage. CCTV near the south foreshore picked it up.'

Bryant rubbed his hands together. 'Good, something to get our teeth into. The data on Cheema is coming in too slowly. Let's go and have a look.'

Before his budget was slashed, Dan Banbury had planned to make the operations room a technological hub where shared evidence could be collated and disseminated to specialists. Now, with its sunshine-yellow walls, whiteboards and mismatched care-home furniture, it resembled a cash-strapped community centre.

The staff waited for Dan Banbury to locate the correct video files. Bryant was happier when everyone saw footage at the same time because he trusted instinctive group reactions and had no idea how to run an MPEG.

'I've two pieces to show you.' Banbury balanced his laptop on an upturned wastepaper basket and tilted the screen towards them. 'The first is from a traffic camera high up on the Somerset House side of the bridge. It's only a couple of frames but you can just make out someone sitting on the edge of the railing, facing out over the water.' He step-framed through an indistinct and unenlightening blob of grey pixels. 'The problem is that the bridge lights are in the central reservation and don't support CCTV. The second piece of footage is from a camera mounted on the south-east staircase. This one caught the actual jump from the edge of its screen range.'

A stanchion of pale stone could be discerned beneath the bridge lamps. It was briefly blotted out by a black diagonal that was probably the stern of a passing barge. A moment later, a much smaller blur slipped past, moving from the top of the screen to the bottom.

Banbury leaned forward. 'That's the body. Let me see if I can slow it down.' He reran the last few seconds. This time the blur revealed flailing limbs.

'Head first,' Bryant noted. 'River suicides usually go in feet first. Look at his arms and legs.'

Land could see nothing unusual. 'What?'

'They're windmilling. He doesn't want to go in. He fell – or was pushed.'

Land's face withered. 'You can't tell anything from footage like this.'

'Thames RP thought it was odd,' Janice pointed out.

'And why would he cut his throat *and* throw himself in the river?' asked Bryant. 'Rather over-egging the pudding, don't you think?'

'Perhaps he wanted to make sure.' Land looked around. 'Are we getting his phone?'

'It wasn't found on his body,' said Longbright.

'Probably forced out of his pocket when he hit the water. I suppose the knife's at the bottom of the Thames, along with every other knife that gets chucked into the river.'

'What about the traffic cameras on the bridge?' asked John May, who had been watching the footage from the door while he removed his coat. In his grey tailored suit and starched white shirt he appeared as immaculate as a maître d'. 'I got you toasted sardine and tomato. Don't pay me in old money.' He threw a sandwich to Bryant.

'We've just been discussing the camera problem,' said Land testily. 'You should get here on time.'

'I already bought him a sandwich,' Colin pointed out.

'He'll be wanting another one.' May seated himself.

'I like to start the day with something substantial,' said Bryant. 'Breakfast like a king, lunch like a prince—'

'Eat like a pig,' said Colin. 'Any ID on him?'

'A wallet with cards and a hundred and fifty quid in it.' Janice checked her pad. 'Lukas George Dickinson, white male aged twenty-four, shares a flat with two others in Waterloo, works in the human resources department of a City bank.'

'Four in the morning,' said Bryant, opening the grease-proof-paper packet and filling the room with an aroma of sardines. 'Where was he until then? What's open that late in London on a Monday night? Have you spoken to the flat-mates yet?'

'They run an artisanal bakery in Borough Market,'

Longbright confirmed. 'I just got off the phone with them. Dickinson left a party in Leadenhall Market.' She opened a screen and marked out the area. 'They saw him at about two thirty and reckon he was pretty drunk then.'

'Don't bakers have to be up at four?' asked Bryant. 'Were they staying up all night?'

'They're young,' said Longbright. 'Dickinson went into the river close to the south side of Waterloo Bridge at four a.m.; his watch got bashed. He was picked up on the south side of Southwark Bridge three hours later. We don't need to listen to the whole thing. You'll just hear their answers.' She played back the phone recording.

'*We hardly ever see him because he works nine to five, although he's got this boss who's a total wankbiscuit and keeps him in the office half the night. Luke's got no friends. I mean, we're supposed to be his friends and even we're not, like, friends.*'

Longbright checked her notes. 'That's Diz. You'll hear Bammer next.'

'Where do they get these names?' Bryant asked his partner.

'Posh boys playing street,' said Janice.

'*Luke told me he hates his job. He suffers from, like, really bad bouts of depression? He's on tablets? But he doesn't like taking them because they stop him from thinking clearly? Yeah? He skipped a couple of days' work last week, which I think was because he broke up with his girlfriend a couple of months ago? And he's not over it? Yeah?*'

'What an annoyingly affected manner of speech,' Bryant grumbled.

'Testimony fits with a suicide verdict,' said May, 'but then there's the footage. I think you're right, he's not a jumper. Waterloo Bridge has an unusually low railing. It's very exposed. He was alone when he walked on to the bridge but maybe there was someone already ahead of him. It's a pity there are so few residential buildings around, no curtains twitching. A driver might have seen something. Are we running checks on passing traffic?'

'There's a south-side diversion on the bridge after midnight,' said Banbury. 'That means delays and passengers looking out of windows. I'll check night buses and dash cams.'

'We might be lucky with a driver or someone on the top deck of a bus,' Longbright suggested. 'I'll put out witness requests and cover social media.'

'Come on, you.' May threw his partner's raincoat at him. 'Let's go and see Giles, find out if he has anything to add. It looks like we're in for a few busy days.'

Bryant did a little jig of happiness at the door. Even at this late stage of maturation he always seemed on the verge of dancing, especially if violent death was involved.

II

CORPSE

By mid-morning the breezeless wet air drew forth the smell of earth and weeds. Soaking misty rain fell on the old railway yards of Goods Way as the detectives headed towards the canal and the coroner's office. Around them, the vertiginous glass stacks of the new King's Cross peered down at the old customs sheds and coal offices like children surprised that their grandparents were now so small and old.

Bryant turned to examine a group of art students who were passing on self-balancing scooters. They were heading for Central Saint Martins, the art college based in the old granary buildings. 'I say, has the term begun?' he asked.

'There's someone in there all year round now,' said May. 'It's big business.'

Bryant sucked his barley twist disapprovingly. 'I miss proper art students with ragged sweaters covered in paint. Look at them, all designer haircuts and hoverboards. They're supposed to be impoverished and disreputable, not' – he waggled his fingers about his face – 'moisturized.'

'They're students. We might learn a thing or two if we talked to them occasionally.'

Bryant stopped dead and studied his partner. 'Do you have any idea what they see when they look at us? Let me give you a clue. In Tanzania they discovered a dinosaur fossil 243 million years old. Add another couple of years on that, and that's how we appear to them. I smell of aniseed and tobacco and you tint the grey out of your hair. We're invisible, and that's the way I like it.'

May was affronted. 'I do not tint my grey.'

'Everyone knows you do. You should learn to enjoy being old instead of trying to knock a few years off by shoring everything up. Character actors always get better roles than juvenile leads. Those women out there who're protesting that all these years they've been getting second-class treatment from men must look at us and assume we're part of the problem. They have no idea that I spent half my life on marches protesting alongside their grandparents. Our pasts don't show up in our faces. To them we're irrelevant and everyone will be much happier once we've been trampled into the dust.' He thought for a moment. 'Having said that, let's go and annoy Rosa.'

'Try to be nice to her today,' May suggested. 'She has to scrub out the morgue.'

'She's temperamentally suited to her profession, I'll give you that.' They crossed the corner of Granary Square, its low fountain jets steaming in the chill air.

'I think she's probably a bit lonely, Arthur.'

'That's ridiculous. How can anyone be lonely in a city of nine million people? They attach themselves to you like barnacles. Look at me, I'm so popular that people actually cross the street to avoid me. They fear being drawn into my gravitational orbit.' He closed up his paper bag of sweets and stuffed it into an already overflowing pocket.

They continued to the cemetery of St Pancras Old Church, and the absurdly picturesque Hansel and Gretel cottage that housed the St Pancras Coroner's Office. Although the back half of the building was a grey concrete block, the original nineteenth-century façade had been retained and in summertime became lost beneath an overgrowth of hollyhocks and rhododendrons. May stepped into the dank tiled porch and rang the bell.

The door was opened by the housekeeper, Rosa Lysandrou. She was clad in her customary shapeless black dress, a yellow duster clenched in her right hand. For a moment she regarded them in silence. Her eyes warmed for May but hardened into black marbles for his partner.

'Hello,' said Bryant, stepping forward, 'I'm Julian and this is my friend Sandy. How bona to vada your dolly old eek again.' He looked at his partner. 'What? That was nice. You didn't say I couldn't be nice in theatrical *polari*.'

'Why is he talking like that?' Rosa asked over Bryant's head.

'He's using a defunct form of London slang to impersonate someone from a very old British radio programme,' May explained wearily.

The housekeeper kept an eye on Bryant while she considered this. 'Is he ill again?'

'Can you not refer to me as if I'm not here?' asked Bryant.

'Rosa, is Giles available?' May pointed around her in the direction of the mortuary. 'Could we have a word?'

Rosa stepped aside. 'I don't know why you cannot phone first.'

'Because if we did Giles would say he's too busy to see us,' Bryant pointed out, 'and it's important for me to get out of the office because sitting around gives me wrinkles.'

May waited patiently for the ritual to play out. They enjoyed annoying each other so much that it seemed a pity to stop them.

Rosa looked at her opponent blankly. 'Go on,' she said at last. 'What?'

'I am waiting for you to say something sarcastic and unpleasant.'

'*Moi?*' Bryant mimed clutching at pearls.

She thrashed the duster at him. 'Why must you always be like this? Why?'

'Oh, because the world is a dark and lonely place and it's fun. Cast your mind back, Rosa. You remember fun. That night on the fairground waltzer in 1983 when the handsome young lad with the gypsy eyes rode the back of your carriage and said to your girlfriend, "You can go free but your mate has to pay." '

She loomed over him. 'After we are called forward by the Lord, you will see that the world is not fun.'

'Maybe so, but I'm going to make sure I have a bloody good laugh until then. If it turns out there's an afterlife, I'm going to have a lot of explaining to do.'

'The wages of sin is death,' warned Rosa, pointing up at the hand-stitched sampler she had placed above the door of the mortuary's chapel.

'A most ungrammatical motto.' Bryant bypassed her, leading the way along the hall. 'I've got my own. "Make life noisy, joyful, rude and strange." Stitch that.' He raised his hand over the door to knock.

'I'm not ready for you yet, Mr Bryant,' boomed a cultured voice.

'That's OK, we just popped by for a chat.' He tried the handle and stepped inside.

The post-mortem facility lay beyond the viewing room and its minuscule doctor's office. It had four autopsy stations, mobile work-trays, steel fridges and a row of head-height windows that looked out on to the remains of the St Pancras cemetery. Kershaw opened the door and raised his gloves in an apology for not shaking hands. 'You can't "just pop by for a chat". It's unprofessional.'

'Lack of professionality is part of my skill set.' Bryant stepped in and looked around. 'I love what you've done with the place. Are those lungs new?' He stopped to admire a garish Victorian rubber facsimile of an opened human body standing at the entrance.

'I got it at a medical antique fair in Chelmsford. We're still trying to think of a name for him.' As always, Kershaw was looking too fresh, too blond and impossibly boyish. 'Where's your PPP? We had kits made up especially for you.'

'Personal protective equipment makes me feel like a five-year-old,' Bryant complained.

'That's how we tend to treat you. Mr Dickinson is over there on the table.'

'Oh. You've already pulled his face off. Is that blood on the floor?' Bryant leaned in with interest. His partner glanced and looked away fast, preferring to keep a respectful distance between himself and the cadaver.

'No, Mr Bryant, I spilled some raspberry yogurt,' said Kershaw. 'Corpses don't bleed. If I ever find a blood spot it means I've cut myself. It's so cold in here I don't notice until I move somewhere warmer.'

'You shouldn't be eating yogurt in here. What was Dickinson wearing when he was brought in?'

'He was togged up for a night out in a rather smart suit. I had to wait for initial identifications before I got stuck into him. I've only just started.'

'Who identified him?'

'An older sister, via Skype from Germany. She intimated that there had been past troubles in the family, but wasn't keen to go into details. As she's the closest relative I would have liked her here but she refused to come in. She said she hadn't seen him in six years.'

'Odd. He would have been just eighteen. How was she?'

'Adipose, pre-cancerous.'

'I mean in herself. Was she upset, unemotional, angry?'

'Oh – I didn't notice.'

'Coroners.' Bryant shrugged at his partner. 'Who else? You said "identifications", plural.'

'Yes, Janice called one of the chaps he flat-shares with.'

'Oh, the bakers. You had him in here?'

'He gave us a confirmation, then he was sick in my litter bin.'

'Where are you up to now?' asked May from the far end of the room.

'I'm just looking at the skull trauma. The river current rolled him into the bridge a few times, doing a fair bit of damage. The star of the show is the pierced throat. I want you to take a good look at it.'

Bryant leaned forward again and studied the wound, which had dried to a neat dark hole. 'I suppose your first thought was the starlings.' These were the piles surrounding the piers of bridges, which had iron spikes protruding from them.

'It crossed my mind, but they're actually quite blunt.'

'Well, it's not a knife. It's the same as Cheema's laceration, perfectly round.'

'That much is obvious. Any ideas?'

'Something with a fair bit of thrust behind it,' Bryant observed. 'What was the actual cause of death?'

Kershaw slipped a loose strand of hair back into its plastic grip. 'He was alive when he fell. He breathed water into his lungs. Thanks to his youth and the fact that his blood alcohol content was probably above 0.125 the temperature shock didn't stop his heart. His jacket was twisted around by the impact, consistent with the fall.'

'Couldn't the pull of the tide cause that?'

'Probably. I just don't think it did.' He covered the body up to its neck with great gentleness. 'You're right about the wound; its depth and length suggest a determined hand. If there were any blood sprays on the fingers of the right hand, as you'd expect in a throat-cutting, they were washed off by the river.'

'You're assuming it was suicide.'

'I'm not assuming anything, Mr Bryant. I leave the sweeping generalizations to you.'

Bryant peered closely at the exposed skull as he clattered his boiled sweet around his dentures. 'He fell in like a man who'd been shoved.'

Kershaw's curiosity was piqued. 'Have you got footage?'

'Only a couple of seconds. Nothing from road-level. Suicides tend to push themselves away from the thing they're jumping off, don't they? They're ready to kill themselves but don't like the idea of added pain, so they try to avoid hitting anything on the way down. Human nature.'

'In my experience— I can smell rhubarb.'

'Rhubarb and custard. I know a woman who makes them. It's better than smelling of dead people.' Bryant offered his paper bag of sweets around. 'Unfortunately, the stabbed throat complicates everything.'

'Rather. To me, a throat wound does not suggest death by one's own hand.'

'Why is that?' asked May.

'It was the same as the puncture on Mr Cheema,' Kershaw explained. 'The edge of the hole is finely cut and puckered inward with no torn skin. In other words, whatever made this was not a solid object. Air came out.'

'So not a poker or a pencil.'

'My first thought was a crazy one: that it might be a self-performed tracheotomy. But as I studied it I realized that I'd seen the mark it left many times before. I think he used one of these.' Reaching over into the instrument drawers beneath his tray, he removed a foot-long steel rod with valves at one end. 'This is a shiny new version of an instrument that has been in use since the end of the seventeenth century. It's called a trocar.' He pointed to the sharpened end. 'This part is the obturator. You pierce the skin and go in through the abdomen wall during laparoscopic surgery. The main part is a cannula, a hollow tube with tiny holes in the side. It allows you to put staplers and scissors inside the body cavity, but we use them to drain body fluids during the embalming process. Originally trocars were used to relieve pressure build-up of oedema. The name comes from *trois-quarts*; six pints of fluid out. This baby is reusable, but we have disposable ones of all different sizes.'

'You really think this was the murder weapon?'

'Without a doubt. It has a very specific, identifiable way of cutting.'

'So he's a doctor?' asked May.

'The problem is that although it's specialist kit you can find them all over the place, wherever there are sick people or dead bodies.' Kershaw studied the instrument with undisguised admiration. 'If you've a strong arm and keep the end sharp, I can't think of a deadlier weapon. I'm amazed no one's ever used one before.'

'Are there any other unusual marks?'

Kershaw removed his predecessor's telescopic pointer from his top pocket. 'A few. There are bruises on his wrist here and here, small but new. A deep graze on the back of his head, just here, probably from the base of the bridge as he entered the water. You really think he was pushed?'

'We don't know who else was on the bridge with him,' said Bryant. 'Two pierced throats – it must have been the same attacker in both instances.'

'I can't give you that assurance,' said Kershaw. 'The river inflicted some pretty serious damage. The cannula penetrated deeper this time. We could be seeing the appearance of a new gang weapon. Why not consider the more obvious solutions first?' As Kershaw said the words, he already knew the answer: Bryant had never taken the obvious route to any solution. This refusal nuanced his opinions but gave everybody else heartburn. 'How did we get the case?'

'It came from someone over at the Serious Crime Directorate,' said May. 'We're still required to fulfil the conditions of our original remit. This would be classified as a case likely to cause "public affright" because it occurred in a communal space.'

'I'm not sure they would have given you this one if they thought you were going to link them.' Giles removed his gloves and binned them. 'People underestimate the power of the river. Go in from a bridge and there's a good chance you'll die. You can't stop people from jumping off any more than you can stop them from being hit by cars as they cross the road.'

'You can if they had their throats punctured first and were pushed,' said Bryant. 'Is it possible to tell whether he did it to himself, or if someone did it to him?'

Kershaw considered the point. 'The movement is the same, but I imagine the angle of the blade might be affected.'

'He didn't tombstone into the water, he flailed,' May pointed out.

The coroner looked doubtful. 'His reactions would have been impaired by alcohol, so I'm not sure you can apply too much logic.'

'Any circumstance that prematurely ends a life must be treated as suspicious, you know that.' Bryant picked up a skull chisel and balanced it on his forefinger. 'Isn't there anything else you can tell from the body?'

'I've not finished with him yet, which is why I hate you dropping in. Can you put that instrument down, please? The volume of water in his lungs is consistent with a single deep intake of breath, even with the trauma to his throat. It was shockingly cold and more water would have been forced in as he gasped. He might well have expelled it through the wound.

Do I need to go over diatomic readings with you? I thought not. I found a tiny strand of blue cotton deep under one nail, no more than six millimetres, but it's not from his jacket. It has a twist and was torn – might be thread from a button.'

'Anything in his pockets?'

'A few coins, some receipts, the wallet and a ballpoint pen.'

'Can I see?' Bryant held out his hand. Donning his trifocals, he examined the blue and white plastic pen. 'There's something on the cap. I need my other *other* glasses . . .'

'Here, let me,' offered Kershaw. 'It looks like the outline of a ship. Hold on.' He slipped the cap beneath an illuminated lens. 'A nineteenth-century sailing ship. Could be advertising anything.'

'I don't suppose you've had a look at his bloods yet,' said May.

'Already filed. Presence of amitriptyline – that's an antidepressant – and, as I said, the BAC was probably north of 0.125 per cent.'

'That's enough to knock out most first-time drinkers, isn't it? How's his liver?'

'No need to look. He likes a drink but he's not an alcoholic. Skin tissue's good. Nails are manicured. He had a big night out, so the alcohol made him more susceptible to bruising and haemorrhaging in the water. And as I said, it would have affected his judgement and coordination.'

'So that's it?' asked Bryant. 'Tag and bag him, just another London statistic?'

Kershaw ushered them from the room and removed the plastic grip from his hair. 'I don't have time to do anything more on him today. I had a fellow in earlier this morning who was killed when a washing machine fell on top of him. He was unloading it, and I'm already being pressured by the delivery company to say it was his own fault. I'm working on sudden deaths that require explanations while my counterparts up the road are seeing sepsis from children with rat bites. The standard of living is falling and the mortality rate is rising. We've exceeded the capacity of this little Victorian building, and I simply do not have the resources to deal with it.'

'You have four tables in there.'

'Yes, because when there's a rush on I get up to three other coroners on contracts working alongside me. Access to medical equipment – your killer could be one of them.'

'So first of all we have to eliminate you lot.' Bryant waved a finger back at the body. 'Throw us a bone, Giles. Could the deaths be related? Give me an opinion.'

'An opinion.' Giles glanced back at the body on the table. 'I think the odds are against you. I agree this puncture is very like the first one but it could have been self-inflicted, so at the moment my instinct – given that we know he was on anti-depressants – is to go with suicide.'

'Tell me you're one hundred per cent certain of that and I'll close up the investigation.' Bryant tapped his boot impatiently, daring the coroner to respond.

'You know I can't do that, Mr Bryant. Not one hundred per cent.'

'I thought not.' Bryant unflattened his trilby and pushed it back on to his head. 'Always a pleasure, Giles. We'll be popping in again.'

'You're a very stubborn man, Mr Bryant,' said Kershaw.

Bryant turned. 'The average person over sixty-five years of age has at least three ailments. I have seventeen, and stubbornness is not one of them.'

'You're a pain in the arse, is that an ailment?' the coroner called, but Bryant had gone.

12

COFFEE

The coffee shop was lined with stools designed for customers of small base and good balance who would not linger beyond the length of a warm cup. Sparrow Martin half rose as soon as she saw Rory Caine push through the door. She waved in the English manner, without attracting attention. He looked around in annoyance and spotted her.

Caine was as ferally handsome as she remembered, but in brighter light she could see he was shadow-eyed and grey-skinned. Playing too hard, working too hard? Both, probably. How easily harmful states fed each other. He had a lanyard around his shirt collar. His suit was sharp but accentuated his thinness. The look was corporate but hipsterish. His black hair was cut in thick waves, shaved at the sides to leave a firebreak before the commencement of a slender beard. He appeared distracted and twitchy.

'Hey.' She thought he was going to shake her hand but he was indicating her shirt. 'You're very – bright.' He clearly didn't mean it as a compliment.

'I work in a bookshop,' she replied. 'We don't have a dress code.'

'Why am I here?' He dusted crumbs from the opposite seat and slid on to it. 'How did you find me?'

'One of your friends told me who you were,' she explained.

'What do you mean, one of my friends? I don't have friends.'

'I didn't want to explain online,' she began. 'I feel a little foolish now. I suppose you read the news. I mean, about Mr Cheema.'

Caine's grey eyes were blank. 'Who the hell's Mr Cheema?'

'He was there the night we met.'

'We've only met once. I don't even know your name.'

'I told you on the phone. Sparrow Martin.' *Gosh,* she thought, *you're unlikeable. I wonder how I failed to spot that last time. Ah yes, tequila shots.* 'Mr Cheema was our driver, the night we shared a cab together. I remember seeing the surname on his dashboard card. It was all a bit of a mess. Don't you remember him?'

'Nobody remembers drivers – you only ever see the backs of their heads. It was ages ago.'

'Yes, the fourth Saturday in October.'

'Why do you even know that?'

'I keep a diary. He was supposed to drop the other girl off first, the one your friend tried to pick up, and there was a bit of an argument, remember?'

'Is that what this is about? Why is this guy in the news?'

Sparrow's eyes widened. 'You really don't know?'

'No.'

'He was hung upside down from a tree and stabbed to death. They're calling it the Hampstead Heath Black Magic Murder. It's all over the papers.'

'I don't read papers.' His contempt was overt. 'When did this happen?'

'The police found his body Sunday morning.'

'On Hampstead Heath? He was probably involved in something weird. Why is this anything to do with me?'

'Because there was another death today.'

She took her phone from her bag, but Caine waved it aside. 'Just tell me.'

'Luke Dickinson – he's your friend, isn't he?'

He crossed his legs, fidgeting. 'I don't know anyone by that name.'

She held up her phone and turned it to him. 'It's online. Remember him now? He got in the car with you.'

'Oh, *him*. Everybody calls him Chucker. I've seen him around. I wouldn't call him a friend.'

'The police pulled his body out of the Thames this morning.'

'What are you talking about?' He reached for his phone and began searching for the story.

'There was only one report but it was in my local newsfeed. He went to a party last night and died on the way home.'

'Who has a party on a Monday?' Caine muttered. He found the news item, scrolled through it and laughed. 'The council is prosecuting the bar for violating its late licence. I thought it closed years ago. Nobody goes there any more.'

Sparrow leaned over to see which article he had found. 'The police say he jumped from Waterloo Bridge and drowned himself.'

'Yeah, I can read, cheers.' He raised the hand with the phone. 'There's nothing in this story. They're holding back the details.'

'I suppose it's too soon to know more.' Everything about Caine made her uncomfortable. 'You see, somebody called me.'

'You mean police? Why would they call you?'

'I'm somewhere on his Facebook page. So are you.'

'His *Facebook* page? He didn't know you. He didn't know any of us.'

'He friended me, along with a thousand other people.'

He looked at her coffee with distaste. 'I don't know how you can drink latte. There's a place opposite that does a decent *cortado*. What phone is that? An older model, yeah?'

Sparrow started to realize that it had been a mistake to call Caine. 'How was he when you last spoke to him?'

Caine was fast losing the little patience he had. His leg was jiggling; he looked as if he was about to fly to pieces. 'I haven't spoken to him, I don't have any contacts for him. I told you, he's not a friend, not anything, just someone I saw around from time to time.'

She tried again. 'He was on some kind of medication, wasn't he? He told me he was.'

'He told you that on Facebook?'

'Yes. We talked a bit.'

'Then maybe he took too much of something and decided to swim home. I mean, really. So you guys were *friends*.'

'I think he just wanted someone to talk to.'

'Sounds like he was just dicking around online. To be honest, he struck me as a bit of a loser.'

'You shouldn't say that,' said Sparrow. 'He seemed very sympathetic. Sensitive.'

Caine swivelled back and forth on his stool. 'Why is it when someone can't handle life we always call them sensitive? Darwin theory kicked in. He's gone, pasted himself into London's history book, that's it, move along.'

The more Sparrow knew about men, the more she preferred the company of bats. 'You don't have to be so mean about him.'

'Why, what do you care? What the hell am I even doing here?' He looked around, tapping his palms on his thighs, eager to be gone. 'Is that it, can I get up now?'

'I think there's something we need to talk about.'

'What? I have nothing to say. I can barely remember his name, let alone yours. What do you expect me to do?'

'Don't you think it's funny that two people who only recently met should die within a day of each other?'

'Yeah, if that sort of thing amuses you.'

'What is wrong with you?' Sparrow asked angrily. 'You *knew* both of them.'

He leaned in. 'I *saw* the driver, that's all. We didn't go to school together. You meet new people every day. Some get sick, some can't handle life, some die. Who knows what this cab driver was into? Or Chucker – what's-his-face – Luke? Maybe it was a double suicide. I'm sorry he's dead but it doesn't affect me, so I don't care. I can't afford to care. You think that's harsh but that's how it works. You give this city the best years of your life and it turns the lost time into cash. If you want to start caring about people go somewhere else, or wait until you retire and do charity work.'

'Thanks for mansplaining business ethics,' said Sparrow. 'I'm going to attend Luke Dickinson's funeral.'

'Are you out of your mind?' He lowered his voice. 'If anyone thinks there's a link between us all – which there isn't, by the way – the press will start creeping around and they'll end up on your doorstep.'

Sparrow persisted. 'But we are linked, aren't we? Whether you like it or not. The five of us, I mean. You know Luke. And you certainly must remember Augusta.'

He eyed her warily. 'What do you mean?'

'You were pretty inappropriate with her.'

'First of all I was pissed so all bets are off, plus it was after a big night out and she was looking at me like she hadn't eaten for a month. What was I supposed to do?'

'Not what you did. I have something else to tell you.' She plucked at her sweater, embarrassed to raise the subject. 'I belong to a wildlife society. We go out late to parks, and on Saturday night I was stationed on Hampstead Heath.'

Caine stifled a snort of laughter.

'Listen to me. I saw something, a man being chased. He was stumbling through the ferns and bushes, but I couldn't see him clearly. It was very dark and everything happened so quickly. I didn't put two and two together until I read about it in the *Evening Standard*. There was no photo, but I think the man being chased might have been Mr Cheema.'

'Did you see who was after him?'

'This guy came charging through the ferns like a serial killer in a horror film. He was wearing a mask. Like a Hallowe'en outfit – I don't know. I only saw him for a split second.'

She waited for a response but none came.

'Well, don't you see? It can't be a coincidence. What if they met up and something happened between them? Suppose they had an argument and Luke killed him and then took his own life? The police are going to be searching for connections, and you and I are both in Luke's social media.'

'You're not going to the police, though.'

'Well – no, not at the moment. I really can't afford to get involved with the police.'

Caine's ears pricked up. 'Oh? Why not?'

'It's nothing, a personal thing. My brother has a history – he has a problem. He's staying with me, trying to get straight. But he's not entirely managed it yet. I don't want the police coming around.'

Caine snatched up his phone. 'How much is there online? Have you had a good look? Is the other girl on there as well?'

'We're just friended, I think. You see why I called? There's you and Luke, and me and Augusta, plus Mr Cheema, so five of us altogether. Five strangers – well, Luke wasn't entirely a stranger to you, but you couldn't remember his name. And now two of them are dead.'

She saw that this time she had given him pause to think. 'You're being completely illogical,' he decided. 'Luke didn't know the driver or he would have said something. So whatever happened between them was after we met. Maybe it was a drug deal that went wrong. It has nothing to do with the rest of us. How could it? Nothing happened. We had a bit of an argument. It was a Saturday night, half the country was probably arguing. Get me off your Facebook page and change your settings. Maybe you can get the other girl to change hers as well. Will you be happy then?'

'Aren't you worried?'

'Of course not. I've got nothing to hide, but I don't want cops tipping up at work asking stupid questions about how we met. Go home and forget about it.' He tapped his hands on his knees, anxious to go. 'The police can't get information out of Facebook without applying through America. It takes months and costs a fortune, and they don't have the resources to do it.'

'I've never been in trouble,' said Sparrow forlornly. ' "Black Magic Murder". It's awful. Do you think he got into black magic, your friend? Did you know about it? People get drawn into cults and psychologically reprogrammed.'

Rory had had enough. 'First off, spare me the ladyscience; second, *he wasn't my bloody friend*. You need to pull yourself together, love. I haven't got time for this.' He rose and strapped his bag on his back. 'I don't want you calling me again. This whole thing is – it's absurd.'

Caine left Sparrow still sitting in the coffee shop and swung out into the street.

He stormed along the pavement in a hot fury. A taxi driver he had barely seen or acknowledged, and Chucker, who had earned his name by once throwing up over the girl he was trying to pick up, a hanger-on who drifted into some of the bars he visited, a friend of another friend he didn't even like. Why did Sparrow think he knew anything? He knew no more about it than she did. The only difference between them was that she was making a fuss. He'd come across her type before, saving wildlife and worrying about complete strangers. This was probably the most exciting thing that had ever happened to her. If it turned out that Luke was a Satanist who went crazy and slaughtered someone, it had nothing to do with him.

Stopping at a bank on High Holborn, he was forced to step over a homeless man who was sitting on a piece of cardboard under the ATM machine. 'Do you mind, mate? I'm trying to withdraw some of my money.'

The man held up a dented Costa Coffee cup. 'Good luck to you, brother.'

'I don't need luck. And I'm not your brother, *brother.*'

Collecting his cash, he paced off down the pavement. He had wasted half of his lunch hour, and would not have time to eat now. With his wallet reloaded, he pulled his ID lanyard from his top pocket and headed back into the office building, dismissing the thought of Luke Dickinson's lonely death from his mind.

13

CONNECT

King's Cross was so damp and penumbral that every light in the Peculiar Crimes Unit building had been switched on, lending it the atmosphere of an ancient steamer heading on one last voyage before the scrapheap.

Inside, the crew members were sifting clues, scribbling notes, pinning photos, making connections, but it was not enough. After the first forty-eight hours, investigation leads start to dry up. In order to make his staff aware of the passing time, Arthur Bryant had wound an old-fashioned alarm clock and kept setting it to ring at the top of each hour. It was making everyone anxious until Longbright surreptitiously removed the clapper. Now she sat in the operations room with her bosses while the two Daves sawed through the hardboard partition at their backs.

'A friend of Luke Dickinson's from work hired the upstairs room of the Cittie of Yorke pub on High Holborn for her birthday party,' Longbright said, 'but some of the guests went on afterwards to a club in Leadenhall Market called Gallon Damage.'

Bryant made a note. 'Interesting name, something to do with drinking eight pints, I assume.' He turned to the Daves. 'Can you two stop doing that for a while? You're like a pair of bad magicians.'

'I've been to that club,' said the Dave with the seventies-style moustache. 'It's full of villains. I've been everywhere, Fabric, Printworks, Corsica Studios – I've pulled a few all-nighters there, I can tell you.'

'Thank you for sharing details of your nocturnal activities with us,' said Bryant. 'We'll know where to avoid.'

Longbright drew a path on her map. 'The club closed at three a.m. Dickinson's flat is south, near Waterloo Station on Frazier Street, so he had to be walking back there, probably getting some air and trying to sober up a bit. Allowing for chucking-out time, that would place him on the bridge at around four a.m.'

'So he'd had a good night out and changed his mind about wanting to live as he was crossing the river?' said May. 'That doesn't make sense.'

Dan Banbury wandered in. 'You're talking about the suicide?'

Bryant was affronted. 'Can you knock before you come in? And take your hands out of your pockets.'

'There's no wall yet, Mr B.' The crime scene manager stepped around the Daves, waving away plumes of sawdust, and unpacked his satchel. 'I've got Dickinson's laptop here. I'm tracking back through his online data. He had a home prescription delivery service for refills of antidepressants. The fellow who sat next to him in their HR department said he thought Dickinson might be heading for a nervous breakdown.'

'That's not going to help our case much, is it?' Bryant complained.

'You're meant to be impartial. I can't just manufacture evidence to suit your theories.'

'I don't see why not, you're a copper.' Bryant rocked back in his chair, amused. Goading staff members to find out what they really thought was part of his stock-in-trade. 'All detectives are naturally suspicious,' he reminded them. 'Did you know suicide was still a crime in Britain until 1961? The hangman John Ellis became depressed and tried to kill himself. He was spared by the judge on that occasion but finally managed it with a straight razor eight years later, in 1932.'

'That just proves how determined suicides can be.'

Bryant dug out his tin of Old Holborn Corpse Reviver, a blend he had specially prepared for him by a little shop in Farringdon, and searched about for his Lorenzo Spitfire pipe. 'You never know what's going on in people's minds. Mr Dickinson worked for a City bank, and banks have secrets. Barings Bank used to be near Leadenhall Market. It was founded in the eighteenth century and destroyed by a young trader who gambled away 1.3 billion dollars and tried to hide it in a secret account. The Bank of Credit and Commerce had employees in seventy countries, and twenty billion dollars in assets. It was trading in arms and cocaine.'

'I have no idea where you're going with this,' said Banbury, trying to sound uninterested.

Bryant ignored him. 'Until recently the Square Mile banks used unprotected messengers to carry bonds between their offices. Over thirty billion pounds passed along the streets each day. Then one morning one of the elderly messengers was mugged. The robber pocketed 292 million quid. The bank put out a story that the bonds were worthless, but the truth is that anyone could cash them just by showing a driving licence to the teller. We all knew who had mugged him, but before we could arrest the miscreant somebody inconveniently shot him in the head. My point being . . .'

He looked from one impatient face to the other.

'. . . that he was either killed by chance, which seems

extremely unlikely even in this increasingly lawless city, or because he knew something he shouldn't. We're not digging deeply enough into his background.' Bryant thought it was worth a look, even if he didn't entirely believe it himself.

'Dickinson wasn't a player,' May said. 'He worked in Human Resources. It would hardly have given him access to millions.'

'No,' Bryant agreed, 'but it gave him control over employees' livelihoods, possibly a motive for murder. He didn't kill himself. When you go out to a party, smartly dressed, you don't usually think of putting a razor-sharp steel trocar in your jacket pocket. A unique weapon, used twice! He might have been a loner but I refuse to believe he didn't have friends, lovers, enemies.' Withdrawing his pipe, Bryant began tamping it with tobacco that smelled like rancid seaweed.

'Don't light that thing in here,' May begged. 'I'll start suspecting you're back to your old self.'

'I rather think I am,' said Bryant, hunting for a match. 'Although I've been having . . . dreams.'

'Everyone has dreams.'

'These happen when I am awake. Four a.m.'s a time for dreaming, isn't it? Too late to be night, too early to be day. And in winter when there are fourteen hours of darkness, it's still a long way from dawn. Janice ran through some statistics for me. Deaths occur pretty much when you'd expect them, late at night after the bars shut, but there are hardly any murders between four a.m. and five a.m. It's when most people are asleep. In the last year of available stats there were none at four a.m. Now we've had two in three nights with the same weapon.'

He arose with the filled pipe and headed towards the little balcony that overlooked the courtyard in the centre of the building. 'Let's see what the others come up with. If anyone needs me I shall be on my Veranda of Contemplation.'

'That thing's unsafe,' May tilted his head and called after him. 'You've not enough to go on, even counting the trocar. And you know it.'

Dan Banbury longed to have a really good conversation with someone about HDMI cables. Unfortunately, as the only truly computer-literate member of staff he was as lonely as a lighthouse keeper. He had already run through Dhruv Cheema's electronic information and had found nothing of interest. Now, with Luke Dickinson's laptop plugged into various home-made applications and random bits of kit, he repeated the routine, digging out all external attacks from Remote Access Trojans and IOT hacks, then starting on personal texts and emails. It would be a long and laborious job, and was the kind of thing he loved doing.

Banbury built an information folder as he ran through the data, and a picture of Luke Dickinson began to emerge.

He spent too much time online. He had a great number of casual friends but nobody close. A number of colleagues actively disliked him. He'd been repeatedly blocked on dating sites. Incoming calls were few. Occasionally one came in from his mother's carer but there were hardly any going back, although a standing order went out to the care home. He had been active on several borderline-illegal websites and constantly checked hook-up apps for available single women, revealing his sexual proclivities in cavalier detail.

Work took precedence over everything else in Dickinson's life. He'd been looking at job opportunities in Amsterdam and Madrid. Most of his calls were to his boss and teammates. His groceries and shirts were bought online. He had plenty of bar and restaurant bills from venues near his office. A few sports events, gym membership, no art galleries, theatre or cinema tickets.

Banbury imagined him coming home close to midnight

most nights, microwaving a low-calorie meal, then going online until 1.00 a.m. The pattern was repeated every week. No wonder Dickinson was depressed.

He noted the most frequently used email addresses and followed their threads. Whenever he studied the electronic spore left behind by a Person of Interest, a phantom figure was gradually fleshed out. Crime scenes showed him a victim's final moments, but the ghost markers he uncovered online revealed how a life had been lived and lost.

The process was a long way from being complete. Banbury bit at his thumb; his nails were a disgrace. He needed more help but none of the others were up to it. Policing naturally attracted Luddites. Looking at his cluttered desk, he wondered what it said about his own life: a dead cactus, a framed photo of a wife and son he spent too little time with, a joke plaque awarded to the Workaholic of the Year that now read like a mission statement rather than a jest, a lapsed gym membership card, a paperback entitled *Fast & Easy Spanish* with the spine cracked at chapter two. With a sigh he returned to the screen.

He found more clues.

Dickinson had a niece he liked enough to buy Christmas gifts for, but he didn't appear to bother with anyone else. He was involved in a legal dispute with his landlord over increased service charges. He spent more than he made and gambled online, but was trying to clear his mounting debts. He suffered from ADD, and his doctor had recently upgraded his medication to a stronger dose.

Banbury sat forward and glared angrily at his laptop. He punched open an app of his own devising that cross-checked social media contacts for familiar names. Information detonated across the screen, fine lines attaching names, places, habits, friends, jobs, bars, money. So much shared knowledge, all given such equal emphasis that none of it was of any use. *Welcome to the information age*, he thought. *Maybe Mr Bryant is better off not understanding it.*

And what was Mr Bryant thinking? After a smoke and ponder he returned to his office and began perusing the ancient volumes he kept behind his mountainously overflowing desk.

'I know you prefer your research to remain untroubled by relevance, Arthur, but an hour ago you were setting alarm clocks for the staff,' May pointed out, 'and now you're acting as if there's no pressure—'

'He went into that water like a man surprised,' Bryant murmured. 'How on earth do you creep up on someone when you're both standing on a deserted bridge? My experiments on body movement—'

'Yes, I know all about those. You threw Crippen out of the window.'

'She was on a bungee rope. I wanted to measure the gravitational effect on her organs but she bit me. Have you spoken to Anjam Dutta? We need to keep searching the camera coverage of both embankments.'

'Who's going to pay for the extra hours?' asked May. 'We'll never be able to sign it off once Raymond sees the preliminary report. He'll say there's no reasonable doubt.'

'Exactly. And what is the one infallible fact we can absolutely guarantee with Raymondo's decisions?'

'They're always wrong.'

'*Quod erat demonstrandum.*' Bryant pushed his book aside, took up his fountain pen and gave it a good shake, flicking ink on to the wall.

'What are you two up to?' Raymond Land was watching them from the door.

'You can't come in,' said Bryant, pointing to a handwritten sign above the door that read 'The Truncheonists'. 'This is a private members' club.'

'What on earth are you talking about?' Land took a step into the room.

'Ah, ah, ah.' Bryant wagged a forefinger. 'No entry without a club card. We can grant you temporary membership for a fiver.'

Land looked back at the sign. 'That's not even a real word.'

'Mid-nineteenth-century slang for a policeman, actually. We could waive the normal club conditions and get you an overseas membership by using your ex-wife's address.'

'She's Welsh.'

'That counts as overseas.' He checked a blank sheet of paper on his desk. 'Oh dear, there's a waiting list. I could fast-track you for a tenner.'

'I'm not going to pay you to be fast-tracked into a club that doesn't even exist,' said Land. 'I'm not a complete fool.'

'Nothing in life is complete. I suppose you're here to feague us.'

'And what's that supposed to mean?' snapped Land.

'It's not *supposed* to mean anything, it does mean something,' Bryant pointed out. 'It's a holophrastic term meaning to ginger up, derived from the practice of putting a live eel up a horse's bottom to make him appear friskier and less worn out.'

Land stared piteously at his most senior detective, then turned to May. 'Perhaps I'll get some sense from you. There's going to be an inquest on Cheema, and that means publicity. I've already had some reporter from *Hard News* on the phone, using the old line about presenting our point of view before they go to press. After the trouble we've stirred up lately we'll have to be extra careful.'

May thought for a moment. 'When you say *we* you mean me and him.'

'So no talking to the press or anyone of dubious character, by which I mean no dowsers, clairvoyants, occultists, flat-earthers, members of the Green Party or people who think lizards have taken over parliament. Leslie Faraday will be watching and waiting for us to make a mistake.'

'I promise you, Raymondo, there'll be no mistakes,' said Bryant solemnly. 'You know how seriously I take my job. How could I not when it involves the final great mystery? "The stroke of death is as a lover's pinch, Which hurts and is desired" – *Antony and Cleopatra*.'

'Do you ever think you went into the wrong profession?' Land asked. 'You'd have made a halfway decent teacher.'

'No,' Bryant replied. 'It's the fatalism of the academic that makes a fine policeman, not the apathy of the educator. Before you absquatulate, indulge me for a moment.'

Land was about to answer in the negative but his detective continued.

'If one malfeasant carried out both crimes, it's not for his personal gratification because there are no corresponding occult elements in the second attack. He hasn't left any obvious way of connecting the deaths apart from the unusual choice of the murder weapon. Why not?'

'Because they aren't bloody connected,' Land replied as if it was painfully obvious to everyone.

'But if they were. A young man is hung from a tree, another falls from a bridge. As far as we know, they're strangers to each other. What if there are others who understand that the deaths are connected?'

Land's eyes glazed. He tried to imagine such a scenario and failed. 'You mean he wants someone to know what he's up to, but not us? What would be the purpose of that?'

'Gang members commit ferocious acts to scare their enemies,' May pointed out reasonably.

'But these don't have any of the hallmarks of gang killings. The victims are too old for a start, and ethnically mismatched.'

'Perhaps it's one man against a gang. Like a vigilante tackling drug-dealers.'

'But they're a saree salesman and an office manager. What could they possibly have in common?'

'That,' said Bryant, 'is what we have to discover.'

Land had had enough. He raised his hands. 'Let's just pop back into the real world for a moment, where people don't turn their offices into clubs or insert eels into horses. I want one of you, preferably not Mr Bryant, to come back to me in the next half-hour with an actionable plan.' He turned to leave, then stopped. 'I don't understand you two. Cheema must have been terrified just before he died, and you lark about as if this is some kind of big joke.'

'Even undertakers enjoy their work,' said Bryant. 'You think they don't make jokes? Of course they do, because they have to. If they didn't the weight of inhumanity which all of us face in this world would come crashing down and destroy them utterly. Don't you remember flash and trash nights at the old nick, when the London Fire Brigade used to come round and douse us with their hosepipes? Everyone used to get involved in water fights, even the local milkmen. It turned into a Norman Wisdom film some mornings. Don't you remember?'

Land looked at him blankly. 'No.'

'Incredible.' Bryant felt suddenly depressed. 'It was how we stayed sane. I'll bring you a plan in half an hour.'

14

ALONE

Patient's name: Arthur St John Aloysius Montmorency Bryant
Unofficial evaluation on patient's suitability for duty
Physician Dr Arnold Gillespie FRCP

Dear Raymond

Thank you for enquiring after my health. My foot is now out of plaster. The next time I get up in the night to fetch a glass of milk I'll make sure I turn the lights on. I knew my wife had been taking her jeep engine to bits in the kitchen but I didn't know she'd left it in the middle of the floor. I have been meaning to talk to her about the matter but her application for the Peace Corps has been turned down and she's currently not to be trifled with.

You asked me how Mr Bryant is doing. If you remember, I had diagnosed transient ischaemia, mood swings and some cognitive impairment, but it seems that to a certain degree these symptoms were the result of the accidental poisoning he suffered, and have now abated. After that I subjected him to a series of complex questionnaires designed to provide us with an insight into his current mental status, but I'm afraid the results are confusing. He appears to have the personality of a fourteen-year-old boy combined with that of an octogenarian, but his thought processes are as unfathomable as those of, say, an octopus.

While he's subject to all of the usual health failings of his age, what I understood least of all was how he maintains the mind of a much younger man. He has none of the signifiers we usually find present. However, I think I may have now found an answer. There's a protein that keeps our neurons from dying, and it can be triggered by maintaining the close friendships that allow us active social engagement. In short, I think the intensity of his working relationship with Mr May is somehow keeping him from dotage.

This is of course a good thing; as far as patient welfare is concerned I am obliged to remain entirely unbiased, despite the fact that Mr Bryant persistently holds me up to ridicule. But it raises a further concern, because the staff member I have found with the most alarming markers is you. Perhaps you could make an appointment with my office to come in. Since your divorce you've been very

'What a load of rubbish,' said Raymond Land aloud, punching *delete* with his fist.

'Knock knock.'

'Yes, you've worn that particular joke out. Come in before I pay to have you killed,' said Land testily.

Bryant took a huge pantomime step into the doorless room, then wandered over to the window. The blackened, bedraggled pigeon stared back at him with his cyclopean orange eye. 'Oh, your little friend's back. I thought you'd got rid of him.'

'I hope you have your plan ready, I'm very busy.'

'Are you? You don't look it. It'd probably be a good idea to put a few bits of paper on your desk and close down your computer screen so that I can't see that you're still trying to fill in your online dating form. Fruit Salad?' He produced some loose chews without their wrappers and picked off some pocket fluff before proffering them. 'So, the plan. Given the unusual nature of Mr Cheema's death I thought we could draw upon some experts in the field.'

'If this is about getting permission to commandeer your usual circle of cranks, don't bother,' Land warned.

'Heaven forfend, *mon petit abruti*. I shouldn't really eat these, they get under my plate.' He spat a sweet into Land's bin. 'You're thigmotropic, I understand that.'

Land glared. 'I have no idea what that means.'

'It's a directional growth movement that occurs as a sensory response to stimulus. You go where you're sent. You do what is required of you, and I respect you for that. Obviously I don't actually respect you, nobody does, but you know what I mean.'

'No I don't, actually,' snapped Land, stabbing ineffectually at his keyboard. 'Do you have anything else for me of a more practical nature?'

'Rather. Luke Dickinson. Given that it was murder, I wonder how you want us to proceed.'

'Well, I'm glad you're finally asking for advice, because I was beginning – wait a minute, what?'

'I want to push for a verdict of murder.'

'Based on what?'

'A piece of new evidence has just come our way. This was found at the spot where Dickinson left the bridge.' He dropped a clear plastic envelope on to the desk. Having been the butt of too many practical jokes in the past, Land chose not to examine it too closely.

'Take a look,' Bryant urged. 'It was on the concrete ledge below the railing, just where he fell. If you care to incline your head a little further towards your desktop and focus, you'll see that it's a jacket button with a small scrap of blue material attached. Dickinson pulled it off just before executing his forward half-somersault.'

'You mean you think he did.'

'I know.'

'No, you don't know, you think.'

'I know.'

'No, you don't know.'

'No, I mean I know I think I know, because I know.'

'I hate talking to you.' Land pushed the bag away. 'People lean over railings all the time. This could be from anyone.'

'It matches the blue thread Giles found under Dickinson's right index fingernail, and it's not from his own jacket, which is replete with the correct amount of buttonage.'

Land waved him away. 'Get it out of my sight. Come up with something more conclusive, otherwise I'll instruct Giles to issue a Death By Misadventure.'

'You can't influence a coroner's verdict,' warned Bryant. 'If there's reasonable doubt . . .'

'Then someone's out there in a jacket with a button missing from it, and all you have to do is find him,' said Land, returning his attention to his non-existent paperwork.

Bryant decided not to argue the point. It was half past five, and he was due in Covent Garden.

Script extract from Arthur Bryant's 'Peculiar London' walking tour guide (Covent Garden, 1.5 hrs, alcohol not included)

Beer had once been highly recommended as a nutritional drink for London children, and anyone could brew and sell it if they paid two guineas for the licence fee. By 1638 the Lamb & Flag was already a public house in

Covent Garden, although it had several other names. Its sign was an ancient reminder of the Knights Templar, the lamb representing Christ and the flag St George. The pub was wedged into a corner of Rose Street and hemmed by Lazenby Court, connected by a narrow, low-ceilinged passageway that left many a homebound drunk with a bruised forehead.

Here England's first Poet Laureate, John Dryden, had been beaten up for writing an insulting satire about the king's mistress. The fact that he was innocent of this act of anti-patriotism did not stop his attackers, and the assault became celebrated as the 'Rose Alley Ambuscade'. There is still an air of ambush about the place; once inside the alleyway, there is no easy way to pass one another.

As he walked into Covent Garden through misty drizzle, tapping his walking stick and occasionally using it to ward off taxis, Bryant hoped his companion would put in an appearance this time. Larry Duggan had a history of unreliability, but Bryant owed him a debt of honour and had agreed to meet. He just hoped it wouldn't take more than a few minutes.

He passed beneath the creaking, leaking pub sign and stepped inside, searching the packed saloon bar. Larry stood out from the crowd. The war photographer still looked as if he passed his mornings at the gym. His scarred features had long ago lost their ability to form a smile or show any kind of emotion. As solid as a railway sleeper, he kept his place at the bar and forced others to squeeze around him. His head almost touched the cabinets of glasses that hung from the bowed ceiling. 'What are you drinking?' he called.

'I'll have an Indian Pale Ale,' Bryant shouted back, removing himself from the coils of his damp scarf. Larry was accompanied by his Staffordshire, Bully, who had legs like a Queen Anne table.

'They used to call this pub the Bucket of Blood,' said Bryant, raising his glass. 'There was a boxing ring in the back. People are too squeamish to stand for that sort of thing nowadays. My old man used to say that a good punch up the bracket never hurt anyone. Of course, he was an idiot. What's up?'

Larry glared into his pint before sinking a third of it. 'Remember how we met at Bow Street Police Station?'

'You helped me out,' said Bryant. 'The building's been decommissioned now. It's going to be a museum. I remember it had white lights outside instead of the traditional blue police lamps. Queen Victoria had asked for them to be changed because the blue lamps reminded her of the room in which Prince Albert had died, and the colour depressed her whenever she saw them on her way to the opera.'

'When you're the head of the British Empire you can do that,' said Larry absently. 'Are you still conducting guided tours around London?'

'I haven't had time lately,' Bryant admitted. 'I heard you lost your job. I'd been meaning to call you.'

'Newspapers don't need staff photographers any more.' Larry's hands made the pint glass look like a teacup. He set it down and wiped his lip. 'Who wants to read about wars? We're in the entertainment business now. Fallujah, Helmand, Syria: ask anyone on the street why they happened and you'll get blank looks. We've been written off as a bunch of adrenaline junkies nobody needs.'

Bryant did not know what to say and was hardly in a position to give advice about making friends, so he sat back with fingers interlaced on the table and let Larry unburden himself. Finally he had to ask. 'Why did you want to see me?'

Larry unfolded a square of paper and laid it on the table. 'Your unit was namechecked in the *Standard* yesterday. It said a man was found hanging from a tree on Hampstead Heath and you're heading the investigation. There was a suggestion that the victim was involved in some kind of ritual, and died in the middle of the night.'

'That's everything we released to the press. Why?'

'Four o'clock in the morning. You know what they call that, don't you? The lonely hour. It's a military thing.'

'Why would it be military?'

'Four a.m. is the time when military police like to break down doors. It's when people are at their most vulnerable.'

'I didn't know that. You think it could be significant?'

'There was a guy in our regiment, a real loner. He didn't get on with anyone. The Falklands have these high cliffs. One night he jumped on to the rocks and bashed his brains out. At least, that's what we all thought he did. Later we heard he'd had a fight with a couple of local lads over an unpaid gambling debt. They broke into the camp and dragged him from his bed. Told him they were going to chuck him off the cliff. They only wanted to scare him, but in the fight he went over. Time of death, four a.m. Seems like we taught them how to do it.'

'There's been another death,' said Bryant. 'A fellow on his way home from a party. He died at the exact same time.'

'So the tactic has been transplanted to here.' Larry ran a hand across his hard, scarred head. 'London's a different place at night. I don't sleep much any more. I go out at two or three, up over Hyde Park, through Little Venice and Maida Vale, all the way to Chelsea and back along the river. There are still a few people on the South Bank. Joggers, City types. Not as many drunks as there used to be. There's a gap around four, when the dolphin lamps go out along the embankment. They don't always stay on until dawn. Then it's more like it was in the past. Better that way. No one about, no one to wind you up. Just water and shadows. Black and oily, like death. Do you ever look forward to dying?'

'Only when I'm in the post office.' Bryant could see that Larry badly needed someone to talk to. The pair had met in South London decades earlier, when the photographer had been sent to film looting after a riot. They had never been especially good friends – Larry was too afflicted with secret troubles – and there was no useful advice he could offer. 'Don't you keep in touch with anyone from the old days?' he asked.

'Most of them didn't make it. They didn't die fighting, they died trying to get their lives started again. I can't settle down. I just feel lost. Being stuck here is like being dead. Sometimes I want to take a rifle and pick people off as they come out of tube stations.'

'You have to talk to someone, Larry. There's an alternative therapy group called the Grievance Service. I can put you in touch with them.' Bryant had no real words of comfort. He was rarely introspective, and grew impatient with those who were. The bar was becoming claustrophobically crowded. He wanted to get up and leave.

'You say talk to people, but if I tell them how I really feel I lose them. There was a girl, but I was on assignment three weeks out of four and she didn't wait around. I guess I made the wrong choice. Have you ever done that?'

'I did when someone I loved died, but it was a long time ago,' said Bryant. 'I still have the unit, and if I feel angry I can take it out on my partner. He doesn't mind. I've known him all my working life.'

'What about women?'

'They've come and gone. Mostly gone. Thanks for the tip-off, Larry, but I'm not the right person to give you advice. I have to be getting back, I've a lot to do.' It sounded callous, but he could not offer more.

'Arthur, I'm telling you this because . . .' The photographer's face betrayed no emotion. 'It's just – things aren't going so well for me right now.'

'I understand that. Well, you can always call me.' Bryant put a crimp in his trilby and donned it, ready to get out, then relented a little. 'I should make more of an effort to stay in touch. We'll meet up again soon, I promise.'

With that, he walked back out into the sifting rain. The thought of the lonely hour had taken hold.

15

BREAK

Mrs Cheema surveyed the room with sadness in her eyes. She had always known that if she could not control her children she could at least keep her home in order. The living room was draped in orange and yellow silk curtains and was bright and inviting, with a tea table covered in fussy gilt cups, a clear plastic cover on the sofa and a grand sideboard – her mother's, kept as polished as her memory – with photographs of many happy children imprisoned beneath the glass.

When she welcomed the unmarried daughters of her friends they only had to look about to see what a marvellous family she had, and wouldn't know that her son Dhruv was useless and his brother Jagan worked nights so he was too tired to check whether the shop downstairs was making a profit. Any prospective bride would coo over the photographs and not notice that her younger daughter Jani was still unmarried and becoming too plump to ever attract a mate. Only Amaya had honoured the family, marrying a nice boy and raising two beautiful grandchildren. And now this shame and horror was being brought down upon her. Thank goodness her husband was not alive to bear witness.

She looked at Jagan and Jani, shaking her head, tears spilling down her cheeks. 'Your little brother – you were meant to look after him. What did he do to deserve this? To die in the woods alone in the middle of the night.'

'He didn't die alone, innit,' said Jagan, shifting his thin legs on the squeaky sofa. 'He was killed, so someone else was there.'

'Don't be disrespectful to his memory! You must know where he went, Jagan. You must know how he got there. He had no money. He always told you everything. He looked up to you. You let him take your car, didn't you? You know they would fire you if they found out. And the police will be looking. They have called me several times, and now they want to film my statement. I have lied to protect you, but now I must tell the truth. That if you hadn't let him take the car my youngest child would be with us still.'

'Mum, that's really unfair,' said Jani. 'He was helping Dhruv out.'

Mrs Cheema was not to be mollified. 'What kind of customer did he pick up? What respectable man is out at that time of the morning? This is on your conscience, Jagan.'

'What do you want, Mum? It's like Jani says, I was helping my brother and now I'm the one who gets blamed?'

'You are the oldest, you are responsible.' She jabbed an accusing finger in his direction. 'You must be able to discover where he went and who his passengers were. You owe it to your brother. You can find out who did this terrible thing.'

'How, Mum? It might not have been a customer. Maybe he had a girlfriend and she was married or something and her husband found out and went mental and did one on him.'

'Why do I think there is something you are not telling me?' Mrs Cheema knew her oldest son too well. Dhruv was the trustworthy one, if a little slow-witted. Jagan was too sharp for his own good, and had to be watched all the time. 'So you let him take your taxi, your livelihood, and then you lie to me and say he was here all night, and now I have lied to the police. So who is in the wrong?'

'You've always picked on Jagan,' said his sister. 'All he does is work, and he can never please you.'

They argued on, the blame and the guilt passing back and forth, but beneath the bickering was a sense of confused loss that ran so deep it would never be understood or healed.

Rory Caine was about to lose his temper. She had seen it many times before, and it was not a pretty sight. Right now he was barking into the phone as if it had made a personal enemy of him.

'No, no, you are not my mate, do you understand? You're a supplier, and in the great food chain of commerce that job title bungs you somewhere down near the sewage outlet, treading water with your mouth open right next to all the other shrimps. If I want to be properly mugged off I'll call in advance so you can put down your pasta shapes, Pritt stick and glitter for a minute and concentrate on dealing with adults, all right, *mate*?'

Caine punched the call off and stared at the phone as if willing it to burst into flame. 'Calling me mate, all glottal stops and trying to get extra with me. Nobody wants to do what they're told any more.' He threw his phone into an armchair and looked back at his girlfriend as if noticing her in the room for the first time. 'Yeah – OK, *what*?'

Victoria Banks had a daily battle on her hands. The object of the game was to gain Rory's attention and make him focus on her questions. Most of the time he did not hear her or was looking at his phone, his iPad, his monitor, his Fitbit or any of the other devices he possessed and could not leave alone for more than a few seconds. He checked his texts in cinemas, answered his emails in restaurants, listened to his earpods in meetings, skimmed web articles and endlessly recalibrated his TV at home, anything rather than look into the face of the person opposite. He preferred the touch of plastic to flesh and was entirely unapologetic about it.

The net result of this was that almost everything and everyone around him disappeared into an indistinct haze, rather as if he was ninety-nine and living inside his unmoored brain. In turn, his inattentiveness also made him disappear as others gave up on him. At first they repeated questions, speaking clearly and loudly as if dealing with a three-year-old in a shop, but eventually they stopped pestering and left him to enjoy the confines of his hermetic world. He no longer bothered with Facebook because there was too much boring stuff about babies and birthdays on it. Now he sought out social networks with no direct contact to real people. Rory was browsing his way through life, and saw nothing at all that interested him.

She tried again. 'Somebody called Sparrow Martin rang me earlier. I don't know how she got this number. She wanted to speak to you. Who is she, Rory?'

Caine stared at her – or rather right through her, possibly into the next building. 'A few phone calls to printers so he can get everything delivered by next week, that's all he has to do.'

'Did you hear what I said? Rory?'

He focused on her. 'Victoria.'

She bristled, having asked him numerous times to call her Vic because she preferred the gender fluidity of the name. 'You don't notice I'm here. Why is that? I'm trying to tell you that someone called Sparrow wanted to know if you would attend a funeral. What's going on?'

Rory raised his dimple, impersonating the act of consideration. 'I really don't know. She's crazy. Sparrow is a needy, overweight girl who wants advice about someone we both vaguely know, and I don't want to talk to her.'

'You've never mentioned her before.'

'Then she can't be very important, can she? Where do you want to eat tonight?'

He rose and paced in front of the curved glass. Beyond the double-height picture windows of the converted gasholder, London's newest area code lay at his feet. The derelict customs houses, factories and industrial waste-grounds of King's Cross had now been fully transformed into retail units, parks and multimillion-pound apartments. Despite the developers' admirable attempts to create spaces of openness and inclusivity, the postcode designated N1C was so effectively separated from its surrounding neighbourhoods by canals, roads and railway lines that it might have been enclosed inside a dome. It existed in an alternate reality where everyone was perfectly groomed, slow-moving, soft-spoken and very polite. Rory loved it. He did not have to know his neighbours or shop for food. His oven was still filled with polystyrene protectors. His furniture retained the smell of newness. Only Victoria's floral perfume upset the balance.

'Do you want me to go?' she asked, looking about. 'You really don't need me here.'

'No,' he replied half-heartedly, 'of course I need you.' His eyes strayed towards the phone in the grey wool armchair. The screen had just lit up and it had started to vibrate.

'Don't you dare, Rory. I'm warning you.'

The phone continued to buzz. He edged towards it.

She wondered how much more of him she could take. He clearly enjoyed shouting at other males but with her he was vaporous and tentative. She wanted to be with someone who would take up space and loom over her. Rory never loomed. After over a year of going out with him she still knew almost nothing about him. How was it possible to have discovered so little when he spent most of his waking hours on social media detailing his life?

'I mean it. If you touch that phone I'm walking out of here.'

Before the dilemma could be resolved, the phone stopped ringing. 'There,' he said, 'are you happy now? You have my full attention.'

The phone rang again, and this time he dived and guiltily silenced it.

Victoria instantly knew he was expecting some new girl to call. What hurt her most was that he couldn't even be bothered to come up with a convoluted, implausible excuse.

'Rory, I think we're through,' she said. 'I'm tired of being a walk-on in someone else's story. I'll drop your stuff off when I remember to get around to it. It's time I had my own life.' Disgusted, she grabbed her coat and headed for the door, slamming it behind her.

'What?' asked Rory, tearing himself from his phone screen, but only briefly.

16

PURPOSE

The first word that sprang to mind when Bryant entered Maggie Armitage's terraced house in Avenell Road was 'cosy'. The second was 'condemned'.

She had painted the kitchen and living-room walls so often that the house was the opposite of the Tardis, being dramatically smaller on the inside than the outside. The rooms had sloping floors and were now finished in lime, teal, gloss red and cream with emerald stripes. A formless mauve sofa lay slumped in the living room beside several pieces of blue plastic outdoor furniture, an upright piano and a painted wooden model of several people falling out of a hot air balloon. Eclectic was too kind a word.

Maggie's neighbours tolerated her with the benign benevolence of people who needed Amazon packages taken in. They told their friends that she was not mad, merely someone who had a tendency to paint outside the lines. North Londoners especially had a remarkable tolerance for the unconventional.

Kiskaya Mandeville usually stood outside the Arsenal tube

station handing out gold-trimmed calling cards that read: 'Herbal Remedies – Tarot Readings – Sofas Repaired'. She was an old friend of Arthur Bryant's landlady, Alma Sorrowbridge, and attended her church, the Redemption of the Faithless Multitude, Finsbury Park. She had cured the late Mr Sorrowbridge's smoking habit and replaced the springs in his ottoman. Now she was in Maggie's house helping to re-upholster Arbuthnot, the squashed ginger tom that the white witch planned to use as her new familiar.

Kiskaya was a generously proportioned Tobagonian lady built with considerably more robustness than her friend's house. She had successfully inflated Arbuthnot's left side and filled him with polystyrene balls. With new orange eyes the cat looked almost alive, although the illusion would have been more complete if both his front legs bent the same way. She was just putting the last stitch into his neck when Arthur Bryant entered.

'The front-door key's in the geranium pot again,' he called. 'I could be anybody.'

'In a metaphysical sense we all could,' said Kiskaya unhelpfully. She shook Bryant's hand with a free finger. 'How is Alma?'

'I don't know, I never ask her.'

'Only when I looked up into the sky last night the stars told me she was not doing so well.'

'Perhaps you misread them, perhaps they were street lamps. I was on my way back from the Lamb & Flag and thought I'd pop in,' he explained, although how he thought Highbury was on the way from Covent Garden to King's Cross was anyone's guess.

Bryant flinched when he saw the tools of the taxidermy trade laid out on Maggie's dining table: ear openers, fleshing knives, lip, eye and nostril tuckers, degreasers, needles and thread. Arbuthnot lay on his side and appeared to be staring into a corner of the ceiling. He followed Arbuthnot's stare but could only see a damp patch.

Maggie entered with a tea tray. Bryant counted three mugs. 'How did you know I was coming?'

'I'm a qualified clairvoyant.' How Maggie managed this reply without a hint of sarcasm was a testament to her good nature. 'I'm still experimenting with traditional methods, cartomancy, scrying, bibliomancy and so on.'

Bryant sniffed a biscuit with suspicion. 'Not seaweed again. Bibliomancy. Remind me?'

'You suspend a key over a bible with a ribbon and wait for it to turn to positive or negative verses, which you have to obey. It's rarely practised these days.'

'I'm not surprised. You'd end up having to dismember concubines and throw babies out of windows. I actually wanted a word with Mrs Mandeville.' Unable to resist the lure of the taxidermy table, he fiddled with a tail stripper.

'Can you put that down? It's not a toy.' Kiskaya unwrapped herself from a sparkly rainbow blanket and took the instrument from him.

'You're just in time,' said Maggie, drawing the heavy green velvet curtains. 'We're about to fire up Arbuthnot and see if he can channel my familiar, Squadron Leader Smethwick.'

Bryant enviously eyed the array of tools. 'As much as I'd love to stay for that and find out who won the war, I can't stop. I just have a question.'

'Maggie was telling me all about your case,' said Kiskaya, hooking Arbuthnot's upper lip over his teeth.

'So much for confidentiality.' Bryant sighed, looking back at the taxidermy instruments. 'Have you ever used a trocar?'

Kiskaya admired her handiwork. Arbuthnot was grimacing unpleasantly. 'That was week one. A very useful tool. You'd be amazed how much gas a cat holds.'

'Have you got one here?'

'We use disposables. Although I might splash out and treat myself if it goes well with the parrot.' She caught Bryant's look as she wired the last of the cat's paws. 'I'm doing a favour for a friend.'

'Is there any reason why someone with a disturbed mindset would choose it as a murder weapon?'

'An interesting question.' Kiskaya attempted to stand the completed feline upright. It looked as if it was wearing a fur coat belonging to a smaller, more misshapen cat. 'Common sense and superstition once went hand in hand, so the Devil's disciples were identified by pricking and setting the accused to running, to see if they bled.' She thumped Arbuthnot's legs. 'Witch-finders who wanted to influence the outcome of their investigations used piercing tools with retractable points and hollow handles. They designed their own special needles with both blunt and sharp points to draw blood from the innocent or leave no mark on the guilty.'

'He didn't just prick his first victim with the trocar,' said Bryant. 'He bled the poor chap dry.'

'The shedding of blood can be regarded as a cleansing process,' said Kiskaya. 'Think of leeches. The trocar may have got him the thing he most desired.'

'Which would be what?'

'The sense of achieving revenge.' She set her tools down and studied her work. Arbuthnot was looking decidedly unstable.

'I think it was something a bit more practical than that,' said Bryant. 'He didn't use occult symbols for the second victim because he'd already got what he wanted from the first one.'

'And what do you think that was?' asked Maggie as the feline fell over.

'Information,' said Bryant. 'In the history of all the world's wars, fear is the oldest technique ever used on captives. I think he was trying to frighten the truth out of him.'

Meanwhile, on an evening as drab as an unloved Victorian painting, the lights once more shone golden in the triangular three-storey building at the end of the Caledonian Road.

Raymond Land had gone home to his rented flat in Wapping in order to take Crippen to the vet, as the PCU's mascot had been off her food since Christmas. The rest of the staff gathered in the partially restored operations room with the day's notes. John May poured teak-coloured tea from an enormous brown china pot brought in by Colin's grandmother. His partner had returned from the Armitage household to finish rewiring a tasselled standard lamp (his latest subversive mission being to replace the operations room's over-bright LEDs with illegal lighting from the 1940s) and was now sneaking a pipe at the window. In the street below, a preacher in yellow satin robes was bellowing at passers-by through a plastic karaoke machine.

The other staff members were hunched around an IKEA coffee table covered in rare books, notepads, doughnuts and chunks of cinnamon pear cake delivered by Bryant's landlady. Meeting minutes were taken by Janice Longbright, because she liked to practise her Pitman and refused to acknowledge the fact that nobody used shorthand any more. It was a scene one might expect to find in digs occupied by Oxford academics in the 1960s, but not in a modern Central London policing unit.

John May walked away from the whiteboards and stretched his back. 'There's a funny smell in here.'

'That would be me,' said Bryant, turning to reveal what appeared to be a stick of wood hanging from his teeth. 'Liquorice root. Maggie gave it to me. Says it's good for the bowels. What else are we waiting for?'

'Cheema's mother has changed her story,' said Longbright. 'She's agreed to record an interview.'

'So she admits the family was covering for her son?'

'It looks like Dhruv Cheema took his brother's taxi out for the night.'

'And I think we've found the vehicle,' Banbury added. 'A white Toyota Prius left unlocked on Redington Road, Hampstead. That's just a short walk from where the body was found. We know it arrived some time overnight on Saturday. According to a neighbour who was coming home, it wasn't there at two forty-five a.m.'

'Did you get a chance to look at it?'

Banbury opened a set of shots on his laptop and turned it around. 'These are only preliminaries, so don't expect much. The interior hasn't been cleaned in weeks. There are hundreds of fibres, hairs, skin flakes and particles of unidentified material to go through.'

'How did Dhruv Cheema swap places with his brother?' asked May. 'Aren't licensed drivers electronically registered?'

'Passengers can see a driver's name and a photograph,' Banbury told him. 'I guess no one asks the driver to turn around so they can check. Brothers and cousins sometimes switch places to keep their vehicles in twenty-four-hour operation.'

'But there'll be a record of the trips he made on Saturday night.'

'It's not an Uber. The set-up is much less sophisticated.' Banbury checked the logs on his screen. Unfortunately his three-year-old had got her hands on his laptop and had added Princess Glitter stickers to it which were hard to remove. 'Cheema's brother is supposed to electronically tag his trips, but the driver has to input them manually. Dhruv Cheema turned off the GPS tracker at three thirty-seven a.m.'

'Why would he do that?' asked May. 'How could he find his way around?'

'I assume he was making the final journey of the night.'

May walked to the map Longbright had stuck to the white-board. 'Where was the last coordinate?'

'Belsize Village.'

Up until now Arthur Bryant had been sitting quietly, a forefinger at his lower lip. Now he raised his hand. 'I have a question. Meera, when you talked to Mrs Cheema, did she say whether her son was religious?'

'Actually it did come up,' said Meera, 'but only because the brother told me he wasn't. He mentioned some of the things they did for their mother's sake, like keeping a shrine at home. Mrs Cheema doted on her youngest son, but didn't have much luck marrying him off.'

'You don't think he was meeting a girl?' Longbright asked.

Renfield looked incredulous. 'In the woods. At four a.m.'

'A chap, then.'

'I thought of that,' Meera said. 'Not according to the brother, who should know.'

Renfield flicked through the notes Banbury had handed out. 'There's no mention here of prints at the heath site.'

'It's the woods,' said Banbury. 'Mud, rocks, leaves, half frozen, half wet. The sort of stuff you see on a walk. Not that I suppose any of you has ever been for a walk.'

Bryant appeared not to be paying any attention to the proceedings. May looked at him in annoyance. 'Arthur, do you have anything further to add?'

Bryant looked up wistfully. 'It all feels so far away.'

'What feels far away?'

Bryant sighed. 'My childhood. I was remembering how we used to play in the street on summer days that felt as if they would never end.'

An uncomfortable silence fell upon the assembled group. The chaotic weeks surrounding Bryant's illness were still fresh in their minds.

'When you have no money you make do with what you've got,' he continued. 'I suppose they're a form of pagan magic.'

May and Longbright exchanged worried glances.

'The rituals you perform with your friends. They're more than just games with sticks and broken toys, they *mean* something. A hole in a hedge can be the entrance to a cave. Children come with complicated rules that can't be broken. We had no money, of course. Nobody did in Bethnal Green or Whitechapel, but we still wanted things. You could steal – after all, most of us bent the laws a bit – or you could find another way. We were just kids . . .'

This was too much for Banbury. 'I'm sorry, Mr B, I'm not sure any of us knows what you're getting at.'

'We made wishes, Dan. And to make them more real we accompanied them with incantations and rituals. The man we're looking for needs something to happen. What makes childishly logical sense to him seems crazy to us. He's no lunatic attacking at random, he has a very clear purpose. I need to show you something.' Bryant bashed at the laptop Banbury had forced upon him, but failed to unlock the file he needed. 'Can somebody open this blasted thing?'

The CSM lent a hand. May found himself looking at a black and white photograph of a piece of pitted grey steel.

'I have no idea what this is,' said May.

'Look at it more closely,' said Bryant.

Banbury explained. 'I told Mr B I was going to Hampstead and he asked me to take some photos while I was out.'

'You went back to Hampstead Heath to shoot this?'

'It's not the heath. It's a close-up of the kerb at Waterloo Bridge, at the spot where Dickinson went over the side.'

'It's why nobody saw the attack, John,' said Bryant. 'The

bridge where you and I have stood discussing cases on so many evenings has been robbed of its innocence. The pavements now have anti-terrorist barriers on either side. It means that drivers no longer see what's happening at the railings because they're too busy concentrating on width restrictions. Look at the next one.'

May twisted his head. 'I give up – what is it?'

'It's the concrete lip on the bridge's outer edge,' Banbury explained. 'That dark spatter, there, is blood. It had been raining but a few drops survived. My sample matches the victim. You see the problem.'

'I'm afraid not.'

'In your version of events Dickinson falls outward and hits the water.'

'He was facing the river, not the stonework,' said May. 'The flailing shot shows that.'

'He turned as he fell,' said Bryant. 'We need to act out the scenario. Colin, would you mind? Sit on the backrest of that chair.'

Bimsley rose to his full impressive height and clambered on to the chair, which looked as if it wouldn't carry his weight for long.

'Colin, fall into the Thames in slow motion.'

Bimsley did his best, taking the chair with him.

'Thank you. Now sit back on the chair in the same position. This time you're not the victim, you're the attacker. Look as if you're thinking about killing someone. Imagine you're in one of Raymondo's briefing sessions. The trocar is concealed in your jacket pocket. Here comes Mr Dickinson, walking a little drunkenly along the pavement. Jack, could you be him?'

Renfield obliged, slowly approaching Bimsley's chair. Bryant's hands framed the scene. 'What does Dickinson see? A man about to throw himself into the river. "You mustn't jump," he cries. The killer looks up. Dickinson – that's you, Jack – steps forward and tries to help him over the low barrier to safety.'

Renfield mimed attempting to save Bimsley's life which, given the antipathy they currently felt towards each other, looked somewhat reticent.

Bryant pointed down at Renfield's boots. 'See, Dickinson is on *terra firma*, feet planted on the pavement, not at risk in any way, just reaching out a helping hand. And you, Colin, you turn around to your left, grab his right arm with your left hand and pull him hard towards you. He's not expecting that. Now, you take the trocar from your pocket with your right hand and stab his throat with the obturator, the sharp point, which is just how you'd do it if you were taking your own life. And now that he's in pain and off balance you simply keep pulling, sending him past you out into the air.'

Bimsley pulled down hard, bringing the surprised Renfield over his knee and slamming him on to the floor on his back. As Renfield climbed to his feet, rubbing his shoulder, he shoved past Bimsley. 'You will bloody pay for that,' he hissed.

Bryant sat back and folded his arms in satisfaction. 'You saw that as Jack went past Colin, his body turned around until it faced out. That's how the blood got on to the outside edge of the bridge. Indeed, it's the only way it could have got there. The second murder is a variation of the first.' He looked around the room, letting the thought sink in. 'We have no reason to believe that it will be the last.'

17

HOME

The glossy photograph was twenty-six feet long and sixteen feet high. It showed a woman in an evening gown of cream satin, as thin as a penitence candle, leaning on her glass balcony with a champagne flute in one elegantly poised hand. She was deliciating in a sunset so over-saturated that it shifted the location's latitudinal coordinates by a good fifteen degrees.

The image was febrile with possibilities. What did she see when she looked down from the thirtieth floor of her glass tower through that contaminating amber light? Palm trees and sugar-cane fields, surely, or the barren humpbacks of Greek islands at the very least? No, this was one trick the marketeers could not pull off. The ArcAngel – the spelling was crucial to separate it from Siberia – overlooked St Pancras Station and the arse-end of the Caledonian Road, but the photograph had been airbrushed free of fried-chicken shops, scaffolding, vans and bawling street drunks. At the building's four corners stood box turrets as grim as prison watchtowers, their sides finished in titanium tiles that reflected the polluted sunsets. The complex had been constructed to provide residents with a vista of the city that would make them forget they had purchased cages with picture windows.

None of this worried Augusta Frost. Drifting about her new apartment, she barely noticed the view. Nobody in the building ever opened the windows because of traffic noise. The flat was silent but for the faint hiss of conditioned air. The television, a great wall of black glass, was so complex to operate that she usually left it off. The three remotes required to initiate the operating system remained in their boxes. Instead she flicked through shows on her iPad.

At 10.30 p.m. her mobile woke her from an aphasic state. Augusta set aside her tablet and listened to the caller. The voice on the other end was hesitant; the unwritten London rule was that only close friends could call after ten. 'Of course I remember you,' Augusta replied. 'How could I not after the way you fended off that arsehole who attacked me? It was pretty impressive. I could never have done that.'

'He needed to understand that he was behaving inappropriately,' said Sparrow Martin.

'Yeah, you taught him that by pushing him out of a moving car. Well done you.'

'I hope you didn't mind me calling. I just sent you a message but you probably didn't see it yet. I wondered . . .' More awkward hesitation.

'How did you get this number?'

'Your address is on Facebook. Well, not directly, but it was pretty easy to find. Do you remember that night?'

'Not entirely, after the amount I'd drunk.'

'The one who jumped on you was Luke Dickinson.'

Augusta started to feel uncomfortable. 'What's this about?'

'He's dead. And so is the driver of our taxi that night. The police are saying they were murdered.'

'That's awful. You say dead – what do you mean?'

'Well, they were found. Separately, I mean, not together. The driver was in the woods and Dickinson was in the river.'

'But it's a coincidence, right? It couldn't be anything else.'

'That's what I thought at first but I don't know. I can't find out all the details. I .was thinking about the taxi. I mean, we didn't know each other before that. It seems so odd. I just wondered if you'd heard anything.' Sparrow felt increasingly foolish trying to explain.

Augusta wasn't sure why Sparrow had called. They had nothing in common, and weren't about to become friends just because someone they'd both met had suddenly died. Her replies were bland and soothing. She could tell that Sparrow was not seeking advice but reassurance.

'It's just strange,' Sparrow concluded limply. 'I don't know what to do. I talked to the other guy, Rory Caine. What a total wanker he turned out to be.'

'Why did you talk to him?' Augusta tried to sound unconcerned.

'Well, it was the four of us, wasn't it? I thought he might know something. You see, I think I may have seen someone, although it was all so . . .' The sentence trailed off. 'I'm being stupid; I shouldn't have called. Sorry. I'm just glad you're OK.'

Sparrow hung up suddenly. Augusta was left staring at the phone. *That was weird,* she thought. *What on earth had she been trying to say?*

She went to the fridge and peered in at a small diet yoghurt, a tub of olive oil spread and a bottle of Gordon's gin, each with its own shelf. In the cupboard were some unnaturally spongy crackers and a can of lentils.

At 11.25 p.m. the delivery boy dropped off a Thai takeaway but had trouble getting through the ArcAngel main gate. By the time he managed to reach Augusta the meal was cold, so she reheated it in the microwave and then burned the roof of her mouth with the first forkful.

At 1.15 a.m. she stood at the window and thought about Rory Caine. After that one encounter he never called her. Hardly surprising, she supposed, after their single catastrophic attempt at sex. She wondered how it had come to this. The smartest girl in her class, the pupil who regarded coming top as a necessity rather than an achievement, the business studies graduate who soared through the ranks of London's most successful property agency, was living in a trophy apartment with Siri for company, just one week away from a birthday party where all the guests would be colleagues. Now that she was finally ready for a new boyfriend she couldn't seem to find one.

Why am I always attracted to bastards? she and a thousand other women in the immediate radius of Old Street tube station asked themselves. *I need to find a decent dating site that's not full of guys in marketing telling me how sensitive they are. I need to rejoin the gym, cut down on my wine intake, increase my steps and drop a size. And I need to get the damned TV working.*

She remembered there was dairy-free ice cream in the freezer. It had no taste but it had no calories. After pouring maple syrup over it and finishing the entire tub she watched a Netflix show about telepathic secret agents on her tablet, took two sleeping pills and fell fast asleep on the couch.

Arthur Bryant seated himself by the partially open bedroom window and directed his pipe smoke out of it. He looked like a man displaced in time. Nothing about him suggested the present. He might have been a Paget illustration: *Colonel Carruthers Awaits the Arrival of Sherlock Holmes.*

Harrison Street was deserted. The distant traffic on Euston Road sounded like machinery in need of oiling, but in the backstreets all was still and quiet. Bloomsbury, once the heart of literary London, was still as calm as any library. Moonlight shone through the courtyard gates of Albion House, casting prison bars across the ground. The yellow-spotted top leaves of the laurel bushes shone like tropical flora. A little snow was falling, drifting theatrically around the street lamps; it might have been shaken from a drum behind a proscenium arch. Like the earlier rain it seemed tentative, almost embarrassed to be here.

Bryant exhaled and looked back at his bedroom, which had finally become interchangeable with his office. Both were a riot of patterns and textures, book-lined and cluttered with memorabilia: a theatre programme for *Orphée aux Enfers*, an alabaster replica of the Vessel of All Counted Sorrows, a length of crimson string, a kite made of yellow satin, a highwayman's tricorn, a clockwork explosive device (possibly defused), a Mr Punch puppet, assorted murder weapons, several London County Council bomb-damage maps and a penholder made from a rat, a memento from a case yet to be transcribed.

His bed had a tall oak headboard with a pair of immensely thick white pillows placed at the centre. The hideous tasselled purple Tiffany lamp on his bedside table was a gift from his landlady, who had insisted on replacing his Victorian candlesticks after he nearly burned the flat down. The paintings were his own, produced in the aftermath of the Water Room case, when for a brief period he had misguidedly thought that his talents might lie in the direction of brush and palette. The woman in his version of Degas's *L'Absinthe* resembled a baboon in a hat, and in *Echo and Narcissus* it looked as if Narcissus was being sick into a pond.

His pipe had gone out, leaving a wildflower fragrance in the room. Bryant sat back and sipped his brandy, letting its spicy sharpness warm his mouth. He was dissatisfied and restless.

He had always savoured his invisibility, but lately he had noticed how most people avoided him and gravitated towards his partner. They sought John May's advice and approval, and hoped that something of him would rub off on them. Nothing of Bryant rubbed off on people. Rather, he shed on them: toffee wrappers, strands of tobacco, inexplicably sticky bits of paper, cinders, crumbs, red wine and static electricity.

By Bryant's own admission he was a necessary evil. Good police officers were like good doctors; they exhibited high levels of curiosity and suspicion, low levels of sentiment and empathy. They believed in fair play but knew that life was entirely unfair, and were able to reconcile the paradox of this knowledge. It led them to believe that at some deeply buried level they were always right. Certitude doesn't protect you from injury, however, and many were lost to stress, depression and addiction.

Not so Bryant. He had somehow soldiered on, reaching the age when most of his friends were either mad or feeling very ill. It was not always easy to maintain stability in a topsy-turvy world, but May was his plumb line, his base rate, the control in the grand experiment. His partner rarely complained, only took chances with reasonable odds and never frightened people. Bryant struggled to understand how they were still friends. Their relationship was no marriage but perhaps an alignment.

It was late and he needed to sleep, but something other than the case was keeping him awake. A vague sense of foreboding hung over him. *Nothing lasts for ever,* he told himself. *At your age you must be prepared for sudden changes.* The most unsettling surprises came at you from directions you least expected.

And he could not sleep because he needed to understand. Why 4.00 a.m.? Why wait until the city is dormant? *Affairs that walk at midnight have in them a wilder nature than the business that seeks dispatch by day,* he thought, paraphrasing Shakespeare's *Henry VIII*. The idea led him to the night play *Macbeth*, in which conspiracies throve beneath the blanket of the dark.

Was it simply that? A dead and silent time when a predator could be sure of locating solitary victims? Bryant struggled to comprehend random acts of cruelty; he sought patterns and connections. Thoughtless acts made a mockery of order. They told him that there was no purpose in trying to understand the world, and he had spent a lifetime believing the opposite. If he accepted that societies were born to fail after reaching the most minimal level of competence, he would have to accept that he had wasted his life. It was not an idea worth pursuing at this time of night, when harmful forces sought out the spiritually confused.

He took his brandy to bed with a copy of *Urban Cosmologies: Disparity and Desolation*. It wasn't particularly restful bedtime reading so he switched to 'The Case of the Slaughtered Stripper'. *When sleep eludes you, embrace wakefulness,* he told himself, and read until dawn.

John May had not opened his mail for days. Usually it consisted of bills, reminders about hospital appointments and brochures for Saga holidays. With a sinking sensation he unfolded the letter and ran a fingertip lightly across the address. Broadhampton Clinic, Lavender Hill, London SW11. The few lines below were bare and unforgiving: '. . . sorry to inform you . . . patient Jane Alice May, née Partridge . . . complications following pulmonary oedema . . . arrangements at your convenience . . .'

Jane, his wife for all too brief a time before her demons overtook her, had been institutionalized for so many decades that seeing the name formally transcribed gave him a shock. He needed to inform Alex. His son lived in Canada, caring for an invalid daughter. His granddaughter April was out there with him.

He had been expecting the letter for years. He told himself that the sense of relief overwhelming him was for the end of her suffering, not the lifting of his guilt. Carefully folding up the page, he set it back on the table. So strong was May's belief in balance that every loss required a gain, every subtraction created the need to add. The letter made him want to be with someone. It was late, but the right time to call Norah.

'I'm glad you rang,' she said. 'I had such a good time with you last week.'

'Are you on-site?' he asked.

'Not tonight. There was no football on so it's quiet out there. Where are you?'

'I'm back at the flat. It's been a long day.'

'Are you all right?' She had a supernatural way of sensing moods.

'Yes. No. I had some sad news tonight. Look, do you want to meet?'

'What is this?'

'Just to . . .' He sought the right words. 'To be with some-one.'

'You want to come to Belsize Park? I'm not a shoulder to cry on.'

'I know that, Norah.'

'Come up.' She rang off.

He glanced back at the folded letter once more, then donned his coat and called a taxi.

Three episodes of *Game of Thrones*, back to back. Colin had seen enough throat-slittings to last a lifetime. 'It's a quarter to three. Can we go to bed now?' he asked, gently lifting the remote from Meera's hand.

She pulled herself upright on the sofa and rubbed her eyes. 'What did I miss?'

'If I tell you, you'll complain about me spoiling the plot.'

'Just give me the main points.'

'A couple of kings died. An old version of Emma Peel turned up. Winter came.'

She looked around for her shoes. 'I have to go home. Why didn't you wake me earlier? Why are there Twiglets all over the sofa?'

'You fell asleep eating them. You don't get enough kip, Meera.' He rose and placed his arms around her waist, dragging her upwards, but she clung around him leglessly. 'You have to help me. Come on, up the wooden stairs to Bedfordshire.'

'You haven't got an upstairs. I want to live in a house.'

'I'll buy you one in about fifty years' time.'

'With a garden.'

'A huge garden and an ornamental fountain, I promise.'

'I can't stay over. My mother will go bananas.'

'Then stay over. We can put her in a home.'

'I should have brought my bike. I can get a night bus.' She was awake now and became a model of practicality once more, dusting herself down, looking for the TfL app on her phone.

'Not at this time. I'll book you a cab.'

'I think I was dreaming about the case. Why is he up at this time of night?'

'Maybe he's an insomniac.'

'Or he works shifts. London Transport. Someone in the public service sector. Security, catering, hospitals, cleaning services. I read that one in eight Londoners works nights.'

Colin checked his phone. 'The cab's here. Want me to come down with you?'

'I'm fine.' Meera swung her bag on to her shoulder and reached up to kiss him. 'See you in a few hours.'

'Stay in the light,' he called after her. It was in his nature to watch until she was safely inside the car.

Janice Longbright slept with a mask because her blinds weren't thick enough to blot out the street lights. It was made of mauve satin and had eyelashes, a perfect copy of the one Lady Isobel Barnett had worn on the 1950s television show *What's My Line?* Like Bryant, Longbright had been born out of time. In her dreams she inhabited a city of misted empty streets and chromium-grilled cars. The river, the stations and the pubs were filled with smoke. There were nannies in Hyde Park, barrow boys in Covent Garden, spivs in Soho and jellied-eel merchants on Cable Street. It was the age before her birth, her mother's world, and therefore fabled.

She had been awoken by the ping of a message arriving on her phone. Dragging her mask over spray-stiff hair, she squinted at the screen. Four missed calls and three texts from Jack Renfield. Presumably he was in a bar with his old mates from the Met. He always chased her when he was drunk. At first she had enjoyed his renewed interest because she had the upper hand, but now it felt as if he was simply trying to take back control. He knew she could not turn off the phone because the line needed to be left open during investigations.

The tone of the text messages decided the matter; she would talk to him at the first opportunity and explain that she had thought the matter over carefully and decided there was no possibility of them getting back together.

Her mind was now too alert for sleep. The next deadline was only an hour away, but there was no one in the office to organize a response. As she rose to make tea, an idea came to her. Taking a pen and pad to the kitchen table, she began to map out a plan.

*

Raymond Land sat on the end of his sofa bed in his pyjamas and dressing gown, watching Crippen asleep in her basket. The vet had found cysts in her stomach, too many to remove. *First Leanne walks out on me,* he thought, *then the cat gets sick. There's only the goldfish to go, and he's already looking dicey.*

He decided to make himself a builders' tea. The kitchen clock read 3.35 a.m. He felt tired all the time. He needed something to distract him from worrying thoughts. He wished he liked music or knew something about art. He had no outside interests to sustain him. Standing at the window with his chimpanzee tea mug looking down into the deserted streets, he tried to imagine a different life. He was trapped between civil servants who treated him with poorly concealed disdain and staff who regarded him as a benign nuisance, like an oxpecker on the back of a buffalo, but he had dreams just like everybody else, although not many hopes.

He had never been outstanding – middle of the class in school, last to be picked for cricket, kindly turned aside by the girl at the edge of the dance floor who badly wanted to dance but not with him, cast in the role of Second Leper in his local church's production of *The Story of Jesus.*

Now he had once again been landed with an investigation designed to fail, so that his superannuated detectives could finally – *finally* – be shipped off to a museum.

But what if he showed them all? What if he did something unexpected? What if he led the team to success by becoming the leader he had always dreamed of being? The very thought of it brought rising heat into his chest.

He looked down and realized he had spilled tea down his dressing gown.

18

PRIVACY

Hugo Blake looked up at the tower block, its name picked out in silver lettering backed by piercing blue lights: 'The ArcAngel 200 City Road'.

There were hardly any lights on in the building. Glass had a way of looking desolate where brick did not. As he walked up to the illuminated entrance, he decided that the best way to get in was the way all smart burglars got into the houses of the rich: through the front door. He remembered an old trick and checked the key pad beside the door handle to see if it would work.

The apartment numbers were illuminated. The key pad was made of brushed steel. Its oval buttons fitted flush. Around the edge of each number was a seal made of clear plastic so that the LEDs behind them could shine through. When residents punched in their code they followed a memory muscle pattern, dragging their greasy fingers from one digit to the next. The City Road was always busy; dust settled all the time. He studied the keys and saw that the left-hand edge of the nine had a thin line of dirt that continued up and across to the five, then to the two and the three, where it stopped. What was the point of keeping the security code secret if anyone with a keen eye could track it?

He pulled the grey cotton hood from beneath his leather jacket and checked his watch. He would be out just after 4.00 a.m., whatever happened.

Punching in the number, he waited for the door lock to click and entered the reception area. The walls on either side were coated in slivers of dark mirror that refracted gold spotlights. The air smelled of antiseptic cleaning spray.

The lift would not work without a swipe card; he hadn't foreseen that and was forced to climb sixteen floors. The staircase had sensor lighting but no cameras; they were all tucked in the corners of the communal areas and were only useful during the day, when a bored guard sat behind an acre of stone and steel in the foyer. Since the property downturn, residents had grown reluctant to pay raised service charges. It meant that half of these new apartment buildings relied on cheap technology instead of night porters and monitors.

He exited at the sixteenth floor and turned into a corridor that reminded him of any large mid-priced hotel. The apartment doors looked solid enough, but he knew their weak spots. Each had a spyhole set in the upper panel, but he had followed the service company's email exchanges with the tenants and knew they had complained about poor visibility. He could tell by the depth of the brass ferrules that the wood was thin.

He rang the doorbell and waited. His right hand ran over the handle of the silver instrument in his pocket. No answer. He checked the corridor and rang again. Now he heard the faintest of footsteps, a rustle of material, bare feet on wood. He had calculated the distance between the bedroom and the front door, and the maximum time it would take her to reach the latch, but she took longer than expected. He suddenly realized why; she was coming from the living room, which was further away.

The trocar was engraved with his name. His fingers removed the cover from its tip and lifted it out of his pocket. The point could be brandished with a single movement.

He had waited long enough. As he threw his weight against the lock he realized he had applied too much force. The door popped open and slammed back. The jamb was made of such soft wood that it splintered apart as the lock tore through it and smashed the occupant against the wall. The plasterwork registered a perfect dent. The girl fell slowly, sprawling face down, her long black hair fanning over the wood floor.

He took out the trocar and crouched beside her, preparing to grab a handful of hair and pull her head back, exposing her throat.

'I need you to tell me—' he began. Something shiny caught his eye and he looked up, glimpsing the flat's shadowed interior. On the kitchen counter was a golden *maneki-neko*, a 'beckoning cat' meant to bring good luck. There were other talismans dotted around: *daruma* dolls and a *koinobori*, a pink paper carp. He reached down and removed the strands of hair from her face.

She was not meant to be Japanese.

He got back to the ground floor at six minutes past four. Outside, leaning against the recycling bins, he felt a flush of extreme heat ripple through his body, as if he had eaten something bad. He tried to feel remorse for the girl lying on the floor of her flat upstairs, but there was nothing inside him. *You made a mistake,* he told himself, *it doesn't change anything.* The most overlooked point about enemies was that they never realized they were the enemy. Hugo knew exactly who he was. He wanted his targets to know it too; it was important that in their final moments they understood he was right and they were wrong.

Attacking the wrong person was a setback, that's all. There were always civilian casualties. He had expected something like this to happen. War was an inexact science. Napalm had been developed at Harvard in 1942, and wasn't banned until Barack Obama's first day in office. There were always some casualties before the scales were balanced.

He wondered if the press had picked up on the jacket button yet. What was the point of leaving behind a clue if they failed to report it? Murders barely warranted a couple of lines in today's papers.

He took a deep breath and realized that he was not going to be sick after all. Once it was over he would be able to rest, knowing that what he had done was not only right but fair.

Setting off into the empty backstreets, he resolved to stay the course until the mission was completed.

'You're not going anywhere without breakfast.' Alma Sorrowbridge placed the bowl before him and folded her arms. In her pink quilted dressing gown, matching curlers and fluffy slippers she was not a woman to be trifled with. 'It's chilly outside.'

'What is it?' Bryant peered down through the steam and sniffed.

'Plum porridge with cinnamon, powdered limes and cocoa nibs.' She placed a spoon in his hand.

'But I've already got my coat on.'

'You can keep it on just this once. I want to see a nice clean bowl.'

'Alma, we're due at a murder site.' John May was by the kitchen door, checking his watch and anxious to leave. 'He's not a five-year-old.'

'Then I'll save it for later. If he keels over it's your fault,' she warned, reluctantly standing her tenant upright and throttling him with an unsuitable scarf. 'Have you been to the toilet?'

'Madam, I do not need to be dressed, coddled, nagged, fed, watered or referred to in the third person,' said Bryant. 'Go and bake something.'

'He's just showing off,' said Alma. 'Have him back by eight.'

The detectives ventured outside. The morning was pur-blind, the sky filled with furious clouds. May held the car door open for him. 'Your laces are undone,' he warned.

Dan Banbury was waiting for them outside the ArcAngel. For once even the CSM looked less than his usual buoyant self. His eyes were dark, his chin unshaven.

'What's the matter with you?' asked Bryant, shaking off his gloves. 'You look like you slept in a bin.'

'Giles needed a favour,' Dan explained. 'I was at the mortuary with him until two a.m. – a car crash in Belsize Park. I couldn't get home so I had to sleep in his chapel of rest. News of this one came in just after seven, when the EMT took over from the police. I'm not good on four hours' sleep.' He handed them coffees.

'You should live closer to town,' said Bryant.

'Raymond doesn't pay me enough.'

Bryant did not mention the fact that he had not slept at all. He unsealed his coffee lid and eyed it suspiciously. 'Is this a soy decaf latte?'

'No.'

'Thank God for that.' He glanced up at the apartment building. 'Look at this place. Just what we need, another stack of hamster boxes starting at a million apiece.' He pulled a packet of Lemon Puffs from his overcoat and offered them around. 'Why wasn't the body left *in situ*?'

'Because she's not dead, Mr B.' Banbury took a biscuit. 'She's been taken to the Royal Free. The building's owners were on the phone threatening legal action within minutes of finding out about it. They haven't sold all the apartments yet and are paranoid about bad publicity.'

'Who's the victim?' asked May.

'Henrietta Takahashi, twenty-six, a Japanese national, piano teacher, found unconscious in her hallway at number 136. Head trauma, serious enough to put her in the ICU but not life-threatening. It looks like she opened the front door and got slammed into the hallway wall. They're going to keep her out until they've repaired the skull damage and made sure she's stable.'

'And what makes you think she's for us?' asked May.

Banbury looked at him blankly. 'There's nothing that directly connects her to Luke Dickinson. She suffered a single blow to the back of the head. It was the time of the attack.'

'Four a.m.'

'On the dot.'

'How do you know?' Bryant warmed his hands on the coffee cup. His name was misspelled on the cardboard sleeve. 'Brian'.

'Because the noise woke her next-door neighbour.' Banbury pushed open the door to the foyer. 'Takahashi's only been in the flat six weeks. She's teaching for three months at the Royal College of Music. That's all I have.'

Bryant stopped to examine the door handle. 'A supposedly secure building with a front-door lock that a moderately bright monkey could open. That's a good start. Any prints?'

'Nothing conclusive yet,' said Banbury. 'The lift operates on a swipe card. I got a spare from the porter. He arrived at eight. Before you ask, I've already checked the staircase. Sixteen floors. It nearly killed me. It would put you in an iron lung.'

Bryant leaned back and studied the ceiling. 'What about cameras?'

'They're supposed to have a state-of-the-art system that backs up everything to the Cloud and doesn't store any physical material, but the subscription charge lapsed while the building was changing to a cheaper management service and it's out of action, so there's no footage to be had.'

'It seems the future is full of flaws. And a woman is in intensive care because of it.' Bryant filched a property brochure from the foyer as they passed through. The lift took them to the sixteenth floor.

May checked along the deserted corridor and saw a couple of dead spotlights, pale green carpet tiles, unfinished paintwork. 'You don't get much for a million these days,' he murmured. 'Let's see what this house of horrors holds.'

They were met by a handsomely suited West Indian manager who introduced himself as Gerard King and shook hands with grave formality.

'The building's owners are Chinese,' he explained as they walked. 'They're very unhappy. They've invested millions in City Road apartment buildings and are worried that their buyers will start losing confidence if news of the attack gets out.'

'It's public news, so it will get out,' said May. 'You've had no reports of strangers wandering around the building? Nobody coming in asking for her?'

'Nobody.'

'How do the keys work? How many are issued?'

King led them to the apartment. 'They're specially made. Each tenant is given two, but they can buy more. I have to be careful about what I tell you. The owners are very litigious.'

'They can yell all they like, the law takes precedence,' said Bryant, looking around for signs of life. 'Anything you say to us will be treated as confidential. Your employers won't have access.'

King hesitated in the hall. 'Gentlemen, these homes are designed for a very specific demographic: single high-income occupants, no pets, children discouraged. It's exclusive.'

'A young woman was attacked in her own home, Mr King,' May reminded him.

'We've had – problems,' said King. 'A con man got in and persuaded one of the cleaners to give him her keys to four of the flats.'

'Was Miss Takahashi's one of them?'

'No, I don't think so. Prices are flatlining right now so there's been some corner-cutting on security. The lifts don't work as they're supposed to. The front-door locks have a fault. People don't feel as safe as they should.'

'You don't sound like a management mouthpiece to me,' Bryant observed.

'I'm not,' said King. 'I'm an architectural graduate getting some ground-floor experience. It's been an eye-opener.'

'Tell me he didn't just kick the door in.' May stopped at the threshold of 136 and stared at the door jamb.

'There are no burglar chains,' King explained. 'They would look too – penitentiarial.'

'Good adjective,' said Bryant. 'So he just had to boot the lock to open it?'

'They're being withdrawn but they haven't all been replaced yet.'

'Then either he was very lucky or he knows about their construction. We'll need details of the company you use.' May followed Banbury inside and saw the oval indentation on the wall. Its edge was rimed with a black crescent of blood. 'You think she was expecting him at four a.m. on a school night? I mean, going to answer the door at that time with no chain on the door.'

'People here don't keep regular hours,' said King.

'He must have waited until she was standing right behind the door jamb.' May crouched and examined the pieces on the floor. 'She went back, smashed her head, then fell forward and hit the floorboards, here. You wouldn't think she'd get away without a traumatic brain injury.'

Banbury had donned plastic gloves and was examining the

wall. 'It could have been worse, but the plaster's soft and female skulls tend to be thicker. The prelim from the admitting doctor says she suffered a split in the lambdoid suture which could easily have pushed slivers of bone into her brain.' He dropped a line from the wall indentation to the floor, then ran it back to the door jamb. 'The way the door caught her, the angle she hit the wall – a decent defence lawyer will argue it down from murder to manslaughter.'

'It's gone eight,' said Bryant. 'No one's missed her yet.' He took a look around the apartment.

'He didn't enter any further than the hall,' Banbury said, 'so could you not go planting your size tens all over the white fur rugs?'

Bryant pointedly ignored the instruction. 'Manslaughter could be right. If he stopped at the door we've no reason to assume he came here to kill her.'

'I can see where he turned,' said Banbury. 'The dust is undisturbed beyond his right heel. A rubber-soled boot. I love tiled floors; you can see exactly where the air has fallen.'

'What do you mean, where the air has fallen?' asked May, watching the pale light that slanted from the white living-room blinds. 'Surely it just drifts?'

'There's a nitrogen dioxide index rating of between four and six in London this morning,' said Banbury. 'We get the highest pollution readings in Europe. The particles settle, bringing down specks of dirt, skin, plastics, carbon, anything that's floating about and can attach itself to something heavier. Bad for lungs, good for forensics. The alarm must have been raised very soon after she hit the wall. He didn't have time to hang around.'

'What about the door?' asked Bryant. 'Can you get anything more from that?'

'The problem with these locks is that the latch isn't quite long enough for the strike plate. If you know what you're doing, you can crack them with a sharp punch using the heel of your hand.'

'So he's a professional.'

'Maybe he's just someone who does his homework.'

'Who reported the noise?' May asked King.

'The girl next door at 138. She was up when it happened. She heard the bang and called the police.'

'What's wrong with these people?' asked Bryant. 'They should all be tucked up in bed at that hour.'

Banbury checked the floor at eye level. 'Haven't you heard, Mr B? Insomnia is a citywide epidemic.'

'Don't tell me. I haven't had a good night's sleep since the old king died.'

'Why didn't she call you, Mr King?' asked May.

'I'm not on nights,' said the manager. 'There was supposed to be twenty-four-hour security but the tenants voted against a hike in the service charge.'

'She didn't go next door and take a look?'

'Would you?'

'Of course I would.' Bryant was amazed that anyone would ask him such a thing. 'Is she in?'

'She's waiting for you.'

'Thank you, Mr King,' said May. 'We won't keep you from your work. Dan, Arthur and I can handle this. Could you find out if anyone has managed to contact Miss Takahashi's family?'

The flat next door, 138, was a mirror-image of its neighbour – the same white walls, the same Italian tiled floor, the same curved breakfast bar, an almost identical sofa with a black marble-topped coffee table. A block of artificial peonies stood in a fat ceramic pot on a pale oblong of wood. There were two abstract paintings consisting of vast umber patches punctuated by turrets of yellow ochre.

Bryant had never seen an apartment so devoid of personality.

The sofa cushions were perfectly balanced on their points, and there was one bookshelf designed to hold six books and a small vase. Only a red yoga mat broke the symmetry. There were no personal items, nothing left lying around. It was a stage set for a phantom film, a show-flat for the world beyond.

The girl seated on the chromium kitchen stool had blue-black hair cropped into daggers. A green and pink tattoo of a fairy peeped out below the lobe of her left ear. She wore a grey dress over black leggings, and had bare feet.

Augusta Frost introduced herself. 'I never even got to meet her. I think she was renting.'

May was surprised. 'You never passed in the hall or said good morning?'

'Nobody says good morning here. Owners don't talk to renters. I sometimes heard her making phone calls on the balcony late at night. Look, I'm afraid I need to get to work. I'm showing a property in half an hour. I reported exactly what I heard. There's nothing else to say.' She cast a worried glance at her phone.

'You didn't open your front door and take a look out?'

'No.'

'Why not?'

'For the same reason I don't go walking through White-chapel at three in the morning. I don't invite trouble. I have enough to worry about in my life.'

'Have you just moved in?'

'No, I've been here for over a year.' She saw what May was looking at and folded her arms. 'I don't like clutter.'

'The walls must be thin. I mean, you being woken up by the noise.'

'I wasn't asleep. I was on the sofa doing some emails. It sounded like—'

There was a sudden thud from the other side of the room.

They looked around to find Bryant lifting a book from the floor. 'I just wondered which edition it was,' he said sheepishly.

May turned back. 'It wasn't enough to alarm you, make you check on her?'

'It didn't occur to me. There are usually around two hundred and fifty emails in my inbox. About a quarter of those absolutely need to be actioned first thing in the morning, so I often tackle them in the night.'

'Well, I don't wish to add to your stress. We'll try to get someone stationed here. Meanwhile, make sure your front door stays locked and keep an eye out for strangers.'

He handed her a card. Bryant gave a theatrical cough.

'What?' asked May.

'Ahem. Ahuerghm.'

'Why are you doing that?'

Bryant rolled his eyes and beckoned with his fingertips.

'Excuse me,' said May, 'my colleague wants a private word.' He headed across the room and grabbed Bryant's arm, pulling him into the study beyond. 'What are you doing?'

'According to that digital thing on her kitchen counter it's eighteen degrees in there, but she's sweating buckets,' whispered Bryant. 'It can't just be the yoga. She knows more than she's letting on.'

'How could she know anything more?' asked May. 'You heard her. They lived next door to one another but never met.'

'Next door. Yes, well, that's the thing.'

John May knew this tone and did not like it. 'There's no reason to look for a link here as well,' he warned. 'If it's the same person, why didn't he try to stab her?'

'Something's not right. The Waterloo Bridge crime scene is less than three miles away. It's another four a.m. attack. And she wants to get us out of here as quickly as possible.'

'Yes, because she has to go to work,' said May. 'Why are we whispering?'

'They didn't know each other.' Bryant started digging about in his pocket for the ArcAngel brochure. 'The building's designer is a gentleman by the name of Jean-Claude Corbeau, and he's a bit too French.'

'What has that got to do with—'

'And then there's this.' He pulled a ballpoint pen from his pocket and handed it to May. On the cap was a blue and white design of a ship in a thunderstorm.

'The same pen Giles found in Luke Dickinson's pocket,' said May.

Bryant took it back from him. 'Only it's a different ship.'

'You actually remember details like that?'

'Of course. There's no lettering. What's the point of a marketing tool with no message?'

'Arthur, it's Dan's job to catalogue everything found in the victim's flat. You can't just nick stuff.'

'It doesn't belong to Henrietta Takahashi. It belongs to the girl out there.' He pointed back towards the living room. 'It was lying on the kitchen counter.'

'Of *this* flat? Then it has to be a coincidence. There could be millions of these pens knocking around London.'

'It links her and Dickinson. You see what this means?'

May blinked. 'You mean – no, this is just you being—'

Bryant brandished the ArcAngel brochure again. 'I was telling you about the very French Monsieur Corbeau. The retro typeface he's used throughout the building is called Art Deco Chic. It's *très élégant* and became very popular in Paris a couple of years back, but it has one fault.'

'How do you even know this—'

Bryant tapped his forehead. 'Eyes. Brain. Do focus. The typeface has two numerals, six and eight, that look almost identical, especially when etched on to pieces of brushed aluminium and seen in poor light. The ceiling panel above the entrance to Henrietta Takahashi's flat is faulty. The front doors are all the same colour and their respective numbers are next to each other in pairs. Don't you see? He misread the number and went to the wrong apartment. That's why he turned on his heel and left the flat so quickly. As Takahashi fell he got a good look at her in the light from the hall and realized what he'd done.'

May looked uncertain. 'I don't know, Arthur, it doesn't seem very likely.'

'It wouldn't be the first time. Just a fortnight ago in Lewisham some chap was shot in the face when he answered the door. Mistaken identity. The shooter apologized.'

May studied the pen again, turning it in his fingers. 'It must be coincidence.'

'It could be,' Bryant agreed. 'It could also mean he'll come calling again.'

May glanced back at the girl. 'Do you want to tell her?'

'I have a feeling she already knows.' Bryant peered around his partner's shoulder. 'Without her cooperation we have no way of protecting her.'

May ran a hand through his silver hair. 'A plastic pen, a button and a puncturing instrument: that's all you have, Arthur. They don't directly link the attacks to one individual.'

'Ah, well.' Bryant shifted uncomfortably.

'What?'

'I meant to tell you last night but I forgot.' He reached into his jacket and withdrew a tiny clear plastic bag. 'The button from the bridge. It was Giles who noticed, not me. It's from Dhruv Cheema's jacket.'

'How did it get to Waterloo Bridge?'

'Either it was in the killer's pocket and magically fell out, or he deliberately left it there to be found.'

'Killers leaving clues? That doesn't happen in real life.'

'Well, this time it did. And why? Because he wants the deaths to be linked, so that the news will get out and frighten someone still living. Now we have a chain.'

May turned the button over in his palm. 'You didn't just *get* this from somewhere, did you?'

Bryant was affronted. 'What, you think I'd falsify evidence to keep the case?'

'I'm sorry.' Augusta Frost came in to interrupt them. 'I really have to go. My boss has called three times since you arrived. She's going to kill me.'

Bryant nimbly stepped into her path. 'Just a couple more questions, then we'll be off. Have you had any reason to feel unsafe lately? Has anyone tried to get into the building?'

'No – no, I don't think so.'

'Has anyone been pestering you?'

'No, no one. Why?'

'Do you remember where you got this pen?'

She took the pen from him and impatiently turned it over, barely glancing at it. 'I really don't remember. They're everywhere. I'm always picking them up.'

Don't tell her too much, thought May, willing his partner to shut up.

'Because there's a good chance that the man who attacked your neighbour was looking for you,' said Bryant. 'You could be in danger. Do you know a man called Luke Dickinson?'

This time the briefest of blinks told them that she was about to lie. 'It doesn't ring a bell. I'm not good with names. I remember faces.'

May took out his phone and turned it to her. 'How about now?'

She looked at the screen for a moment. This time her eyes betrayed nothing.

'If you've ever seen him before, or even think you might have done, you need to tell us, Miss Frost.'

She looked squarely at May. 'No, I'm afraid not. I didn't even ask for your ID. Are you sure you're detectives?'

Bryant bridled. 'We have to ensure your safety. If you can think of anyone who might mean you harm, you must let us know at once.'

'Fine, of course.' Augusta started heading to the door, relieved. 'I'm perfectly fine. Quite capable of looking after myself.' She checked her watch again. 'I'm already incredibly late for work. I hate to rush you out.'

19

SHIFT

When they got back to the PCU, Bryant went to Raymond Land's office and explained Janice's plan.

'No,' said Land emphatically. 'Turn everything upside down, just to pander to a whim? It's out of the question. The logistics alone would be a nightmare. Absolutely not.' He slapped the desk for emphasis.

'It wasn't my whim, it was Janice's,' said Bryant. 'You like her. It's a good idea. We can start tonight. Everyone else is in favour.'

Land was outraged. 'How could you agree such a thing without my approval?'

'We didn't want to bother you, my old cullion. The others don't take pleasure in seeing you upset, so we took a vote and it was unanimous.'

'Don't I get a vote?'

'Yes of course. I voted on your behalf *in absentia*.'

'But I was here.'

'Not really, because when I fast-tracked you for the Truncheonists I put you down for overseas membership, so you're not technically residential.' Bryant eased himself on to the corner of Land's desk and counted out on his pudgy fingers. 'Try to concentrate. The killer left the button from his first victim at the scene of the second crime. And we found a pen similar to the one on *that* victim at the next site, sort of, because it was in the wrong flat. Or rather, the right flat. The important thing is that everything is starting to link together.'

'You're doing it again,' Land warned. 'Pens, buttons, black magic, explaining away an attempted murder by saying the killer got the address wrong – you're turning this investigation into something it was never meant to be.'

'All I'm saying is that we have more chance of tracking him down if we run shifts around the clock. We have to be ready for him.'

'Darren Link thinks this latest attack was nothing more than a botched burglary.'

'Is that it? You're taking advice from Link now? I still haven't forgiven him for placing this building under quarantine.' Link was a superintendent at City of London's Serious Crime Directorate, and a harsh critic of the unit's operational style. He watched its staff members as a hyena might trail behind a limping zebra.

Bryant tried once more. 'We need to operate night shifts until we catch him. He goes to ground during the day, Raymondo. Please, give it a chance. We've never operated a night service before.'

'With good reason,' said Land. 'I'm in bed. Besides, you know what happens when coppers switch to nights. They can't conduct prisoner interviews at night so they get up to mischief, turning over their governors' offices, dragging each other out of cafés and eating Chinese with the restaurant workers before wandering around the capital looking for someone annoying to arrest. You lot are enough trouble in broad daylight. I can't stay up all night.'

'We won't need you.' Bryant, ever the master of charientism, cheerfully waved the thought away. 'You can pack your empty briefcase on the dot of six as you usually do and leave us to keep the place operational from dusk to dawn.'

'But that way I'll never see anyone.'

'Exactly. Good, isn't it? Don't worry about me, I don't need much sleep.'

Land was unconvinced. 'You're no spring chicken, Bryant. People who don't get a full eight hours die two years before those who do.'

Bryant ticked off his fingers. 'Yes, but if the average lifespan is a biblical seventy years that's 5,840 waking hours per year, giving you a total of 408,800 hours, compared to my 6,935 waking hours per year which means I get 485,450 hours in total awake across my lifetime, which is 76,650 extra hours, or let's see, 210.5 extra days not counting leap years and allowing for a lie-in on Sundays when I'm awake and doing something useful. Whereas you don't do anything useful at all.'

Few things muddled Land more than his detective's assaults on logic. 'Stop confusing things. You know I failed my Maths O level. You've already got the press talking about black magic, and if they decide the deaths are connected they'll be spreading nonsense about Satanists operating in London. Look out of the window.'

Bryant obeyed. The pigeon on the ledge outside studied him with interest. 'What am I looking at?'

'There are two photographers lurking in the doorway of the fried-chicken place.'

'So there are.' They were underdressed for the weather, kept warm by their excessive weight. One watched the PCU's windows as he took a cigarette from the other, who was festooned with telephoto lenses.

Land shied away. 'Do you want them to see us working through the night?'

'We could turn the lights out.'

'I will not have this place turned into some kind of ghost train ride.'

'*Sutor, ne ultra crepidam*,' said Bryant. 'Don't pass judgement beyond your expertise.' He slapped Land on the back. 'We're going to restore the fine tradition of London being open all hours. Don't you long for the days when Samuel Pepys would send his servants off for jugs of porter and a few dozen Thames oysters at one in the morning? Did you know there were once so many pearls on the banks of the river that a street-sweeper used them to make buttons for the first pearly king?'

Land tried to find an adequate answer but the words escaped him. 'No,' he said weakly.

'It's good to see you two having a lively discussion,' said May, passing by. 'Has Arthur told you Janice's idea?'

'He's telling me about oysters and pearly kings,' said Land with a sigh.

'Right-ho.' May decided this was one conversation he could afford to duck out of.

'Look, Raymond – may I call you Raymond?' Arthur placed a matey hand on his boss's back. 'Four a.m. is the time when people are in their most vulnerable state. Now, let's assume—'

'I hate it when you assume,' said Land.

'—that our killer is indeed linked to the neighbour, Augusta Frost, either personally or indirectly. Why is Frost trying to hide the fact? She knows more than she's saying. She lied to us this morning. Is she protecting him, or someone else?'

'Can't we just haul her in here and shout at her until she tells us?' asked Land.

'What a brilliant idea, why didn't I think of that?' Bryant replied. 'We could waterboard her. I know Sir Winston Churchill said that the best argument against democracy is a five-minute conversation with the average voter, but the last time I looked we were still in one, so for now we'll have to pretend that London is not a police state and treat her with a modicum of respect.'

'You cannot switch the unit to nights without Home Office approval,' said Land doggedly. 'What would we do about the phones?'

'We'll take turns to monitor voice messages during daylight hours.'

'What about' – he tried to think of another obstacle – 'statutory meal breaks?'

'It's King's Cross, chum, one of the few places in London where you can get a fettuccine Alfredo at three in the morning.'

'But if Link tells Leslie Faraday about this . . .'

'Let me deal with him,' replied Bryant, relishing the thought.

Leslie Faraday, the porcine Home Office liaison officer and budget overseer of London's specialist police units, proudly considered himself the enemy of innovation. He was a man who had never knowingly broken a rule in his life. It is the destiny of such people to be the accidental instigators of anarchy, and so it proved with Faraday, who inspired the staff of the PCU to seek out new ways of horrifying him.

'Crippen's sick,' Land announced suddenly. 'I have to take her back to the Cally Road vet. It doesn't look good.'

'I'm very sorry to hear that,' said Bryant. 'Can you manage?'

Land nodded forlornly.

'You'll see, it will all work out. You mustn't worry so much.' Bryant rose from the desk corner and indicated that Land should do the same. 'We'll be here to support you, even if everything goes horribly wrong. I'm so glad we could have this little chat.'

Once again, Raymond Land felt defeat slipping over him

like a shroud. As he walked out into the corridor he tried to imagine a future that did not involve humiliation and regret.

Then he realized that Bryant had ushered him out of his own office.

As the unit made plans for its first night shift, Bryant felt his old sense of elation returning. They had been pushed around by Whitehall mandarins and civil servants for too long. The unit had permission to act under its own authority but rarely exercised the right to do so. In an era of counterbalances and accountability they were in danger of becoming cautious. It was time to shake things up a bit. He wandered back to his office, thinking how best to proceed.

'Don't make that face,' said May, passing by with a chair in his arms.

'What face?' Bryant asked, his aqueous blue eyes filled with false innocence.

'The one that warns me you're about to do something illegal or unhygienic.' He stood the chair down. 'We're setting up an information centre in the operations room, all incoming data to be displayed the old way, pinned all around the walls. I just saw Raymond leaving. Has he decided to go home?'

'He's taking Crippen to the vet again. He'll be back. Despite all his moaning he doesn't want to miss anything traumatic in case he has to write a report on it later.'

They headed to the operations room and found the staff milling there with an air of expectation.

'Will we need to keep the window blinds down at night, Mr B?' asked Bimsley, cracking his knuckles.

'No, Colin, it's not the Second World War.'

'If we're all in here how are we going to stop him from doing it again?' asked Meera. 'We need to get out on the streets.'

'You need to figure out which streets first,' May pointed

out, 'and the only way you'll do that is by pooling information here.'

'Takahashi's condition has stabilized,' said Longbright, pinning her report to the wall with the others. 'Her mother is with her. I spoke to the neighbour again. Frost wasn't happy about being interrupted at work. She refuses to accept that she's in any danger and insists the attack has nothing to do with her. She also says she doesn't think you're real detectives.'

'Arthur, you could be wrong about this—' May began.

'I am not wrong,' said Bryant vehemently. 'He's made his first mistake. Whatever he was planning next has to be reconsidered. We need to go back to the beginning and reconstruct events in the light of what we now know. Dhruv Cheema was found inside a willow tree. According to Maggie—'

Everyone groaned. Bryant raised a silencing digit.

'—the willow is traditionally associated with the grief of death because it hangs down lifelessly. It's a funeral tree. "Under the willows we wept and mourned." In Greek mythology the goddess Circe hung dead bodies inside willows. And in *Hamlet* Ophelia's corpse is found beneath a weeping willow. The choice of the tree may not have been an accident. My personal opinion—'

Everybody groaned again.

'—is that it was done to send a signal. That said, the items he left at the base of the tree all have a meaning for him. The dolls, the stones, the candles and the beads were baptized in blood. That's the thing about magic; the individual items don't have to be special. It's the way in which they are gathered together and arranged, their meaning to the owner, the words which are spoken over them, the nature of the ceremony and the exact time: those are the things which are important.'

'Then why didn't he do the same thing the second time?' Meera asked.

'He didn't need to,' Bryant replied. 'He'd already succeeded with the hardest part.'

'You've been reading too many books, mate,' said Renfield. 'It's a gang thing. Cheema was a bit sketchy, pissed someone off and got paid back big time.' He glared at Bryant, who chose this moment to potter out of the operations room with the kettle.

'Jack, you don't understand,' Longbright began. 'If Mr Bryant has any reason to suspect—'

Renfield cut across her. 'You always take his side, have you noticed that? Even when he makes no sense. I try to talk to you and you don't listen. Don't you see how he divides you all, just so he can get his own way? He thrives on chaos. He won't even get rid of the two Daves because he needs to keep everything nicely off balance. And you all fall for it.'

Longbright bristled with anger. 'Mr Bryant is unconventional but his methods work. We're all outsiders here in one way or another but he puts himself on the line for us. I trust him. We all do. If you hate it so much why did you come back?'

At that moment Bryant reappeared with the filled kettle and frowned at Longbright. 'Janice, can you get on with something useful? There's no time for chat. We've a lot of work to get through.'

As Renfield left the room, he smugly glanced back at her.

Bryant walked over to the wall of loose pages that might have blown in through the window and become stuck there for all the sense they made. 'Do any of the victims seem shady to you? They're all ordinary Londoners. I need to understand what connects them.'

'*You* need to?' snapped May. 'We're meant to be a team.'

'I'm not much of a team player,' Bryant replied. 'I'm quite happy working alone.' He pushed away from them and left the operations room.

'Blimey, what's got into him?' asked Bimsley, frowning.

'He's not sleeping,' said May. 'Something's wrong but he won't tell me what it is. If I had to take a guess I'd say that bloody witch-woman has spooked him again.'

Dan Banbury stuck his head around the door. 'John, can I have a word with you?'

'Sure,' said May, 'come in.'

'Not in there.'

Banbury stood with him in the corridor. 'I did a search of Dickinson's flat. Some personal-use recreationals, nothing too dicey, but there were messages to a girl on his laptop. She's near here. She's – well, she's a working girl.'

May frowned. 'So why the secrecy?'

Banbury stuck his hands in his jeans pockets. He looked uncomfortable. 'It could involve people who've worked with the PCU,' he said.

'How closely?' asked May.

Banbury made a helpless face. It was a look that was easily interpreted. *Very closely indeed.*

20

TEXT

Across the city, over the Thames, three people met in the café-bar of a theatre. The industrial steel terrace of Waterloo's Young Vic was built around an old butcher's shop that had miraculously survived a bomb blast during the Blitz. Half saved, half lost, it functioned as a mnemonic for that tumultuous era. On a dim, soaking January lunchtime the building receded into the London landscape. The three of them, Sparrow, Rory and Augusta, selected one of its darkest corners and settled around a coffee table. It seemed like a good place to avoid drawing attention to themselves; at this time of the day the front half of the café was filled with mothers and children.

Once again, Rory was unsettled and already impatient to leave. Augusta was similarly distracted, keen to be anywhere other than here. Yet both had turned up: a measure of the situation's gravity. Sparrow took a notepad and pen from her bag, eager to be of practical use.

'I'm sorry, perhaps if we just run over the salient points? I'm a long way from where I work,' she explained. 'I can only stay for a few minutes.'

'Yeah, I need to be near my office too,' said Rory, tapping at his phone, 'but apparently I was outvoted.'

'Can you put that thing down while we talk?' Augusta knew he would ignore her. Maybe he paid more attention to his girlfriend, although that seemed hard to imagine.

Rory gave an impatient sigh and dropped his phone on to the table. 'If this is about Luke again—'

'Please, listen to Augusta,' Sparrow asked.

'Last night a girl in my building was attacked,' Augusta explained. 'The police interviewed me. They said there's a possibility that someone was trying to get to me and picked the flat next door by mistake. I've started to think maybe it does involve us.'

'Wait, I'm having déjà vu.' Rory raised a hand to his forehead. 'I'm flashing back to when was it? Oh yes, *yesterday*, when I got stuck in the same bloody conversation with this one.' He pointed at Sparrow. 'Did you know the girl?'

'No, we'd never met,' said Augusta.

'What has it got to do with me?'

'It happened at four a.m., just as it did with Luke and that driver.'

'Sounds like you chose a bad neighbourhood.' Rory raised his hands. 'I mean, come on. Loads of people die at four a.m. They must do, right?'

'She lives literally next door to me,' said Augusta. 'What if someone mistook her for me?'

'What did you tell the police?'

'I tried to downplay it. Said I wasn't worried. Which I'm not, obviously, but . . .'

Rory's eyes strayed towards his phone. 'Are you going to do this every time somebody dies in London?'

'Don't you see?' said Augusta. 'We only met once, all of us, and just for a few minutes.'

'So it must be something else. I already discussed this with her.' He pointed dismissively at Sparrow again. 'Nothing happened that night. That's why we never had any reason to mention it to anyone. It's boring; there's nothing to tell. Although I did mention it to Victoria.'

'Why would you do that?' asked Augusta.

'Because I was supposed to stay with her that night and I didn't, did I?'

Sparrow looked from one face to the other. 'Am I missing something?'

'After you were dropped off, Rory came back to my place,' Augusta admitted.

Sparrow's mouth fell open. 'You'd only just met him. And he was *drunk*.'

'It's none of your business,' said Rory. 'Anyway, I wasn't there long. I didn't stay.'

'He got another cab afterwards,' said Augusta. 'Can we just go through it? So, Rory: you and Luke got into the shared taxi with the two of us because Luke ordered the wrong one. Is that right?'

Rory's phone lit up. He absently scrolled through his messages. 'I already told you. We would never have met you otherwise.'

'So we were only together as a group for about – how long, fifteen minutes? Actually less, because Sparrow pushed Luke out of the car, remember?'

'It has to be just a coincidence, it can't be anything else,' said Sparrow. 'Why should we be targeted? We haven't done anything wrong.'

'Rory,' Augusta begged, 'put that down for a second.'

He looked up from his phone. 'I just had a text that may be relevant.'

Augusta held out her hand. 'Show me.'

He raised the phone and turned it to them. The message said simply: 'HELL IS EMPTY, AND ALL THE DEVILS ARE HERE.'

'Who's it from?' asked Sparrow.

'I don't know. It sounds like a threat.'

They looked at each other as another phone registered an incoming message. 'I've got the same,' said Augusta. She raised her phone to show the others.

'I didn't get one.' Sparrow stared at her darkened phone screen, puzzled.

'Call it back.'

'No, *you* call it back,' said Rory.

'Fine.' Augusta put the phone to her ear and listened. 'One ring. It's blocked.'

'He knows who we are,' said Sparrow forlornly.

'He knows who *we* are. You didn't get one,' Rory snapped. 'Anyway, who's he? There is no *he*. It's probably a hack and everyone is getting some kind of automated spam.'

'What kind of spam mentions hell?'

Rory shrugged. 'I don't know, Jesus spam, like those mad churches that run out of old cinemas. Maybe Augusta and I got it because we're executives.'

'And I just work in a bookshop, you mean?' said Sparrow. 'Is it the sort of stuff your agency produces?'

'We handle a lot of direct social media. It's not surprising we've all got the same message. You get a higher conversion rate with an 8/10 relevance score, so the four of us would be in the same target demographic.'

'Thanks, Rory, I needed a lesson in marketing,' said Augusta. 'So we ignore it. Somebody out there knows who we are and hates us, and we're not going to do anything about it.'

'What can we do?' Sparrow asked. 'Should we go to the police?'

Augusta dropped her phone into her bag. 'And say what?

We don't know anything. We'll only make things worse for ourselves. We shouldn't even be calling each other.'

'This is absolutely bloody ridiculous.' Rory got to his feet, ready to leave.

'What if he does something?' Augusta asked, but the others were already rising. 'If anything happens to me, you'll know you're next.'

'Go back to work, both of you,' said Rory with a sigh. 'Augusta, you need to take a Valium or something. I don't think we should meet again.'

They left the café heading in different directions.

As Sparrow turned off the Cut, heading towards Waterloo Station, Hugo Blake stepped out in front of her.

'Hey, I didn't mean to make you jump.' He kept his distance until he could judge her mood.

'Have you been following me?' She looked him over with a mixture of alarm and concern. He was wearing the same clothes she'd seen him in last time, and appeared not to have slept.

What was there in his eyes that gave her permission to trust him? To seize upon any half-hearted explanation and accept it as the truth? His arrival took away her anxiety, to the extent that even if she proved to be wrong about him things would somehow turn out well enough. She knew he could not really hurt her, in the way that animals know an owner's intentions are not harmful. So she listened and found herself nodding.

'Things are difficult for me right now. I wanted to see you so I went to the bookshop. Don't go mad. The girl there told me you were meeting friends here, and I just wanted to see you. I'm sorry, it's going to creep you out now.'

'No, it's just – I've never had a stalker. You're too late. I have to get back to the shop.' She gave him another once-over.

'Oh, for God's sake. Do you want to walk to the station with me?'

They cut through the hidden hipster enclave in the narrow, shadowed streets behind Waterloo. As they walked, he unthinkingly took her arm. 'I'm not good at explaining myself, Sparrow. I thought about how we met. Remember the conversation we had about *The Tempest*?' His voice was as soft as rain now. 'You said Prospero wants to control everything, but he can't because people are too messy. He creates order from chaos. He builds his own world.'

'But for all of Prospero's great magical strength and knowledge, the only thing he's learned is how to control others. He's obsessed with revenge.' She pressed her arm more deeply against him, feeling his warmth. 'It was always my favourite play. What would have happened if Prospero hadn't learned to forgive? If he'd not broken his staff, and had chosen to see his revenge through to the end? What would he have been left with? Nothing.'

Blake nodded faintly. 'The island would have destroyed him. He would have been left with blood on his hands and power over no one. He chose forgiveness over retribution. He deserved to have justice.'

She wondered, were they still talking about Prospero? 'Should I be afraid of you?' she asked, stopping to look him in the eye.

'No,' he replied. 'No; others should be, but you shouldn't.'

For a moment Sparrow thought she had misheard. Time seemed to slow down, but she let the comment pass. 'I have to catch my train,' she said.

'Another day, then.' He stood at the side entrance to the station and watched her go. When she looked back, he was still there.

Augusta watched the other two leave, and tried to tamp down the anger rising in her chest. Someone had managed to get into her building and smash through her neighbour's front door, and all the police could do was send over a couple of old men to poke about in her stuff. Rory treated the whole thing as if it was a joke. As for Sparrow, she was either a simpleton or hiding something. Why didn't she get the text message they had both received?

On the way back to her office Augusta called a security company she had used before and arranged for someone to come around after work. The others were burying their heads in the sand. Luke was dead and her neighbour was in hospital. It was time to strike first.

She reached the ArcAngel building at 7.15 p.m., and the locksmith buzzed her intercom soon after. He had been on his way home when he'd received the call, and said if he picked up some more kit he could maybe do something for her.

'Know the easiest way to get into someone's flat?' he asked her after examining the door. 'All you need is a screwdriver. You put the sharp end over the keyhole, like so. Then give the handle a good whack with your fist. It often punches the lock right through.' The violence of his mimed action caught her by surprise. 'You could have a French bolt, extends twice the length into the mortise.'

She knew when she was being upsold. 'I think I'd just like the regular lock replaced for now.'

'Suit yourself, but a child could open one of those.'

'Then give me one a child can't open,' she said with more sharpness than she'd intended.

He replaced the lock, fixed a chain to the front door and checked that all the window locks were in good working order. Although she took out a credit card, she suggested cutting a deal by paying him cash in hand, and he accepted the reduced payment.

While he was working on the door he made a phone call to his son, then explained that he would have to leave in a few minutes to pick him up. If she had any problems, he could come back.

Reassured, she opened a bottle of Albariño, ran herself a bath and checked her emails.

When she went into the living room an hour later, the locksmith had gone, the carpet had been swept and the flat was fully secure. It was important to be self-sufficient; if you started whining to the police nothing would ever be achieved.

We were just five strangers, she told herself. *Nothing happened that night, and there's nothing to connect us.*

21

NIGHT

Approaching midnight, the black and grey striped concourse of King's Cross Station remained almost as busy as it had been during the day. Some Italian students appeared to be having a picnic under the station canopy. A homeless girl sat with her arms on her knees next to a lengthy cardboard message explaining her circumstances. A Jamaican family dressed in home-made ecclesiastical vestments were warning everyone that hell awaited sinners. A phalanx of bachelorettes in tiny silver dresses, strappy shoes and bunny ears marched past, heading to their next destination like soldiers on a final tour of duty. Inside the station, tourists were still lurking around the Harry Potter trolley that had originally been set there as a joke by the station guards, then monetized when queues appeared. As flinty-eyed and mean as it had ever been, London was good at making everyone pay.

The bars on the Caledonian Road were now shutting but there were still plenty of people on the street, drinking and laughing as if they were in Nice or Seville, not standing on a litter-strewn Victorian pavement in fine soaking rain.

Up in the offices of the Peculiar Crimes Unit the mood was sombre and enervated. Raymond Land stood watching raindrops coursing down the second-floor window and dug a sodden tissue from his sleeve. He blew wetly into it.

Longbright patted him lightly on the back. 'Crippen has had a good life,' she said. 'It'll be better if she doesn't suffer.'

'She's a member of the unit. Two days ago she was happily rubbing herself against my legs and coughing up hairballs in the kitchen. You forget how quickly things can change.' Land sniffled through a fresh nasal blockade of Kleenex.

'Really, do we have to have this ghastly sentimentality?' On the far side of the office Bryant sat hacking at his pipe with a lethal-looking letter opener. 'We're English. Not caring is in our blood. Cats have short lives. It's how they punish you for getting attached to them. She couldn't last for ever.'

'You've managed.' Land blew again.

'If she doesn't pull through we'll get you another one,' said Bryant. He waved the knife in Land's direction. 'It's impossible to use up cats, they just keep reappearing. Didn't she have lots of kittens?'

'At your insistence they were all found new homes,' said Land accusingly. 'I'll miss her. She kept me company at night.'

'So did your wife and she left you as well.' Bryant dug deep into the pipe. A hardened lump of tobacco pinged from his blade and struck the clock.

The operations room was as cluttered as a charity shop. The entire rear wall was covered in paperwork, photographs, printouts, statistics, witness statements and scrawled questions from Bryant written with a fat red felt tip, some of them incomprehensible. Banbury and Renfield had agreed to handle the morning shifts. As the remaining six worked on,

Colin passed around a plastic tray of sausage rolls. 'They may be past their peak,' he warned. 'I found them.'

Raymond Land raised his glasses and cast a suspicious eye over the tray. 'What's in them?'

'Meat. Do you want one or not?'

'I'm a vegetarian.'

'Since when?'

'Since now.'

The night shift was having an unexpected effect on Land. With each passing minute he became more miserable. Rocked back in his chair and gradually withdrawing into his jumper, he looked like a time-lapse film of a dying houseplant. 'When Leanne left me I thought things would get better,' he told anyone who might be listening. 'Now I'm living in a basement flat that looks like a gas chamber with a sofa. Yesterday I found a dead mouse in my toaster. There's mildew everywhere. When was the last time you saw mildew? My bed looks as if it came from a care home. The woman next door is learning the accordion and the landlord's dog has dysentery. I ask myself what was it all for. Don't you sometimes ask yourselves that? No, of course not.'

'Raymond, you're tired,' said May, looking up. 'Why don't you go home and get some rest?'

'I'd rather stay. It's cleaner here.'

'We get it,' snapped Bryant impatiently. 'You're unhappy. We're all unhappy. What do you expect? We're citizens of a nation that thinks *Abigail's Party* is a comedy. Go home.'

The unit chief looked as if he might put up a fight for a moment, then caved in. 'Well, if you think I won't be needed.'

'Of course you won't.' Bryant was instantly more cheerful. 'Meera, what's happening with the intel on Jagan Cheema?'

Mangeshkar looked back from the wall of head shots. Her glossy black hair had been tied back to reveal a small symbol tattooed at the nape of her neck. 'We're meeting up with a contact later,' she explained.

Land looked at his watch. 'How much later? It's the middle of the night.'

'He's working as a barman,' said Meera. 'His shift doesn't finish until two thirty.'

'That's late. I hope it's a good job.'

'He's on a minimum-wage, zero-hours contract. So no, it's not actually a good job.'

'Everyone's so touchy.' Land turfed another handful of used tissues out of his coat pocket. He had his arm half into the sleeve when he saw the bags. 'What's all that in the corridor?'

'It's my stuff,' said Longbright, who had changed into a yellow jogging suit. 'A yoga mat, my make-up box and some clothes.'

'You're not moving in.'

'We all need to stretch.'

'Are you going to be holding a yoga class in here after I've gone? Why stop there? Get out your massage board and essential oils. Can somebody grab that phone?'

'It's my mother,' said Meera, putting her hand over the receiver. 'She wants to know where I'm staying.'

'Tell her here,' said Colin.

'I don't want to start lying to her. I'll forget where I'm up to. She's not someone you mess with.'

'So you're not staying here?' asked Longbright, cocking an eyebrow at Bimsley.

'Wait,' said Bryant, listening in. 'Ask her if she knows anyone who practises Tantra, would you?'

'What's that?' Meera asked.

'It's a Hindu science that offers ways of expanding and liberating the soul. It was always likened to black magic. It crossed my mind that Dhruv Cheema's killer might have staged the ritual for his victim.'

'You are not drafting my mother into this,' Meera warned. 'Do I have to ask her?'

'Go on.'

'Arthur, I can't read what you've put here.' May tapped at the pages.

'It says "Who is Cristina Prifti?"' said Bryant. 'Her name crops up in Luke Dickinson's accounts.' He followed a felt-tip trail across the tacked-up pages. 'Four times a hundred and fifty pounds, every three weeks. Personal payments, so not dental work. What do you think, some kind of service?'

'Sex worker,' said Longbright, turning her laptop screen towards him. 'Quite pretty. Based very near here. John, don't you know the community support officer up at Market Road?'

'I can call her,' May replied.

'No,' said Meera loudly, pocketing her phone.

'I'm sorry?' Bryant had tuned out for a moment and was now lost.

'My mother. She doesn't know anything about the occult. Now she's going to spend her evening googling "Tantra" and deciding I've become a Satanist, and she still wants to know where I'm staying.'

May wasn't listening. 'The neighbour, Augusta Frost. What are we doing about that situation?'

Longbright pinched another sausage roll. 'She doesn't want us to put a PC in the corridor, so I called Islington to make sure there would be someone outside the main door of the building all night. I'll liaise with the constable.'

Bryant held up the matching pens. 'Did you get anywhere on these?'

'Still working on that,' said Colin. 'There are thousands of similar designs in circulation.'

Bryant pinned up a sketch he had made of the symbol. 'I'm sure I've seen this blasted thing before.' He tapped the prow of the ship with his pipe stem. 'I need a book.'

'Arthur, don't just vanish into your library,' said May, but it was too late; the unit's most senior detective was already heading for his room to find a match and settle in his armchair with a few abstruse volumes.

Meera took Colin with her as a back-up. The Carmen Bar was tucked inside a maze of freshly cobbled alleys behind the main road to King's Cross Station. It was still crowded with customers, most of whom were huddled beneath square canvas umbrellas like sheltering ducks.

Jay Savage had the narrow-eyed side glance of an East End wide boy, and looked out of place in a bar mainly used by students and office workers. Dressed in too much of everything, from Burberry to North Face, he curved the peak of his Superdry baseball cap by storing it in a coffee mug overnight and smoked with his cigarette cupped inside his hand. He kept watch over the customers, assessing threats and opportunities, looking so much the part that no one ever imagined him to be an undercover officer.

'How's the cocktail business, Jay?' asked Meera.

Savage bumped her fist in a complex gesture of recognition and laughed. 'Drop me out, I'm rubbish at mixology. They make me use a blowlamp to roast the gin garnishes. Last night I set fire to the curtains.'

'Did you get us any background on Dhruv Cheema?'

'The family's clean but the older brother's got some pretty sketchy interests.'

'What kind of interests?'

Jay glowered out from beneath his cap. 'Moving stuff about. I don't know how deep he's in, but his fam's involved and there's money changing hands. The lads are buying themselves a lot of bling.'

'Are we talking about moving drugs, money, people, what?' asked Colin.

'Stick this on.' He leaned closer. 'Artefacts.'

'What kind of artefacts?'

'They come from private storage facilities and freeports in places like Kazakhstan, then make their way to private collectors around the world. Some of them pass through the UK to collect forged paperwork. Jagan Cheema's mates have a company that looks like it might be involved. The word is they just fell out with each other. Jagan's in there somehow, on a minor level.'

'Have you picked up any rumours about last Saturday night?' asked Colin. 'Anything on the little brother?'

Savage dropped his cigarette butt and stood on it. 'Just random static. You know he was driving Jagan's taxi.'

'We've got that.'

'People are saying that little Dhruv took the hit for dodgy Jagan. Mistaken identity.'

'So you think Jagan knows more than he's telling us?' asked Meera.

'He knows how to keep his mouth shut.'

'What do *you* think happened?'

Savage pulled his cap lower as a woman he recognized from the bar walked past. 'I think someone was hired to send Jagan's mates a serious message and got their wires crossed, whacked the brother by mistake.'

'Is there anyone else we should be talking to?' Colin asked.

'Dhruv Cheema kept pretty much to himself. He was the family favourite, the youngest son, working long hours in the store, keeping himself clean.'

'What about Luke Dickinson?'

'Not my territory, bruv. The Met has a couple of people in the Square Mile for that sort of thing.'

They moved as the bar staff came out and began stacking chairs. 'Fair enough,' said Colin. 'Can you stay on this for a few days?'

'If your boss has a word with my boss, yeah.'

'You still working for Darren Link?'

'Technically I'm part of his unit. He thinks the bar's running an illegal immigration service, and it would suit us to take them down for another case we're building, so I'll be here for a while.'

Colin and Meera made to go, but Savage called them back. 'There's one other thing. Jagan's mates. One of them has been mouthing off about a shipment that was supposed to go through the laundry last month. A piece of it went missing. Maybe that was enough to get his brother killed.'

'Thanks,' said Colin. 'Good accent, by the way. I'd have taken you for a Dagenham lad.'

'I've always been a bit of a mimic,' said Savage. 'I can give it ESL, LME or RP.' When Meera looked puzzled he explained. 'English as a Second Language, London Multicultural English or Received Pronunciation.'

'I'd never have known you were from Budapest. Very cool. Is there anything you need?'

'*Szilvás gombóc*,' said Savage. 'Plum dumplings. At home we fry them in sweet breadcrumbs. I can't get them here anywhere.'

'Not sure we can do much about that but I'll ask around,' said Colin. 'Stay in touch.' The pair headed off into the rain-misted alley.

22

PUNTER

Arthur Bryant closed the blue leather-bound book and replaced it on the shelf behind his chair. *Type Foundries of the Netherlands* was never going to be much help to him. He examined the spines of the others in his stack. *A Popular History of Greek Seaweeds*, *The Illustrated Catalogue of Antique Barbed Wire*, *Victorian Spoon Boxes Volume III* and a biography of Nell Gwynne entitled *Oranges Are the Only Fruit*, none of which were terribly useful right now. He was sure he had seen the symbol in one of these volumes.

He drew a further stack towards him and lifted off the top book, *Fleek's British Naval Commanders of the Seventeenth Century*. On page 127 he found an engraving of four ships: the *Association*, the *Eagle*, the *Romney* and HMS *Firebrand*.

Bryant took out one of the pens and held the design against the drawing of the ships. It was identical to the *Romney*. On the following page was a portrait of an admiral, periwigged and Neroesque. The text read: 'Sir Cloudesley Shovell rose in the ranks of the Royal Navy from cabin boy to Commander-in-Chief and Admiral of the Fleet, battling pirates and enemies of King Charles II until his ill-fated ships were smashed on the rocks of the Scilly Isles.'

He read on. Having lost his life and all his ships in one of the greatest marine disasters in British history, Sir Cloudesley Shovell had been commemorated in a public house. Overleaf was a monochrome photograph taken at night. The admiral was hanging on a pub sign. The Ship & Shovell, WC2, London's only pub split into two halves.

Bryant's nicotine-stained forefinger sped beneath the sentences. The disaster had spawned its own mythology. One tale concerned a sailor on the flagship who had tried to warn the admiral that his fleet was off course, but had been hanged from the yardarm for inciting mutiny. As a result it was said that no grass could ever grow on Shovell's grave.

There were other bizarre tales: that Shovell was still alive when he reached the shore of Scilly at Porthellick Cove, but was murdered by a woman for the sake of his priceless emerald ring, and that the woman who stole it confessed on her deathbed thirty years later. After two and a half centuries the treasures of the lost fleet were rescued and sold at Sotheby's. Now only the pub lived on, together with its logo of the admiral's flagship and the inscription of its year of demise, 1707.

Bryant turned to a more jocular book, *Mine's a Large One: The Connoisseur's Guide to London Boozers.*

On the upper floor of the pub's greater half was a private club for those associated with the disaster, later reserved for exclusive use by naval officers, which finally became a cocktail bar with a four a.m. licence. The names of the last two of the four ships that sank under Shovell's command had been emblazoned on the bar's advertising material, along with the pens that had been found on Dickinson and Frost.

Now we're getting somewhere, thought Bryant. *I can be there and back in an hour.*

*

The idea that there were still prostitutes on the streets of London seemed anachronistic in the age of online liaisons, but there were pockets of nocturnal activity in the underlit backstreets. Family men were wary of leaving electronic trails.

In Dalston, Barking, Dagenham, Finsbury Park, Edgware Road and Paddington the working girls hid in plain sight after dark. Bayswater had so many that the Chinese who controlled London's crystal-meth trade had come up with a nickname for the lower quality drug they imported into the UK: 'Bayswater Basic'. Drugs drove the street market. Most of the girls worked for gangmasters, but those who were free to choose the life set up online identities. The ones outside were only there because they needed urgent cash; why else would anyone stand all night in winter drizzle at the dead edges of a public housing estate?

John May had a list of London streets he hated, and Market Street was near the top. Neither as contemptuously ugly as Old Street Roundabout nor as blandly boring as Kensington High Street, it existed in a liminal landscape that had long ago replaced its cattle trade with baser appetites; the drug-dealers had finally been moved from pavement corners but the prostitutes survived thanks to Norah Haron. She fought for them, which was a good thing, but May sometimes wondered how far she would go to protect them.

There was a time when the girls of Market Street were as tough as crocodiles, but they weren't so young any more. At one end of the street a couple of them nodded off on kitchen chairs. That's why they tried to conduct their business in parked cars; they looked forward to a warm-up and a sit-down. Some still remembered the PCU detectives from the old days at Mornington Crescent, back when vice control fell under the PCU's local remit.

Norah Haron had been the building manager of a Soho brothel when she was twenty-six. Now she ran an online cosplay costumiers and worked thirty hours a week as a community support officer, liaising with the English Collective of Prostitutes to ensure the rights of sex workers. John May had become friendly with her because the girls were in her ward, and he had occasionally been able to help her protect them from harassment. How their friendship had passed into something more mystified him. He knew that he should not have allowed it to happen, but it had. They had spent several nights together, but their relationship was now passing into unknown territory.

As Norah walked towards him she raised a hand in greeting. She looked like a business executive returning from a night out, sleek black hair tied in a chignon over the turned-up collar of an elegant green woollen coat. She was too smartly dressed for the neighbourhood. The street light above her threw a fierce whiteness over bare grass and a brick wall. They might have been meeting on a stage set.

'I wasn't expecting your call.' Her voice always came as a surprise to May. She sounded wrong, too refined.

He kissed her cheek. 'For someone with two jobs you always manage to look so . . .' He gestured at her, unable to come up with anything appropriate.

'Everything's always been in pairs with me, John. I'm a Gemini, I had two husbands, two kids, two jobs. How's Janice?'

'She's well.'

'You never told me she used to be a nightclub hostess. One of the girls mentioned it.'

'Yes, in Soho. She loved the work but the clientele tended to follow her home. She still keeps a house brick in her handbag as a memory of those days.'

'How did she end up in the police?' Norah's steady breath condensed and vanished. She was always cool and calm.

'I suppose it was inevitable,' May replied. 'Arthur and I

worked with her mother. When Janice left the club trade she joined Vice.'

Norah led the way across a corner of cropped grass, so glossily green that it might have been Astroturf. 'Has that partner of yours managed to upset anyone today?'

'Not to my knowledge.'

'Did I tell you? The last time I bumped into him he was carrying a three-foot-long pike.'

'A spear?'

'No, a fish. Stuffed, I presume. He was trying to find a taxi outside the swimming baths. He doesn't like me, you know.'

'Why do you say that?'

'When a man like Mr Bryant doesn't like someone, you'd have to be blind not to notice. It's your lucky night. Cristina turned up just after you called. You didn't explain what she's supposed to have done.'

'Nothing bad, I hope. One of her punters is dead.'

'She's a good girl, keeps herself straight, only works when she's short at the end of the month. You know I have to detail everything that happens up here, so I'd appreciate you keeping my name out of any report you make on her.'

Three girls were waiting on the pavement at the rear of a sports centre, where the public grounds ended and private gardens began. Cristina Prifti was slender, boyish, smoky-eyed, with a white-blonde pixie cut and very crimson lips. She sat on a garden wall in red tights and a fuzzy pink Top Shop cardigan which she had redesigned by removing half the buttons. She was massaging the toes of her right foot. A dog barked somewhere, an unanswered call that quickly fell silent.

She looked up at them. 'I would rather be in trainers but I get more work in heels.' She had the clipped speech of someone who had learned English in Central Europe.

'Have you run out of cash?' Norah asked, studying the girl.

Beneath the make-up Cristina was pale and tired. It was a look she had seen all too often. Some girls wore away, fading a little more each time she saw them until the light disappeared from their eyes.

'It's me who has run out of places to hide it.' She wriggled her foot back into her shoe and rummaged in her bag for a cigarette. 'He takes everything from me.'

May and Haron sat on the wall beside the girl. Cristina studied May apprehensively. 'I'm surprised to find you out again tonight,' Norah said. 'I thought you were cutting down your hours.'

Cristina shot her a bitter look. 'I can't move online without a hotel deal, you know that, and I haven't got enough to cover the up-front money.' Most of the hotels that rented out rooms to the girls would only do so if they paid extortionate deposits. 'But business is bad, I think. Nobody has any money after Christmas. Everyone wants to cut a deal.' She found her cigarettes and offered them around. May shook his head. 'No vices? Good for you.' She lit her own and exhaled into the night air. 'I'm still trying for a baby and the NHS can't help. I need five thousand for the treatment so I'll carry on until then.'

'You could send your boyfriend out to work,' said Norah.

'You try telling him that.' She turned to May. 'I don't want to be in this place. We only get the ones who won't go online in case their wives find out.'

'You've been seeing a fellow called Luke Dickinson, is that right?'

'You want me to talk about him?'

'It would help.'

'Is it worth anything?'

'You mean money? No.'

She shrugged. It was worth a try. 'Luke is a good person, I think. Underneath it all.'

'How many times have you seen him?'

'Six or seven, I don't know.' She waved smoke from her face. As it dissipated he briefly saw her as a younger woman, before all this had started. It softened his heart.

'Was it purely business?'

'Of course, just business. I keep a distance from *them*.' She nodded towards an overweight man in tracksuit bottoms and a hooded jacket, trying to strike a deal with a desperate-looking girl sitting on the back of a bench.

'Did he ever talk about himself?'

'All the time, mostly bullshit. Talk, talk, grinding his teeth, you know? Too much of this.' She tapped the side of her nose. 'Every time he calls me, I go over there.'

'To his flat?'

'Yes, to his flat. You think I only work here? This is low-life. I only do this when I have to.' Cristina jetted more smoke into the night air. 'He talks about his work, his friends, trying to impress me. I say then why do you go with a girl you must pay for? You know what he says? "It's easier this way, so I don't have to think about women." For him I have to look expensive. I have a blue and gold Chanel dress, very beautiful. Not an original but a good copy. Chinese.' She dragged at her cigarette as if it was the last one she would ever see.

'Cristina, I'm afraid Luke Dickinson is dead.'

A beat and a blink. Then she regained her composure. 'This is perhaps not such a surprise.'

'Why not?'

'Oh.' She shook her head. 'You see these boys working so hard, living so fast – they use everything up. They are not happy. He tells me he cannot sleep because of bad things that happened in his life.'

'What kind of bad things?'

'I don't know. Something a long time ago.' She flicked

away the cigarette. 'I think he gets into trouble. He went out with some friends and something bad happened.'

'Did he tell you the names of these friends?'

She corrected herself. 'Not friends, people, he says people he has never even met before. That's all he tells me. I am sorry for him. And sorry for me too. A good job gone.'

'He didn't confide in you about anything else?'

Cristina studied him from kohl-dark eyes. 'Men don't want to *confide*. We are not their mothers.'

'He didn't mention his job, his colleagues?'

'No, no. We talked only about clubs, where he goes for fun, and the pubs he likes in the West End, because he was going there one night after seeing me and he likes getting drunk. He tells me this. Wait.' She held up a black-varnished nail. 'Wait, wait. Oh my God. I remember something very bad. He told me one thing. He saw his father die. When he was little boy.'

'What happened?'

Cristina pulled a face. 'How should I know?'

'Why would he tell you that?'

'He was very – what you say – "melted". Is that a word? He said to me, "Cristina I am broken," and I said how, and he said, "I saw my father die." So there it is. People are private. They have sex with you but they stay private. You are policeman, you must work it out. I have to work.'

May thanked her and left with Norah, heading up to the main road. He glanced back at Cristina silhouetted before the street light, as posed as any catwalk model.

'Can you do me a favour?' he asked. 'Keep close to that girl and see if you can get anything more out of her. She might say something to you that she wouldn't tell me.'

As they walked, Norah linked her arm in his. 'John, you know how much I owe you. I'll talk to her.' She checked her phone. 'Do you have time to grab a coffee?'

He took her hand and kissed it. 'I have to get back.'

'Saturday, then. Some dinner.'

'I'll try, Norah. The case comes first.'

As he left, May dropped the arrangement into his electronic diary without thinking. It was the same night he had agreed to see Blaize Carter, the firefighter he occasionally dated when their shifts matched. As he walked back to the unit, he went through every step of the investigation and tried to imagine ways of breaking beyond the dead ends, but nothing came to mind.

Talk to your partner, he told himself as he reached King's Cross. *You're a team. He's infuriating, but you work better together.* But even as he had the thought, he knew it would not be possible to explain about Norah.

There were some things he could not tell anyone.

23

SECRET

It was past midnight when Arthur Bryant reached the Strand and walked through the broad, low brick tunnel that led to the Ship & Shovell.

The pub's crimson mirror-images faced each other on the slope of Craven Passage, beyond flights of narrow steps leading down from the Strand. One pub, divided into two halves. He had been there a few times before; the Phobia Club had held their monthly therapy sessions upstairs until somebody lost a tarantula.

Only the left side of the pub was open at this late hour. The ground floor was devoid of drinkers but raucous laughter came from upstairs. The only door was shut, so he rang the bell and heard the click of a lock released. Stepping inside through a fold of red velvet curtains, he crossed the empty bar.

'I'd like to see whoever's running the club,' he told the barman, laying his polished acacia walking stick on the copper-topped counter.

'Not going to happen, mate,' said the boy without looking up from his phone.

'It'll happen if you don't want to be closed down.'

He looked up now, and clearly did not like what he saw. 'We haven't done nothing.'

'That's a double negative and I don't need you not to have done nothing to find something.' He flicked his ID on to the counter. 'Where is he?'

The lad pointed upstairs.

'Thanks. You should use Clearasil on that rash.' Bryant ascended a narrow ship's staircase towards the sound of merriment and walked down the dimly lit hall to a doorway.

In the crack of the door appeared a face. It would have been hard to imagine anyone looking more dissolute and unhealthy than the sweating gentleman in the black silk waistcoat who slowly appeared before him. He had the discolouration of an elderly halibut and was clearly three drinks from a heart attack.

'I'm afraid this is a private members' club,' he explained, failing to shut the door against Bryant's stick.

'Then you'd better work out the fastest way to sign me in while I check your late licence.' Bryant held up his battered PCU identity card. 'This has the magical power to turn off your lights, your pumps and your revenue stream.'

'Police, eh? We don't want any trouble. You'd better come in.' He released the door.

Bryant took in the surroundings. The long room was tricked out with the usual trappings of a Victorian pub, including red velvet sofas and gold chandeliers, but at the far end was a small curtained stage complete with footlights. In the middle of it stood an open coffin on a pair of wooden trestles. Presumably there was a corpse inside because Bryant could see it was wearing black boots. This detail was hard to miss as the boots were two and a half feet long, and pointed upright.

'Are you the landlord?' Bryant asked.

'I'm Clemence Gilpin, the president. What can I do for you?'

Bryant scrunched up one eye. 'What are you running up here?'

'This is the Tivoli Variety Society,' said Gilpin. He gestured to the ladies and gentlemen in the room, most of whom were dressed in late-Victorian evening wear and were half-cut. 'We're dedicated to the art of popular music hall perform-ance. Do you want to become a member? It's only five pounds.'

'No thank you. My old man's drunken rendition of "Don't Buy any Seafood, Mother, Dad's Coming Home with Crabs" left a permanent scar on me. Why is there a coffin on your stage?'

'One of our oldest members, Mr Peacroft, died this morn-ing. This is his wake.'

'Is that legal?'

'Sir, it was once entirely commonplace.'

Bryant donned his spectacles and had a good look. 'So was putting felons in pillories and pelting them with dead cats. What's wrong with his feet?'

'Mr Peacroft was a gentleman of, ah, restricted height.'

'You've got a dead dwarf in here? Wait a minute.' A smile crept across Bryant's face. 'Was he a polydactyl?'

Gilpin beamed with delight. 'You exceed expectations, sir! He was not, but his hero was. Technically, Little Tich was not a dwarf but a midget. He became the toast of Europe.'

'And he was born with six fingers on each hand and six toes on each foot. May I see?'

'Certainly.' Gilpin led the way to the stage. 'Our monthly meetings normally feature a stage performance, but we decided to forgo tonight's out of respect for Mr Peacroft. You can understand my reluctance to admit you.'

Bryant recalled having seen footage of Little Tich's acro-batic music hall act, which involved him balancing upon a pair of greatly extended boots. The corpse in the coffin was wearing a white silk top hat and matching tuxedo, a red bow tie and a feather boa. The other members crept forward, pleased to see that the policeman in their midst was an aficionado.

'Did those boots belong to Little Tich himself?' asked Bryant, admiring them.

'Sadly the originals are in the Victoria and Albert Museum, but Mr Peacroft had his own identical pair made, and wished to be interred with them. I personally dressed him.' Gilpin cast his head to one side, admiring his handiwork. 'I think he'd be pleased that he's finally made it to the stage.'

Bryant picked up a plastic ballpoint from the counter and toyed with it. 'I need your help. Do these belong to you?'

'They're from the events company that connects promoters to venues like this,' Clemence Gilpin explained. 'They put their logo on flyers and badges. I believe they're called Sink & Swim? Something like that.'

'So they have nothing to do with Admiral Shovell?' He pointed out of the window to the hanging sign painted with Sir Cloudesley's portrait.

'I think they started out here. The pub used to be called the Ship & Shovel with one "L", but there were too many of them about. It was a common name for any public house near the river. I heard the brewery wanted to create a more interesting backstory. That's how myths get started, isn't it?'

'I suppose a seafaring nation deserves to celebrate its admirals, even if they sank their fleets,' Bryant said with a shrug. 'I need to contact the people who distribute these things.'

'That's easily done,' said Mr Gilpin. 'There's a chap we deal with. I can send his details to your phone.'

'Write it down. You've enough pens.'

On his way out of the pub, Bryant tried the number and got a recorded message. The offices of Sink & Swim opened at 9.00 a.m. As he climbed back up the staircase leading to the Strand, he found himself wondering what other peculiar events were unfolding across the city under cover of darkness.

Cristina went looking for Norah Haron. She found the community support officer sitting in a silver Audi parked outside a steel-sided warehouse at the end of Market Street. Haron unlocked the door when she saw Cristina approach.

'Listen, that officer—'

'John May? He's a decent man. Anything you tell him—'

'I did not tell him everything.'

'What did you leave out?'

'He asked about Luke Dickinson. I tell him Luke has done something bad. This is what he tells me, yes? But I think about this and I remember what he says. Because you know it is hard to listen to a man, you just have to look like you listen. And what he says to me was this: somebody did a bad thing here.'

'Here? Whereabouts?'

'The club.'

'Who was it?'

'A driver.'

'What do you mean, he did a bad thing? What driver?'

'This I don't know. He says he sees a taxi driver do a bad thing, hurt someone very badly, and now I remember because of the Keys.'

Haron glanced out of the window. The warehouse stood alone on the former landfill site that had been created by the demolition of the area's slum terraces. By day the ground floor sold wholesale bathroom fixtures. By night the rear half, an old ballroom dating back almost a century, opened its doors as a nightclub. Over the years the Keys had been forced to move from one derelict warehouse to another as each property was bought up. The club flew beneath the radar of fashionability and was therefore never very busy, so the authorities tended to ignore its negligent door policies.

'Yes, the Keys club,' Cristina confirmed. 'This is where he was, and where he saw the bad thing.'

'How long ago was this?'

'Some time before Christmas. Maybe late October, early November.'

'Did Dickinson see someone hurt one of the girls?'

'Maybe. I don't know. But it was right over there, outside the club.' The girls had been known to take customers behind the warehouse, but it was risky because there were sensor lights.

'We can't tell anyone about this,' said Haron. 'If they think something happened here they'll clear you all off Market Street.'

'Why?' asked Cristina.

'Because if a murder victim witnessed a crime on this spot just before he died his story won't only bring the police, it'll bring the press. You can't go anywhere else, Cristina, you know that. The council has placed all the other streets off limits. The factories have gone, it's all residential now and they don't want you on their doorsteps. You're only allowed to stay if you keep within your territory and I keep delivering my weekly reports.'

'Then what can we do?' asked Cristina.

'Don't make matters worse,' Haron replied. 'What a punter tells you is confidential information. We have to make sure it stays that way.'

She looked back at the Keys club. Even when it was open it looked closed, as if it always had something to hide. She had never been inside, and never intended to. Whatever had happened there was no business of hers. The last thing she needed right now was more trouble.

24

REMEMBERING

The old parquet-floored ballroom formed an immense oval. Winding baroque staircases led to a balcony of flaking gilt. The walls had been sloppily painted in purples and crimsons, the colours of diseased hothouse plants and old medical plates. The bar counter had an immense mirror, leprous and damp-spotted, angled behind it. A pair of dusty mirror balls hung overhead. Against the walls stood salvaged crucifixes of stone and wood, tin crosses filled with coloured light bulbs, old mission signs and church boards. The intended effect was not of piety but excess, even though the two states overlapped.

Rory Caine had not intended to come back to the Keys club, but had been drawn by the memory of that night.

When the barman caught his eye, he jabbed a finger at his empty glass. He had drained four Estrella bottles in quick succession, matching them with four rum chasers. He didn't know why he came here; he hated the place. A half-derelict building lost among the cavernous storage facilities behind Tufnell Park.

He needed to think. If Sparrow was right and they were all being targeted perhaps the police did need to be informed, not about everything but at least about that night. He knew enough now to fill in most of the blanks.

Back on the fourth Saturday in October, the Keys had been much fuller than it was now, and Caine and his drinking buddies had been out on a binger. Luke Dickinson had hovered at the edge of their group, hanging on every word, an anxious courtier seeking to curry favour.

Caine knew at once that a girl was standing close behind him. He could sense her just beyond his vision, watching and listening, getting ready to speak. Glancing up at the great tilted mirror, he saw her more clearly. He liked to make entrances into the lives of others, so he slowly turned around.

She said her name was Vi. That was all he knew or wanted to know. She was very young. She wore a vintage dress over leggings and silver slippers, and a man's leather jacket. She smiled at him hopefully from beneath the ragged black curtain of her hair.

Rory never smiled or looked pleased to see girls. He expressed no pleasure or affection because it made him look weak. He had been self-conscious of his sex appeal for so long that he had come to regard it as a veneer to be maintained, much as one would keep a sports car waxed.

He bought her a drink and briefly touched her waist. Luke butted in to ask her age and couldn't resist pointing out how much younger she was than Rory. He launched into some tale of office bravado, and when she tried to comment he held up an index finger, warning her to let him finish.

Luke laughed loudly and sycophantically; then they were ordering more rounds, back-slapping other mates, heading in and out of the toilets, wiping their noses, talking too fast, calling the barman over for rum chasers. They held a drinking contest that involved placing upturned shot glasses on their foreheads. Others came and went. Vi's sense of excitement must have faded as she realized she was participating in a spectator sport, just another girl watching men at a bar drink themselves into insensibility.

Rory didn't recall everything about the evening, just the moments that had incensed him at the time and still made him angry now. They had all been shouting at each other above the music, and a lot of the conversation was swallowed up. It was all trash talk. How did they manage to carry on so loudly for so long about nothing at all? Whenever the girl spoke their laughter stalled for a moment, as if an outsider had wandered into the room. He had participated in that little snub, not quite ignoring her but never giving her more than the most minimal attention. He had lost interest because she seemed strange and unsynchronized to their mood. Despite this, it amused him to keep her hanging on in hope.

When she came to the ungendered bathroom to fix her lipstick she caught him in one of the open stalls with a groove of paper at his nostrils. She pretended not to notice and examined her eyeliner in the mirror, taking a selfie to remind herself how it looked. That got his attention. He had shouted at her and held out his hand for the phone.

'I'm in that,' he warned. 'Give it up.'

'What, you doing a cheeky one?' Mock innocence showed in her eyes as she enjoyed a moment of power. 'I might Instagram it. Insta-half-a-gram, more like.'

He made a grab for her phone and the sudden force of his lunge shocked her, so she held it further away and fled into the corridor, laughing in fright. Swearing, he stumbled after her.

Vi headed back to the bar and stayed beyond his reach. More shots had been poured out beside the beers and gins. She drank hers straight down, then his, while his mates whooped and warned that there'd be trouble.

They argued but he toned it down in front of the others,

not wanting his friends to see how furious he was. Then someone told a joke and it was admittedly very funny and she laughed, and they were all right again, and he even snaked an arm around her waist, pulling her a little closer to his side in a gesture of ownership.

And so it went, the head-back laughter mixed with sharp looks and mean stares, the mood like distant lightning in an overheated landscape. The barman rang a bell for last orders and one of the others got his round in because Rory had called him on it, so they drank faster, and the harsh lights rose.

Suddenly he could see how shabby the room was, the peeling plaster in the corners, the battered furniture, the tarnished counters. The lights were deliberately unflattering, designed to make everyone appear jaundiced. Luke looked pale and sweaty; he had bloodshot eyes and the skin of an incipient drunk.

Rory felt dizzy, dyspepsia setting in. The air stank of beer. 'Let's go,' Vi said, pulling at his arm, which was a mistake. He shook her off.

'I'll book a taxi. Give me your phone,' he instructed, holding out his hand to her.

Her fingers tightened over the Samsung. 'I haven't got an Uber account.' She looked like a child denied pocket money.

'Just give me your bloody phone,' he said, but she backed away. It would only take him a second to delete the photograph. He lunged at her again, looking playful to his mates, dangerous to her, but she had buried the phone deep inside her jacket and walked away.

On the other side of the city, someone else was thinking of the same October night.

Sleep eluded Sparrow Martin. Rain spattered the window of the ground-floor flat she had taken over from her parents in the Barbican. Visitors found the maze of post-war concrete tunnels gloomy and confusing, but she loved living there. Tonight, though, the rooms felt claustrophobically over-stuffed with her family's old furniture. She went to an armchair and sat with the new Kate Atkinson propped in her lap, but when she read her mind drifted back to the night the four of them met. She had started to think of it as 'The Event'.

Sparrow had booked a carpool taxi from the Strand because she couldn't cope with the home-going conviviality of the night tube. The people carrier was already occupied when it pulled up. Augusta Frost said she was relieved to be sharing with another female because she'd been surrounded by idiot men all night. She'd been to several bars in Covent Garden, where she and a girlfriend had hooked up with a couple of ridiculously tall Dutch lads on a birthday weekend.

For Sparrow the night had unfolded with all the desper-ation of an unplanned New Year's Eve: a party in Maida Vale with the lights up and the music down, and a club in Charing Cross Road as crowded as rush hour. She had been talked into staying by a woman who worked part-time in the bookshop.

When the driver picked her up, he explained that they would probably stop to pick up more passengers. Sparrow's finger had traced spangles of rainlight on the car windows. She looked out at the lamp-yellow streets lined with ran-domly ordered shops: nail bar, electronic repairs, noodles, coffee shop, fried chicken, pub. *A limited choice,* she'd thought, *rather like men.* Once she would have seen how they looked at girls like Augusta and felt a twinge of jealousy. Now she watched them from an anthropological viewpoint, like observing monkey troops.

'This creepy media guy was talking about his daughter as if she was his girlfriend,' Augusta had told her. 'How was yours?'

'A TV producer described his vinyl collection to me in great detail and offered to get me on a quiz show,' said Sparrow.

The driver checked his rear-view mirror. 'I am picking up

passengers here,' he had said, pointing through the smeared windscreen.

Sparrow peered out but saw nothing but dead offices, building sites, tall halogen lights. 'Where are we?' she had asked. 'I can't see where we are . . .'

'The back of Tufnell Park,' said Augusta. 'There are always murders around here.'

'Murders,' she had repeated. 'I think I read something . . .'

It could only be because of that night. She needed to talk to someone. Augusta said she never slept. Sparrow reached across the bed for her phone.

Rory set his shot glass down on the bar of the Keys club. The lights blazed across the emptying dance floor and the last few customers were heading to the coat check. It had been the same on that night two months earlier. He tried to recall the exact sequence of events.

There had been an argument about transport and the lateness of the hour. Luke had said he'd called the cab. 'It's on its way, I can see it.' He raised his phone screen.

Rory had looked around. 'Where did the girl go? Is she in the toilet?'

'No idea. Maybe she pushed off without you.' Luke was chemically loaded and twitchy. 'Do you want me to look? Shall I look?'

'Allow it, mate. She's well annoying.'

'You were giving her a bit of a hard time about her phone.'

'She took a selfie in the lavs with me in the background doing a bit of the old hooter nonsense. She'll be posting it all over the shop. If anyone from work sees that I'm a dead man.'

'Let's go. Maybe she's waiting upstairs,' said Luke. 'The car's two minutes away. It says here two minutes, yeah?'

Outside it was raining just enough to mist the air and slicken the roads. Apart from a few working girls in the next street there was no one else around. The shutter for the main entrance had already been half lowered.

'Where's the cab?' Rory kicked a kebab box into the gutter.

Luke checked his phone again. 'I think we lost that one. Yeah, gone. He didn't wait. There should be loads of others knocking about. I've got another company.' Rory stared angrily at Luke, who stared at his phone, then rang a number.

Rory made a what's-going-on? gesture. Luke put his hand over the phone. 'You have to call the number, it's not online.' He listened for a minute. 'Jagan in a white Toyota, plate ends in JHT,' he told them.

'That's old school, no wonder he's cheap.'

'He says he's right here somewhere.'

'I don't see any car.' Rory went back to his messages and let Luke sort it out. A moment later, the Toyota pulled up a short distance away from the entrance.

'That's not ours,' Rory said.

'It's the right number plate.'

'It's a people carrier for a carpool. You've booked a sharesy, you muppet. Cancel him and get another one.'

'I can't, that's what I ordered. Wait.' Luke ran out into the road, ducked down and peered inside, said something to the driver and ran back. 'There's two girls in there; one of them's fit. Don't fancy yours much.' He laughed and ran back into the road, and Rory reluctantly followed.

Augusta and Sparrow had complained at the way the boys pushed in, but not enough to stop them. The driver sat silent and motionless, staring forward through the windscreen, waiting for them to settle.

'You want to wait for that girl?' Luke asked. 'She might still be in the toilet or something.'

'She's not, is she? The doors are closed. She's gone home.'

'Not being rude, mate, but what are you doing with her?' said Luke. 'She's underage, innit.'

'Nothing happened,' Rory said. 'Let's go. I don't want to sit around here for hours.'

The impassive driver waited for mutual agreement, then set off.

'No, wait.' Rory slapped the back of the driver's seat. 'You'd better go around once. Take the slip road here.'

Both of the girls started to complain. The driver turned and circled past the rear of the club but they were all arguing now, voices rising, a storm breaking inside the car.

'You're going the wrong way,' said Rory. The driver stopped for a moment, then laid his arm along the seat and reversed into the slip road behind. They heard something that sounded like the slap of a hand against the boot. The driver hit the brakes but it was undramatic, the kind of stop you make when you don't quite know if you've hit something.

Luke was out first. The driver was twisting around to try and see, and the girls were asking what just happened. Then Luke came back and asked for him, and told the others to stay in the car, there was nothing wrong, it would only take a minute.

Rory went around the back of the Toyota and froze. 'Did he hit her?'

Luke dropped to one knee. 'Give me a hand.' Vi lay on the tarmac with her legs buckled under her. She mumbled unintelligibly. It was hard to tell if she was concussed or just drunk.

'What if she's broken a bone or something?' Rory asked. 'You're not supposed to move people.'

'Just help me, will you?'

Together they lifted the girl to her feet. Her leggings were ripped and her left knee was bloody. Her head rolled back. She said something that sounded like, 'Don't tell my dad.'

Luke reached down and gingerly touched the bloody knee-cap. Vi yelped. 'It's just a graze,' he said. 'You bleed more after you've been drinking.'

'Take her round the corner, just sit her against the wall until she sobers up, yeah? He doesn't know how to bloody drive. He could have broken her leg.'

'We should take her home,' said Luke. 'I mean, she's vulnerable here. It's not a good area.'

'Yeah, we could book her into a suite at Claridge's for the night.'

Luke rose and stamped his feet. 'You don't give a toss, do you?'

'Strangely enough, I don't. She's not supposed to be here. You take care of it.'

Luke part walked, part carried Vi to the corner and sat her down against the shadowed side of the building, where the eaves would shelter her from the pattering rain. He lit a cigarette. Rory bent down, slipped his hand into Vi's jacket and fumbled around.

'Hey, get off!' she shouted suddenly, batting his hands away.

'What you doing, man?' Luke asked.

'Nothing,' said Rory.

'You're not having my phone.' She swore at him. 'He nearly ran me over. Give me a drag.' She held out her hand for Luke's cigarette, drew on it until it sparkled, then had a coughing fit.

'For Christ's sake let's just go.' Rory pulled out a twenty-pound note and held it before her. 'You need some cash to get home, yeh?'

'The cab won't wait,' said Luke, worriedly looking back.

Rory reached down and held her face. 'Can you hear me?'

Vi groaned, raising her head. Struggling to focus, she reached out to touch his cheek.

'It's OK, she's fine,' he told Luke. He opened his wallet and put the twenty away. Vi drew up her knees and sat hunched over, groaning.

Luke rose and headed back towards the car just as the

larger of the two girls, the one called Sparrow, came to see what was happening.

'What's the problem?' Sparrow asked.

Vi moaned and clutched the side of her head.

'What's the matter, don't you feel well?' asked Sparrow.

'Eye hurts,' said Vi. 'Got some grit in it. Their fault.'

'Hang on a minute.' Sparrow found a bottle of Optrex in her bag. 'Do you know this girl?'

'She was hanging around us,' Luke said sheepishly. Rory made a noise of disgust. Vi attempted to stand and gave up. She took the drops and tried to clear her eye. The taxi's remaining passenger was looking out of the back window in annoyance, tired of the delay to her homebound trip.

Luke, Rory and Sparrow headed back to the car. 'I think she should come with us,' Sparrow said, looking back with concern.

'Can we just go now?' Augusta called, shoving herself down in the seat as Luke climbed in.

Rory got in the other side of the vehicle. 'She can get a bloody night bus instead of a cab,' he snapped. 'A total pain in the arse. The perfect ending to a really shit night.' He tapped the driver on the shoulder. 'Your fault, mate, bashing into her like that. You'll lose your licence if you're not careful.'

The driver ignored him and pulled away, and everything should have settled down but the atmosphere had soured and the lateness of the hour had started to bite. Nobody was pleased when the driver suddenly pulled over and jumped out, walking back.

'Where the bloody hell is he going?' Rory asked.

'What's happening *now*?' asked Augusta.

'I think he wants to give her a lift,' said Sparrow. 'Where does she live? Is she going in the same direction as us?'

Two minutes later the driver returned and climbed back into the vehicle.

'What was that about?' Luke asked him.

'You cannot leave people in that state,' he said. 'We could have taken her.'

'No, mate, she's nothing but trouble,' said Rory. 'What did she say?'

'She had already gone,' Cheema replied, pulling back into the main road.

'You can get on to the next street from the back of the building,' said Luke. 'She'll get a bus just down from there.'

'I should never have bought her a drink,' Rory said. 'Following me around like a dog – it's pathetic. I don't need the grief.' He turned and placed his arm across the back of the seat. 'So, girls, where are you off to now?'

Two months ago the car had vanished into the rainswept night, Rory thought. And now two of the people in it were dead.

25

LATE

Arthur Bryant removed the apostle teaspoon he had been using to wedge open his office window, and mopped rain from the sill with the only handkerchief he owned that was not covered in sulphuric acid burns. The building was quiet. The pipes ticked as the heating went off.

London became a more extreme version of itself after midnight, but the street scene below felt even stranger tonight. A young woman was standing outside a closed tobacconist's with her fists held at her sides, screaming incomprehensibly. The homeless boy cocooned inside shards of cardboard in the doorway tried to ignore her. A few yards away, two furtive young men were swapping something suspicious from their coat pockets. There was harm in the air.

He was waiting for the kettle to boil when John May appeared in the doorway, slapping water from his trousers. He looked around for somewhere to leave his umbrella. 'Dickinson was seeing one of the girls on Market Street. She reckons he was in trouble. He'd done something bad, but she doesn't know what.'

'Market Street. I can't believe there are still girls working up here.' Bryant dropped bags into two mugs. 'The sale of sexual services on that spot goes back several hundred years. So do some of the ladies, if memory serves. Anything else?'

'She says Dickinson saw his father die. He never told her what happened. It shouldn't be too hard to find out. How come you're not with the others in the operations room?'

Bryant stirred the mugs with his apostle spoon. 'They've all been assigned tasks. I've been trying to think through some ideas.'

'If you have any thoughts about who we're looking for, you need to start sharing them with me,' said May, lowering himself into his armchair.

'I'm not sure night shifts were such a good idea. I can't talk to anyone out there because they're all asleep.' When his laptop pinged he opened the message and read it.

'What's the matter?' asked May, looking over.

'An old acquaintance of mine.' Bryant looked up with wide blue eyes. 'A combat photographer, Larry Duggan. He's shot himself. I was just with him.'

May's brow furrowed. 'How? Where?'

'We met up in the Lamb & Flag. He'd lost his job and was suffering from depression. Apart from extracting his thoughts on the case I barely listened to him. I was too busy thinking about my own needs. He took a train to Devon, sat on the clifftops and blew his head off with a shotgun.'

'How awful. Who sent that?'

'Regional news. He wanted to talk to me. I cut him off.' Bryant felt a rare pang of shame. Why had he not seen the risk and done something?

'You weren't to know that he might kill himself.'

'That's the point, John. I could have known if I'd paid more attention. I'm not an idiot, I've read Thucydides and Pope and Proust, but I'm lost with people.' He tapped at the window frame with his spoon. 'Dying alone. It doesn't bear thinking about, but I suppose some people think about nothing else. This is what it's going to be like, entering the night. Watching your friends fade away until you're the only one left, marching on alone in the dark.'

May had let his head rest back and closed his eyes. 'You're right, you'd be more cheerful if you died.'

'You don't understand. You're younger. I need to work. I need a fresh lead, a new angle. I need – a biscuit.' He reached up to a bookshelf, felt along the ledge and produced a packet of Florentines.

'I'm younger by three years,' replied May. 'That's nothing when you're past seventy. It's like going into the park and comparing a couple of trees.'

'At least people still listen to you. I see them exchange condescending smiles above my head.' He took two Florentines for himself and absently handed over the packet. 'Wait till they start using the plural pronoun on me. *And how are we feeling today?* They'll get the ferrule of my umbrella where they least expect it.' He gave a deep and ancient sigh. 'I look out there and feel as if I'm the last one who remembers what this city was once like. Its habits and customs were stitched into its fabric, brick and paper, copper and stone. Tudor Street smelled of newspaper print, Shad Thames smelled of cloves, Soho of hops and garlic and hot bread. Remember when London's livery was red? The colour was everywhere, in guards' tunics, buses, telephone boxes. Everyone had direction and purpose. I wonder if that's how Larry felt.'

May was not fooled. 'You say it keeps changing but you change with it. You used to play Gilbert and Sullivan all the time. Now you listen to Ambrose and his Orchestra. You've moved half a century forward. You're now only ninety years out of date.'

Bryant dropped into his own armchair. 'After my illness I

wasn't sure if my memory would come back, but it did. Some-times the weight of it all – especially at night . . .' He lost the thread of his argument and stared at his book-strewn desk. 'Winston Churchill said, "The longer you can look back, the farther you can look forward." That's my skill, and my curse.'

'I have to tell you something, Arthur,' said May, sitting up. 'My wife – Jane died on Monday. I only just found out. I was waiting for a time to tell you.'

'John, I'm so sorry.' Bryant looked up. 'I liked her. You weren't there.'

'She stopped recognizing anyone a very long time ago. I'm told she just went into a deeper sleep than usual.'

'Oh dear. We may lose Crippen too.' The staggering impro-priety of this remark was allowed to pass without comment. Bryant tried to manufacture a more appropriate response. 'Is there anything I can do?'

'No, I don't think so.'

Bryant felt helpless. He needed to give his partner something practical to think about. 'Is it your job to tell the family?'

'I'll talk to Alex and April, although she won't remember a time when her grandmother was well.' May toyed with a pen cap, turning it over in his long fingers. 'You know, I look back at the brief, disastrous period of our marriage and wonder why I didn't spot her symptoms. She hid them so well. Alex should come to his mother's funeral. He'll make some excuse, of course. It hurts me to say it, but he's been a disappointing son. Well – I thought you should know, that's all.' He studied his partner for a moment. 'I should have told you earlier.'

'I understand,' said Bryant. 'Why don't you go home for a while? It was too ambitious to try and run a unit like this through the night. I can manage here. I'll stay until we pass four o'clock. I'm not sure how I'll feel if the phone doesn't ring. Glad that there's someone alive. Angry that he's got away.'

'You should be happy that you still get results,' May

pointed out, yawning. 'Look at the people you know from the old days, all those historians and safecrackers and conspiracy theorists. They're mad but at least they're your friends.'

'Of the kind that follow you down the street shouting at you. I suppose you're right. Morning will bring a clearer head. My rising senses will begin to chase the ignorant fumes that mantle my clearer reason.'

'That's the spirit. If the phone doesn't ring just after four, we won't stop looking for him. We have some promising new leads.'

Bryant shook his head sadly. 'It should have been straightforward, John. A cab driver killed on the heath. A hate crime, perhaps, or a lunatic who should have been picked up at daybreak. Except the victim's not a cab driver and the crazy has a plan, and the attacks don't make sense. We're about to find out if this thing is truly over.'

He looked across at the carriage clock on the mantelpiece, watching as the minute hand moved inexorably onward. In his heart he knew that something bad was coming, and was powerless to stop it.

Augusta Frost padded about the flat in her dressing gown, waiting for the microwave to heat some hot chocolate. When it was ready she changed her mind and poured a glass of white wine. She'd been planning to start a new Netflix series but the TV had decided to update its software and now it had become confused. Her iPad was still charging, so when Sparrow called she almost welcomed the distraction.

'This is almost getting to be a habit,' she said, sinking on to the sofa with her wine glass. 'I didn't think you'd be up this late. Do you know how to change sources on an amplifier?'

'I think they're all different.' Sparrow sounded uncertain. 'I only watch stuff on my laptop.'

'What did you make of that little meeting? He's a piece of work, isn't he?'

'Who, you mean Rory? I don't like him and I don't even know him.'

'Pretty men are all the same. They think you're hanging on every word.'

'What about the text message you two got?'

'All right, don't rub it in. You're not on the list.'

'Luke couldn't still be alive, could he?'

'No, Sparrow, his death was on the news so it must be real.' She picked at a cushion.

'It means somebody has your contact details. Rory didn't seem bothered. I still think we should go to the police, just to register a complaint. After all, it was a threat.'

'No it wasn't. It was phrased not to be. It sounded like a quote of some kind.' She dug around on the sofa, following the cord of her iPad. 'Have you got your laptop open?'

'Yeah, give me a moment. What was it again?'

' "Hell is empty, and all the devils are here." '

'I thought it sounded familiar,' said Sparrow. 'It's from *The Tempest*. The spirit Ariel is quoting the king's son Ferdinand as he abandons ship. He's the first one off as it starts to sink.'

'So it's, like, advertising a show?'

'No, Augusta, *The Tempest* isn't a show, it's Shakespeare.'

'Whatever. So it's not someone being weird, just a theatre thing. That's a relief.' She reached for the Albariño bottle.

'You don't sound very upset about your neighbour getting attacked.'

'Of course I'm upset! Our security's appalling.' She refilled her wine glass. 'The service charges are outrageous and they still can't keep out undesirables.'

'You don't think something happened that night, do you?'

'You mean when we met? Like what?'

'I don't know. The whole thing was strange. The driver going off like that, Luke and Rory arguing – and then after.'

'You mean when Luke tried it on,' said Augusta. 'I did nothing to encourage him. He actually assaulted me. He tried to climb on top of me. You still shouldn't have done what you did.'

'I don't regret doing it,' Sparrow told her. 'You should be thankful.'

'Yes, but you could have killed him.'

'Don't be so dramatic. We were at the lights. I just opened the door and kicked as hard as I could. I knew the driver hadn't put the central locking on.'

'I suppose it was quite funny,' Augusta conceded, recalling Sparrow with her boots planted on Luke's shoulders, shoving him out on to the tarmac. 'I thought for a moment you'd broken his neck.'

Luke had fallen badly, bumping against a black iron bollard, but moments later he had jumped up and started swearing at them, watching angrily as they accelerated away.

'You don't think it was Luke who killed the driver, do you? Because he blamed him in some way?' Sparrow asked.

'For what? Driving off? If he was that sensitive he'd have come after you for kicking him into the road.'

'You're right. Forget it, I'm not thinking clearly. I had no bat duty tonight. I think I'm becoming nocturnal. I'd better try to get some sleep.' The line went quiet for a moment. 'You know it's nearly—'

'I know what time it is,' snapped Augusta, hanging up.

She finished her wine, then went to check the new lock on the front door. It closed smoothly, the heavy bolt sliding into the mortise with a satisfying click that made her feel safe. She went to bed and fell asleep at once.

Her dream was strange and smothering. She was back in the night taxi but now the vehicle's engine was not electric but clockwork, whirring and clicking as they bumped over some railway tracks. Luke flew out of the door and was lost from view. The driver started to turn around. His fear at seeing the open door quickly turned to anger, and he shouted at her. The clicking grew louder.

She awoke.

The red numerals on her alarm clock read 3.58 a.m.

All she wanted was one good night's sleep. Now that the heating had gone off the bedroom air was cold. It was also disturbed. Something was fluttering and there was a draught. Or perhaps not; after a moment she could no longer feel it. Her curtains were heavy and let in no light. City nights were purple, grey, aquamarine, indigo, sulphurous yellow, and light had to be blocked.

The last glass of wine had left her with a muzzy head. She lifted herself from the pillow a little and looked down at the carpet. Had she really thrown her overcoat on the floor like that? She was sure she had hung it up. It must have fallen from its hook.

The coat moved.

She wondered if she was still asleep, but the rags of her dream had already flickered away.

She looked back at the coat. As she watched, its empty sleeves filled out and extended across the floor. Its shoulders arched and slowly rose up as if something monstrous was being created inside it.

She tried to pull herself upright in the bed but her vision sparkled. Breathing deeply, she slowly sat up. She needed light. Her temples ached.

Something dark and misshapen was shuffling across the floor towards her. The shape of a head appeared from inside the coat like a tortoise revealing itself. She found the cord of the bedside lamp and pushed at the switch, flooding the bedroom with light.

A pair of darkly glittering eyes, wide and maddened, stared just inches from her own. Before she could make a sound, one broad cold hand covered her mouth. The other drew out something that sounded like a knife being sharpened.

From the corner of her eye she saw what first appeared to be a sword. Then she remembered how the others had died. The tube had an ivory handle and a chased silver point that shone like a dagger made of moonlight. She could read a name on the side of it. *Hugo Blake.* The worst part was that the name meant nothing to her. She would go to her death without knowing why.

Colin Bimsley swung past the detectives' office. Bryant and May were both fast asleep in their respective armchairs. He rapped his knuckles loudly on the desk, startling them. 'I just tried Augusta Frost's phone and got a dead line. Same with the house phone. There's an officer outside the property but he says no one has been in or out. What should I do?'

'Colin, sorry, nodded off.' May rubbed at his face. 'Get them to send someone senior over from Islington. They can get there before us.'

A moment later the phones in the operations room began ringing. Renfield and Longbright picked them up. 'Augusta Frost,' called Longbright. 'I've got the Angel nick on the line. Their officer is calling from City Road.'

'Has he been up to check on her?' asked Renfield.

'No – I – wait.' She raised a finger, listening.

'What's happened?'

'Frost's apartment.'

'What about it?'

It was rare to see Longbright flummoxed. 'He says it's gone,' she replied.

26

BLAZE

The main access to City Road was blocked so Banbury gave May directions that would get them through the Islington backstreets. They found themselves caught in a slalom of bollards, speed-bumps and chicanes that would challenge a rally driver. Thin, persistent rain blinded the sides of the car, forcing May to guess width restrictions.

'The building's been evacuated,' Banbury said, hanging on to the door handle. 'They don't know the cause of the fire. There was talk of a terrorist attack but the report's just been downgraded.'

'I was reading Samuel Pepys's diary the other day,' said Bryant, watching the streets pass. 'He wrote in his diary that a substance mixed from a single grain of gold, *aurum fulminans*, could, when put in a silver spoon and lit, give a blow like a musket and strike a hole downward through the spoon without the least force upwards. He was probably talking about explosive mercury. The advancements in the field are very exciting. There are so many materials you can use to create explosions.'

May braked hard to avoid colliding with a Deliveroo bike. The lid came off Banbury's coffee.

'Saltpetre, charcoal and sulphur . . .' Bryant enumerated.

May swung the wheel hard. The tyres squealed. Banbury's flat white went over his trousers.

'Potash, antimony, magnesium . . .'

As Banbury tried to re-cap his cup it leaped out of his hands, dispersing its contents more evenly. May hunched himself over the wheel and drove on with grim determination.

'Thermite, barium peroxide. Remote electronic detonation, channelled blast zones . . .'

'Mr B!' Banbury finally exploded before reining himself in. 'Please just . . . stay back behind the barriers when we get there. Please don't go wandering off.'

'Why is he talking to me as if I'm a child?' Bryant asked his partner.

'Arthur, I agree that explosives are a fascinating topic but let's see what we're dealing with first.' May bounced the vehicle out into the opened section of the main road.

As an anti-terrorist unit raised its pavement barriers, a haze drifted across the tarmac like cannon fire from a distant battlefield. A pair of fire engines blocked the eastbound lane, their hoses twisting and fizzing under pressure. The police and Emergency Medical Team worked methodically; the silence was broken only by the crackle of headsets.

'Good Lord, I can't even see the building,' said Bryant, peering out. 'What has he done?'

A dull orange glow shone through the smoke drifting down from the ArcAngel. The cyan lights of police vehicles strobed the ground floor. May climbed from the car and approached someone he recognized.

Senior Fire Officer Blaize Carter was bulked up by the fire-retardant coat she had grabbed from the station. Her kinked auburn hair was netted to allow for the strap of her breathing apparatus. She lowered the mask and immediately pushed May back.

'We picked up a running call and got here first. Bells went down at four oh seven a.m. You can't stay this close, John. We don't know what's happening with the outer walls yet.'

May looked up but the smoke was obscuring everything. 'I thought the codes were more stringent after Grenfell.'

'In theory. The building's fitted with AFAs but, you know.' She rubbed her forefinger and thumb together. 'The cheapest alarm system always wins. This one is notorious for shorting out. It has plastic housings that buckle and break the battery contacts.'

May craned his neck to see. He couldn't spot any flames. Apart from the haze of smoke the building appeared un-harmed. 'How severe is it?'

'It's pretty localized. Fire is a tiger; after a while you get a feel for where it's going to move next. This isn't going anywhere. The interior fire doors are preventing through-draughts.'

'Do you know what happened yet?'

Carter held out her arms to keep a rubbernecker behind the lines. 'It'll take a while to get clear answers,' she called over her shoulder. 'The gaffer says the walls are untouched but we need to check for electrical faults, so the barriers are staying up. There's no gas connected, it's all electric, so no obvious cause. It was a topical combustion that didn't spread. Looks like it started in the living room, which is suspicious.'

'Why?'

'There was nothing in there to cause a fire. The kitchen's untouched. Residents are home at this hour but a lot of the flats are empty, so there's hardly anyone to evacuate.'

'You found the occupant?'

'I'm afraid so. The EMT has already taken receipt of her. No other casualties.'

'Wait, was it smoke inhalation? Is she dead?'

'I'll try and find out for you.' She raised a hand and listened to her headset. 'Sorry, I'm wanted upstairs. We need to make sure everyone's accounted for.' She walked back, reconnecting her helmet. 'Hang around here for a few minutes.'

The pall of smoke thinned to reveal the glossy photograph of the woman in her cream satin evening gown, leaning on her glass balcony above the city. In her retouched world everything was still immaculate.

May looked for his partner and found him with Banbury, searching for scorch marks on the outer walls of the building. 'The apartments on either side don't even have smoke damage. How could he be sure he'd done the job?'

'What do you mean?' May asked.

'Committing arson is an act of anger,' said Bryant. 'He went back up, found a way in and killed her. Why? Because she didn't tell him what he wanted to know? Or is he just so consumed now that everyone he targets has to die? He clearly torched the place.'

'We don't have that data yet.'

'I don't need data, just my instincts.'

They waited, but after twenty minutes of inaction Bryant grew impatient. 'What's happening?' he asked. 'Can we go up?'

'I know it probably appeals to your pyromaniac sensibilities, Mr B,' said Banbury, 'but fire isn't your department. Let someone else be in charge for a while.'

They talked to the young officer who had been posted outside the foyer all night. 'No one went in,' he said. 'I was looking up at the flat and all of a sudden it disappeared behind a cloud of smoke.'

'No bang?' Bryant asked.

'Nothing.'

'You didn't try to go up there?'

'No, I called it in.'

'The fire service didn't receive the call until seven minutes past four. Why did it take you so long?'

The constable grew defensive. 'I didn't know what was happening. I tried to find someone who could help. I was caught by surprise.'

'Not good enough. Nothing should surprise you.'

The haze drifted away like the aftermath of a firework display. After another ten minutes Blaize Carter emerged and came to find them.

'What have you got?' asked May.

'As we thought, a localized burn area.' She removed her helmet and apparatus. 'Definitely arson, something low tech kept around the flat, bathroom cleaners, hairspray, cooking oil, anything containing alcohol. It'll be easy to prove once we go through the discards. Fires burn much faster than they used to because apartments like these are built open-plan.'

'Do you have an exact time when this happened?' Bryant asked.

She turned to him. 'The neighbours say it was four a.m.'

'So most of the flat is intact? Any other clues?'

'There was one odd thing. In the bathroom, the lint trap of the spin dryer had been removed and was lying on a counter. Lint's highly flammable.'

'Did anyone see the body?'

'The team leader bagged her. She died before the fire was started.'

'Because her throat was pierced.' Bryant rubbed angrily at his forehead. 'Does anybody else know about this?'

'I don't think so.'

'Make sure they don't. I don't want it getting out, not to anyone. If it does I'll know where it came from.'

Blaize was about to say something she might have later regretted, but changed her mind. 'Fine. I have to finish up here. I'll speak to the team.' She turned to May and slapped him on the arm with a glove. 'Don't forget we've got a date on Saturday.'

May froze. 'Damn. I don't think I can make it. Let me call you.'

A sense of shame descended upon him as he watched her go back to join her workmates.

There was nothing more that could be done for a couple of hours at least, so the three of them headed back to the unit. The ArcAngel was tarnished with a single burst window. The roads were still wet and empty; the circadian engine of the city had yet to begin turning once more.

'If this gets out there'll have to be a press conference,' said May, turning towards King's Cross. 'Remember what happened last time? Colin put a *Daily Express* reporter in a dustbin.'

'Someone will have already picked up the fire call but they won't know about the body,' said Banbury. 'Let's keep it that way.'

'So he killed her, poured cooking oil over her and lit the lint,' said Bryant. 'Whether she told him something or nothing he still killed her. He's beyond reason now.'

May dropped the CSM outside the unit, then drove around the block to take his partner home to Harrison Street. He pulled up outside the gate to Albion House and opened the car door for Bryant, hauling him out. 'Go and get some sleep,' he instructed. 'You look done in.'

Mercifully, Bryant had not quite reached the mental age that turned any exit or departure into a lengthy ritual of patting down pockets and searching for lost items. Within moments he was at the gate with his key in his hand, although the askance look on his face made May hover. 'What is it?' he asked with a sigh.

'There's nothing you haven't told me, is there?' Bryant looked unusually serious.

May was mystified. 'No, of course not.'

'You see, I've got quite a few of the pieces but there are a couple of very odd blanks.'

'No, I don't see at all.'

Bryant paused a moment longer with his key held before the lock. 'There's someone missing and it's not the killer. But you know that, of course.'

'How would I know, Arthur? As usual I have no idea what you're talking about.'

Bryant looked sadly at him, then turned away to open the gate.

'See if you can get back in by ten,' May called, getting into the car. 'At least you'll have had some sleep.'

As May drove away, their conversation started to bother him. Too tired to drive home, he headed back to the unit to find a sofa and some earplugs.

27

SCENARIO

The PCU's night shift had ended at 6.00 a.m., by which time Raymond Land looked as if he had been subjected to immense gravitational force. It seemed impossible that anyone's face could sag so far and fast overnight.

After returning home from the vet he had cleared out Crippen's food, basket and litter tray, then sat on the end of the sofa bed, unable to sleep, before giving up and returning to the PCU. Janice had packed him off to the attic, where he had availed himself of an ancient armchair. After a brief restless sleep he emerged and headed downstairs in yesterday's rumpled clothes, where he found the operations room in a state of siege.

With the dawn had come the first of the calls, and now the scorching lines had been temporarily suspended. Someone had broken confidence. The unit was not prepared to publicly acknowledge that the cases were linked, but the press were happy to make the leap and wanted verification.

Bryant came in looking surprisingly refreshed. 'Ice,' he told Longbright. 'It tightens the pores and sharpens the thinking.'

'Do you put it on your forehead?'

'No, in your brandy. Who told the press? It was either someone in the Emergency Medical Team or that young PC. No matter, the damage is done. Why don't you have an investigation procedure in place yet?' This last question was tossed at Renfield. 'What have you been doing all night?'

'It couldn't be locked down without your approval,' said Colin. 'We couldn't ask *him* to do it.' He nodded at Raymond Land.

'We don't have enough staff to handle the situation,' Land complained, wandering from table to table in an effort to be useful and getting in everyone's way. 'The Augusta Frost case has to take priority over the others now. I don't want to acknowledge that they're linked until you have absolute proof. Street attacks are one thing, but now he's entering people's homes. We'll cause sleepless nights right across the city.' He stared at the scribbled messages on the whiteboards. 'Who can make any sense of this? What am I supposed to tell Leslie Faraday when he calls?'

'I'd rather you didn't tell him anything. Go home, Raymondo,' said Bryant. 'Have a nice soak in a bath.'

'Will you kindly stop telling me to go home?'

'I promise we'll get the investigation schedule up and running. We'll call you once we've collated everything.'

'It'll take more than a few paper clips to sort this lot out,' said Land gloomily. 'Look at the state of this room. It smells like an Algerian barber's in here.'

'That'll be my hair oil,' said Colin, hastily gathering papers.

'We'll clear it all up,' said Longbright. 'Just as soon as—'

'Crippen died,' Land said suddenly, loudly, pulling out a sodden tissue. 'I have to go and collect her. The vet had to put her to sleep.'

'Oh no.' This was from Meera in a very small voice.

'I'm very sorry to hear that,' said Bryant. 'I thought she was looking off colour. I could arrange for her to be cremated.'

'I'm never going to trust you with another cremation urn, not after what you did with our last coroner,' said Land. 'I'll take care of her. She was only thirty-six in cat years.'

'She had a good life.' Bryant found a doughnut in his pocket and ate a piece. 'I could have used her for all kinds of experiments but I hardly ever did.' He saw the miserable look on Land's face and felt suddenly sorry for him. It was not a sensation he welcomed. 'Please, Raymond, do go and get some rest. I'll send someone for Crippen. It was kind of you to make her final days so peaceful.'

'Call me when you need me.' Land headed forlornly for the door.

'That won't be any time soon,' said Meera after he'd gone.

'Raymond is your boss,' Bryant reminded her. 'He may seem useless and out of his depth but . . .' He tried to think of something positive to say. '. . . we always know where we stand with him. At any given moment you can see every one of his thoughts with perfect clarity. It's like watching goldfish in a tank: shall I go through the little castle or over the pirate chest? He's like the placebo in a medical trial, ineffective but necessary in order to obtain an accurate result.' He turned to his partner. 'Has Dan been allowed into the ArcAngel apartment?'

'He's just arrived there,' said May.

'He won't find the weapon.'

'Why not?'

'Because the killer hasn't finished with it. He's more dangerous now than when he began.' Bryant held up one of the plastic pens. 'These were made by a company that runs events for dozens of clubs and bars. They're probably shipped out in thousands. They can't be the only link.'

'Luke Dickinson and Augusta Frost tick a lot of the same

boxes,' May pointed out. 'Both professionals on decent salaries in fancy flats. He was an insomniac who visited prostitutes and suffered from bouts of depression, she was stressed and taking an antidepressant called Paxil. We have no evidence that they knew each other, but they have dozens of contacts in common.'

'Which seems to get us closer, but doesn't.' Bryant dumped the rest of his pocket doughnuts at the tea station. 'There should be a handful of names recurring on that whiteboard by now. If we were a Scandinavian cop show I'd be striding about in a memorable jumper telling you to pick up so-and-so at once. Janice, don't you have a single solid link between Dickinson and Frost?'

'There are hundreds if you factor in Twitter, Instagram, LinkedIn, Facebook, Tinder and other networks.' She pushed back her chair and stretched. 'I've added parameters of geographical proximity, age, job type, special interest groups and so on to reduce the search area, but it's actually making the matrix more confusing because there are no factors common to all of them.'

'I can show you what to look for,' said Banbury, shifting his chair.

Longbright gave him a strange look. 'You smell like a bonfire.'

'Did you get a confirmation on Dickinson's father?' asked May.

'I spoke to the sister.' Longbright walked to one of the whiteboards and drew a link to her name. 'She says that when Luke was ten their parents split up. He and his father were walking through Battersea Park on their way back from a funfair, when the father stepped into the Thames, leaving his son on the pavement. He drowned himself, Luke had therapy, he and his sister were raised by the mother. The sister handled it better, but of course she wasn't there when it happened.'

'Hm.' Bryant tore off a piece of doughnut. 'Interesting.'

'I know that sound,' said May.

'The glimmer of an idea. I do hope I'm wrong. Four attacks in five nights, all at a time when people are most vulnerable.' Bryant tapped insistently at the board. 'Isolation, the urban disease. There are eight million single households in the UK. In Japan, women over sixty-five are deliberately getting themselves jailed in order to make friends. You wait, it'll catch on here next. He doesn't want to spare them; he wants them to feel alone at the end. How did he manage to get back into the ArcAngel without the duty plod spotting him?'

'There's no footage from the building,' said Dan Banbury. 'I should be able to get CCTV from the street before noon.'

'He'll be prepared for that,' said Bryant.

'How do you know?'

'Because he's a schemer. He's been watching them. Maybe he has an accomplice. But he's not a professional; he makes mistakes and gives in to his emotions. He hasn't got what he wants, and it's driving him insane. So what is he after?'

'Crazy people make plans too,' said Banbury. 'Have you ever seen their diaries?'

Bryant wrinkled his nose and squinted hard at the board. 'Find me some common interests in this group. I've never used social media so there's no point in me looking. In fact I'm not entirely sure what it is.'

'You've never been on Facebook?' said Meera. 'How do you stay in touch with people?'

Bryant fixed her with one of his looks. 'First of all, young lady, I don't want to stay in touch with people. And if I do have something to say, I go and see them. We order beverages, I say something, they say something and I say something disagreeable back. The discussion of moral and philosophical problems between two or more people is known as a Platonic dialogue and cannot be instantly monetized, repackaged, sold on or turned against the participants. It doesn't need a safe space, trigger warnings or crowfunding.'

'Crowdfunding,' said May.

'Whatever,' said Bryant.

Janice tapped a Sharpie against her teeth. 'Mr Bryant's right. There may be another way to track them down.'

'Oh yes?' May put down his tablet and paid attention.

'The old-fashioned way. Create a victim profile with the help of an expert. One of your lot.'

'I assume you are referring to my Rolodex of defrocked academics, delusional mountebanks and fully paid-up members of the maniac community.' Bryant held up a tattered black leather book stuffed with multicoloured Post-it notes. 'Well, there might be someone here who could be useful. Perhaps I can persuade one to come to breakfast. They can normally be won over with the promise of clean socks and a hot meal.'

Bryant reached for his phone and began checking his address book.

Hugo Blake sat on a bench in front of the walled garden at Kenwood House. The Earl of Mansfield's neoclassical villa rose majestically on the crest of the hill between Hampstead and Highgate. At the bottom of the grass slope, rain stippled the dark lakes and bowed the trees. It was so green and fresh in this shadowed vale that terrors could finally be held at bay, if only for a brief time. Protected under a black umbrella, he listened to rain pattering through the ivy pergola on to the flowerbeds. He checked his phone: 10.15 a.m.

He had never doubted himself, never felt for a second that what he was doing was wrong. War was based on the concept of justice. But he could not afford to make any more mistakes.

He had still been patrolling the peripheries of the ArcAngel building, trying to solve the problem of access to the Frost girl, when he saw the locksmith's van arrive. Guessing that it might be someone coming to repair the door he had smashed, he moved closer and heard the name spoken at the intercom. It felt like a chance too lucky to be trusted.

Blake stepped in, apologizing to the locksmith and explaining that there had been a mistake; his wife had forgotten that he had agreed to take care of the problem. He handed the locksmith more than his callout fee in cash. Once the van had driven off he called Frost on the intercom and explained that he could return to do the job in a few minutes.

He had a metal carpentry box, tools and locks back at the house. He certainly knew how to reinforce Frost's apartment door, but it was still a risk. He didn't like factors beyond his control.

He needn't have worried. When Augusta Frost opened the door she remained glued to her phone and barely noticed him. She chatted and texted the whole time he was there. She had been so unsuspecting, so offhand and inattentive that he almost felt sorry for her. A person who had placed herself at risk like this should, he felt, be more aware of the fact. Studying the pale nape of her neck and the dark roots of her hair as she turned away, he almost changed his mind and let her live.

He played out each scenario:

1. She admits her crime and accepts her fate.
2. She denies any involvement and belatedly realizes her guilt.
3. She insists she has no idea what he's talking about right until the end.

He wanted her to turn and look at him. He needed to find fear, understanding and acquiescence in her eyes at this point, the termination of her life.

But she did not turn around. While she ran her bath and fretted over phone messages he simply wanted to kill her.

He looked for a hiding place, and decided on the space under the bed in the guest room.

When Augusta realized he would be some time and half-heartedly offered to make him tea he declined, saying he would try not to disturb her. Once the lock had been fixed he showed her the London bolt he'd added, confident that she had never seen one before.

'Sorry,' she said halfway through his explanation, not looking up from her phone, 'I need to sort this out, bit of a crisis.' She bullied him down in price and left the cash on the hall table, wandering back into the bathroom with her phone.

He had not expected that it would be so easy. He opened and closed the front door, then stowed his gear in the guest wardrobe and slipped under the bed. Then it was simply a matter of silently waiting until the appointed hour. His only fear was that he might fall asleep and snore.

Ultimately, Augusta Frost chose Option Three.

This created a problem. It denied him the satisfaction of revenge and sowed fresh seeds of doubt in his mind. She admitted one thing: that she had briefly met the others. It meant that either they had all agreed to lie, or one of the two still alive was the enemy.

He folded his umbrella and felt the rain on his face. He could hear it falling in the trees, a distant murmuring that cleared his head.

From the very beginning he had never expected to survive his actions. He had imagined being gunned down by police snipers or simply turning the trocar on himself. That was before he had met Sparrow. Assuming the other three had not lied to him at the moment of death, only two remained, which gave her and Rory Caine equal odds of being guilty. But which of them was it?

He had started to believe that it must be Sparrow. Why else would fate complicate matters by making him fall in love with her?

28

BACKSTAGE

May dropped his partner off at the Capannina, Camden Town's last remaining old-fashioned Italian café, which had half-height nylon net curtains and plastic tomatoes on yellow Formica tables and smelled so strongly of frying bacon that the diners took a Proustian memory of breakfast away in their scarves and sweaters.

Frankie Matthews was sitting at the window. A tall, well-built African woman with cropped red hair, immense hoop earrings and watchful, amused eyes, she was dipping a fat chip into a fried egg, her plate overloaded with beans, sausage, black pudding, mushrooms and triangular-cut white sliced bread.

'Caught me stuffing myself, I'm afraid,' she apologized, pushing out a chair for him. 'They used to keep the teaspoons on little chains here, that's how rough it was, but you can't beat it for a proper heart-stopper. I need the carbs today.'

'Oh, you're working?' asked Bryant, settling his hat on the next chair.

'I'm doing a Pinter play at the Ambassadors. There's supposed to be a practical meal in the second half, but the director has cut it. I tried to sneak a packet of crisps into the production but she said Pinter would never have advocated the use of potato-based snacks in his plays. Instead I have to drink endless cups of tea. It's murder on the bladder.'

'A good play, though?' Bryant waved at the waitress.

'I've no idea.' Frankie mopped a floppy piece of toast around her beans. 'Apparently it's an aesthetically stylized piece set in the moral vacuum of the bourgeoisie. Not that you'd know it from the set. Two call-centre chairs, a salvaged sideboard and a gas fire. I think if you're paying eighty quid a ticket you want a bit of sparkle. People keep asking me what it's about. I tell them it's about two hours, and you could take out one of those if you closed up all the gaps. The director says she wants the theatre full of sexual tension and subconscious Oedipal desires.'

'And is it?'

'No, it's full of pensioners. Do you know' – she pointed at him with a chip – 'there are young Asian slam-poets appearing in the pub next door to the theatre who are saying something relevant about the modern world while we're dragging Pinter's corpse across the stage every night? I'm sorry, Arthur, I've been told not to rant but you've always been sympathetic.' She paused for a moment to catch her breath and swallow, watching him with amusement. 'I assume you tracked me down for a purpose.'

'I need some advice on a murder case. But please, shovel that lot in first. I can wait.' He ordered while Frankie demolished her breakfast. It felt as if he had known her for ever. Whenever they bumped into each other the actor was dashing off to a studio or a theatre, either to teach drama or to play a singing teapot (*Beauty and the Beast*, Dominion, Tottenham Court Road), a Fairy Godmother (*Cinderella*, Hackney Empire) or, when times were a little tougher, Shopper Considering Vegetables (*EastEnders*).

'Isn't it a little odd, asking a thespian for advice about a murder?' asked Frankie.

'I seek out people with the right expertise, and you know a bit about motivation.' Bryant nicked a ketchup-smeared chip. 'Have you ever played an accomplice, victim or witness to murder?'

Frankie chewed pensively. 'I tend to play survivors. Lady Macbeth, Mother Courage, Goneril, Masha in *Three Sisters*, Hedda Gabler. Men have outbursts of violence but women can sustain their cruelty. Wasn't it Hannah Arendt who talked about "the banality of evil"? I'm not sure that many people are actually evil. We always talk about Hitler being mad but he acted with knowledge and enthusiasm. A combination of blind intention, low intellect and power-lust. Maybe that's why there aren't enough strong female stage roles. We never had power.'

'You had Margaret Thatcher.' Bryant sat with his hands clasping the edge of the Formica table like G-clamps, waiting for his tea. 'You think the person I'm looking for is powerful? I hadn't thought about a woman.'

'I suppose you're going to tell me it's statistically unlikely, to which I would say' – she leaned forward and looked into his eyes – 'maybe it's because they get away with it more often.'

'You could have a point there,' Bryant conceded. 'Actors are night creatures, wouldn't you say? What's it like keeping odd hours?'

'The worst part is having to come into the West End during the evening rush hour.' Frankie offered him a piece of her sausage. 'This director insists on giving us notes after the show so we always end up going home late. But you quickly adapt. My wife changed her shifts so we can spend some time together. You see a different crew when you're on lates. People are friendlier. I suppose you could say London's front-of-house by day and backstage after midnight.' She stirred her tea mug.

'That's when the real work gets done. Cleaning and repairing, dismantling and putting stuff up. Those huge sets they build in Leicester Square for film premieres have to come down by two a.m. After a while you get to know the riggers. Sometimes as I walk home it feels like they're dismantling London, as if it's just one big stage set that's rebuilt overnight.'

Bryant knew the feeling. As a sleepless child in the East End he had watched bakers, fishmongers, market gardeners, drivers and milkmen. 'The city has to renew itself and get ready for another daytime performance,' he said. 'Do you ever feel vulnerable when you're alone at night?'

Frankie speared the last mushroom with her fork, then pushed her plate away. 'I'm surrounded by people all the time so it's a relief to walk through quiet streets. They empty out the moment the bars stop serving. It's not like Southern Europe, where they all stand around chatting until it gets light. The English secretly can't wait to get home. They want to be indoors. I walk beside the river, gather my thoughts, take stock. I suppose it's like your job, vocational. Why do you ask?'

'People are being killed halfway through the night.'

'But you don't know why.' She dabbed her mouth with an unabsorbent napkin. 'There's not always a reason.'

'There's a reason all right, but I have yet to find it. They're known to each other on thingie. You know' – he mimed typing – 'social media, but we can't find any specific connections. No one has come forward, which suggests the killer is working alone and unsuspected.'

'Then he's getting something he wants or needs. Most characters are motivated by gratification.'

'I have no idea what his needs might be.' Bryant looked out of the window. 'It's not a sexual impulse, and not for monetary gain as far as I can see. His motives are hidden from us.'

'So it's revenge, a bit Jacobean, a touch of Webster's *The White Devil*, but with a twist.'

'What do you mean?'

'I once appeared in an amateur all-female version of *Hamlet* in Sheffield. Ophelia's lines were made up of Titania's speeches because she'd learned *A Midsummer Night's Dream* by mistake. A friend of mine playing Claudia dropped out of the production after a ladder broke in half, gashing her leg. We found out later that Rosencrantzia had sabotaged it because she was sick of having her lines stepped on. She never spoke to anyone about the problem; she just took action. What I mean is, your victims may have no idea why they've been singled out.'

'The attacks aren't random, Frankie. He researches and prepares. He's in control, he's good at thinking on his feet, but clouded by emotion. What kind of person does that suggest to you?'

'I don't know ... someone who's damaged and sees his victims as the enemy. If I was looking for character motivation I'd go for sexual jealousy, self-absorption, isolation, anger. A classic revenger. Don't you have a profiler who works out this sort of thing for you?'

'In Europe and America, not so much here.' Bryant finished his tea and rose. 'I hope the play turns out well. Break your ankle.'

'You mean break a leg. I'd rather break my contract.'

'Be thankful you're still working. I am.'

'I never forget it for a second, darling. Do you know how many good roles there are for mature black women who can't sing?' She raised a thumb and forefinger, making a zero. 'If things get really desperate I'll try out for *The Mousetrap*.'

'I think you'd get bored very quickly.'

'Not half as bored as the audience.' She waved him off. 'Call me if you need any more thespian advice, darling.'

29

ADMISSION

It had not taken the other pupils in his school long to figure out that Vincent Dillard's surname was one letter away from an insult, and they applied it mercilessly. Consequently Vincent developed no further than immaturity. His thin skin was a liability in most careers, but in journalism it proved disastrous. After alienating the editors of most national newspapers he now found himself working for Janet Ramsey, the editor of *Hard News*, in charge of the department she had christened 'The Assassination Bureau', an innuendo-laden name-shaming section of sub-journalism that replaced empirical data with rabid opinions.

Dillard's remit required him to express outrage and disgust at what was happening in the world, but he found the English hard to rile. Oh, they complained and rattled their newspapers in front of the fire, and took out their annoyance on the roses or said something sarcastic on Twitter, but they rarely headed out to the streets and never thought of storming the palaces of power.

The *Hard News* website had a dedicated trio of investigative reporters on the payroll, but Dillard had not been able to ingratiate himself with them, so he worked freelance and alone. He was not a likeable man. When he tried to sound interested he came over as prying, and when he turned on the charm he was as creepy as a spider. Today he was looking for a break in the story of the 4.00 a.m. killer, and the logical place to start was in Whitechapel. The Cheema family's saree shop was a vast cavern of emerald, saffron, ruby and turquoise materials, much of it studded in sequins and glittering brocade.

The reporter congratulated himself on thinking of the store, although he was not the first on the scene; a Berlin film crew had already visited and had been sent packing. Dillard stuck out like a white male in a saree shop. He decided to brazen it out when the girl approached him, but he knew that as soon as he opened his mouth he would be regarded with suspicion. The old argot of the East End had developed a spicy new tang as it absorbed slang from other cultures, becoming a mixture of cockney, Bangladeshi and West Indian, whereas he sounded as if he was from the wrong part of Essex, which he was.

'Is there anything I can help you with?' the girl asked.

'I'm not here to buy, miss,' he replied. 'You must be little Jani, yeah? I'm wondering if you could tell me anything about the death of Dhruv Cheema.'

Jani Cheema's smile faded. 'Absolutely not. I will get my mother—'

She turned to leave but he grabbed her arm. 'I'm trying to do the right thing here, love. I thought it was only fair to give you a chance to present your side of the story—'

She pulled free and walked away. 'There are no sides, there is no story, now get out before I send for my brothers.'

He skipped along after her. 'Oh, so you *are* one of the daughters. What was your brother doing in his taxi, cruising around so late at night? Up to no good, was he?'

'You have to leave right now.'

'I'm going, I'm going.' Dillard stalled, playing out his line. 'I just wondered, if he wanted a hook-up why not use an app like Tinder or Grindr instead of going into the woods after leaving his taxi—'

'This is none of your business.'

'It's in the public interest to know if cab drivers can't be trusted. And if he left his taxi to go and have some fun in the dark—'

'It was not his taxi!' she cried in exasperation.

'So it was his brother's.'

Jani's mouth shut fast. They both realized at once what she had done.

'I should leave you to grieve,' said Dillard, backing away. 'I'm sorry to have intruded upon your time and privacy.'

Outside, he walked around to the alleyway at the back of the building and looked up at the first floor. That was where the family lived, the two brothers and the unmarried sister. A new kitchen, expensively kitted out. He climbed on to a fence strut and peered over into the back garden, where a television box had been thrown away. Massive screen, very high-end.

Dillard thought it through.

The police had to be aware that Dhruv had taken his brother's car. Perhaps they hadn't released the information at the family's request. Thoughtful of them, obstructive for the press.

There was no sign of the vehicle on the street. Behind the shops were a row of garages, but their doors were all locked.

Dhruv Cheema had needed the taxi to get to his rendezvous with the killer, but obviously couldn't have driven it back, so it must have been left there and impounded. Dillard had picked up some ground chatter about the brother's contacts. It started to sound like gang business. The more he thought about it, the more obvious it seemed. There were plenty of unemployed young Indians here, and who knew what they got up to under cover of darkness? Jagan Cheema was being protected by his mates.

There had been several arrests in the area last month. He ran a few searches on his phone. Not drugs or girls – they had a family business, why risk it? Something more distanced, illegal but indirect. A safe way of making money below the radar. Money laundering had become more covert of late, since the government had been forced to push for clearer accounting. Something else.

One search result caught his eye. Looted Egyptian arte-facts, clearance through London's East End, ongoing investigations. Rumours only, no arrests so far. Why hadn't anyone at the SCD spotted this?

It wouldn't take long to discover where Jagan Cheema hung out. Dillard decided that it was a good place to start.

Sparrow Martin had booked the day off, not because she had planned anything special but because she needed space to think. Now she opened her new bat notebook and took out a pen. Perhaps she didn't care about bats quite as much now, but they were still her favourite mammal.

Seated in the room she had laughingly christened the stu-dio because it was the only one with decent light, she tried to understand what was happening. That ridiculous meeting at the Young Vic café, Rory refusing to take anything seriously, the creepy text message the others received, the nagging sense that this was happening because of something they did. The deaths of people who knew each other. What was the likeli-hood of that happening?

At the top of the page she wrote 'Dhruv Cheema'. It had started with him and the ridiculous masked figure she had glimpsed chasing him through the woods. Who knew what their fight was about? Men fought.

Next she wrote 'Luke Dickinson'. He must have been attacked by the same person, or perhaps a gang. Somehow they had managed to drown him. The press were offering no further details about the deaths, and there had been no follow-up stories.

She rang Augusta and waited three rings for an answer before halting the call. She couldn't keep pestering her. She knew that the most obvious and logical thing to do was go to the police. But what could she tell them that they didn't already know? She hadn't seen the face of the man in the woods, couldn't give a useful description. The thought of being dragged into the spotlight horrified her. What if she was wrong, and had completely misinterpreted what she saw?

The phone made her jump. It was Pamela, from the Ladies of the Night. 'Hello, Sparrow? I'm so glad I caught you. I hope your fright last weekend didn't put you off helping us with the bat-boxes tonight? We're terribly behind schedule.'

'Actually I was thinking about giving it a rest for a while,' said Sparrow.

'We won't be bothering with the Brandt's bat this time. It can survive perfectly well without us. We'll be back to our usual hour, at dusk, meeting by the top gate at Kenwood Park. We could really do with your help.'

She gave in, as she knew she would. 'All right, I'll come along this time.'

'Jolly good. Before I forget, somebody called me yesterday morning asking questions about you.'

'What kind of questions?'

'To be honest, I couldn't really hear him. There was a helicopter overhead making the most frightful noise. He wanted to know where you worked. I told him I couldn't give out your number and he hung up.'

Sparrow rang off and looked around the room, wondering how secure the windows were. Bars would make the place look like a prison but she would at least feel safer. Not for a while, though; the landlord lived in Belgium, and the managing agent still hadn't arranged to have her leaking toilet cistern fixed.

She needed to remain watchful until the police had caught this man. She needed to do a lot of things. The page on which she had planned to map an investigation had turned into a tick list that began with 'Buy new duvet' and ended with 'Move to Hastings'. The midday light was so low that she had to switch on her desk lamp. The room was full of bats: furry ones, cuddly ones, rubber ones. *Never tell anyone what you like because they'll buy you it forever,* she thought gloomily.

Something metallic clattered outside the back door. Pushing back her chair, she walked across the room and listened. All she could see through the stippled glass panels were brick walls and the outline of her recycling bin.

She knew the most stupid thing to do was go and look, but it was daylight and she had no intention of becoming a prisoner in her own flat. Her hand hovered over the handle for a moment before she decided she was being absurd, and she drew the door back. A black shape flowed smoothly out of the bin – next door's cat had something disgusting in its mouth.

She returned to the notebook and uncapped her pen.

They had been strangers before that taxi ride. Could Luke and the driver possibly have met somewhere before, then pretended not to know each other in the taxi? If they had it meant that whatever happened only involved them, and she, Augusta and Rory were safe.

The more she thought about it, the further she spiralled away from any likelihood of uncovering the truth. Luke and Cheema had met in the past, so their ride together was either planned, or merely coincidental and awkward. She tried to create a scenario with pictograms. The unstable Luke had booked Cheema's cab and killed him before taking his own life. But the woman next door to Augusta was also attacked.

None of it made any sense. She threw down her pen in disgust and poured herself a beer, sitting back to listen to the falling rain.

A new noise came from outside, like a tin can slowly rolling about on its side. The most ordinary sound in the world, and yet it sent prickles across her shoulder blades. *This is ridiculous,* she thought, *go to the police and tell them what you saw Saturday night. You could be withholding evidence.*

No more excuses. She rose and pulled her raincoat from the cupboard, wrapped herself in a scarf and checked her phone. There was a police station still operating at Snow Hill, between Smithfield Market and the Old Bailey, just a short walk from her flat.

The hill was the site of a London aqueduct, and there remained a marble drinking fountain outside St Sepulchre's Church. On days of public celebration the conduit had run with red and white wine. Not any more, sadly.

The police station was housed in a listed modernist building of Portland stone with a central column of tall, mullioned bay windows. It was built on the site of the Saracen's Head, a famous coaching tavern demolished in 1868. Only a blue enamel badge above the doorway revealed the building's present purpose.

The station was devoid of visitors. Sparrow approached the duty desk sergeant and asked to talk to an officer, but the thought of an official interrogation began to undermine her resolve.

The sergeant pushed a sheet of typed paper at her. 'Just fill in the nature of the inquiry,' he requested.

She hesitated. Writing 'I saw a murderer' would set the cat among the pigeons. She settled on 'possible witness to a serious crime' and returned it.

*

The long-legged, bullet-headed officer who came striding across the waiting room three minutes later only made her feel worse. Darren Link was a superintendent at the City of London's Serious Crime Directorate, but he made everything his business, and the girl sitting alone with a batgirl handbag on her dimpled knees looked like she needed his help. Link was a zealot who believed in cleaning up neighbourhoods street by street, and did so with evangelical fervour. Not long after he graduated from Hendon Police College he had been slashed in the eye by a junkie wielding a shattered fence post. His left pupil had healed in two half-discs that caught the light separately, giving him a disturbingly robotic appearance. Link believed in punishment before rehabilitation, yet he was not unsympathetic to those in trouble so long as they showed repentance.

He led Sparrow Martin to an interview room and listened while she explained how she had come to be on Hampstead Heath in the middle of the night. She described what she had seen there, and when she came to a stammering stop he asked her why on earth she had taken so long to come forward. Unnerved by his aggressive attitude, she began to tell him about the others.

Darren Link listened carefully, but not out of compassion. The PCU had been handed the case on a platter and had somehow failed to locate this witness. The maverick unit was the bane of his life. Despite having the highest strike rate in the city they refused to follow government recommendations. They ignored protocol, contaminated evidence, lost witnesses and missed deadlines. The more the girl talked, the more frustrated he became by the unit's failure. Now she seemed to be rambling on about Facebook and bats. He cut her short.

'Would you be willing to go on record, verifying that you saw the victim moments before his death, and that you were not subsequently interviewed by any investigative body?'

Sparrow shifted nervously on her chair. 'I didn't tell anyone what I had seen because I didn't really put it all together until later—'

'But nobody came to take a statement from you.'

'No, they didn't but—'

'That's all I need. It shouldn't take more than a few minutes. Please stay here while I make the necessary arrangements.' He would have to build his case carefully and make sure it was watertight. But he would have them. He rose from the table and left her alone.

Sparrow started to regret having come to Snow Hill.

She had always found it difficult to make friends, but it had never bothered her until now. She tried Augusta but there was no answer, so she called Hugo Blake and asked if she could meet him in an hour.

Blake was waiting for her in the Black Friar, down by the river at Blackfriars Bridge. It was a sepia-toned Arts and Crafts pub built on the site of an old Dominican priory, surroundings in which he seemed even more lost and out of place. 'I called the bookshop and they said you had the day off,' he explained, buying her a pale ale and seating himself on a comically low stool beneath a frieze of processional monks.

'I'm trying to sort some stuff out.' She shucked her coat and looked about. 'Things are weird at the moment. My brother's staying with me but he keeps going missing, along with any money I leave around. He's always had substance-abuse problems but it's got worse lately, and I really don't know how to deal with it.'

'I thought maybe you didn't want to see me any more.' He studied his open hands.

'I'd make time for you. Anyway, it's lunchtime and a girl has to eat.' She reached out and touched his fingertips. 'I'm not stupid, you know. I can tell you've got troubles. You were in the army, weren't you?'

'How did you know?'

'You're going to laugh at me.'

'I won't, I promise.'

'The way you sit.'

He did not laugh. 'What do you mean?'

'With your back arched so that you can't slouch. My father always did that. Both of my parents are ex-military. We moved around all the time. What did you do?'

'I was in the medical corps.'

'You were a doctor?'

'No. I was mostly in Afghanistan, debriding wounds and cleaning bodies. After they were brought in I had to make them ready for shipping out. You can't risk leaving a corpse intact on a flight. They have to be cleared of infection, drained and refilled with inert fluid.'

'That must have been awful.'

'I repaired them as much as I could. I made them look peaceful. Most were intended for closed-coffin services because there were often head traumas, but we tried to get them in a fit state. Limbs can be amputated and replaced but—' He stopped himself, looking up at her in surprise. 'I'm sorry, I don't normally talk about this. I never told my son anything.'

'What happened to his mother?' she asked. 'You said something before—'

'She left me,' he said. 'I wasn't entirely surprised. Let's talk about you.'

'Me? To be honest I'm a bit freaked out at the moment. I can't get hold of someone. I think something may have happened to her.'

He looked her in the eyes. 'Tell me.'

She laughed. 'No, you'll think I'm a crazy lady.'

'Then tell yourself and I'll just sit here listening in.'

Without intending to, she told Blake the whole story, starting with the Saturday night when she went looking for the Brandt's bat. He listened in silence, frozen and blank-faced as she described a version of him that he barely recognized. Then she told him of the night last October she shared a taxi with three other passengers, going into as much detail as she could remember. When she had finished she waited for him to speak, but he simply stared and said nothing.

'Well,' she said, anxious for a response, 'what do you think?'

30

CONTACT

'Is he dead?' Meera peered into the detectives' room. Arthur Bryant was stretched out on the sofa with his eyes shut and his mouth wide open. 'It's the way he would have wanted to go,' she whispered.

'I thought he was the one who didn't need to sleep,' said Colin. He pulled a feather from a cushion and dropped it over Bryant's mouth. It went in and didn't come out.

'What if he really is dead?'

'We already lost Crippen.' She took a party blower from his desk and blew it in his ear. Nothing happened. 'Oh my God, he really *is* dead.'

'No, his hearing aid's on the windowsill, next to his teeth.'

'Very Steptoe-ish.' She shook him awake.

Bryant sat bolt upright. '*Jetez des pierres aux corbeaux!*'

'What?'

'Stone the crows. I dreamt I was French. A nightmare, obviously. Hang on.' He reinserted all the appliances needed to keep him up and running, then gave the pair his fullest attention. The effect was like someone putting their

257

hand up a ventriloquist's doll and bringing it to life. He looked around and smacked his lips together, bedding his teeth in. 'What seems to be the problem?'

'You're wanted in the operations room,' said Colin, scratching at his facial stubble. 'We've come to a standstill.'

Bryant pulled himself to his feet. 'Go and see if there's a good strong cup of tea knocking about. I'll be right there as soon as I can find my other shoe.'

The operations room looked as if it had been attacked by wolves. Chairs and tables had been shifted, stacked and remodelled into makeshift areas of repose. Meera had brought a sleeping bag. Empty pizza boxes and hamburger cartons were stacked among piles of coats, bagged evidence, internal paperwork, witness statements, dossiers, files, folders, laptops and an immense Black Forest gateau delivered by a strange young woman from Tower Hamlets who called herself Ambrosia and explained that she was a huge, huge fan of the PCU and not a stalker or anything creepy like that but she had made them a lovely cake. Banbury conducted a test on it and declared it safe to eat, but by that time Colin was already on his second slice.

'It's the day shift, you're not supposed to be here,' Bryant reminded his staff.

'We've got too much ground to cover,' said Janice. 'The handovers risk missing vital evidence. Someone needs to be in the building all the time. Even the two Daves are in.'

He checked each of them in turn. 'You can't work around the clock and expect to be at your peak.'

'Your boss hasn't been at his peak for decades and he always gets a good night's sleep,' said Meera unhelpfully.

Bryant clapped his hands. 'Let's get organized. Democracy works much better when everyone does what I tell them. Colin, I don't want you wandering around in your undercrackers any more. Being part of a twenty-four-hour shift doesn't mean you can dress for bed during the day.'

'These are trackie bottoms,' said Colin indignantly. 'You were wearing your pyjamas under your suit the other day, Mr B. And you keep leaving your teeth around.'

'I can't find anything in this mess,' John May complained, entering the operations room like a leading character who had missed his second-act cue. 'How can you expect to make judgement calls in here? Look at the place – it's a tip. The overlapping shifts really aren't working out. We have to rethink this, Arthur. It's worse than when we were under siege. Meera, can you clear away everything we've finished with?'

Meera looked around with a level of theatricality she had learned from her bosses. 'I'm sorry, is there a dog in here? Oh no, there isn't. I must be the next lowest person. I'm Indian; we don't clear things up.'

'I'm sorry, I didn't mean—' May began.

Meera raised a hand. 'It's fine, joking, I'm on it.'

The night shift had adversely affected everyone except Janice Longbright, who had been used to working in hostess clubs until 4.00 a.m. Working overnight suited her. While everyone else looked frayed and haunted, she shone. She had switched into full Doris Day mode and looked resplendent in a mauve wool bolero jacket and slacks, more like a 1960s starlet auditioning for a film about the Soho underbelly than a North London police officer preparing to tackle a pile of eye-reddening paperwork.

'Do you remember before we had laptops, when we spent all our time on stakeouts and patrols?' said Renfield, reading her thoughts.

'We had a lower success rate.'

'It was more fun.'

'You were a desk sergeant then, weren't you?' said Colin without looking up.

Renfield turned to face him. 'Yeah, I was. What of it?'

'Nothing, mate. It's just not – you know, a proper job.

While we were out there on the street you were back at the station logging domestics.'

Renfield's formidable eyebrows lowered. 'It stopped me from getting my head kicked in, which will happen to you in a minute.'

'Hey, you two, knock it off,' May warned.

'Hang on.' Longbright tapped her screen with a gonk pencil. '*Sun-Raj International Export Company Provides Export-Import Solutions in Diversified Product Ranges.* That's the most meaningless phrase I've ever ... *Managing Director Raj Ranganathan.*'

'That name came up earlier,' said Colin. 'I saw it written down somewhere.'

Longbright began rifling through the loose pages on her table. She held up a statement. 'Raj Ranganathan sent some emails to Jagan Cheema. His company was under investigation by the Serious Fraud Office. In the last one he says the matter has been dropped. Should we get him in?'

'No,' said May. 'We do it the old way. Go and see him on his home turf.'

'Good idea,' said Bryant. 'I'm going to try another old way. If you've finished with me I'm heading off to contemplate.' He rose from his table, stretched his aching back and headed out of the operations room.

'Don't use the downstairs one, it's blocked,' Meera called after him.

Back in the inner sanctum of his office, Bryant closed the door and settled himself behind his tumultuous desk. He needed to think without interruptions. His natural instinct was to track down a cross-section of contacts who worked exclusively at night. He knew plenty of nurses, orderlies, carers and officers who hardly saw the light of day, but right now he needed someone less orthodox.

Flicking through his address book, he earmarked a few

names. There was an agoraphobic English professor who spent the dark hours walking virtual streets with similarly afflicted friends, via an online map that allowed them to play football on the walkway of Tower Bridge and race bizarre vehicles through Hyde Park. Bryant noted that next to his name he had added 'Nervous breakdown'.

He moved on. Station guards Rasheed and Sandwich spent their nights working in the London Underground, where no diurnal pattern existed. Stanley Purbrick was a conspiracy theorist who took his acolytes on night jaunts around the city trying to prove that a system of secret passageways linked churches to the headquarters of Satanists. A girl known only as GPS, the codenamed head of the Rough Sleepers' Community, spent her nights finding shelter for vulnerable teens. And there was the insomniac Dr Harold Masters, formerly an art historian at the British Museum before he spectacularly blotted his copybook, who met with fellow academics in the dead of night to discuss abstruse theories about Tang dynasty tomb figurines. None of them would be of much help here.

Bryant decided that his best bet was Stanhope Beaufort, an architect who regularly went nightwalking around the city's ghost streets, through the hidden alleys and marginal spaces of the Square Mile. He placed a call and arranged to meet him, then filled his Lorenzo Spitfire with Old Warrior Plug and ran a further search on the colleagues of Jagan Cheema, hoping to find some reason why they might have mistakenly targeted his brother.

He was still waiting for the pinwheel on his screen to stop turning, wondering what he'd done wrong this time, when Giles Kershaw rang in with the results of his preliminary exploration of Augusta Frost's body. He confirmed that she had been killed with a trocar, then sprayed in a mixture of lighter fluid and oil.

Bryant was frustrated and ashamed. That she had died, that they were trailing too far behind the perpetrator, that others might yet suffer. The post-mortems of botched investigations always read the same: 'flaws in the system', 'unfortunate mistakes', 'errors of judgement'.

He swore this one would be different.

31

WHITECHAPEL

Script extract from Arthur Bryant's 'Peculiar London' walking tour guide (Whitechapel, 2 hrs, no weapons)

Whitechapel seems to exist in multiple dimensions.

Once the home of wealthy merchants and members of the East India Company, it has housed French, Jewish and Bangladeshi immigrant communities, welcoming all into its teeming, pungent backstreets, and all have left their imprint. I'd like to have shown you Dorset Street, the infamous 'worst street in London', but it's now buried under a cul-de-sac of squeaky-clean offices.

For nearly two centuries Whitechapel became the sanctuary of paupers and those who preyed upon them, until an estate agent noticed that it was within walking distance of the City of London. Now developers are frantically planting glass towers between the crumbling brick terraces. The new tenants will breathe filtered air in cool grey sanctuaries while below them burst the scarlet, azure and emerald satins of rowdy shop life.

At one edge of Whitechapel was Petticoat Lane, although in a typical London paradox there was no such street. It had once been called Hog Lane and is now Middlesex Street. It remains as chaotic and filthy as it ever was. Some say it gained its name because traders would steal your petticoat at one end of the market and sell it back to you at the other.

For those sensation-seeking visitors hoping to feel a frisson of Victorian evil, it's still the home of Saucy Jack. For the fashionable, Whitechapel hosts basement cocktail bars and blank white galleries. But to those who work there it is still a ramshackle market operating from within the battered shells of the twisted old houses that line Commercial Road.

Longbright took Renfield with her to Whitechapel because he knew the area well. Jack flipped through the pages of the *East London Advertiser* as they walked between the market stalls. 'Says it all, really.' He held up the page to show Longbright. 'Your hot topics tonight: Wormwood Scrubs murder, acid attacks, council corruption scandal, West Ham FC. Take your pick.'

'I remember my dad bringing me up Petticoat Lane one Sunday morning,' said Janice. 'There were stalls selling pets down this end. He fed me a salt-beef sandwich while he took back his bird of paradise. He'd bought it after he'd been in the pub all afternoon. Mum told him to return it.'

'Why?'

'It was a pigeon covered in blue paint.'

'Did he get his money back?'

'No, it suffocated, like that woman in *Goldfinger*. The shop has to be along here somewhere.'

Raj Ranganathan's store front covered the ground floor of a three-storey building with rotted windowsills and peeling stucco walls. A silver plastic sign announced the presence of the Sun-Raj International Export Company, but shared its space with Peet's Anteeks. The unlit ground floor smelled of sage, argan oil and sandalwood. Every corner was crammed with brass urns, ungainly pottery and carpets of dubious authenticity.

They entered and reached the centre of the tiled shop floor, where they heard furious shouting. Renfield caught Longbright's eye and ran for the back of the store. Here they found three men, one attempting to attack the second, being held back by the third. Longbright saw no weapons, only clenched fists. Renfield was taller and broader than all of them. Even so, angered men sought closure in damage, so she kept well back.

'You're a total salad, Jagan, how could you screw this up?' shouted the attacker.

'Calm down, mate.' Renfield pulled out his ID, placed a broad hand on his chest and pushed him back towards the man trying to contain him. 'What's this about? You're Jagan Cheema, right?'

'Who wants to know?' said Cheema, smoothing down his hair and straightening his jacket. He was grateful that the attack had been stopped, but nobody wanted to see the police. 'That's Raj, and that's Akim, his brother,' he explained. 'Raj attacked me.'

'This is nothing to do with you,' shouted Ranganathan, pointing angrily at the officers. 'This is just business.'

'Don't give me any ear-piss, sonny,' warned Renfield. 'It's our business if it involves throwing someone down. Who wants to go first?'

The three all began bouncing around and shouting at once.

'You.' Longbright pointed at Jagan. 'Why is he threatening you?'

'I don't know,' said Jagan, looking at his torn sleeve. 'He's a crazy man.'

'*He* knows.' The other brother pointed at Jagan. 'He was supposed to do a job on Saturday and he didn't bloody turn up, innit.'

'You're the taxi driver, right?' said Longbright.

'Yeah, so?' Jagan was a heavier, less skilfully crafted version of his brother, with a sidelong, wary look that implied duplicity. He couldn't resist checking the line of his suit in an overhead mirror.

Raj cut in. 'He let his stupid brother take his cab out on Saturday when we needed it back.'

'What, so you had to thump him?' Renfield asked.

'He was booked for the night. He owes us. So now the cab—'

Akim took over, pushing Raj back. 'It's nothing, it's our problem, OK? We can sort it.'

But Jagan Cheema wanted the last word. 'My brother is dead, man. Show some bloody respect.'

The Ranganathan brothers exploded. Jagan sprang back and turned to the officers for help. 'They've taken my car,' he said.

'We found the Toyota on Redington Road in Hampstead, and forensics just returned it to Mr Cheema,' said Longbright, 'so why have you taken it?'

'He works for us; it doesn't belong to him,' said Raj, glaring at Jagan.

'I let Dhruv take it out on Saturday, OK?' Jagan replied. 'You know what happened. Hey, shove your job, man. My folks need me in the shop. I ain't paying you nothing back 'cause you owe me.'

The Ranganathans raised their outraged disbelief to an altogether higher level. Renfield snatched at Jagan's collar. 'Let's get you out of here, then they won't have anyone to shout at, yeah?'

'He belongs to us,' said Raj, jabbing his finger at Cheema.

Renfield stepped across his path with ominous calm. 'You don't own anyone, so back it down. Where's the car?'

'It's gone,' said Akim too quickly.

As the desk sergeant of Albany Street Police Station, Renfield had spent his life rinsing low-rung hustlers like the Ranganathans. He stepped closer, darkening the room with menace.

'It's at a mate's,' said Raj, his tone guarded.

Renfield pointed at Jagan. 'He brought it back because you needed it, so why is it now in someone else's hands?'

'Someone – wanted it,' Akim finished lamely.

'Do you always answer for him?' asked Longbright, taking out a pen. 'Don't look at your friend, I'm talking to you. Write down an address for us.'

'He has nothing to do with this.' Akim tore a page from a desk pad and wrote down the number.

'Come on, you, outside.' Renfield seized Jagan's collar again and dragged him from the store.

Longbright led the way to a litter-strewn stump of an alley, still cobbled and bricked, as if the modern world had run out of ideas and allowed the past to return in its side streets.

'You think they had something to do with your brother's death?' she asked. 'That guy looked ready to kill you. Are you working for them?'

'I make a few deliveries, that's all. To dealers.'

'What kind of dealers, sonny?'

'Antiques. Modern stuff. Most of it's made in Morocco, dining chairs like Egyptian thrones, all legit. I sometimes drop smaller bits off at posh houses.'

'Is that what your brother was doing in Hampstead the night he took your car? Did he take over your bookings as well?'

Jagan's attempts to avoid giving out information were starting to fail. He was like a soldier acceding territory. 'I'd done five shifts in a row so I took the night off.'

'What were you supposed to do?'

'Leave the car at an address in Hampstead. The Ranganathans were going to bring me a new vehicle on Sunday.'

'Are all the trips electronically recorded?'

'It's not what you'd call a sophisticated operation, OK?'

'Who has your number?'

'We drop cards off at most of the big clubs, so it could be anyone.'

'You told your brother he could borrow the car if he left it in Hampstead,' said Longbright. 'That's why he took jobs in the area.'

Renfield looked at the ground and shook his head. 'What's going on? If we go back into the Sun-Raj and take their place apart, what are we going to find?'

'I don't know, man. You can try asking Raj but he won't tell you.'

'Forensics found nothing in your car,' said Longbright. 'Do you want to find your brother's killer?'

'There's nothing you can say or do that will bring him back, right?' Jagan held up his hands in defeat. 'I'm not going out there to avenge his death, man. Have you seen what happens to families around here when they start smearing each other? I'm out of the cab business now. I'll go and work in the store.'

'A bit sudden, isn't it?' Longbright tutted. 'A career change, just like that?'

'My brother was in my car the night he died. Don't you have any respect for the dead? You've got the address – go and look at the taxi.'

'I have a better idea,' said Renfield, hauling Jagan along the pavement with him. 'You can lead the way.'

John May's fingers brushed the serrated edges of the photograph. Nothing in the modern world quite matched the power of these neat monochrome squares. This one showed his wife Jane in happier times, sitting on Box Hill, looking out over the North Downs with a picnic before her, laid out on a checked tablecloth with the same precision she applied to meal tables at home. With hindsight he could see the beginnings of her changing mental state: the refusal to catch the camera's eye, the hand that tightly gripped the hem of her dress. Some broken-stemmed flowers – cowslips, he thought – had been strewn carelessly about. The sun was setting, lengthening shadows.

That summer had been a time of endings. It was the last photograph he had taken. Their marriage had not been in trouble then. Neither of them could have known that Jane's illness and his own lack of understanding would tear them apart. When he thought back to the way he had handled the situation he felt ashamed. Nobody had realized how carefully she hid her symptoms. Her medication had changed constantly as doctors failed to agree on a diagnosis. He should have fought more for her. He had mourned her illness so often that he found it hard to mourn her death.

Placing the photograph back in his jacket pocket, he went to the office he shared with Bryant. One of the Daves was attempting to put up a smoke detector with a tool that looked suspiciously like a roller-skate key.

'Where's my partner gone?' he asked.

'I saw him a few minutes ago, squire.' Dave One pointed daintily with the device. 'He had his castle on.'

'His what?'

'His castle and moat – his coat.'

'That's not even proper rhyming slang,' said May testily.

'It's what we say up Green Lanes.'

May knew that the old drovers' route, always referenced in the plural even though it was singular, housed much of London's Turkish community. 'You've been living there all this time and you've never once brought us a tray of baklava? Where was Arthur going?'

'Last time I saw him he was with that mad woman. Bugger.' The skate key slipped and the detector fell out. A rawlplug bounced off his head.

'The mad one. Can you narrow it down?'

'Crimson hair, cheap bracelets, looks like a Munchkin.'

'Smells of garlic,' added Dave Two, who was standing nearby, rewiring a plug with the end of a pastry fork.

'Ah, Maggie,' said May. 'Where were *they* going?'

'To Atlantis, I think.'

'A mythical underwater kingdom.'

'That's what he told me, Mr M. Don't crucify the messenger.' Dave went back to eviscerating the smoke alarm.

May was prepared to put up with his partner's peculiar operational methods most of the time, but now the random disappearances were starting to get to him. *Fine,* he told himself, *let him do what he wants. The rest of us will get on with the real work.*

32

WEALTHY

Maggie Armitage and Arthur Bryant had tracked Percy Pinner to the Atlantis Bookshop because the occult booksellers tended to hang out together, seeing as no one else would talk to them. They usually sat in the back of the Atlantis smoking dope and outlining plans for a new world order, but only occasionally tried to put their ideas into practice as the results tended to be uniformly disastrous.

'He killed again.' Bryant handed Percy the mortuary photograph of Luke Dickinson.

'No more paraphernalia?' Percy asked, looking around for other pictures.

'No, just the first time.'

'Then he achieved the desired effect from the initial crime and now he wants something else. How many times has he attacked?'

'Four altogether. Three are dead. The fourth is in hospital.'

'And clearly you haven't been able to find him. I don't know how I can be of help.'

'I'm not sure either,' Bryant admitted, 'but I try to keep an open mind, even if it means going cap in hand to a bloke wearing a *Game of Thrones* T-shirt. There's a common feature to the deaths. He pierces their throats with a medical instrument.'

'All I know is that he's no magician,' said Pinner. 'But he certainly wants people to think he is. And that's the paradox; if he's succeeded, then the magic has worked.'

'The strength of magic lies in what people believe.'

'Exactly. You say a medical instrument is involved?'

'A device called a trocar.' He took the photograph from Maggie and showed it to the bookseller. 'It comes with limited career choices. Morticians and coroners, mainly. We've already checked the main morgues and mortuaries.'

Pinner examined the image. 'Anyone who has to remove body fluids and make corpses presentable would know how to use one of those,' he suggested.

'Have we missed someone?'

'If I were you I'd try army medical units,' said Pinner, handing the photograph back. 'Working in the field is traumatizing. There was an author who came back from Helmand so profoundly altered that he never wrote again.'

'How does the change manifest itself?' asked Bryant.

'Depression, emotional numbness,' Percy replied. 'But there are other side effects that don't get talked about. I've heard of people developing unusual belief systems in order to cope. Dealing with the dead makes you superstitious.'

'I never imagine you lot on public transport,' Jagan Cheema said as they waited for London's deepest, slowest tube lift to surface.

'Yeah, it's like seeing your teacher at the shops,' said Longbright. 'Where are you taking us, Cheema?'

'These people are seriously rich. I delivered to them a couple of times.'

'And you were supposed to drop the car there on Saturday, but sent your brother instead. Were you expecting it to kick off? Is that why you sent him?'

Jagan regarded Renfield with disgust. 'I wouldn't do that to family.' Guided by his phone, he led the officers along Heath Street. It was the time when nannies collected their charges from private nurseries.

They were now very near the site of the first murder. Even though it was only a short distance from the city centre Hampstead was colder than the rest of the city. Janice wished she'd worn her padded PCU jacket instead of grabbing her summer tunic.

They turned off into a maze of narrow ivy-walled streets overlooked from every angle by greenery. The effect was like strolling through a model English village, except that the apparently modest country homes standing back from the road were no longer owned by artists and musicians but energy traders and trust fund managers. There was no street life, unless one counted the odd trotting fox at night. Windows were shuttered and barred, walls studded with yellow octagonal boxes that indicated alarm systems.

Attempts to keep the modern world at bay had been partially successful; Hampstead was one of the few areas in London that still had its original gas lamps, now wired for electricity. Jagan checked his phone and led them towards Admiral's Walk, carrying on across roundabouts, triangles, dog-legs and the odd gnarled oak. It was the kind of area that had defiantly built its roads around the trees.

'The Admiral's House,' said Jagan, indicating the corner.

Longbright knew that Constable, George Gilbert Scott and John Galsworthy all had associations with the grand edifice that appeared before them, tucked behind the trees. Her teacher had once made it the subject of a school visit. The house had been owned by a naval lieutenant who, according to legend, always fired a broadside from his rooftop cannon to salute a British naval victory. From its quarter-deck to its flagpole, the nautical appurtenances of the white stuccoed building appeared to owe less to the Admiralty than to the film set of *Mary Poppins*. With good reason: P. L. Travers had lived nearby, and had based Admiral Boom's home upon it.

'They lent your motor to the guy who lives here?' asked Renfield, incredulous.

'No, he lives *there*,' Jagan replied, pointing to a nearby mid-eighteenth-century brick house of less individual appearance.

'What would someone who can afford a gaff like this want with a manky old Toyota?'

'I don't know. He's one of Raj's regular clients.' Jagan stopped before the front garden gate.

'Is that his name?' Renfield pointed to a brass bell plate on the door frame. 'Hunstanley Rostov?'

Jagan nodded meekly, his fight gone. He stood back while Janice rang the bell. The door was opened by a pale young woman in an absurd maid's uniform. She might have been supplied by a casting agency for an Edwardian drama.

'There is nobody here,' she announced.

'Where is Mr Rostov?' asked Renfield.

'He is out of the country.'

'When will he be back?'

'We have no date for his return. He lives in Moscow.'

'He had a car delivered here.' He held up his ID card. 'We want to see the vehicle.'

The young woman hesitated in the way of employees who must weigh a request against possible retribution. 'I don't know – I would have to get permission for that.'

Before Renfield became intimidating Janice jumped in. 'We'd like to see it now. Does he have an assistant or someone else who can help us?'

'Yes, but she is in Paris. Mr Rostov does not like people coming into the house when he is not here.'

'We'll clear it with Mr Rostov. This is a police matter. We'll make sure you don't get into any trouble.'

The maid reluctantly stepped back to let them enter, then led the way through a mausoleum of marble, mahogany and brass. Busts of Napoleon and Lenin guarded the central stairway. Looming from the far wall was an oversized painting of Putin, bare-chested and riding a stallion. Whether the piece was intended to be satirical or show loyalty was hard to tell; it looked as if George Stubbs had been commissioned by Mills & Boon.

The maid led them to a sleek steel lift and let them enter. 'There is a mechanic at work on the vehicle. Perhaps he can help you.' She pressed Minus Three.

'From the outside it looks like there are only two floors,' said Janice.

'There are five. Two above and three below.'

'I've heard about these,' said Renfield. 'Iceberg houses.'

'When I was a kid only poor people lived in basements,' said Longbright.

The door opened to reveal a vast blue concrete space with a false sky of twinkling LEDs. At the far end was a cinema, its furnishings swathed in orange velvet. Shallow steps led into an illuminated azure lap pool that resembled a glamorous sheep dip. At the other end of the open-plan floor several cars – a Bugatti, a Rolls-Royce Silver Cloud and an exceedingly rare black and grey Daimler Majestic Major – were arranged in the garage. Janice struggled to understand how watching a film in an atmosphere of chlorine and petrol was in any way luxurious.

The battered white Toyota was parked beyond the other vehicles. A man in grey overalls started when he saw them and began to walk away with studied nonchalance.

'Hey, mate, wait there,' called Renfield angrily. It was the worst thing he could have done. The mechanic put on a burst of speed and jumped into the Toyota, starting the engine.

'Wait, Jack, don't—' Janice called, but it was too late. Renfield had set off like a charging bull. The electronic shutters at the top of the basement's winding ramp had already begun to open. What did he think he was doing? Was he going to try and run after the vehicle on foot?

Then she realized that he had spotted the key box on the wall, and was grabbing the keys to the Daimler.

Vincent Dillard's feet had gone numb. His trainers were not designed for keeping out Hampstead's frosty January air. Perched on a freezing wall, he blew on his hands and withdrew his notebook once more.

'Maid opened door to officers,' he scribbled. The Indian guy was Jagan Cheema. He'd seen the blonde woman's ribbed black jacket and boots before; she looked a bit too glamorous for the Peculiar Crimes Unit. Her sidekick was a bruiser with shoulders like a door. 'Maid admitted officers and suspect,' he managed to write before his biro clogged. The maid hadn't extended Dillard the same courtesy, so he was stuck here waiting for something to happen, trying to figure out his next move.

Some rich old trout in an ankle-length mink came by to threaten him with police removal. 'I know your type,' she warned, stabbing a bony finger in his direction. 'We don't want immigrants here.'

'What are you talking about, you daft cow,' he said, pointing behind her. 'There are your immigrants, in those houses.' Dillard's suggestion as to what she could go and do next wiped a few months off her lifespan.

Clambering off the wall, he thumped some life back into his paralysed legs. He felt exposed here; the streets were so postcard-orderly that pedestrians stood out. He wanted a fag but had just flicked away his last dog-end, and didn't want to vacate the spot in case he missed anyone leaving. He was about to call his editor for advice when the garage door opposite whined and began to roll upwards.

The white Toyota accelerated up the ramp with such reckless energy that it caught the hem of the rising door, cracking the top of its windscreen. The dented roller-door jammed and now another vehicle was emerging behind it, a vintage Daimler that scraped its roof against the door base with a horrible whine as it emerged. Dillard tried to see who was driving. *That's definitely the PCU,* he thought. *Not known for keeping a low profile.*

The cars turned into Windmill Hill, one tailgating the other. Dillard knew neither car could move too quickly through the narrow walled streets. He could beat them on foot and grab some shots on his phone.

Half of the roads looped into dead ends suffocated with thick green foliage. Others were connected by artisanal footpaths. He knew the area well; he could keep pace with them. As he made the turn into Windmill Hill he hoped that the Toyota wouldn't turn down towards Frognal or Holly Hill. He would lose them on either of the wider thoroughfares. So long as they stuck to the backstreets he had them covered.

The Toyota driver panicked and turned right on to Branch Hill, into a labyrinth of deceptive, confounding culs-de-sac.

'I've got you now,' Dillard said aloud, pulling out his phone.

'He knows the width of the streets,' said Longbright, trying to find the clasp of her seatbelt. 'You've not got much clearance.' The pavement disappeared and the way ahead narrowed sharply, enclosing them between high brick walls and trees.

'How much do I have left?' asked Renfield, concentrating on pacing the Toyota.

'About half a foot on either side. You've already buggered the roof.'

'He's got plenty of others to choose from.' Renfield winged a green plastic recycling bin, sending it spinning across the tarmac.

'A Sweeney, *really*?' asked Longbright.

'I didn't do it on purpose.' The Toyota swung a sudden left, catching Renfield by surprise. He missed the corner and removed an urn of chrysanthemums from a garden wall with the right wing of the Daimler, scattering foliage and leaving an untidy spot.

'Maybe we shouldn't be going after the taxi,' said Longbright, growing nervous about the consequences of this escapade.

'We need it because nobody wanted us to find it.' Renfield gritted his teeth and looked over his shoulder as he reversed, then shot forward into another switchbacked street. A Filipina nanny pulled her old-fashioned pram back up the pavement as the Daimler's white-walled tyre mounted the kerb. Some low chestnut branches tore and clattered over the bonnet. Pigeons burst out around them.

'He's getting away,' said Longbright unhelpfully.

'I can still see him. Once he gets on to West Heath Road he'll be bordered by woodland. There are only a few roads he can turn into.'

The Toyota added a burst of speed, so Renfield put his foot down. The two vehicles feinted at each other, the Daimler held back by the Toyota, which slammed on its brakes to force a distance between them. It was like the car chase from *Bullitt* relocated to a miniature village and directed by someone with an underactive thyroid, although the Daimler did manage to burst a potted rose bush and crunch over its shattered pottery.

'Oh, no. It's two-lane.' The road opened out ahead. As

Longbright was thrown against the passenger window she saw vehicles taking turns to let a bread van pass. The Toyota driver had spotted the same obstacle and suddenly reversed. He swung sideways and clipped his way into a narrow side street, removing the awning struts from a wool shop.

'Let's see if this thing does pavements,' said Renfield, turning the wheel sharply and mounting the kerb. The Daimler was essentially a chromium-trimmed Challenger battle tank, and succeeded in mowing down several pieces of street furniture as if they were made from lolly sticks.

Longbright glanced back at the debris. 'Maybe we should call this one in to the Met, see if they have any ground officers on motorbikes.'

'I'm not letting him go now,' Renfield replied as a Wall's Ice Cream sign bounced over the bonnet and an alarmed pensioner stepped into a hedge.

The two vehicles were almost bumper to bumper when a bicycle pulled out ahead. The Toyota swerved, the Daimler swerved harder and a display table of gluten-free fairy cakes went to the winds. Then the bicycle was gone and the route was suddenly clear of vehicles.

Which might have resulted in a win for the Toyota except that Vincent Dillard was standing in the middle of the road with his phone raised to his eye, preparing to get a full frontal of the slowly speeding vehicles. As he seemed disinclined to move, the Toyota was forced to veer left into the pristine garden and alabaster portico of a bay-fronted property worth £12.5 million, which promptly fell apart to reveal plastered-over breeze blocks.

Unfortunately, as the driver deviated he drove over Dillard's right foot, effectively ending any future career the reporter might have had planned as a flamenco dancer.

The mechanic decided to do a runner, which saved him from the whiplash that would have resulted had he stayed in his seat, for this particular customized Daimler, while a superb performance machine in every other respect, had the stopping distance of an Airbus A380 and ploughed into the back of the Toyota, vaporizing it.

He was brought down before he could find a way over an eight-foot trellis fence by Renfield, who simply launched himself like a lump of granite leaving a trebuchet and landed on him from a great height.

'You do realize that legging it makes you look a bit sketchy?' asked Renfield, mainly out of curiosity, his great palm pressing the driver's head into a fertilizer bag.

The driver's eyes pleaded with him. 'I was going to the shops.'

Renfield glanced back in Longbright's direction with an amused look. 'What were you doing with the car before you decided to go to the shops?'

'Checking the engine. I'm a mechanic.'

'Sorry, mate, but no, you're not.' Renfield turned over his hands. 'Not with those nails. You couldn't tell a carburettor from a carbonara.'

'I just delivered it. I was told to clean out the inside and leave it in the garage.'

'So why did you run?'

'They paid me five hundred quid.'

'What, to deliver it a distance of seven miles?'

'Yeah, on the condition I didn't have an accident.'

'Well, you've had one now,' said Renfield. 'I think this voids your contract. Sorry, chum.'

Longbright climbed out of the limousine, which had lost its right wing, the radiator grille, one of the headlights and both nearside hubcaps. Its windscreen was cracked and the roof looked like an elephant had fallen asleep on it.

'That's not coming out of my wages,' she said, looking back. 'There'd better be something really special about this taxi.'

33

FLÂNEUR

'Canal towpaths are a good place to start,' said the architect Stanhope Beaufort, swinging his crowbar.

They had alighted from the train at Cambridge Heath and were walking through the fractured hinterland of East London. Beaufort had shaved off his beard and lost a phenomenal amount of weight since Bryant had last seen him, during the investigation of a vanishing public house called the Victoria Cross. 'Choose any spot where the lighting is inadequate and you'll find them in the dead of night,' he continued, 'the conductors of furtive activity. Usually it's drug deals. Occasionally there's something more interesting going on.'

In the early-evening gloom they passed beside a series of cavernous railway arches, somewhere off the Regent's Canal between Bethnal Green and Hackney. The area had changed radically since Bryant lived here. Now it looked like a smashed jigsaw puzzle. Victorian terraces and new flats were pushed up against gasholders and warehouses, lone buildings had been chopped into workshops, galleries and penthouses, a patchwork of ingenuity and enterprise. London was adept at putting new flesh on old bones, but it had no truck with sentiment either, and was happy to demolish the past for the present.

Bryant stopped while Stanhope hiked his trousers up. 'I haven't invested in new clothes yet,' the academic explained. 'I've been on a weight-loss programme.'

'I'm glad you've settled that,' Bryant said, relieved. 'I didn't know if it was a diet or cancer.'

'I know old people lose their filters, Arthur, but you might make an effort to spare my feelings. It's hemp oil and sprout tops. I feel energized.'

'You look like a deflated balloon. Given the open-plan nature of your office I imagine flatulence presents a logistical challenge. May I ask why you're dieting?'

'I've met a young lady, if you must know. Very personable. She won't go out with someone who can't see his laces. Where were we?'

'I was asking you about liminal spaces,' said Bryant. 'These sausage rolls are still hot. Are you sure I can't tempt you?' He opened an oil-stained paper bag and an enticing aroma of rendered meat enveloped them. Beaufort struggled with his conscience for a nanosecond, then seized one.

'I don't see how I can help you. I'm not sure what you're on about.'

'I get that a lot,' Bryant replied, munching his roll and sending crumbs everywhere. 'I wish I could explain the way detection works but I don't truly understand it myself. It's rather like baking a cake. You have to assemble all the ingredients first, but you never know where the yeast will come from. There's another four a.m. coming. Our killer is using the darkness to hide his activities. I remember a talk you gave, "Nightwalking In London". You said that the city nights used to be far more dangerous?'

'Well, it was murkier then, and parts of the city were off limits to the gentility. When people needed to clear their heads they would lose themselves in the darkness. Night-walking was a pastime, a method of lucid dreaming, but London's no longer a city for the *flâneur*.'

'Instead we have an epidemic of insomnia,' said Bryant.

'I'm afraid we architects are partly to blame for that. Too many bright lights. In the name of safety we established the rules of isolation.'

'They're working late.' As they passed between Broadway Market and the canal Bryant peered through various ware-house windows. He saw earnest young women and men in open-plan offices painted like nurseries, transfixed by the cold light of their screens.

'They don't measure time in the same way that we did. Machines don't need downtime. We can trace loneliness to the seeds of modernism.' Stanhope was now in full expansive lecture mode. 'Think of Wells Coates and his *machine à habiter*, the Isokon building in Hampstead. Today we regard it with delight but at the time it was voted one of Britain's ugliest buildings. Collective housing for left-wing intellectuals, with common spaces and built-in furniture.' He raised his hands high, picturing the scene. 'Think, create and live together, the prototype for a new kind of communal city, that was the dream, but it didn't work. You couldn't expect a group of argumentative radicals to put into practice what they championed in theory. We have the technology to create almost anything that can be imagined, so the steampunk exterior of Lloyd's hides the Adam Room inside it, an eighteenth-century dining hall exported in its entirety from the original building. We can hollow out two-hundred-year-old terraces and hide offices behind the façades, and tunnel under houses to create vertical gardens and artificial beaches. Luxury is a concierge flat where you're left like a mouse in a box awaiting experimentation. It changes people, of course. How can it not? We're breeding an army of psychotics.'

Bryant balled his paper bag, tossed it towards a bin and missed. 'Do you really believe we're doing that?'

'Believe it or not, pricing families out of the city centre seemed a smart theoretical idea. By replacing them with an endlessly renewable young workforce you dissipate the state burdens of age, illness and poverty.' Beaufort looked for somewhere to wipe his oily fingers and ended up using his trousers. 'The city becomes a financial battery farm and the suburbs do the same for families. Look at you, Arthur, and the way you were raised in Bethnal Green, in and out of each other's houses all day long, picking up information in the corner pub while the wives ran networks of hearsay and advice. Nobody lives like that any more.'

'It wasn't all good,' said Bryant. 'The woman next door insisted she got pregnant from a polio jab. They were uneducated people, terrified of poverty, the men drunk and violent on Saturday nights. One night my father went to the Skinner's Arms and somebody hit him with the fireplace grate, but he wouldn't press charges because they were pals.'

'But the way they lived was genuinely communal, not some liberal fantasist's architectural dream. The by-product of efficiency is solitude.'

Bryant chewed thoughtfully. 'The last victim's colleagues said she mostly stayed in her apartment chatting on social media. Surely she must have had some real friends.'

'Must she? Thirty-five per cent of all Londoners say they have no friends outside of work. We used to toil until we were too tired to do anything but sleep. Now we grow as fractious as abandoned pets when we're left alone. People don't stay here for long. The turnover in London is higher than in any other European city. It's a toxic environment. We're suffering from an illness that can only be cured by reconnecting the landscape to communities.'

'Do you think someone could be driven to murder by loneliness?'

'I have no doubt at all, Arthur. Luckily you have John to anchor you and a vocational career you still enjoy. Now, this is what I wanted you to see.'

He stopped before a fence made of wood pallets, placed over a low arch. 'This is just to keep out the curious,' he explained, sliding his crowbar under the crosspiece, gently easing out the iron hook that held it in place. Setting the door aside, he bade Bryant follow him.

Bryant found himself standing beneath a curved roof composed of interlocking amber bricks. He could see arches and waterways folding with the impossible infinities of an Escher print. The air was brackish and mossy. Pigeons scuttled on some distant lofty perch.

'We're in part of the catacombs that were created when waterways, horses and railways all needed storage space,' Stanhope explained. 'The land was seized by the state back in the 1960s, but ownership of these common areas is still in dispute. The council sanctioned the site for the homeless, but no one outside knows it's here. There are places like this all over if you know where to look.'

Dozens of tiny lights shone within a city of domed nylon tents. No sound came from any of them. 'The night lights are part of a security system, just in case there's trouble,' Beaufort explained. 'There's no sense of time in here. Most of the occupants are law-abiding and organized, working on ways to escape the poverty trap. They're good at it, too.'

'So they just eat and sleep here?' asked Bryant.

'No, Arthur,' said Stanhope, laughing. 'They're running ethical companies and eco-businesses. But some are also using their skills to exploit others on the Dark Web. Imagine two cities occupying the same space: the one you live in by day, and the ghost city of the night.'

'I'm not sure I appreciate your point,' Bryant admitted.

Stanhope took Bryant gently by the arm and led him away from the glimmering nylon domes. 'I don't want to tell you your job.'

'But if you had to . . .' Bryant encouraged.

'The man you're looking for lives in this world, not yours. You don't have any way into it, so how will you ever find who you're looking for? You're bound by PACE* and all the other parliamentary regulations. How were you trained to handle every criminal case?'

'Through the five Ws. What, why, when, where, who. And how, of course.'

'The way we gather information has changed. The internet lies; it assumes intimacies that don't exist. When you become active on a social network you find friends you've never heard of, enemies you've never met. It's a gift to the unscrupulous and means that your killer can get his information in a thousand different ways. He doesn't follow the rules of the majority. He won't answer to you.'

'I always thought we were good at finding people who lived under the radar,' said Bryant, disappointed.

'You were, old chap,' said Stanhope, 'but the world you knew and loved so much is fast disappearing. You've been asleep, Arthur. It's time you awoke.'

* Police and Criminal Evidence Act.

34

CODICES

It was getting late. Colin felt inside the rain-spattered plastic carrier bag and lifted out yellow polystyrene boxes, noting the handwriting on them. 'Lamb doner for Meera, chicken salad for Janice, some kind of tofu rubbish for Dan, mine's the mixed kebab with extra chilli sauce, John, the kleftiko's for you. I'm assuming Mr Bryant is making his own supper arrangements.'

Meera peered dubiously into her box. 'Is this processed?'

'No, I saw him cut the sheep's head off. Of course it's processed. It's been through the process of cooking. It wouldn't be edible otherwise.'

Raymond Land dampened the room by entering it. 'Russia is three hours ahead of us,' he said, staring hard at each of them in turn. 'Did you know that? So it's getting on for three a.m. there. Not a time to make phone calls, but I just got one from Moscow. From a gentleman seeking information about a classic car.'

'What car would that be?' asked Renfield as lightly as possible.

'A 1962 right-hand-drive Daimler Majestic Major. The owner recently had a small scratch polished out of the bonnet for four thousand five hundred pounds, so you can imagine how expensive it would be to replace, oh, say, three-quarters of it.' He swung the accusing beam of his attention on to Renfield and Longbright. 'Through the backstreets of Hampstead? What were you two imbeciles thinking?'

'The driver was trying to escape from them,' said Bryant from the doorway, appearing like a superannuated gunslinger ready for a duel. 'They were following my instructions.' It was a risky gambit, seeing as he hadn't been there.

'He's a person of no interest,' cried Land. 'We weren't after him.'

'Let me bring you up to speed on this, Raymondo. John, tell me if I've got it right. The taxi Dhruv Cheema borrowed from his brother on Saturday night was supposed to be dropped off at Admiral's Walk in Hampstead. Instead it was abandoned on the edge of the heath because Cheema's last fare killed him. The car's owner, Raj Ranganathan, has a history of handling stolen goods, and is in the export business. Suddenly he wants his car to be taken to Admiral's Walk and left there. What does that suggest to you?'

'I have absolutely no idea,' said Land.

'A general statement that could be applied to any part of your working life. You may not but I do. Janice, did you ask Jagan Cheema if the car had been in for a service recently?'

'No,' said Janice. 'I'm sorry, it didn't occur to me.'

'Dan, if you'd do the honours.'

Banbury came forward and laid a series of monochrome photographs on the table between them. 'The car came up clean in forensic tests but at Mr Bryant's request I searched the Toyota again and took these.' He indicated a photograph that showed a series of grey rectangles with rounded edges, arranged in rows.

'What am I looking at?' asked Land as the others crowded around.

'I told him not to search inside the car but *inside* the car,' said Bryant.

'They were in the taxi's door panels,' said Banbury. 'He wasn't ferrying stolen goods. The car itself was the contraband.'

'In 2006 the so-called Jordanian codices were supposedly found in a cave in Jordan,' Bryant explained. 'A collection of twenty lead books possibly linked to the Kabbalah. A piece of leather found with them was dated to the first century. Obviously if they prove to be genuine they could change our thinking about religious history. However, the Jordanian Department of Antiquities has been busy debunking them, with good reason, because experts are convinced they're forgeries.'

'Do we have to have another of your history lessons?' Land complained before the others shut him up.

'The lead pages are bound with distinctive metal rings,' Bryant continued. 'Forgeries of this quality are surprisingly valuable. Some were dismantled and sold on the black market to Israeli dealers. You're looking at part of one of the dismantled books.' He tapped his biro at the shots. 'The pages are flat and flexible, and were sealed in protective plastic covers.'

'The Toyota went into a body shop owned by Raj Ranganathan last Thursday and was there for about four hours,' Dan explained. 'I kept thinking, why a Toyota? It turns out—'

'The door panels are easier to remove,' said Banbury.

'There had to be something hidden in the car,' Bryant continued. 'I couldn't decide if we were looking at smuggling or fraud. It turns out to be both. When the vehicle got rear-ended the passenger door broke open. Dhruv Cheema was meant to drop the car off in Hampstead but never made it because he got a call from a fare. When he got to the pick-up point our killer was waiting for him.'

'I don't see how you could possibly know that,' said Land.

Bryant raised his hands in a gesture of obviousness. 'How do the strong prey upon the vulnerable? By getting to know their weaknesses. What do school bullies look for in their opponents? A hairline crack, a fracture that will expose the inner child. Dhruv Cheema had a secret he couldn't tell his family. Over to you, Meera.' He slid a fork in the direction of her lamb doner.

'I asked around online and finally found Dhruv Cheema's girlfriend. She's from Bangkok.' Mangeshkar moved her meal out of reach. 'They were planning to run away together, but he needed to make some money first, which is why he kept asking to take out the taxi. He nearly had enough saved to disappear.'

'Which made me think,' said Bryant. 'If the killer discovered an easy way of getting to Cheema, maybe he had a way of reaching Luke Dickinson too. When Dickinson was ten years old he saw his father commit suicide by drowning himself. You remember Dan showed us two pieces of footage from the bridge, one of a man sitting on the railing and the second one of him falling into the river? What if they weren't the same person?'

'I still don't understand what you're getting at,' Land admitted.

'The killer does his homework. He makes sure he knows exactly who he's dealing with. So when Luke Dickinson walked on to the bridge, the man who was planning to kill him sat on the railing, looking as if he was about to jump. No matter how drunk he was, Dickinson couldn't let that happen. He tried to help but got pulled over the side instead, windmilling on his way down. Cheema couldn't resist one more fare; Dickinson was tricked into being a good Samaritan. He's not just exploiting their weaknesses, he's tapping into their fears. Cheema was afraid of confronting his family. It drove him out to make money. Dickinson had been left with a fear of drowning.'

'What about the girl, then?' Land asked. 'Augusta Frost, what was her weak spot?'

'That should be easy to find out,' said Longbright. While the others ate she called Frost's mother. They tried to listen in but were forced to wait until Longbright had rung off.

'Well?' asked Meera.

'I thought she wasn't going to come up with anything, but then she remembered that when Augusta was small she had an electric blanket. It shorted out and badly burned her legs. After that she was terrified of fire.'

'Could anyone else have known about it?' asked May.

'She spent a lot of time online,' said Longbright.

Land walked over to the whiteboards. 'I don't know where all this pop-psychology is taking you.' The diagrams arranged before him looked like lithographs for Victorian improvement: *The Vessel of Common Sense Founders upon the Rocks of Ideology.* 'We're probably going in a completely wrong direction.'

'Quite understood,' said May. 'We don't want to force the facts into the theory.'

'I mean, what if he's just a violent, brainless nonce who can't sleep and hates people?' asked Land, seizing the chance to extinguish any fancies.

'Wise words as ever, my vermicious friend,' said Bryant. 'But I agree with my partner. Until we understand his motivation we have no hope of catching him. Miss Frost's fear may have been fire but her real weakness was inattentiveness. On the one occasion I met her she was so concerned about getting to work that she barely talked to us, and refused to take the threat to her life seriously.'

'Meanwhile, this nutter may be getting ready to attack again while we sit here doing nothing,' said Land. 'Why aren't you getting more intelligence from the street?'

'We have a surfeit of intelligence but hardly anyone involved in the case has had any dealings with the criminal community or the police,' said Bryant. 'They're hard to find.'

'Mr Bryant, if you can spare a minute?' Banbury interrupted, dangling an iPad in one hand.

'If it's something to do with that device I might need to go for a smoke first.'

'I'm building a bespoke suspect ID program. It's just that Dhruv Cheema thought he had hidden his girlfriend from his family, but she's here in plain sight.' He held up the screen, which showed an incomprehensible sequence of crimson dots. 'He's got two laptops and an iPad all using anagrams of his name and birthday as passwords. His deleted search history was sold to a site in the Ukraine—'

'Then why don't you have the name of the person we're looking for?' Bryant snapped. 'The one system you can't crack is the oldest and most secure in the world. It's untraceable but also unverifiable.'

'Is this to do with cognitive networking?' Banbury asked, puzzled.

'No, it's called talking. Cheema was killed first. He was lured to the edge of the woods, and whoever strung him up used the trocar to torture information out of him. Your pretty screen can't give us the kind of information we really need. It's too logic-based. The killer started with Cheema because he knew what drivers do. They listen.'

'Wait, you're saying the other victims were just *passengers*?'

'Well, he didn't meet them in his mother's saree store.'

'You don't kill to get information,' said May. 'Cheema was murdered outright, like the others.'

'Maybe not. If you puncture someone in the throat and

hang them upside down they're going to bleed out quickly. Think of what we know about him: he's driven by anger and makes mistakes. He wanted to frighten Dhruv Cheema into giving him information. Either Cheema died before he could tell the truth, or because of what he admitted.' He looked at the others. 'The killer hired Cheema's taxi. Perhaps he rang it from a burner or just flagged it down. We need a date and a pick-up location for the original ride.'

'Wait, what original ride?' asked Land, lost.

Bryant rolled his eyes and groaned. 'He's a *driver*. So what do you think his attacker might want to know?'

Land looked at him blankly. 'I have no idea.'

'Really? Incredible.' He turned to the others. 'Let's start on the assumption that at some point the taxi was booked late at night to take a group of people home.'

'Why would you assume that?' May asked.

'Because, my dear fellow, it was an illegal cheap carpool service, and you're more likely to use one of those when it's raining and late and there are no black cabs or Ubers around. So if the taxi dropped the victims off at their respective addresses, moving from the centre of town outwards, perhaps we can follow the route back.'

May checked his phone. 'In that case the drop-off running order would be Augusta Frost in City Road, then Luke Dickinson in Waterloo, which pulls them back to somewhere between the West End and here.'

'The busiest two-mile strip in the whole of London, and we have no date for the trip. Suppose Jagan was driving? What if *he* took the cab out the first time and picked them up? It would mean the wrong driver was targeted. The killer wouldn't have been able to get information from Dhruv Cheema because he didn't know anything.'

'Which means that Jagan may remember something,' said May. 'Let's talk to him.'

Bryant had not quite finished with Banbury. 'You know, just because a computer can make connections using fancy algorithms doesn't mean the killer did. This fellow is visiting old school vengeance on his victims. He tortured a man to death for information he didn't have and is tracking the others down one by one.'

'My program will get there first,' said Dan stubbornly. 'One day soon this technology is going to make us obsolete.'

'I wouldn't be too sure about that,' replied Bryant. 'I work better with a cup of tea inside me. That thing doesn't.'

'Did he just threaten me?' Dan asked, slipping his tablet back into its cover.

The detectives headed back to their own office. May rang Jagan Cheema.

'You're still up, then,' May said as his call was answered. 'I have a question for you, Jagan.'

'Wait, am I on speaker? Who you got there?'

'You don't need to know,' May replied, catching Bryant's eye. 'Did you ever think your brother might have taken the fall for something you did?'

'Man, you can't say that, my brother is dead and it's disrespectful—'

'So you keep saying. I'm sending you a couple of photographs. I need to know if you had these people in your cab. I'll hold.'

Bryant dropped into his armchair, secretly marvelling at his partner's technical agility. He thought of trying something similar with his own phone, but remembered that the last time he had asked Siri to set an alarm it had called him an ambulance. He waited while Jagan received and examined the shots.

'No, I never seen them.'

'You're quite sure about that?' said May. 'I need all the dates your brother took the car out on night shifts, going back to when he first started borrowing it. Text them to me in the next half-hour or we'll come over there and pick you up.'

'The killer must be very frustrated about not getting the answers he's looking for,' said Bryant after May had cut the connection. 'Cheema wasn't supposed to bleed to death. Frost's neighbour wasn't supposed to get a fractured skull.'

May studied the phone thoughtfully. 'Are you still checking British Army records?'

'It's going to take days. Apparently we can't access their database without a special set of permissions.'

'Still worth a try.' May glanced at his watch. 'Just gone one. Three hours to go. I want to look at Jagan Cheema's bookings in detail. This time I'll start from when he first had the cab.'

'That's four years of receipts,' Bryant pointed out, 'and they're incomplete because he told Janice they often left the meter off.'

'Do you still think he has no connection to any of these people?' May asked. 'That they're total strangers who have no idea why they've been targeted? The only similar situation I can imagine is that of ideological murder. A terrorist attack.'

'But victims of terrorism are targeted by chance,' Bryant pointed out.

'So, couldn't it be chance here?'

'It doesn't feel that way.'

'Not very scientific. So let's concentrate on finding a link between Dickinson and Frost. They *must* have interacted with the killer, otherwise why would he go after them?'

'Why are we still disagreeing about the basics?' asked Bryant.

'Because investigations are always marred by bad luck and poor judgement. We track everyone and miss everything.'

'Then we need to return to basics. Examine the evidence;

discern the motive. *Lex parsimoniae*: the simplest solution is the correct one. How can there be no suspects? Stanhope says this is a ghost city, overlapping layers that never touch. He says I'm out of touch, that I don't know what's going on any more. I know one thing: we're more connected and more isolated than at any time in the past. Do you remember we used to go to local neighbourhoods and stand in the street, just letting people come up to us with information?'

'Yes, and a lot of it was spectacularly wrong,' May pointed out.

'But that's how the system always worked in this country. You were convicted on hearsay and judged by a magistrate with no formal training. And for most felons it still works the same way. Every new piece of technology gives rise to something that negates it, so that the law stands still.'

'Arthur, the trouble with you—' began May.

'Nobody wants to hear a sentence that starts like that,' said Bryant.

'—is that you know too much about the past and not enough about the present.'

It was the kind of comment that made him furious. 'But don't you see?' he cried. 'History is all around us. Look at where we are! The Caledonian Road, a two-mile stretch famous for its bricks, its cattle, its prison and, most of all, its *movement*. The Piccadilly and Victoria Lines run beneath the road, and above it run the bus drivers and rail workers and the Cally cabbies. More taxi drivers operated here than anywhere else in London. They had to live where they worked because they stabled their horses at home. It was a lower-middle-class profession, and there was always passing trade for the criminally minded. That's why the illegal cabs and their punters are still here. It's the past that shaped these crimes.' He looked up at his London reference books, arranged according to an arcane system only he understood.

'Each arriving generation is susceptible to the same old dangers. We're dealing with an age-old problem that's been given a modern twist; the crimes are non-sexual and seemingly motiveless, and the only thing we can be absolutely sure about is the time when they happen. I don't know if he'll attack again but whether he does or not, I can't help feeling he's beaten us.'

35

PAINTING

Sparrow had agreed to meet Hugo later because she needed to understand what was happening, both to herself and to him. She had forgotten about the bat patrol she had promised to attend. That evening, as they left the Ship & Shovell and walked unsteadily down the tilted alleyway towards the river, Hugo looped his arm in hers as though he had been doing so for years. As it had on the night they first met, snow danced in the air about them. The uplighters on John Adam Street revealed columns of drifting stage confetti.

Sparrow wanted to explain her feelings but something held her back. Hugo was as silent as a farmer. He spoke little about himself. It was as if he had a sorrow that could not be shared, a wound too deep to be healed. She could sense it within him, unbroachable, and was anxious to avoid any subject that might upset their fragile equilibrium. A few minutes earlier they had shared a kiss that felt so awkward and wrong that she had very nearly pushed him away and fled in fear. She had never thought of herself as someone who might be in thrall to a man with secrets. Yet here they were, still walking together, the backs of their hands brushing against each other.

They reached the end of the street, turning down towards the darkened park and Watergate Walk, the flagstoned alley-way that passed behind Victoria Embankment Gardens. The river glittered darkly beyond. She knew he was more comfortable talking to her when he was away from the light.

'You've been very quiet.'

He had no answer. They stopped before the York Water-gate, the Italianate monument that marked the original edge of the Thames. It looked like a stone gateway to another world.

'I didn't expect this to happen.' Still holding her arm, he turned to face her. His eyes were unreadable.

'What do you mean?'

'You – being like this. It's not what I'd planned. Will you come somewhere with me?'

'When, now?'

'I want to show you something.' He held her close to him.

She felt the effects of the alcohol in the cold night air, and shifted her weight to steady herself. 'Where?'

'Back at my place.'

She laughed and shook her head. 'Oh no, I don't think that's a good idea. Not tonight.'

He brought his face close to hers. 'It's on your way home. I just want to show you something. It would only take a few minutes.'

'Can't you just tell me?'

'It would be better to show you. Please. I'll get you a cab after.'

His persistence put her off. But then he said, 'No, you're right. Not tonight, bad idea.'

And of course that perversely made her change her mind.

*

'Nothing,' said John May, checking his phone. 'It's after four. It's over.' He rose from the table in the operations room and rubbed at his face. 'What a nightmare. How are we ever going to find him now? Where are you going?'

Arthur Bryant stopped on his way to the door and hauled open one red eye. 'Look at these. They're like bruised plums. If I don't get some sleep soon, the next time I nod off might be the last. I'll walk home, although the air pollution out there could take years off my life.'

'You haven't got—'

'Joke. It was a joke.'

May looked up at him. 'Aren't you concerned that he's stopped? There have been no reports coming in from anywhere.'

'I'm not concerned, I'm jolly glad. You can't be sure he's finished. He seems incompetent or mad or both. He might have decided to skip a few days, or it may be that no one will discover his victim before daylight.' He gathered his scarf and trilby from the coat stand. 'If there's any news please call me at once.'

May watched his partner leave with trepidation. It was always a risk letting him out of his sight. The air smelled of stale food. Meera was clearing away the night's debris.

'Why don't you get off home?' he said, opening a window.

She stuffed meal boxes into the bin. 'I guess it wasn't such a great idea, trying to keep this place running all night without the staff. Everyone's knackered. What do we do now?'

'We keep going,' May replied. 'There are still three people dead and three grieving families.'

'Do you think it's up there, among that lot, and we're missing it?' She pointed to the collision of information that had been scribbled over the whiteboards.

'It's possible we've overlooked something. Let's start afresh later. Go and get some rest.'

As Meera left, she passed the detectives' office and saw

that Bryant was still there, looking as if he'd forgotten something. 'Goodnight, Mr B,' she called. 'You look terrible.'

'Thank you, Meera. You're young, you can stay up all night without suddenly turning into a haunted painting.'

He stared back at the overcrowded bookshelves, wondering what he had been intending to look for. Something relevant to the investigation? 'Ah, that was it,' he said aloud, '1642.' He began searching through the shelves.

May dropped on to the sofa in the operations room and closed his eyes for a minute. Just as he felt consciousness starting to slide away, his phone rang.

'I knew you'd still be there,' said Blaize Carter. 'I'm on nights this week too. How is it going?' Her voice was a balm, warm and comforting.

May looked up at the chaos of files, maps and photographs spread out before him. 'I honestly don't know any more. Nothing is going as we planned. Did you get anything else from the fire site on City Road?'

'We had a confirmation on the oil. The looping splash path tells us it was squeezed out of a bottle. He'd moved the body in front of the sofa, which is flame-retardant. I think he wanted to be sure that the body would burn without the fire spreading anywhere else.'

'That seems to fit,' said May. 'He has a plan.'

'It's gone four. I suppose it's too early to tell if—'

'Nothing's come in yet. Somebody has to wait here in case it does.'

'I'd better go. Listen, John . . .'

'Yes?'

'Are you sure you can't make Saturday night? I was going to invite you over and cook something.'

Guilt crept over him. 'I can't, Blaize. Arthur needs me here. We're going to be working right through.'

'But I just spoke to Arthur – I rang his number when you didn't pick up. He told me you're free. Why does he keep your diary?'

'He doesn't,' said May, rattled. 'Let me call you back.'

He left the operations room and went to the office he shared with Bryant. His partner was back behind his desk, poring over a stack of art books. 'Why are you still here?'

'Oh, Rembrandt,' said Bryant airily. He seemed to have regained some of his old energy.

'Did you tell Blaize Carter I was free on Saturday night?'

'Well, we'll probably be knocking the night shifts on the head so I thought—'

'I'm not free. And I'll thank you not to interfere with my private life.'

Bryant looked hurt. 'I'm sorry, I didn't think you might have other plans.'

'I have a private life outside the unit. You should respect it.'

'My dear fellow, I would never have said anything if I'd known you were going to make such a fuss.'

May knew the real reason for his anger, but pushed the thought aside. 'What are you doing, anyway?'

'Tell me something. Why do you think British cinema is so awful?'

'Is it? I don't see what this has to—'

'Humour me for a moment, please.'

May thought. 'I'm sure I've seen a few good British films. *Passport to Pimlico*, that was one.'

'It's nearly seventy years old. Let me tell you why. The British are visually illiterate. How could we be otherwise? We cherish the written word at the expense of the image. We don't know how to read what we see. *The Shooting Company of Frans Banning Cocq and Willem van Ruytenburch.*'

'I'm sorry?'

'We called it *The Night Watch* because Rembrandt's

painting had been coated in dark varnish. I went to see it in the Rijksmuseum in Amsterdam. The Dutch, lovely people, frightful food. It's a painting of a group of arquebusiers, civic military guardsmen. But there's a controversial theory that it hides a murder which can only be understood if one studies certain elements of the picture. It's one of those conspiracy theories people love to expound upon, but there are several strange anomalies in the painting.'

May was rapidly losing patience. 'It's late, Arthur. I have absolutely no idea what you're on about.'

'I do wish people would stop saying that. So, visual literacy. The painting.' He tapped its image with his pen. 'A group of people with a single connection, the militia, are gathered together in one place, and are accused of hiding a murder. You see my point.'

'Yes, vaguely, but not where it's going.'

'A group of people, numbering up to five.'

'Why five?'

'That's how many you can get in Jagan Cheema's Toyota. I'm positive they were passengers in his car, John. They had to be. If it was a ride-share there's no reason why they would have known each other beforehand, which is why we can't link them. The killer started with the driver either because he thought Cheema was the culprit, or because he knew it was one of the passengers in his taxi and didn't have the other names he needed. Taxi drivers listen, so he terrifies Cheema, trying to extract information, then realizes that he's gone too far and that his target has bled to death.'

'And all the black magic paraphernalia?' asked May. 'What about that?'

'He wanted to disorientate Cheema and get news out to the others, to let them know he's coming after them, that they can't escape.'

'You say he's looking for a culprit – what kind of culprit?'

303

'In his eyes they've committed some kind of crime, with or without the driver's involvement. Now he's killing them. It's a bit of a mad theory, but it fits from just about every angle.'

'You're only guessing there were five in the car when this mysterious event occurred. There could have been fewer.'

'But to think that would be complacent. There could still be two more victims.'

'And he kills at four in the morning to catch them off guard?'

'No.' Bryant touched the glossy reproduction of the Rembrandt painting with reverence. 'I'm wondering if he lost someone at that time. Someone he was close to.'

The idea was feasible. 'Someone he loved.'

'A girlfriend. What if Cheema ran her over and the others agreed to keep quiet about it? It would mean he couldn't know which of them was responsible.'

'But the driver would ultimately be at fault.'

'What if even the killer doesn't know what happened? Only that *something* occurred?'

'Wait.' May's head was starting to ache. 'Where can we possibly go from here?'

'We could start by looking at pedestrians killed in road accidents over the last couple of years.'

'Why pedestrians? Why not another driver?'

'Because if you kill someone in a car crash you can't cover it up.'

'So you think they thought they'd got away with it.'

'Yes, but one aggrieved person was determined to make sure they didn't.'

May looked back at the painting and sighed. 'I don't know how you got from Rembrandt to this, but you may be on to something.'

'Stick with me,' said Bryant, flicking his scarf around his shoulders. 'It's not much fun but it's educational.'

May patted him on the back. 'This time you really should go home and get some sleep.'

Bryant looked down into the deserted street. 'I'm not going to get much sleep knowing he's still out there.'

36

TANK

Sparrow awoke to the seesaw sound of a train horn. She took stock of herself. There were hemispheres of tender tissue on either side of her throat. She had a headache, and her mouth was dry. She was not gagged. Her hands were free, but he had disabled her by placing her ankles over each other and joining them with a single plastic cable tie. She picked at it but knew it would prove impossible to remove. She could see nothing. The floor was cold and metallic, and reverberated faintly when she kicked it with her heel. There was a roll of padded nylon beneath her that opened into a sleeping bag.

He planned this, she realized with a lurching stomach. *He knew he was going to bring me here. He knew the first time we met because he planned everything.*

She tried to ignore the throbbing in her head and recall the night before at his flat. A set of spartan, claustrophobic rooms, bright and tidy and dead, filled with cheap furniture and too many lights.

'I'm sorry, Sparrow. I need something from you. I have to know the truth.'

'I don't understand. About what?'

'I was there. In the woods on Hampstead Heath. I was the one you saw. The one in the pig mask. It was all I could find. My son bought it for Hallowe'en.'

She had frozen for a moment, then tried to pull away.

'It was four in the morning. You weren't meant to be there. I'm telling you this because I care about you.'

'Let me go, Hugo.' Her voice had been clear and firm, the kind she used on children in the bookshop.

'You saw me, but I saw you, Sparrow Martin. I saw you. Remember?'

He handed her the bat journal. It was creased at the corners and smeared with mud.

Once again she glimpsed the scrabbling victim, the larger figure rising through the ferns behind him in the ridiculous mask, a silver spear held in one fist. No, not a spear, some kind of weapon. For a few moments it had remained motionless against the trees, outlined in the moonlight. In a spurt of panic she recalled her first assumptions: that it was a perverse game meant to be acted out in secret, something she could not afford to see in its entirety.

She knew now that Hugo had been there on the heath, and that he had killed a man. She should have recognized the odd upright way he carried himself. She did not allow herself to flinch.

'I wore it to frighten him. I told him exactly where to find me.' He gently took her other arm. 'You know what I remember most? As I climbed back up the hill to the main road afterwards I remember thinking *I am a killer now*. In the army we were taught how to kill a man in self-defence but I never had to. I wasn't that kind of soldier. I ran a mobile mortuary. It was a shock to realize that I could take a life just like the others. I can't stop now, not until I know the truth.'

She struggled beneath his hands. 'Please, Hugo. Just let me go. I won't tell anyone, I swear.'

'The notebook had your name and address.' He pulled her closer. 'I couldn't remember where Cheema parked. I reached the main road that wound through the woodland and finally found the taxi. I'd had a plan but suddenly it had gone and I was operating blind. Alone.'

He had closed her windpipe with his strong broad thumbs.

'I was going to move the taxi but I realized I'd forgotten to take the keys from him. I couldn't go back because there was a chance that you might still be there.'

Sparrow did not have the strength to fight him. She crushed her eyes shut in fear, waiting for the worst.

'I had to find you, just to talk to you. I hadn't been prepared for this. I'm so sorry.' His thumbs pushed down.

She remembered hearing the beat of her heart, her blood pulsing with a dull throb. She was floating lightly and feeling no pain.

And she had awoken here.

She listened carefully, trying to decipher the distant noises. A faint thrum of traffic, a fast-fading siren. It was daytime. Why was there no light? She was somewhere below ground level; the sounds all came from above and there was an overpowering smell of petrol. Beneath it the air had a damp acidity, as if her prison had been scrubbed clean.

Sparrow tried to remain rational. She told herself she could work out where she was so long as she stayed calm. He had rendered her unconscious to stop her struggling, not because he wanted to hurt her. He had provided her with bedding, and had not gagged her because he was confident that no one would be able to hear her. There was a dead sound down here that suggested a sealed chamber of some kind.

She knew she should explore and discover the dimensions of her prison, but merely repositioning her ankles was painful. There was no chance that she would be able to stand up. She had one small advantage: thanks to her nights spent bat watching she had no fear of the dark.

There was nothing else on the floor, no food, no latrine. She had to assume he would soon be coming back. The question remained: who was he? She tried to recall their conversation at the end of the night, but nothing useful came back. He was damaged and angry and had done something terrible in the past. He had tracked her down, and he had kissed her. Why had she been spared when the others weren't?

Her need to remain calm and rational was upended by the outrage of betrayal. She had lowered her guard enough to trust him. Whatever else happened now, she knew she would never trust again. She needed to take back control, and the best way of doing that would be to escape.

Feeling around, she dragged herself across the floor to find a wall. It was not far away but oddly curved, so that there was no right-angle with the floor. She was in a tank of some kind.

Now she began to grow fearful; tanks could be filled.

Script extract from Arthur Bryant's 'Peculiar London' walking tour guide (London's Bridges, 2.5 hrs, umbrellas supplied)

The original Hungerford railway bridge was named after a popular market and had been built by Isambard Kingdom Brunel in 1845, a great lattice of riveted steel more suited to spanning New York's East River than the Thames. Later, a rickety boardwalk was added to one side of the rail tracks, connecting the riverbanks so that pedestrians could cross. The southern buttress still has a staircase leading to the original steamer pier beneath. The bridge's walkway was narrow, eerie and underlit, and after the horrific murder of a young man who had ironically survived a London terrorist attack, two new pedestrian walkways were constructed, and the whole crossing was renamed the Golden Jubilee Bridges. However, we Londoners are the ones who decide what to call buildings and bridges, not architects, and the name refused to stick. It remains the Hungerford Bridge.

The skateboarders who slammed and slid beneath the elaborate graffiti pieces on the South Bank had chosen this spot as a place where their old boards should go to die. The bridge's downstream crossing had a flat concrete stanchion far beneath it, and it was here that they constructed their gimp park, hurling their broken-backed boards and turning the inaccessible spot into a cemetery for planks that had been kickflipped to death. Council workers descended from time to time and cleared away the debris, and were booked to do so at 8.30 a.m., but when they arrived on Friday morning they found something else and called the police.

The body of a man in his mid-twenties lay there, awkwardly splayed with one leg folded beneath the other. The night's brief snowfall had turned to sleet, then rain, and had washed away his crown of blood. He lay face down among a nimbus of boards until the workers arrived and were forced to scare away some Italian skaters who were leaning as far back on the railings as they dared, taking selfies with the corpse in the background.

Colin Bimsley routinely monitored the local police digital channels, and heard the call come in. The victim had a wallet, a phone and a name: Rory Caine. He also had a circular throat puncture and a roughly estimated time of attack that made Colin place an immediate request to take over the case.

After the settling of jurisdictional arguments, Caine was taken away by the EMT. The watchers on the bridge dispersed, and because the rainbow-coloured graveyard had now become a crime scene the broken boards were not cleared away, much to the delight of the skaters.

37

HOSPITAL

The knocking continued as Arthur Bryant made his way to the front door, searching for the belt of his red quilted dressing gown. He took off the chain and opened the door a crack.

'Oh, Mr Pitt, it's you,' he exclaimed, surprised. 'I do hope this isn't going to take long because I took one of my pills ten minutes ago. You can't have come to complain about the noise because I haven't been making any.'

Brad Pitt was Bryant's neighbour. His real name was Joe, but due to a misunderstanding on Bryant's part it had been so firmly replaced by the name of the Hollywood star that even Joe's wife had started calling him Brad. 'Not this time, Mr Bryant,' replied the cable-muscled man in the XXXL Arsenal shirt and Doc Martens. 'Although I'm not too happy about the chamber pot full of red ink you threw out of your bedroom window the other night.'

'Ah yes, I should probably have warned you about that,' Bryant admitted.

'Because I put my head out to see what the banging was and got a faceful.'

'Yes, I was getting rid of the dregs.'

'And then I got hit with the chamber pot.'

'It slipped out of my hand. Luckily it was made of enamel so it didn't get too damaged.'

'I would have come up but the window fell down and trapped my hand.' He held up three bandaged fingers. He waited for a response with remarkable patience.

'It was the Black Death,' Bryant explained. 'It hit London in 1348 and spread through poor neighbourhoods like this with alarming rapidity. I was researching contamination patterns and wondered if the unhygienic disposal of waste among those living in overcrowded and impoverished dwellings increased the infection rate.'

'Are you saying I'm unhygienic?' Joe sucked in his stomach to create what he hoped was a menacing demeanour.

'I thought the spatter configuration might reach you but not because you stuck your head out of the window. You ruined my experiment.'

'You ruined my shirt.'

'I find that hard to believe. Besides, the ink was water-soluble, probably. Was there anything else?'

'I thought we'd agreed that if you did anything weird again I'd come up here and pull your ears off.' He took a step back and mustered his dignity. 'That's not why I'm here. Your flatmate—'

'She's my former landlady.'

'She's in hospital.'

Bryant was dumbstruck. 'Why? I thought it was odd that she hadn't woken me up. What's happened?'

Joe pulled at his pocket. 'I've got the ward details here. She was taken ill last night, a suspected stroke. She tried to get hold of you but couldn't get through. She's in University College Hospital.'

'My dear fellow, thank you so much for telling me. This is dreadful. I'll go at once.'

The white UCH building was less than a fifteen-minute walk away. He pulled his tweed trousers over his striped pyjama bottoms and hurried there.

Alma Sorrowbridge looked so much smaller in her hospital bed. When Bryant came in she struggled into a sitting-up position and anxiously smoothed her hair back in place. She had a bruised eye and a pale pink plaster on her forehead. 'Oh, Mr Bryant, you shouldn't have come, you've work to do,' she told him. 'Your breakfast, I made peach and clove porridge last night and put it in the fridge. Did you have it?'

Bryant sat on the edge of the bed and took her hand. 'Stop worrying about me.' He handed her a creased paper bag and a book. She took the bag and focused on the cover of the novel. It was Cervantes' *Don Quixote*. 'I thought I'd better bring you something long and demanding, in case they keep you in and you have trouble sleeping.'

Alma peered into the bag. 'What's this?'

'Just some bees.'

She turned the bag upside down. Fifteen bright yellow furry bees fell out. They came with rolly eyes and green wire clips. Bryant began attaching them to the edge of Alma's pillow. 'I thought they'd cheer you up. What happened?'

'A stupid thing. I slipped, that's all. I was cleaning the kitchen window and blacked out. Gave my head a bit of a bang.'

'You should leave those jobs to me,' Bryant admonished.

'If I did that they'd never get done.'

'Have you seen a doctor yet?'

'Yes, they did some tests when I came in. They're doing some more today.'

'Do you have everything you need? I can bring you clothes?'

'The ladies from my church are coming in this morning. I was going to change your sheets today.'

'Oh, don't worry about that. If they get dirty I'll use a sleeping bag.' He gently rubbed the back of her hand with his thumb. Her skin felt like tissue paper. He knew she had always dyed her hair, but now he could see white roots for the first time. He realized he had no idea how old she was. He didn't know much about her at all because he'd never asked. 'I'll speak to the doctor,' he offered.

'Could you ask him how soon I can leave? I can't stay here. I've far too much to do.'

'Your baking can wait,' he said gently. 'Alma, I'm sorry I missed your call. I seem to have mislaid my phone again.'

'Please stop fussing.' She patted his hand. 'I know how busy you are, Mr Bryant. I just took a tumble, that's all.'

'If anything ever happened to you I'd never forgive myself. And I really think it's time you called me Arthur. I only insist on last names for the first forty years.'

'I couldn't do that. And I'm fine, really. The Lord looks after me.'

'But I want to look after you.'

She gave a weak laugh. 'Silly boy, you can't even look after yourself. It's my job; it's what I'm meant to do. You are the cross I have to bear.'

'Now you're talking nonsense. I'll get the nurse to bump up your meds if you're not careful.' He detached himself from her and rose. Looking back from the blue paper curtains, he saw her sink back into the pillow, surrounded by yellow bees, and thought of all the things she had done for him, the endless meals, the little kindnesses, the unswerving support. He had done nothing in return. He had not even been there when she had fought in the courts to keep their old home in Chalk Farm. He had always been too wrapped up in his work.

It was time for a change.

Doctor Lisiewicz explained that it wasn't a stroke. 'Mrs

Sorrowbridge suffered a temporary interruption of her blood flow known as a TIA, but there's unlikely to be any lasting damage. Even so, we'd like to keep her in for a few tests. Then she'll need to take it easy for a few days. Are you her husband?'

'Certainly not. She's my landlady, and quite respectable. What are you implying?'

'Will you be able to take care of her when she's released? Or do you have a carer of your own who could look after her as well?'

Bryant was indignant. 'I'm a working police officer, you quack, not an enfeebled pensioner. I can manage perfectly well. Will she still be able to cook?'

'She should be fine.'

'Thank God for that. Mind you, she's probably stocked the freezer until the Final Judgement, an apocalypse she is anticipating with the greatest fervency. I dare say her church ladies will be around like a shot, sprinkling holy water on everything, including me. They think I'm a Satanist, you know.'

'But you say you're – a policeman?' asked Doctor Lisiewicz uncertainly.

'Same difference sometimes,' Bryant assured him.

He arrived back at the unit a little after 9.00 a.m., and found May asleep in his armchair. 'I got coffees,' he said loudly, unsnapping the lids as noisily as he could. 'Yours is the faddish one, coconut decaf.'

May opened one eye. 'I drink soy latte.'

'It's all the same, beans and nuts. Alma's in hospital.'

May sat up and pulled himself together. 'What's wrong with her?'

'The doctor says she had a disruption in her brain activity. He wants to keep her in for more tests.'

'I'm sorry to hear that. Will you be able to cope?'

'If one more person asks me—'

'There's been a development. I'm waiting for Giles to call. I tried ringing you.'

'Ah, yes, my phone. I found it. Well, parts of it.' He dropped several pieces of plastic casing on to his desk, along with a few more bees. 'It seems to have fallen to bits. Shoddy goods if you ask me. Can I get another one?'

'You know, detectives spend their entire careers waiting for the one murder case that will make all their sacrifices feel worthwhile,' said May. 'This investigation has left four dead, and you can't manage to keep a phone in one piece.'

'So there's been another victim.'

'Rory George Caine, twenty-six-year-old white male, found with throat trauma and defence cuts on his palms. He lives in Bermondsey, works in Holborn and has a very upset ex-girlfriend who was nevertheless hoping he might call on her. She lives somewhere off Portobello Road, so we have no idea how he ended up where he did.'

'Which is where?'

'In the skateboard cemetery off Hungerford Bridge. Here's a live feed.' He turned his phone to Bryant, who made a show of squinting at the screen for a moment.

'I haven't got the right glasses. How did he get down there? Was he thrown, did he slip?'

'He was directly beneath the walkway. I had these blown up for you.' May turned to his laptop and opened a file of larger screen grabs.

'It looks like some kind of avant-garde art installation.'

'Except there's a dead man at the centre. The cameras on the bridge struts only cover the main pedestrian sections. Dan has some video from the attending officer's body-camera which he sent to your phone.' He patiently set up the footage on his laptop.

The camera dipped over the railing to reveal a male body

splayed upon the bridge's steel deck. 'Frost and Caine allow us a better chance of finding connections between them all on social media,' said May, stifling a yawn.

'You haven't been home?'

'No, Janice, Colin and I stayed on. We let the others go.'

Bryant headed to the window with his coffee. 'That leaves one more potential victim.'

'You could be wrong about who was in the car. There may not be any more to find. Anyway, our job isn't to prevent bad things from happening but to deal efficiently with the aftermath. It's like asking doctors to diagnose cancers before any symptoms appear.'

'So we don't bother looking any further?' Bryant asked.

'I didn't say that. I just don't think we'll get to the bottom of this by talking to booksellers and actors.'

'You never minded in the past,' Bryant muttered, hurt. 'It's how Churchill worked.'

May glared at him, which was a peculiar experience for them both because May never glared. 'You're not Churchill. And I've always minded. I've just never said anything.'

His partner's words wounded him. May had supported his unconventional methodology in the past without complaint. 'I'm not some kind of deranged academic you have to protect while others handle the real investigation,' he replied hotly. 'I get results.'

'Until you don't any more. It looks like we've reached that point now.' May dragged his fingers through his silver hair and got to his feet. He appeared to be at the end of his tether. 'Do you understand what's really going on here, and has always been going on ever since the unit began? It's about class. Whenever you consult academics instead of relying on foot soldiers, the Met teams think you're making fun of them. The ordinary men and women working the blues and twos hate us, especially when you come swanning in at the last minute and make them all look bad.'

'I don't swan intentionally,' said Bryant. Shamefaced, he concentrated on scraping a bit of egg off his scarf.

'Well, I'm relying on you to do it this time because God knows we haven't got anything else.'

Bryant decided it was best to leave the room before his partner could say something he might regret.

38

MISSING

Sparrow tried to explore the tank on her knees, but moving about in this fashion was too painful to continue for long. Her feet were bare and the floor was painfully cold. She still felt half-asleep, and wondered if she had been drugged. Outside and somewhere above the day was unfurling. A single pencil beam of light from a rivet hole illuminated a spot on the floor. She heard a road drill, and later a vehicle-reversing beep.

The floor of her prison was made of welded steel and was wet in places. There was a circular drainage trap at its centre, but without light she could find no way of opening it. She could smell traffic fumes. Her biggest fear was that this would become an oubliette, a locked and forgotten spot about which Hugo would tell no one.

To stem her panic she felt around for her belongings. She emptied the pockets of her jacket; her phone had been taken but there were coins, a comb, a sparkly pencil, her wallet, and nestled in the lining – surprise of surprises – her Swiss army knife. She had bought it with some vague idea about learning woodcraft while she was out on bat watches, but had never used it. Instead it had snagged on her jacket pocket and torn its way through the stitches, falling into the bottom of her coat. It was a miracle he hadn't noticed the weight.

She retrieved it and cut through the cable tie in seconds. She needed goals: find the exit, check out the drain, use the knife somehow. A few months ago she had played a quest game in which she and her colleagues had been locked in a room with a one-hour time limit set for their escape. For that she had needed puzzle-solving abilities, but at the end of the hour the door was opened, revealing a scene not worth escaping to: Caledonian Road in the pouring rain. She told herself she would be less likely to panic if she treated this as another game.

More than anything else she needed light. If she could not see, there was nothing to do but wait and hope that someone would catch Hugo before he returned.

The thin thread of daylight glimmered at the bottom of the wall on her left. Following it to the roof, she stood on tiptoe and tried to reach it. She was just able to brush it with the tips of her fingers. The edges of the hole were rusty; she could see red flakes drift down when she touched it. So, a rounded metal object in disuse, under the ground. A storage tank. Unfolding the knife, she picked at the edges of the hole, enlarging it very slightly. Then she began to yell.

After half an hour she lost her voice and was forced to stop. She needed water, she needed to pee, she needed to get out.

As the full horror of her situation began to bite, a sense of panic tightened around her like the wings of a gigantic bat.

By shortly after 9.00 a.m. on Friday everyone had reassembled in the PCU's operations room with the exception of Dan Banbury, who was on his way back from the St Pancras

Mortuary. He had spent the night mapping all links between the victims via their social networks, and had now passed the collected information to Janice. Colin and Meera had cleared the whiteboards of obsolescent material, Meera had sprayed a disgusting air freshener through the room to remove the lingering memory of Crippen's litter tray, and even Renfield was lending a hand. The ill feeling that existed between the unit's most senior detectives had subsided and everyone was trying to work together, which was never a good sign.

May's phone buzzed. When he saw who was calling he slipped out of the office.

'John, I'm sure you're busy but I need a moment of your time,' said Blaize Carter. 'It's a personal matter.' There was tension in her voice.

'About what?' May asked, his defences rising.

'I know you're seeing someone else on Saturday night. I really don't care but I'd rather you were straight with me.'

'Who told you that?'

'It doesn't matter—'

'Just tell me.'

'Someone in your office overheard you confirming the date.'

He could not bring himself to lie again, and remained awkwardly silent.

'I had to talk to Jack about the fire victim and he mentioned it in passing.'

'Jack *Renfield*? I don't see how he could know anything.'

'It's a police unit, John, everyone knows everything. So is it true?'

Seconds passed. 'I have a meeting with the Market Road community support officer that evening,' he admitted.

'Norah Haron? You're seeing Norah Haron?'

'I wouldn't say *seeing*.'

'I suppose you know she's under investigation at the moment.'

'What for?'

'Financial irregularities in her funding. She's been accused of taking bribes, John.'

'I haven't picked that up.'

'Well, she's kept it from you then. It wouldn't be a good idea to get close to her at the moment.'

'She has a tough job, Blaize, she gets criticism from all sides.'

'Not from you, it seems.'

May held his breath, waiting. He had no idea what he should say.

'Oh come on, John, we're both adults. You know what I think? I think you're never going to change. I don't want to be your enemy, so let's just keep the relationship professional from now on. You need to look at the company you keep, because people like that rub off on you. Look, my break's over, I have to go.' The line went dead.

May felt a hot flush of shame. It took him a few minutes to track down Norah Haron.

'I'm getting some static about you,' he said. 'Is there anything out there I should know about? If we were linked and it turned out you were holding something back—'

'John, I've given you everything I have,' said Norah.

'Did you speak to the other girls? If Cristina remembers anything else about Luke Dickinson it could change the course of the case.'

Haron sounded tired and impatient. 'I already told you I'd get in touch if there was anything fresh.'

'I'll take your word on that. We'll talk more on Saturday night.'

As May rang off, the dead weight of doubt began to press down on him. He returned to the operations room, where his partner was instructing the team.

'Dhruv Cheema took his brother's car out around a hundred

and twenty times, and he usually pooled the trips to make more money. Jagan Cheema says that most of the cash runs would have involved picking up groups from the West End and distributing them around Central London.' Bryant broke off when he saw his partner in the doorway. 'Ah, John, can I have a word with you?'

'Not right now,' said May, distracted. 'There's something I need to sort out.'

'What's wrong? Good heavens, you've the complexion of a potato.'

'Just don't today, OK?' May collected his briefcase and left again.

'What's wrong with him?' asked Meera.

'Woman trouble,' said Renfield with a smirk. 'Not very professional, is it?'

Disturbed by the altered atmosphere in the operations room, Bryant wrapped things up and returned to his own office. One of the pleasures of working at the PCU had always been knowing that the staff liked and supported one another. Now a malignant air was settling through the place, unfocusing the investigation.

Something else was bothering him. Leslie Faraday, the Home Office liaison officer, had been ominously quiet this week, despite all that had happened. While he considered the possibility of a fresh government plot, he looked in on Land.

'Raymondo, my pleonasmic pal, I hope you got some rest.'

'What do you want?' asked Land irritably.

'Oh, nothing. I just saw you sitting there backlit by whatever it is that passes for sunlight in this neighbourhood and thought to myself, Blimey, Ed Sheeran's looking rough. I wondered if you'd heard from Leslie Faraday at all.'

'Oddly enough I have, and I've had his even dimmer brother Nigel on the phone as well,' said Land, who was always bemused by Bryant's ability to anticipate problems. 'Nigel is running an anti-corruption campaign aimed at the police in general and London's special units in particular. They want assurances from us that every step we've taken in the investigation has been documented, backed up and independently verified.'

'Don't be ridiculous, of course they haven't. We don't have the staff for that sort of thing, or the inclination.' Bryant was aware that the unit had a long, ignoble track record of providing bafflingly incomplete evidence. 'It's never been a problem in the past.'

'No, because we've always had Margot Brandy looking out for us.'

'I don't like that use of the past tense. What's happened?'

'She's being transferred to Manchester,' said Land. 'They're severing our connections by removing those who look upon us favourably. We're a non-partisan organization. It's their right to do so if they think we're biased.'

'Even if it means we can't close the case? If they don't want this unit to continue running, they should at least have the guts to say so.'

'They've just said so.' Land swung his chair away, presumably so that he did not have to look his most senior officer in the eye. 'They've got something on us. I don't know what, but it's enough to place us on the list of departments to be reincorporated.'

'A euphemism for the dustbin of history, no doubt,' said Bryant dismissively. 'We've been there before and always managed to survive. I can make some calls—'

'Just stop it, will you?' Land shouted, surprising himself as much as Bryant. 'How many more favours do you have left to call in? Are your ancient parliamentary pals going to overlook four very public deaths and no leads?'

Shocked by the outburst, Bryant could only pop a Fruit Gum into his mouth and remain silent.

Janice came by Land's office with a note in her hand. 'It may be nothing. A woman called Pamela Hickson has just reported a missing person. She didn't turn up for a meeting last night. Usually reliable, not answering her phone.'

Land raised his hands in a defeated shrug that demanded more information.

'They belong to a group that maps out bat habitats in parks,' Janice explained. 'They meet on Hampstead Heath, very near the site of Dhruv Cheema's murder, and now one of their number has disappeared.'

May put Pamela Hickson on his office speakerphone.

'Her name is Sparrow Martin,' said Hickson. She sounded relieved to get the call. 'She's normally very trustworthy, and has never failed to turn up before. I rang her flat this morning but there was no answer. Her mobile sounds funny, as if it's a dead line.'

'Where does she work?' May asked.

'In the Belsize Park Bookshop. I already called them. She hasn't come in. She's usually the first there because she opens up.'

'You must be a good friend to worry about her after this short a time.'

'No, not really. But I remembered something she said. We were on the heath last Saturday night, quite deep in the woods.'

'What time was this?' May asked, leaning forward.

'Well past midnight. Sunday, technically. She came running up to find us. She told me she'd seen something, but we all thought – well, it can be quite eerie being there by yourself, and the imagination plays tricks. We usually split up, you see. It makes tracking easier.'

'You mean she was a witness?'

'She just said she saw someone behaving strangely. That's all I could get out of her.'

'Did she tell the police?'

Hickson thought for a moment. 'I get the feeling she's not comfortable with the police. I told her she ought to report it. And now she's gone.'

Less than half a mile away from the unit, Sparrow Martin waited in her underground cell, not knowing whether she would still be alive by the time the light faded on this new day.

She had now tried everything she could think of. She had attempted to remove the drain in the floor, but there were no screws or bolts protruding. It seemed a smooth, tight fit. She had tried enlarging the rust hole further, to no avail. She had rapped on the wall with the end of the knife, but no one had come.

Exhausted, she fell back on to the sleeping bag and wondered whether he had made the hole himself, so that she would be able to breathe. If that was the case, it seemed that he might be planning to let her die slowly.

'I don't know what you want!' she yelled as loudly as she could. 'I don't know *anything*!'

39

SPY

It was unclear to Colin Bimsley when his antipathy towards Jack Renfield first began. Perhaps it had always been there. The former desk sergeant had been the butt of many a cruel joke over the years, and they had left their mark. His reluctant acceptance into the unit had been proof that he was as good as any of them, but the old fault lines had soon reappeared. One would have thought that the pair could have become good friends, sharing such similar backgrounds, but in the weeks since his return Renfield had grown prickly and secretive. When he was needed he went missing, and when he attended briefing sessions he took a back seat, leaving the decisions to others.

So Colin had done the unthinkable: he had run a check on his own colleague, and found that he had been taking regular meetings outside of the unit. And when Renfield once again ducked out of the briefing on Friday morning, Colin followed him.

Renfield walked quickly over to Tavistock Square, past the Portland stone buildings that still bore the scars of one of

London's worst terrorist bombings. He entered the central garden, passing the bust of Virginia Woolf, moving between ivy-covered oaks and peace memorials.

Colin followed, careful to keep his distance.

There, standing beside a statue of Mahatma Gandhi, was the budget overseer of London's specialist police units, Leslie Faraday. Renfield shook his hand and they walked to a nearby bench. Colin looked for somewhere to hide his conspicuous bulk. He slipped behind a holly bush, but it was a fair distance from the pair. Luckily there was very little traffic circulating around the park, so he was able to catch parts of the conversation.

'You were supposed to report to me last night.' Faraday dug into his briefcase and flourished an envelope as suspiciously as Jeffrey Archer handing over a payment. 'I don't have an open chequebook, you know. I need to justify the expense.'

'I couldn't get away.' Renfield swapped the envelope with one of his own. 'That should be all you need: failure to follow procedure, missed evidence, I don't know what . . .' A van drove past, blotting out some of the conversation. '. . . irregularities are an everyday occurrence. There's more than enough there. So you can pull me out at the end of tomorrow.'

Colin was dumbfounded. Why hadn't he realized what was going on sooner? Whenever Faraday set foot outside City of London Police Headquarters he stirred up trouble. This time it appeared that he'd gone further and infiltrated the unit itself.

'When we put you back into the PCU, the deal was to stay on until we agreed to release you,' said Faraday. 'You wanted to be there because of Longbright, so now you can stay on until we're sure we have everything we need.'

'Janice has nothing to do with it,' said Renfield. 'That's my private life.'

'You surely don't think she'll want anything to do with you after she finds out what you've done, do you?' Faraday lit a cigarette and carefully put the spent match back in its box. 'You'll be free to go back to your old job, of course, but not until we've built a cast-iron case against them. I need you to stay there, Mr Renfield. There may be other tasks for you.'

'You never mentioned that.' Renfield pushed his fists deep into his pockets and looked around. Colin ducked back. 'I nearly got caught out yesterday.'

'Then don't do anything stupid. Use my private line if you need to speak to me urgently. I'll see if I can find you a little extra cash for your time.'

Faraday rose and walked quickly away up the path. Renfield watched him go before heading off in the opposite direction.

Colin had never been fully in control of his anger. He had always managed to thrash it out of himself at the Bethnal Green Boxing Club, but as he stepped out in front of Renfield it got the better of him.

'So, how was Mr Faraday?' he asked with dangerous amity.

'It's none of your business, little boy.' Renfield tried to walk away but Colin blocked him.

'Tell me I didn't just see you selling us out for slush money from the Home Office, Jack. Because if I did, that would be a pretty big deal, wouldn't it? That envelope's got to be packing a fair wedge. A bit old school, though. Nobody uses cash any more. It's too grubby.'

Renfield was taut with resentment. 'If you start with me, Bimsley, you're going to end up in the river.'

Colin placed an unfriendly hand on his shoulder. 'Was stringing Janice along part of the deal? I don't suppose she'll be surprised to hear about your sideline.'

Renfield moved with such speed that he caught Bimsley

entirely by surprise, closing his hand around his opponent's throat and slamming him back against the Gandhi plinth. 'Keep your bloody mouth shut.'

There was no one in the park to witness the confrontation. Colin neatly broke Renfield's hold and pulled free. 'When you spent that month away from us, where did you go exactly? Not back to the Met. Faraday recruited you, didn't he? Nothing ever ends well with that man. Know what Mr Bryant calls him? The bacillus, because he's invisible to the naked eye but highly toxic. Don't you get it? He paid you in cash because when this is over and he's got the evidence he needs, he'll make sure you go down.'

Renfield looked as if he might strike again, but held back his fist.

'Jack, you once told me that you wanted to be respected. You were earning it with us, so why go looking for a shortcut?'

Renfield dropped his arm. 'I've been promised a position in the Home Office Liaison Unit.'

'Except that it won't happen. You've got nothing in writing, have you?'

Renfield stayed silent and immobile.

'Faraday doesn't give a shit about you. He'll shunt you off to West London on airport surveillance, where no one will ever see you again. It's not too late to change your mind.'

Renfield spoke through clenched teeth. 'I already made up my mind.'

'If you're happy, fine,' said Colin. 'Well done. You've just been mugged off by a civil servant with the mental agility of a sock. I was trying to give you a way out.'

'Wait, *you* were going to give *me* something? I'm the one who can close you down.'

'Tell you what, mate,' said Colin, 'you're the one with the problem. What you're doing to Janice? That's sexual harassment in the workplace. She's been fighting off blokes like you all her life.'

Renfield was heavy but fast. His right fist smacked Bimsley's mouth and the left slammed into his stomach, doubling him over. He dropped one knee to the gravel path, trying to draw breath. Renfield stood over him, watching and waiting.

'You all think you're something special, don't you? But you're not. You work for a bunch of flaky old men playing at criminal investigation. You're hated, all of you, by everyone who's a real officer. You're a laughing stock. Remember what I said. One word from you before this is over and they'll be fishing your body out of the Thames.' He turned and walked away with deliberate nonchalance, as if daring Bimsley to come after him again.

It was, Bimsley reflected as he spat blood and pulled himself to his feet, not the best way to start the day. He knew he should talk to someone senior, but part of him wanted Renfield to realize his mistake before it was too late. Nobody liked seeing a fellow officer screw up. Wiping his bloody lip with a McDonald's tissue, he headed back to the office. It was his fight, and he would decide when to act.

One of the caretakers let Longbright into Sparrow Martin's flat in the Barbican complex. 'I don't think she was here last night,' he said, pushing open the front door. 'I know Miss Martin, she's a nice quiet girl. I volunteer at the concert hall, and came past at around eleven fifteen last night. Her lights were off.'

'She might have gone to bed early.' Janice stepped inside and looked around. A circuit through the flat revealed a bed neatly made up with cushions and stuffed animals, mostly knitted bats. Chiroptomania, the love of bats, another word Mr Bryant had taught her. After years of working with him she now had the vocabulary of an Oxford don.

Longbright had long ago developed a sixth sense about apartments. You could quickly tell whether the resident had a close relationship with family and friends, whether they were gregarious or isolated, content or dissatisfied, coping or failing. Those without good community connections often made war with their surroundings, putting bars at the windows and chains across doors. Widows had handrails above their bathtubs, installed when their husbands were becoming ill. Singles had gym equipment but no dining table.

Sparrow Martin had left clues about herself in the kitchen: ready meals for one, a calendar on the refrigerator door that suggested she filled her evenings with too many language courses and yoga classes. A Batman notepad lay on the counter with a shopping list and a hasty scribble: '10.00 p.m. Watergate.' Longbright could only think of two Watergates; one was in America, the scene of the crime that led to Nixon's impeachment. The other was on Victoria Embankment, a public thoroughfare. She stood before the fridge, puzzled. If that had been where Sparrow was abducted, how did he move her? Perhaps he didn't need to. Perhaps she chose to go with him. If they got a cab, they had two choices, Victoria Embankment or the Strand.

Longbright called the Public Carriage Office and put out an immediate request for information. She had a time and place to work with, and one clear description. When it came to finding passengers fast, the black cab company network was astonishingly efficient. It took less than twenty minutes to get a positive ID. They had hailed a taxi on the Strand and taken it north up Holborn Kingsway.

She caught a tube at Barbican and came back to King's Cross, walking up from York Way until she reached the turn-off.

The Keys club was a magnet for unlicensed taxis; drivers could collect drunken fares as they left without jackets and suddenly discovered that it was cold and wet outside. The building stood alone in a half-developed industrial estate of storage depots enclosed by stockades of steel stakes and razor wire. Since the collapse of London's club scene venues had relocated to the city's marginal spaces, where rents were cheap and no neighbours would complain.

She walked past the building's steel delivery doors and roller shutters. Large circular bins stood at the back, beside a pair of storage sheds and raised concrete platforms where the petrol pumps of the old garage had once stood.

If Cheema had come here to find fares, could all of the victims have been inside the Keys? Had they decided to share, or were some of them already in the vehicle? What could happen on a late journey home that was serious enough to inspire such violent retribution?

On the steps at the rear of the building she sorted through drifts of plastic and found several blue and white ballpoint pens, each of them with a ship symbol. The same symbol turned up on club flyers with the initials S&S printed on them. She dug out her phone and checked the Sink & Swim website to see if they held club nights at the Keys. There was at least one a week, but it was impossible to know which event the victims might have attended.

She was about to call the unit when she heard the sound of metal on metal. Backing up, she circled the sheds, waiting for a helicopter to pass before listening again. It was close by; she could feel a faint vibration, a thudding through the soles of her boots. It was coming from somewhere beneath the ground.

One of the two concrete pump platforms had a circular steel lid riveted over it, but the other was not sealed in the same way. Instead, an iron bar had been passed through a pair of rusted hoops on either side of the lid, pinning it in place. Longbright crouched down and listened again. The ringing of metal made her jump back.

She needed her house brick. Hauling it out of her bag, she hammered the end of the bar, pushing it back until it had cleared the lid.

The same bar was sharpened at one end for the specific purpose of raising the cap. When she had finished levering it off she took out her pocket torch and shone it downwards.

'Police,' she called into the darkness. A steel-rung ladder led to one of the old storage tanks. 'Is anyone down there?'

Someone tried to speak but the voice from below was faint and hoarse.

'Sparrow Martin? Are you OK? You're not hurt?'

Longbright knew she should phone in the discovery before going any further, but it was more important to help the girl. She climbed down part of the way, trying not to inhale petrol fumes.

The dirt-smeared girl looking up at her was squatting in the dark, shielding her eyes from the sudden burst of light. 'He took my trainers,' she said forlornly.

Before climbing down, Longbright quickly called the unit. 'Let's get you out of here,' she told Sparrow, reaching the bottom of the ladder and holding out her hand.

'I have a knife but I couldn't get the lid open,' said Sparrow. 'I fell down the ladder.' She pointed down at her bloodied shin like a child looking for sympathy.

'Well done for carrying a knife. That's not something you'll hear a police officer say very often.' She held Sparrow's arm and steadied her. 'Did you get a good look at him?'

'I know him,' said Sparrow forlornly. 'His name is Hugo Blake. I was with him last night and then I woke up in here.'

'Did he force you, drug you?'

'No, I – It's complicated. He pressed on my neck. I think I passed out. It was like he'd done it before. I have a really bad headache.'

'I'm not surprised. You've been inhaling petrol fumes.'

Longbright pulled hard, bringing her out of the shaft. 'Get clear of the top and wait there for a second. Stay in my sight, OK?'

Sparrow heaved herself out and sat down heavily on the concrete platform, resting her throbbing head in her hands.

Longbright descended once more and quickly checked the tank for evidence. She decided to leave the few remaining items where they were, ready for Dan to inspect. When she got back to the top of the ladder and climbed out, she looked around.

Sparrow Martin had disappeared.

40

SOLDIER

Dan Banbury was downloading CCTV footage in the operations room when John May caught up with him. 'Look at this,' said the CSM excitedly. 'It's from one of the Hungerford Bridge cameras mounted on the walkway masts. There's a little pixelation at the edges but it's a pretty impressive image, very little compression-artefacting, no stepping on the diagonals, good deep blacks.'

'I must get you over to retune my TV,' said May. 'Can you run the whole thing?'

'This is quarter-speed,' said Banbury. 'Here he comes.'

They stared at the screen as a hooded figure appeared with his arm around a second man. In a single smooth gesture he lifted the body over the bridge rail, dropping him off the edge of the screen.

'A big lad, he looks like a boxer in training,' May said. 'A grey hood. Is that all we get?'

'We're looking for more,' replied Banbury. 'Time of death, four a.m. on the dot. The other guy is unconscious. A dead weight like that takes real strength to lift. I've started tracing the pair back via the CCTVs. I've got a clearer shot of them on the north side of the river, coming along the passageway beside Charing Cross Station. He's not hard to spot. He keeps his arm around the guy, holding him up. It reminds me of those photos you see when soldiers carry comrades off battlefields. I'm assuming he avoided staircases, which would put him on Villiers Street or under the railway arch leading to Northumberland Avenue. It won't take me too long to trace them right back; I'm just waiting for the footage to be downloaded. My best guess is that he met Caine under the bridge and rendered him unconscious. I've known army chaps who could manage it with a single punch but I've never actually seen it done.'

Meera swung into the operations room. 'Janice found the missing girl but she's lost her again,' she said. 'We have the name of her captor. I told her we're on our way.'

May looked to the coat stand for a clue to his partner's whereabouts. 'I've no idea where he's gone,' he said. 'Has anyone else seen him? No one? Then we'll have to go without him.'

They pulled into the forecourt of the old garage eight minutes later to find Longbright distraught and out of breath.

'I don't know what happened.' She pointed back at the petrol tank. 'I got her out of there. She went ahead of me. I was only down in the tank for a moment. By the time I climbed out she'd vanished.'

'Would she have taken off by herself?' asked May, looking around at the bleak, blank landscape. 'How far could she have got?'

'No, she was grateful to be rescued, groggy from the fumes down there but otherwise OK. He must have been watching from somewhere nearby when I got the lid off the tank.'

'He had to have a car,' said May. 'Could she walk?'

'Only just. She has bare feet. She was confused and exhausted.'

He headed over to the tank. 'Nothing in there?'

'Nothing of his that I could see. She was kept there overnight but not injured in any way.'

'I wonder why not.' He straightened up and looked around. 'We have to let the Met go wide with this. I don't care how it makes us look, we've lost control now.'

'No,' said Longbright, wiping a smear of oil from her cheek. 'We should hold off for a while longer.'

'Why?'

'They'd have to assemble a team and start over. It'll take too long for them to get up to speed.'

'They're going to do it anyway, the second this gets out. Where the hell did Arthur go? Why is he never around when he's needed?'

'He didn't tell me—'

'I'm here,' said Bryant, strolling across the remains of the garage forecourt with his hands in the pockets of his voluminous overcoat. He looked like a senior on his way to the shops, stopping to take a look at a traffic accident.

'You found us,' said Longbright, feeling vindicated.

'Oh, I just happened to be passing.' He looked around.

'We lost the girl,' said May.

Bryant appeared not to hear. 'This is where they got the pens. It's where the event occurred that inspired this whole rampage.'

'What?' May was thrown. 'How do you know that?'

His partner raised a hand and pointed up. 'Wait for a moment. There's a breeze coming.' They followed the line of his finger. Above the building a flag unfurled. It read: 'S&S @ Electric DJ Wite Noyz'.

'I presume the name at the end refers to a young person who possesses the ability to play records in a consecutive

339

order,' said Bryant. 'Rory Caine was picked up here on the night of Saturday, October the twenty-seventh. The club shut at three, so we can assume the taxi was outside around then. Jagan Cheema had dropped off a fare in Covent Garden and was on his way back when he stopped to collect two men, Luke Dickinson and Caine. As we suspected, he already had a couple of passengers on board, Augusta Frost and Sparrow Martin. They'd been to various cocktail bars in the West End and were a bit merry. Can I get a lift with you? My knees are playing up.'

'So you found all this out and didn't tell us?' asked May, throwing open the car door.

Bryant held out a crumpled scrap of paper. 'I just made a few phone calls. Rory Caine's ex-girlfriend still had his clothes at her flat, so I asked her to search through them. She found this in his jeans.' He climbed inside the car with a grunt, handing over the receipt. 'I very nearly missed it. Cheema handwrote them on Sun-Raj International notepads so they're not technically claimable as taxi receipts. He keeps as much as he can off the books. That's it, Rory Caine to Jagan Cheema; we only needed one connection for the rest to fall in line.'

It seemed to May that he was being kept in the loop out of politeness. 'You got a confirmation from the brother, didn't you?' he said, knowing that someone must have talked to Jagan Cheema.

Bryant waved the others towards May's car. 'He admitted he was driving on the night that turned them all into targets. Specifically, he remembered a couple of incidents. After they were all on board, he reversed to get out of the road and brushed against a drunk girl who'd been walking behind the vehicle, knocking her over. He and his passengers got her back up. She was unhurt but angry about tearing her leggings. Jagan was worried that he might get reported so he went back to check on her. But she'd already run off, and he forgot about it.'

'You said a couple of incidents.'

'The other one happened on the journey to City Road, which he thinks was the next stop after the club. One of the lads tried it on with one of the girls and got literally booted out of the car. He hit the pavement hard.'

'We have a name,' Longbright said, 'although it may be an alias.'

May drove to Balfe Street and parked behind the PCU building as Longbright checked her phone messages. 'OK, there are only two Hugo Blakes listed in London. One is eighty-seven years old and the other is a Frenchwoman.'

'So in her case, "Hugo" is probably short for Huguette.' Bryant pulled himself out of the car by grasping either side of the door. 'If Sparrow Martin was in collusion with the other victims, it would be in the killer's best interests to get rid of her. Instead he locked her up overnight, and was presumably coming back for her when Janice arrived.'

'I don't think he's going to hurt her,' said Longbright.

'You can't be sure of that,' said May.

Bryant stood before the unit's optical security monitor and wrapped his scarf over his face until the system became confused and unlocked the door. 'We can't be sure of anything until we've done some more digging,' he said, heading for the stairs, 'but I think I can work out where he's taken her.'

Hugo Blake had watched the PCU team depart from a safe distance, knowing that they would never think of looking in a neat council flat with a brightly painted door and fresh curtains at the windows, a sublet of a sublet owned by a Serbian and a Croatian, once bitter enemies, now business partners running illegal apartment rentals all over North London.

Blake had been briefly happy here with his son, but now it

was time to give the place up and move on. He had a thousand other spots in which he could hide, the kind of places that weren't considered valuable enough to protect and patrol.

Having the girl with him made it more difficult. He had threatened Sparrow Martin enough to keep her silent for now, but he knew she would be searching for an opportunity to escape. He had pulled the hood of her Puffa jacket up so that it covered the top half of her face, and had connected her sleeves with a plastic tie so that it appeared she had folded her arms, but anyone taking a more than cursory look would see that something was wrong.

He could not hurt her. The irony had not escaped him; she had done nothing wrong after all, but she had seen him on Hampstead Heath. She said she would never tell anyone but he knew it was panic talk, the kind he had heard from the prisoners captured by his unit, the ones who would say anything to save their necks.

He dreaded the night. That was when the past returned to haunt him. Twenty-six of the soldiers from Nine Platoon had gone out on patrol in Afghanistan's Helmand Province. A third were killed or seriously wounded by improvised explosive devices. He had been moved to night raids. He remembered the kicked-in doors, the men cowering in corners, their women and children huddled in separate rooms. Four in the morning, when civilians were at their most vulnerable. He had watched them pleading for mercy and had seen them next on gurneys.

For his last tour of duty he was switched to the mobile morgue. The others avoided him because he was the one who cleaned up the bodies, and touching the dead was like passing on bad luck. The smell of death was in his clothes. For a while he joked that he could take care of anyone so long as he had a needle and thread, a scalpel and his trocar. The jokes wore thin. The shunning took its toll.

Then came the fight, the discharge, the return to London,

where things had moved on and nothing made sense any more. His wife against him, his son changed, his skills useless, his friends gone.

What he had seen over there had robbed him of all the things that made him human. Relearning was like being reborn, but it was all too late. Another irony, for he had become a peacetime killer, using the techniques that had been hammered into him for so long.

He needed to keep on the move, to find a fresh place to hide, to think through his actions. So much had gone wrong that there was now no way to put it all right. He knew he would have to deal with the girl, even though he could not bear the thought of any harm coming to her. But he had to do *something*, because if he failed to act she would be his downfall, and he would have failed the boy.

41

CLOSER

Script extract from Arthur Bryant's 'Peculiar London' walking tour guide (Central London, 2 hrs, no refunds)

Tottenham Court Road in 1880, ladies and gentlemen. Grand and Gothic, brick-built and filled with horse-drawn omnibuses. The crossing point of three parishes, St Marylebone, St Pancras and St Giles-in-the-Fields. An area coterminous with the ghosts of buildings lost: the old wildfowl shop with gold letters on black glass, where a Christmas goose could be taken down from a rack of fifty fat birds, and the baroque five-floor building standing alone on Bozier's Court that was demolished to 'improve the view'.

That view changed as almost all of the buildings fell, and searchlights crossed the sky and shrapnel bounced and sparkled on the pavements, and couples made love in darkened doorways, fearing each night would be their last.

And now, newly unveiled, a glass box of a station and a dozen new blank-faced buildings that look as if they've been tentatively mapped by a child with a single pencil and a minuscule allowance of paper. A road of nothing because nobody lives here any more. A parody of personality, a caricature of community. Once there were families who feasted and fought together. Now there are only unintentional visitors, drifting between shops like drowsy pollinators.

Arthur Bryant stopped dead on the street, causing a young woman staring at her phone to crash into him.

'If you'd care to stop checking that your friends have seen your latest online rodomontade perhaps you'd be better able to navigate a pavement,' he admonished.

'You what?' said the young woman, looking up for the first time.

'Boasting, madam, you're too busy doing it to see where you go.'

'All right, Granddad, don't piss yourself.' She snapped her fingers, dismissing him, and returned to her phone.

Bryant looked about and sighed. Tottenham Court Road on a wet afternoon in January. A victim missing. A murderer on the loose. Alma in hospital. The cat dead. John angry and upset. Dark undercurrents everywhere. He was close to an answer now, but the key was understanding, and they were almost out of time. Merely pointing a finger would do no good. He needed to be sure, and to do that it was necessary to reverse the investigation and begin at its roots.

Hugo Blake, a man with an unbearable burden. Life has failed him. The city treats him with unthinking cruelty. Only revenge will silence his voices. He commits a murder almost by accident. Things go from bad to worse. He doesn't know what to do next. He makes mistakes because he has no more planned moves . . .

Overhead a surveillance helicopter hung motionless in the

sky, its unsettling low drone raising the anxiety levels of an already disturbed populace. Bryant turned off into the backstreets, lost in thought. He did not care if the others thought he had abandoned them. He needed to explore one final avenue.

May and Longbright found the barman everyone called 'Rogan' Josh working at an oyster bar in Borough Market. The market had survived since the twelfth century and backed on to Southwark Cathedral. Its canopy, supported by great pillars of blackened iron, had allowed it to retain a dank, sepulchral atmosphere. A few City workers were drinking Guinness at upturned barrels outside the bar, but most of the stalls were closed today.

The two police officers entered a high-ceilinged room that smelled of the sea, full of tall tables, chalked blackboards and boozy laughter. There were pint pots of shrimp, oyster shells, plates of chopped ice and scattered quarters of lemons.

Josh was half-Goan, half-Australian, and pulled weekend shifts at the old Regency Ballroom. 'I keep a diary 'cause I do fill-in work. Let me check,' he said, bouncing back behind the bar. 'October the twenty-seventh? Yeah, I was on shift at the Keys until closing time.'

Janice handed over her photographs of the victims. 'Do you remember serving any of these people?'

Josh studied them carefully. 'Not the girls, but these guys were propping up the bar all night.'

'You sure about that?'

'Yeah, they were pretty boisterous so I kept an eye on them.'

'Was there any trouble? Did anything unusual happen?'

'I thought it might kick off but no, nothing crazy.'

'Why did you think it might kick off?' May asked.

'There was a girl.' Josh shrugged. 'Small, cropped black hair, dark red lipstick, black leather jacket, I think.'

'You've a good memory.'

He laughed. 'I remember the pretty ones. She hung around with the guys for a while. There was something going on, a bit of rivalry. You get a sense for these things.'

'Was she with one of them?'

'No, I don't think so. Just circling. The usual flirty stuff. I remember thinking she was too good for them. There was a ton of gak flying around. Not that they were doing it on the premises because that would be illegal, wouldn't it? This one guy, he was loud.' He pointed at the photo of Rory Caine.

'Did they all leave together?' asked Longbright.

'I think maybe the girl left first, then the others went after. I can't be sure.'

'The two men, did they argue, were they friends, what?'

'I don't know, man, there are just two stations on a long, busy bar. I would only have noticed them if they were throwing punches, and then I would have called Danny. He's the doorman, a bit of a Nazi but he sorts out the aggressive ones.'

'Would he have passed them into the club?'

'Yeah. Weekdays he works behind the bar in the Dog & Duck in Soho.'

By the time they arrived in Soho's Bateman Street it was raining torrentially. January had decided to work through its entire catalogue of adverse weather conditions, like a shop assistant choosing fabrics for an unimpressed customer.

The Dog & Duck was marooned in a pocket of the past. The venerable hunters' inn had amber tiles and a bar no wider than the height of a man, but was now surrounded by junk-food outlets. Old Soho's historical character had been forensically preserved until the day someone decided to rip out a listed fireplace and discovered there was a minimal penalty for doing so.

They found Danny the bouncer under the pub's awning,

having a smoke on his break, holding his cigarette backwards in his fist like a true East Ender, a habit dating back to when workmen were mindful of others in shared rooms.

'I remember them because I remember everyone,' he explained, tapping the side of his tattooed head. 'It's my job. I'm highly trained. If there's trouble inside I have to identify the cause. My work is no different to yours. Absolutely no different.'

Longbright decided to let that pass. 'Do you remember what time these guys arrived?'

'Eleven thirty or so, after the pubs turned out, when everyone arrives.'

'Did they come in together?'

'There was three or four of them, these two' – he tapped May's photos – 'and another guy.'

'What did he look like?'

'Short, black beard, hair shaved off at the sides, long on top. Black hoodie, black stretch jeans, trainers, a bit Spanish-looking.'

'What about when they left?'

'Wait, I need to think, access my memory cells. I guess you have to go through the same process all the time, right? I'm with you, bruv. Not easy, is it? Let me think. They hung around outside. It was raining – that's it, they had trouble finding a cab. We closed up – I'm always one of the last out – and they was still outside. Then a cab came, but there was a couple of girls in it and *that* guy—'

'Rory,' said Longbright.

'Yeah, Rory, he goes, "You've booked a sharer, you muppet," and the other one goes, "There's girls on board," or something like that, so they get in, and I'm waiting for Rogan to finish closing off the till, it's all electronic so there's nothing for him to do, basically a monkey could do that job, and while I'm waiting I see this girl heading towards the cab, and the cab driver reverses and boomps, the girl falls on to one knee, and the guys get out and make sure she's OK, and she's really pissed off and swears at them, a right old mouthful, and one of the girls gets out too, everyone making this big fuss, then they all pile back and the cab heads off but stops again and this time the bloody driver gets out and walks back, well mugged off, and he asks me, "Where did that girl go?" And I say I don't know, mate, try round the back, and he checks around the corner but she's gone, which she could do without going past me 'cause the pavement by the old garage goes to the main road where the night buses run. So the driver goes back to his cab and drives off. End of.' He tapped the side of his shaved head. 'See? Mind like a steel trap. If we were granted powers of arrest I could have taken care of it and saved you the trouble. Or just give us tasers.'

May caught Longbright's eye and took out a photograph of Jagan Cheema. 'Was this the driver?'

'Yeah, that was him,' said Danny. 'I never forget a face. Well dodgy. I'm good with mugshots. I couldn't get into the force because you know, criminal record. Domestic violence so no chance.'

'Thank you,' said Longbright. 'You've been very helpful.'

'Power to you both,' said Danny, genially raising a fist. 'Put in a good word for me, eh? You never know.'

42

TOXIC

Jagan Cheema was waiting for them in the PCU's depressingly lavatorial interview room.

'So, where are we now?' asked John May, seating himself before Cheema and prodding him awake. 'Try to pay attention. We've already got you for handling stolen goods, fraud, trafficking and generally behaving like a dick. That leaves us with the passengers in your taxi. Let's go back to the night you *were* driving, Saturday October the twenty-seventh. What was your first stop after the club?'

'I think it was City Road. I can't be sure.' He twisted on the chair. 'I didn't see anything, OK? Is this gonna take long?'

'Every time you lie to us it'll take a bit longer,' said May. 'City Road can't be more than ten minutes from the club, fifteen at the most. What did they talk about in the car?'

'No idea, mate. I wasn't listening.'

'Did they discuss the girl you reversed into?'

'What? No. It was just the kind of bants you always get from punters in a cab. I just tuned out.'

'No one else could have heard what they talked about

except you, yet the killer found a way to you. What happened to the girl you bashed? Where is she now? Why hasn't she come forward?'

'I don't think she's the person you're looking for, mate. Murder's a bit extreme for a bruised knee.' Jagan flicked a finger at the interview camera's screen. 'You gonna erase this? I don't want it getting out.'

'Worried about your reputation?' May pulled his chair closer. 'Think, Jagan. What could you have overheard that was worth killing for? Passengers talk to each other as if the driver isn't there. They *must* have said something.'

Jagan stared at him in defiance. 'If they did, I didn't hear it.'

Longbright put her head around the door. 'John, can I have a word?'

'What's up?' he asked, stepping out, pulling the door shut behind him.

'We have to get over to St Thomas's,' she said. 'This is one for the books. Rory Caine is not dead. The EMT got a pulse out of him. He's awake and talking.'

Harry Prayer was, emphatically, not a tramp. He might have been wearing a grubby dressing gown, an evening shirt, jodhpurs and rainbow beard-braids but he described himself as a gentleman of the road. He turned down offers of accommodation to remain free, which at the moment involved attempting to sell children's action figures recycled from soft drink cans. Unfortunately they invited the attention of Disney's copyright lawyers, so he had now abandoned his spot on the pavement outside Oddbins and had taken to lurking in alleyways off Islington's Upper Street. When Bryant came searching for him, Prayer popped out from behind some bins and called him over.

'I'm in a bit of a situation,' he told Bryant, taking his arm and hurrying him along the pavement.

Bryant attempted to ask a question without breathing in. 'What sort of situation?'

'One that involves an ecclesiastical charity ball and a shipment of tainted prawn rings,' said Harry mysteriously. 'I was just the middleman. I can't be seen in public until things cool down. The Catholic Church has spies everywhere. First Disney, now them. By the way, I'm sorry about kipping in your basement like that, but you did tell me I was welcome.'

'Next time let someone know you're there,' said Bryant. 'You nearly gave my DC a heart attack. I'd have called you if you had a phone.'

'I do but I'm ex-directory.' Prayer flicked a piece of fish from his dicky.

'Anyway, my own phone fell to bits.'

'Do you suspect tampering? I've seen priests hiding. They could be taking down my circle of contacts.'

'Harry, I thought of you because I need to be introduced to someone.'

Prayer looked at him suspiciously. 'What for? I'm not a dating agency.'

'I'm on an investigation. You're going to the Grievance Service, aren't you?'

'You know I am, you put me on to them in the first place. I come here every Friday afternoon. What's going on?'

'I just want you to take me in with you. I'll do the rest.'

'I can't be seen with a copper. I've got my reputation to consider. Let me think about it and get back to you in a month or so.'

'Harry, don't waste my time, I'm old. Take me in with you or I'll arrest you.'

'What for?'

Bryant eyed the itinerant and sniffed. 'Failure to report an offensive aroma.'

'Yes, sorry about that, I've got a tin of sardines in my pocket.'

'Unopened, I hope.'

'Not entirely. I like the juice.'

'Just sign me in as a friend.'

They made their way to the decommissioned police station that stood on the north side of the street. Across the decades, the London Borough of Islington had overcome its failings only to be hollowed out by success. Once it had been the home of the Silver Hatchet gang, and running battles were fought between the police and criminal families. Now most of the churches and municipal buildings had been chopped into flats and bars, and blue-collar crime had been replaced by white-collar drugs. The undulating, tree-lined street was once more struggling to keep its dignity.

On the steps of the old police station, Bryant stopped and looked up. It was the kind of substantial Victorian brick building that went unnoticed on London streets, but it possessed the graceful serenity of an elderly lady at peace with herself. The basement was leased from the council to house the Grievance Service, a complementary therapy unit that held alternative anger management sessions, acting as a pressure valve for people whose tempers overran their reason. Harry Prayer led the way, identifying himself on the intercom and waiting for the buzz of the door lock.

'The first session will just be finishing,' said Prayer as they entered and signed in. 'The police aren't welcome, although I'm sure they monitor the place. When you're this angry about life you're bound to be on somebody's radar.'

Bryant peered through the wire glass at the therapy group. Its members were sitting in a circle on red beanbags, listening intently to one of their number. He tentatively pushed open the door and entered with Harry at his back.

'I wanted to fill a bottle with petrol and light a rag in it,' said a threadbare-looking lady of middling years. 'Burn the place down with all of them screaming inside.'

'A rather strong response to slow service in the post office,' said the therapist, making a note.

'What interests you in here, if I may ask?' Prayer whispered.

'I've been reading a book,' replied Bryant. 'It's given me ideas.'

'Yes, they can do that,' said Prayer. 'I'm not allowed in Islington Library any more. I wet myself in the reference section. Dante. I got carried away.'

'Best to stick to a Dan Brown,' said Bryant.

'We want to be noticed, not invisible,' said the lady, who was close to tears. 'Surviving is not living. I don't want charity.'

'Does anyone have something they'd like to say to Mrs Johnson?' asked the counsellor, who had pencils in her hair and was digging about in a chaotic handbag. An eager hand went up. It was ignored.

'Anyone?'

When no one else was forthcoming, the counsellor wearily pointed. 'Mr Adams.'

'Bombing is too risky. She should have followed the cashier home, then waited for her child to leave the house before kidnapping it.'

'There are a few weaponized individuals in here,' warned Prayer.

'I know the type I'm looking for.' After listening for a few more minutes, Bryant pointed out a young woman with short pink hair, kohl-rimmed eyes and a lip ring, sitting apart from the others. 'I think she may be able to help me.'

As the session broke up, Prayer made the introductions. 'This is Arthur Bryant, he's . . . an interested party. This is Glennie Wiseman.'

They sat in a corner of the room on the kind of kitchen chairs Bryant felt confident about getting out of. Wiseman was baby-faced but tough, like one of Oz's Lollipop Boys, with a brisk, direct manner. 'I did two tours in Afghanistan,' she explained in the kind of broad Glaswegian accent that Southerners instantly formed the wrong opinions about. 'I know I don't look old enough to have done that but I started young.'

'Why did you join?' Bryant asked.

'There weren't many options left. I had a lot of problems at home, and it seemed a good way out.'

'You returned, though, and you're here.'

'Yeah, but you come back toxic without realizing it. You're not the person you were. There are types of PTSD that go undiagnosed. I had trouble settling. I couldn't find decent work because I had no qualifications. I would do anything, shelf-stacking, driving, jobs that didn't involve dealing with the public.'

'Why not the public?'

'Because I want to kill them,' Wiseman said. 'I quite want to kill him right now.' She pointed at a surprised Harry. 'He stinks.'

'You say *kill* . . .'

'OK, not kill but you know what I mean. I want to grab them and shout in their faces: Do you know how lucky you are? You're here whining about not getting the right coffee and my friends are so damaged they can't walk to the shops unaided.'

'Didn't you have any friends or relatives who could help you?'

'I went into the army because of them. My family don't want anything more to do with me. I only meet other damaged people. I can't afford to go out.'

'You talk about being angry with the public . . .'

'Which is why I'm here.'

'Would you ever carry out a threat you'd made? Now, I mean?'

Wiseman thought for a minute. 'It's hard to say. They teach

us to watch out for stress triggers. I probably wouldn't do anything unless . . .' She stopped.

'Unless?' Bryant repeated gently.

'Unless I lost someone I cared about.' Wiseman sat back and folded her arms. 'Then I would plan my revenge like a military campaign. I'd wipe them off the face of the earth.'

Harry left his old friend with the young woman for a few minutes. They chatted quietly, then Wiseman wrote on a scrap of paper and handed it to Bryant.

'Well, she was very helpful,' said Bryant as they left the building.

'Glennie went off her meds and knocked a hospital receptionist unconscious,' said Prayer. 'Now she has compulsory attendance here. How is this going to help you?'

'You'd think it wouldn't be hard to find a murderous army mortician operating in a tiny area of North London, would you?' he asked. 'I know roughly where he is, but I want to know *why* he is.'

'I'll never understand how a man as intelligent as you fails to explain anything properly,' said Prayer, patting his pockets. 'Can you spare a tenner?'

'No, but you can have whatever's in my pockets.' Bryant rootled about and produced a handful of soft, grubby notes.

'These are rupees,' said Prayer, dismayed.

'There's a couple of hundred.'

'That's just over two quid.' Harry shrugged and pocketed them. 'Why are you not here with Mr May?'

'He's annoyed with me,' said Bryant. 'I don't understand it. I couldn't be more accommodating.'

'But you two never argue.'

'I knew when we finally did it wouldn't be over anything small.' He patted Prayer's shoulder, then hastily wiped his hand. 'Thanks for your time, Harry. I hope the priests don't catch up with you.'

43

MEAT

At the same time, John May and Janice Longbright entered the private room in St Thomas' where Rory Caine lay. There were dark brown stitches in his throat and the right side of his face was blackened with bruises. His head had been shaved, and a white plastic skullcap had been fitted over gauze and presumably more stitches. Ellen Shaw, the ward sister, remained to supervise with the proviso that she could terminate the proceedings at any moment.

'No one,' Caine whispered as they came in. 'Mother, girl-friend, no one.' His voice was thickened by medication, like an audio track running too slowly.

'What do you mean?' asked Longbright.

'Just – you.'

'You've only been here a short while.' Janice studied his vital signs monitor. 'The doctors get their hands on you first, then us, then your family and friends, that's the way it works.'

'My mouth is dry.'

May poured some water into his beaker. 'Did you see him before he attacked you?'

'Asked my name. Pushed me, did this.' He tried to point at his throat stitches.

'How deep is that wound?' Longbright asked Shaw.

'Only surface,' said the nurse. 'It didn't extend to the hypodermis. He was wearing a thick roll-neck sweater. It probably saved his life.'

'Go on, Mr Caine,' May urged.

'Picked me up, threw me. Over railing.' Caine coughed and drank a little more water.

'Had you ever seen him before?' asked May.

'No.'

'So you don't know why . . . ?'

'I don't know why. Ow.' He gingerly lowered his head to the pillow once more. 'Crazy man.' He tried to raise his right hand but it was in a blue plastic cast.

'Stay still, Mr Caine,' warned Shaw.

'Can you give us a description?' asked May.

'Big. Bald. White. Forty, maybe older, don't know.' He gave an aggravated sigh. 'He looked like . . .'

Silence. 'Yes? Looked like what?'

'A murderer.'

'You don't have any idea why—'

'Sparrow.' He shut his eyes.

'Sparrow Martin?' asked Longbright. She knew that testimony taken under the influence of medication could not be admitted, but pressed ahead. 'Do you know where she is?'

More silence. He appeared to have fallen asleep. Shaw tapped Longbright on the shoulder and pointed at the door.

'You were together in a taxi, all of you,' said May. 'Luke Dickinson, Augusta Frost, Sparrow Martin and the driver. Mr Caine, what happened that night?'

Suddenly his eyes opened. 'Nothing.'

'You *do* know what's happened to the others?'

'My head. Can't talk any more. Talk to Sparrow.'

'John.' Longbright drew May back. 'We can't use any of this.'

'We're just doing what Arthur would do. You know what he says. Getting to the truth is the only thing that matters.'

'Do you want me to call him again?' Longbright felt increasingly caught between the pair of them. She did not want to take sides.

'No. He'll reappear when he's ready. Get some rest now, Mr Caine. We'll be back.'

Caine had sunk back into the pillows and closed his eyes once more.

'We're done here until his medication is reduced,' May said. 'He obviously doesn't know Sparrow Martin has been taken.'

The nurse stepped back to allow them out. 'You missed your friend,' she said.

May stopped. 'What do you mean?'

'The old fellow with the hat who smells of tobacco and aniseed balls. One of your lot.'

'What do you mean?'

'English.'

'Very funny.' Shaw was Irish.

'He was here just before you.'

'Arthur already saw this patient?' May was shocked. 'What did he want?'

'I thought you'd know. Isn't he your partner?' Shaw gave him a pitying look. 'If you boys can't keep track of each other there's not much chance you'll be catching many villains, is there?'

'Has he ever done this before?' Longbright asked as they headed out into the wet grey ribbon of Euston Road.

'You know how he likes to disappear, but this is different. You don't suppose his hallucinations are back?'

'I hope not,' said Longbright. 'Didn't he accuse his dry-cleaner of being Lord Byron?'

'George Bernard Shaw. Byron was his milkman. I wonder where he is. Call Dan Banbury and see if he's hidden any transmitters this week.' Banbury had a habit of dropping GPS trackers into the linings of Bryant's pockets whenever he vaporized another phone.

Longbright called the CSM. 'I was going to stick a bug in the lining of his hat but I've been having some problems with the range,' Banbury explained.

She rang off. 'It looks like we're really on our own.'

'He's avoiding me,' said May with certitude. 'In all of our years together he's never once done that.'

Script extract from Arthur Bryant's 'Peculiar London' walking tour guide (Smithfield & Clerkenwell, 1.5 hrs, no vegetarians)

Smithfield, once known as Smooth Field, is one of Central London's most historic and least understood spots, a strange, secular world with its own rhythms and residents.

It has been occupied since the Bronze Age, and was favoured by the Romans. Religious orders arrived. The Priory of St Bartholomew was founded by a fool, the court jester to King Henry I, and a great hospital for the poor was built, but from worship and healing something malignant grew. Smithfield was an execution site where Catholics and Protestants were tortured and burned. The area, always poor, found use as the perfect spot for resting cattle. By the eighteenth century thousands of sheep and cows were being brought to the market, but by the time they had been walked to London they were thin and sickly, and needed fattening. Their waste was dumped into the Fleet waterway and eventually stopped it.

On market days the locals were in danger of being

trampled or tossed by bulls, which were known to blunder through the backstreets, even crashing into shops. At night rapine and murder took place under the blanket of darkness in Smithfield's mean alleyways.

London ran on meat. As the market rose it employed a great workforce and grew a vast dome. The airy colonnades of the underground cold stores were filled with hanging carcasses. The cellars were connected to railway lines, to speed supply and satiate the city's appetite.

The market porters are known as 'bummarees'. It's an eighteenth-century term still in use that feels as if it might be Indian in origin. Bummarees are still initiated by being stripped naked, dumped in meat trolleys and pelted with eggs, flour and rotting offal.

During the Second World War Churchill's boffins planned to take over the market's cellars and create portable aircraft landing strips from icebergs. When you add sawdust to water and ice you can make a shatterproof material called pykrete. The plan was never actioned.

Smithfield's history is still layered through its passages and alleys because it escaped the greatest conflagrations: the Great Fire and the Blitz. But in 1958, two and a half acres of labyrinthine basement caught fire. The building's linings were impregnated with decades of animal fat, and turned into a relentless inferno with only one escape channel – through one of London's most familiar landmarks, the ornate Poultry Hall, which burned to the ground.

Today Smithfield remains a paradox; because its meat market still operates through the night, yet always appears forbidding and deserted, it is the perfect place to hide in plain sight.

Sparrow Martin desperately wanted to be home. She was no longer sure that Blake could guarantee her safety. He was pacing across the chamber now, muttering under his breath, clutching at solutions and discarding them. She could hear odd echoes, clangs and thumps, and recognized an unpleasant odour that somehow reminded her of being in her mother's kitchen.

This time her wrists and ankles had been bound with tape, pieces pressed lightly across her mouth. He had grabbed her as she emerged from the opened petroleum tank and bundled her into a car. At first she had lashed out, but further pressure to her neck was warning enough. He had swiftly bound her, pulled up her hood and pushed her low in the passenger seat, ordering her to stay down. He had sworn she would be safe, that he just needed some space to think, but it was clear that he was undergoing some kind of breakdown. He would rant, then try to stroke her arm. Each time, she flinched and pulled away.

It was a short drive from one safe house to the next. After extracting a promise that she would behave herself, he parked behind some sacks of builders' debris, reached back and pulled the hood from her eyes. She recognized the building at once.

He led her through the ornate painted arches into Smithfield Market. She stumbled shoeless across bare wet concrete and down a stone staircase, feeling the temperature drop with each step. What was she now, she wondered, a bargaining chip? She told herself she was not scared but if he really was without a plan it seemed likely to end badly for both of them.

The staircase opened out into a vast stone undercroft, the ceiling arcing away into the gloom like a structure from a Gustav Doré print. The building was in transition, preparing for its new role as a museum, but the basement still housed the meat store and held the thick, musty smell of animal flesh within its stone walls. When they turned the corner into the main hall she froze. The limbless carcasses of bulls, sheep and pigs, all as solid as tree trunks and monstrously pink, were strung from S-hooks in every alcove like votive sacrifices. They might have been hanging in a gallery created by Damien Hirst or Francis Bacon.

Sparrow tried not to look. The dark irony of interring a sensitive vegetarian in such a cell did not escape her.

He sat her against a stone wall streaked with calcified stalactites, and stepped back with his palms open to show her that he meant no harm.

As he returned and dropped down beside her she tried to push herself into a corner, but he just wanted to remove the tape from her mouth. 'Things went wrong right from the start,' he told her. 'Maybe I should let you go. What would you do if I did?'

'Nothing, Hugo, I swear. I don't care what you've done or why. I just want to be left alone.'

'Alone,' he repeated, as if the word was newly minted. The figure beside her might have been made of bricks. Blake suddenly seemed restrained and helpless, a man contained by his own devils.

'Who are you?' she asked softly. 'What did you do?'

He considered the question, looking off into the dark. 'Don't believe what they tell you about the army. I had a good war. A lot of personnel went through Northern Ireland, Bosnia, Kosovo, Basra, and loved the life. But we had tough, terrible times. I'm proud of being a survivor. It was my wife who didn't make it. She gave up on me. The boy was all I had left. Seb was doing badly at school. I didn't know what was wrong. He explained, and I tried to understand.'

He removed a tobacco tin from his pocket and lit a crumpled dog-end, leaning his head back against the wall. '"Few

die well that die in a battle". *Henry V.* Know that quote?
You'd be amazed how many soldiers do. Shakespeare should
have added, "Few live well after it." '

'What do you mean?' she asked.

'I came back and everything fell apart. I thought I'd be able
to pick up from where I left off, but things had moved on.
Armies are built to kill people and break things. Once you've
learned that, it's impossible to make sense of civilian life.'

He's confused and that makes him unpredictable, she
thought. *He doesn't want to hurt me but he's likely to.* She
was quite capable of staying calm, but Hugo was strong and
his moods were moving like spring clouds. He pressed his
palms over his eyes. 'What have I done? You should get out,
just get away from me.'

'My legs . . .' she said, trying to sit upright.

He tore at the tape and pushed her towards the staircase.
'If you tell them anything I will have to terminate you as I did
them, do you understand?'

'I don't know anything. I swear to you, Hugo, I don't know
why you're doing this.'

She tried not to stumble as she walked towards the staircase,
not daring to look back. There was a rustle of movement behind
her and she turned to see him striding forward. He grabbed her
arm, gripping it painfully. 'You must know something. Just try
once more. What happened that night, in the taxi?'

'The taxi?' She was confused.

'I know you covered it up, you struck a deal with the
others, swore never to mention it. Just tell me who it was.'

'I don't . . . There wasn't . . .' She tried to think clearly.

'There were four passengers in the car that night. How
many of you were responsible?'

'Responsible for what? Nothing happened! I had supper
with some people from work I don't even like, I got stuck in
a nightclub, it was raining, I couldn't get a cab. There was a

364

driver outside touting for work. We went via King's Cross and collected two drunk idiots. We had an argument with them. I pushed one out of the car when he wouldn't leave the other girl alone.'

'You killed my son.'

Sparrow twisted in his arms, trying to look into his eyes. 'What are you talking about? Nobody was killed.'

'You took him from me. He was not in control of himself. He went to a club and died. Severe skull trauma.' Hugo looked past her at the peeling walls, the skinned bodies.

'Nobody hurt your son,' Sparrow cried. 'You've made a mistake. We didn't do anything.'

Hugo shook his head violently. 'I know that. I thought a man with a knife at his throat couldn't lie, but the driver said it wasn't him, he hadn't been there, it was someone else, one of you, I'd got the wrong man. So I pushed the trocar deeper into his throat, but he bled out and still said nothing.'

Only his eyes were visible in the spectral light. 'Once I thought I saw my boy silhouetted against the lamps in my street. I heard him calling to me, I saw his breath appear as he spoke. He was so thin and exposed. I told him I knew he was dead. You could have saved him by showing a little kindness. If we can't even do that for each other what is the point of being alive?'

'You said you'd made mistakes,' she said, trying to sound reasonable. 'What if this was the biggest one of all? What if you got the wrong people?'

'I don't know any more. But there's no going back now.' He pulled her towards him. 'You have to stay with me until this is over. We'll go together.'

He's mad, she thought, *he's got it all wrong. If I insist I'm innocent of whatever he thinks we did, he'll kill me too.*

She had no choice but to let him lead her back into the shadows.

44

BURGLARY

'Well, this is an honour. I haven't seen you for a few years.'
Norah Haron sat back in her chair and lit a cigarette. Here in
the cobbled courtyard of Bloomsbury's Pied Bull Yard she
was the picture of propriety, cocooned in a suspiciously real-
looking mink, sipping hot chocolate beneath one of the
outdoor heaters. The yard was a pleasingly elaborate fake,
tucked in behind the upmarket shops that faced the British
Museum. 'You've lost a little weight. Probably work stress.'

It was just after six, and some of the area's office workers
were having a glass of wine before heading home. In her
boots and padded PCU jacket Janice Longbright felt like a
lumpen interloper among them. All she needed now was for
her radio to crackle and make everyone jump. 'You look
very – respectable,' she replied.

'That's because I am.' Norah rolled a gold lighter between
manicured fingers. 'This can't take long. I'm meeting members of Camden Council here in a few minutes to discuss this
year's funding. I suppose this isn't a social visit.'

'Not exactly. I hear it's hard to get a spot on Market Street these days. How do you allocate spaces to your girls?'

There was a hard amusement in Haron's eyes. 'They're not *my* girls. You know very well there are four spots allowed on that corner and two on the opposite corner. We could fill them many times over. They're handed out according to need.'

'That's interesting, because I heard they're being reserved according to how much the girls pay you.'

Haron ground out her cigarette, the look of amusement leaving her features. 'It's not a hobby, Longbright. These are women in debt and in trouble. There's a big demand. You know I have the full blessing of the council. I'm very well respected in the chambers.'

Longbright ignored her. 'You have a Polish girl, Cristina, says something happened outside the Keys nightclub.'

'There's always trouble near the club.'

'I didn't say it was trouble.'

'How could it be anything else? How do you know about this?'

'I've been putting calls out to all your girls,' said Long-bright, as if it was obvious. 'What, you think nobody keeps their numbers on file?'

'I guess it takes one to know one.' Haron stared back at her, stone-faced.

'Obviously if you knew and failed to pass on the information it would breach the terms of your arrangement with the council. I mean, if the rumour was true.'

Haron sipped her chocolate. 'I have to listen to a lot of nonsense, usually very late at night. Now that I think about it, one of them did say something, but it was all very vague.'

'Too vague to pass on to your police unit? I assume you know we're looking for witnesses in that area.'

'Witnesses to what?'

'I'm afraid I'm not cleared to give you all the information we have. There needs to be a border between us and you.'

'Oh? You used to be a hostess – isn't that what they called them? – at a Soho club called the Purple Pussycat. Don't tell me there was always a border between you and your clients.'

'I always knew where to draw the line.' Longbright opened her bag and removed a folded printout. 'It says here you're currently under investigation for providing incomplete accounts for your funding.'

'You're concerned about my tax filing system, is that it?' Norah smiled, the lines around her eyes deepening slightly. 'I didn't know such things fell under your jurisdiction.'

'I'm concerned about more than that.' Longbright leaned in and held Haron's gaze. 'Your Russian boyfriend is about to be deported for misappropriating online user data.'

'We're not together any more. You see? You don't know the first thing about me.'

'That's true. When I look at you I don't see what men see.' She examined Haron for a moment. 'The professional image is slick enough, a little gauche perhaps, but you could pass. You're a good mimic. You can see how it all works, but you don't quite understand why.'

Haron smiled tightly. 'Perhaps you can tell me what part I'm missing.'

'Miss Stefanov – let's use your real name from now on because simply reversing your first name is a bit obvious, isn't it? Norah Haron, the Gemini with twin names? There's a chain of trust that connects us all, but you've broken it.'

'How exactly?'

'You're sleeping with my fellow officer, and hiding information from him because if he finds out that one of your girls is a material witness he'll not only have to stay away from you, but will have to close you down. You'll be toxic. You'll lose your go-between status and end up back where you started.'

Haron studied her for a considerable time, then tapped out another cigarette. 'So tell me what I should do,' she said. Her pragmatism was almost admirable.

'It's not in your hands any more.' Janice closed her bag with finality. 'I'll decide what to do. If I find you've withheld any information from John May, you will be arrested and charged. Do you understand?'

A portly man and a woman in a boxy blue blazer had entered the yard and were walking towards them. 'It looks like your next meeting has arrived. Interesting that they don't conduct it in council chambers, where there are cameras. I wouldn't bother committing to anything long-term if I were you.'

Longbright pushed back her chair and stepped away, leaving Haron to take her meeting.

'Are you sure you know what you're doing?' Arthur Bryant peered around the hedge and waited for the all-clear. He couldn't have looked more suspicious if he'd been dressed as a cartoon burglar.

'You know better than to question my professional abilities.' Felix Lightly blew gently into the keyhole of the building's municipal blue front door. The low-rise council block was so devoid of distinguishing features that it might have been a stack of Portakabins, and was buried behind a thicket of unkempt hedges. 'It's nice to be working together again, Mr B. I haven't seen you since we broke into that school.'

'*We* don't break into places, Felix, you are helping the police gain access to a suspect's property. I'd do it myself except that I seem to have lost my skeleton keys.'

'Doesn't your partner have any?' He twisted his blank and popped the front-door lock.

'I don't want to involve him.'

'Can you give me a reason why I'm doing this?' He tapped and cleaned the lock. 'Just in case anyone asks.'

'I got a tip from an army vet. Someone she knew lives here.'

'How do you know it's the person you're looking for?'

'I may be wrong but the location is right. The club where the whole thing started is just across the road.'

'Fair enough. I could do with some goodwill from the rozzers at the moment.' Felix stroked his neatly waxed handlebar moustache, then removed his pick and peered at the strike plate again. 'I've got a case pending. You could help me out of a hole.'

'I'll help you into one if you don't get a move on,' Bryant warned.

'I had to get through a Bluetooth lock the other day. A very nice piece of kit. You use an app on your phone to lock it and can set it to open with a timer. It's completely foolproof.'

'Presumably you managed to get in?'

'Piece of cake.'

'What did you do?'

'I stole the phone.'

Felix Lightly was one of the last of Britain's venerable old-school burglars. He had a coat full of hooks, jemmies and keys, and the kind of cockney swagger that only now existed in pockets of Essex and old Ealing comedies.

'You're lucky you caught me,' he said. 'I just come off a well booky little job. I get a call from this fella, can't divulge his name, says he needs to get back something he bought for his wife before she files for divorce, a mid-nineteenth-century French cameo brooch inset with sapphires and emeralds, worth a packet. He's the owner of this grand old country house called Tavistock Hall, huge bloody place with a gravel courtyard and a circular fountain, very sheesh.'

'I know it,' said Bryant. 'John and I once solved a murder there.'

'Right, so, he's beggin' it, desperate for me to help him out, but it sounds like he's got it all sussed, and I can't see why he needs me on the job at all. So I meet up with him and he's tiny, dressed in a red hoodie, looks like the dwarf in *Don't Look Now*, gave me quite a turn. Hang on.' He took out a set of Allen keys and began inserting them into the lock. 'And I can see the problem. He's too short to get the window catches unlocked. This is the middle of the day, right, the wife's on holiday with her Soho House coven so we've got the run of the place. Look at the state of this lock, my granddad could open it with a bent pin and he's on a ventilator.' He twisted the keys and the door swung inwards. 'So we reach an agreement: he gets some private letters he needs plus the brooch, which we'll fence and split the take. I have to open the locks and seal 'em again after, so he needs a professional. I do my part, he whips in and gets the stuff, I'm still up the ladder, and as he comes out he hands me the brooch and somehow we fumble the pass and the brooch falls between us, and I see it splash into the pool of the fountain. So we go down and I roll up my sleeves and start looking for it, and all I find is stones and coins, all the stuff people can't resist chucking in whenever they see an expanse of water belonging to toffs. And I says, "It must have gone down the drainage pipe," but luckily he knows where it comes out so we go down there, I take the grille off and start fishing about in the muck. I'm doing that for half an hour before I realize he's buggered off.'

'Well, *of course* he'd gone,' said Bryant impatiently.

'What do you mean?'

'He didn't own the hall, there weren't any letters, but he knew about the brooch and he needed you to help him get it. So to be rid of you he palmed the brooch as he handed it to you – you were presumably hanging on to the ladder at this point – and dropped a pebble into the pond. It's called persistence of vision, Felix. Your mind played a trick on you and told you that you'd seen it fall into the fountain.'

'Blimey,' said Felix, 'you can't trust anyone nowadays.'

'That's the trouble with the criminal fraternity, you're all so naïve.' Bryant entered the building, stopping to tip a scrap of paper to the hall light. 'Second floor, Flat Three.'

The flat was opposite the lift doors. 'Now this is more interesting.' Felix bent over the door lock. 'The regular strike plate is cheap rubbish, but your suspect knows that so he's reinforced it with an anti-tamper restrictor *and* he's added an extra portable lock made of chrome-plated carbon steel.'

Bryant gritted his dentures. 'Is that going to be a problem?'

Felix pulled down a magnifying lens from his headband and peered through the door edge. 'No, because every lock has the same weakness.'

'Which is?'

'It's only as strong as the door.'

Felix produced a small circular saw and cut a neat semi-circle. Then he turned around and kicked like a horse. The lock remained in place but the rest of the door swung in.

'I guess he'll know he's had a visitor,' said Bryant. 'Everyone in the building must have heard you.'

'There's no one else around,' said Felix, stepping inside. 'To my professional eye this looks like one of the last occupied properties on the estate. The council is rehousing all the tenants. There's too much criminal activity here.'

'That'll be you then.'

'I'm in a traditional trade. You should thank me for not joining the Brexit brain drain.' Felix took a bow.

'I just thought your approach would be more sophisticated.'

'A fair point. After all, you are looking at the felon who once burgled the Duchess of Devonshire's country seat. Purely an academic exercise. She wanted to see if I could lift her Klimt.'

'Yes, but you went to jail for keeping it,' Bryant pointed out.

' "Property is theft," Pierre-Joseph Proudhon, French anarchist. In you go; I'll just be outside. Don't do anything illegal.'

A tiled kitchen, a basically furnished living room, one bathroom, two bedrooms, one of them barely larger than a single bed. Everything beige, white or caramel, the colours of cheapness. An apartment suited to a single parent and a small child. The walls were thin, the windows small and mean, the fittings utilitarian. What kind of life would an energetic kid have in here, where no noise could be made and there was little more space than a jail cell?

'Where are you, Hugo?' Bryant asked aloud. 'What happened to you?'

In the kitchen he found clues. A dinner service with a floral pattern that Blake had recently purchased, leaving the price stickers on, cupboards kitted out with brand-new culinary tools. Most of it had never been used. One mug and one plate had been washed up and left on the draining board. An empty fridge, a stack of identical ready-meals in the freezer.

'It's sad that people still grow up in places like this,' Bryant murmured. 'Our old flat in Whitechapel was about the same size. No bathroom or toilet, though.' He studied the unopened bills, a school letter, a summons, flicked them back on to the kitchen counter and looked about for further evidence. Different sized trainers in the hall. 'Two people here, not one. A man and a boy.'

'What's that, Mr B?' asked Felix.

'Just talking to myself,' said Bryant. A father and son. But there was something else. A loss. He looked around, opened cupboards, lifted rugs. The living room next. TV guides torn from newspapers, stacked beside an old easy chair. Half of the furniture had been bought by a couple, the other half added at a later date by a man. A magazine rack contained copies of *What Car?* and *Military World* but also an issue of *PC Gamer.* Drawers were in disarray. All personal items had been taken away. *He changed locations in a rush*, Bryant thought.

When he went to the main bedroom he saw that there was something missing from a top shelf, drag-marks in the dust where people always kept bags and suitcases. Climbing unsteadily on to a chair, he felt about and retrieved an army luggage tag. In the bottom of an old-fashioned wardrobe he found a shoebox of photographs and a scrapbook.

The smaller bedroom had been preserved untouched. Old movie posters and stickers still covered the walls, along with Freddie Mercury, David Bowie, Sam Smith, a Greek temple, a Roman statue of Sporus, Aztec ruins. Bryant took photographs on his phone. A stack of schoolbooks sat on a stool beside the bed: *1984, Howards End, Twelfth Night, The Tempest, Gormenghast, His Dark Materials.* Beneath them was an old essay: 'If you could be any character from Shakespeare's plays, who would you be?' The writer had been awarded an A+. The handwriting was small and laboriously perfect, as if copied from a book on calligraphy.

He began to form an image of the bedroom's occupant. He leafed through an incongruous mix of magazines, stopping at an ancient issue of *Vanity Fair.* Something wasn't right.

'This is the first time I've actually seen you working, Mr B,' said Felix, replacing the last of the tools in his bag. 'I can hear your brain turning over like a bit of rusty farm machinery. Found what you need?'

'I've found all the pieces but they don't fit,' said Bryant, stretching out his fingertips. The story was here, if only he could make sense of it. 'There's still one bit missing, but I'll be blowed if I can see what it is.'

'You'll have to get the others to help you.' Felix headed out with his burglary kit. 'You've got a good team there; you should use it.'

'That's the one thing I can't do,' said Bryant. He took one last lingering look, then pulled the mutilated door shut behind him.

45

CORRUPTION

'He's like some mythical creature, a Will-o'-the-Wisp, able to come and go without anyone seeing him,' said Raymond Land. 'How is that possible?' He looked like the startled survivor of some kind of disaster, a factory explosion perhaps, or a bridge collapse, unkempt and bewildered and waiting for help.

'We'll catch him,' May assured his boss.

'Not the killer, you imbecile, your partner. Like some human equivalent of Brigadoon, periodically visible to passing strangers, then poof – vanished, and he's meant to be here, bailing us out of this nightmare. That girl could be dead by now.'

'And she could still be alive,' said May. 'The others are covering the streets around the Keys club.'

Land stuck his hands on his hips and looked around. 'Well, let's see. Janice is following a lead, Dan's on all fours in the operations room trying to rewire something and presumably you're not a mirage, so who's out there? Renfield, Bimsley and Mangeshkar, the PCU's elite homicide team, two former

PCs and a bloke who doesn't want to be here. That's "covering the streets", is it? Perhaps we can send the two Daves out as back-up. It's pathetic. The Met's in the middle of being reorganized into a new acronym so they can't spare anyone, not that they'd help us if they could, and we haven't got anyone to begin with because one half of our senior detective team has gone off to Narnia again.'

'You could do something,' said May.

'I'm overseeing the operation, aren't I?' said Land testily. 'Executive management. Someone has to do the strategic thinking. You have to get your partner back, John. Whatever happened between you, you have to put it right.'

May was stumped. 'He executed the others but took her. Why?'

'She's the last of the five in the car. Maybe that's your answer. She's his only way out. He knows he's going to be caught. I had a mate in the army who said: "Always leave yourself an option." She's part of his endgame.'

'You could be right,' said May.

'Try to sound less amazed,' Land suggested. 'I want you to find Bryant. It's not that I don't have faith in your abilities but I'd feel much happier if our final moments in full employment were enjoyed by all staff. Isn't there anyone you can call?'

'I tried Maggie, but she hasn't seen him today. We all know Arthur has a habit of wandering off, but I'm sure he's trying to close the case as quickly as possible.'

'Why do you always stick up for him?' Land snapped. 'He's left you here to carry the can. There's a girl out there probably terrified out of her wits, and if she dies it will be laid on us. Faraday's threatening to send a team over to padlock our doors—'

'He tried that before,' said May. 'We took the handles off.'

'You think this is all a game, do you? All this death and no one accountable? This isn't another East End territory fight, it's a psychotic who can strike anywhere, and that means nobody is safe.'

'You mean white people aren't safe,' said May, 'which is why the Home Office is suddenly interested.'

'You dare to level that accusation at me?' said Land, taken aback.

'I'm not saying you're racist, Raymond, but it doesn't help if you just parrot Home Office policy.'

'Who do you think pays our wages?' Land had had enough of this. 'You're living in a bubble, May. The new HO recruits have written us off as a bunch of delusional liberals. It's a new world now. Past achievements count for nothing in the mind of a twenty-five-year-old civil servant looking for career advancement.' He raised his hands in surrender. 'I've gone out on a limb for you again and again but you know what? I'm done. If you can't figure out why Bryant is avoiding you, you're blinder than I ever imagined.'

'What are you talking about?' asked May.

Land rounded on him. 'You think we don't know about you and Norah Haron? Your little liaison has jeopardized the entire investigation.'

May was appalled. 'My private life has nothing to do with any of this.'

'Are you honestly going to tell me you have no idea what she's been up to?' Land grabbed a handful of papers from his desk and thrust them at May. 'She's played you for a complete fool.'

'If I thought for a second that any sort of line had been crossed—'

'Oh, we're far beyond crossing a line now,' Land replied. 'When did she suddenly start contacting you again?'

May tried to think clearly. 'I'm not sure. About six weeks ago?'

'She set you up. When this gets out you'll be retired immediately. What on earth were you thinking?'

'Tell me what she's done,' May pleaded. But his heart already knew the answer. He had simply pushed the idea to the back of his mind.

Land could barely contain himself. He looked as if his eyes were about to burst. 'Do you need it spelled out for you? Haron pays her girls to keep their mouths shut, and is sleeping with you to obstruct the investigation.'

And there it was, the simple truth slapped down before him. May felt a terrible sliding sensation in the pit of his stomach. Everyone knew the PCU broke the rules and got away with it. How could he have allowed such a thing to happen?

'I've let you get away with every kind of rulebook infringement imaginable but this will go down as corruption, plain and simple,' Land said. 'Talk to Janice, not me. She's been out there trying to save your arse. When this comes down, you'd do well to remember how much you owe that woman.'

May left the office in a state of shock. The enormity of his failure had yet to sink in. He could not allow himself the luxury of examining it while Sparrow Martin's life was in danger. The only important thing now was to find her.

It is almost impossible to hurry law enforcement's foot soldiers. They work at their own pace from the start to the close of an investigation, and it is only with hindsight that the case adopts a finite shape. Its course is uniform, marked by stretches of inactivity and small bursts of advancement. Which is why, as Colin Bimsley sat down on a low garden wall beside his partner and carefully unwrapped a beef pie so that its guts didn't drop out, he possessed little sense of urgency. He and Meera had been set a task and were simply seeing it through, although it didn't stop them complaining.

'What's the point of doing interviews on a bloody industrial estate?' said Meera. 'Nobody lives here. You could die
screaming blue murder and not be heard. There's no physical
evidence left. Who have we talked to? Three security guards,
two dopeheads and a mad bloke dressed in a shower curtain.'
She accepted the pie from Colin and took a tentative bite.

'You heard what Dan said. He doesn't leave anything
behind. Even the petrol tank was clear.'

Meera considered the problem. 'He's got to be somewhere
nearby. Everything that's happened has been in a really tight
radius. You know how much store old Bryant sets by geog-
raphy. Sparrow Martin is twenty-three. She's strong and
healthy. She'd knock him unconscious. She won't do what he
wants unless he threatens her. He can't take her anywhere
without attracting attention.'

'Right,' Colin agreed. 'So he needs another spot like this,
where she can yell her head off without being heard. I can't
think of any places around here.'

'Tube tunnels.' Meera wiggled a piece of gristle from her
teeth.

'It's nine p.m. The stations will still be crowded – getting in
and out would be impossible. It has to be a private residence,
or a spot that's closed to members of the public.'

'How far away? Dan lifted some tyre tracks. Let me try
him again and see if he has a vehicle ID.'

While Meera checked with the unit, Colin wandered to the
rear of the warehouse. A thin but persistent rain was dropping through the lamplight. He blew on his hands and rubbed
them smartly, peering at a darkened doorway that he was
certain had been shuttered before. Some shadows were so
deep that they looked as solid as walls.

From within one a young black security guard in a boiler
suit pushed open a door. He was hauling an immense grey
plastic crate on wheels, trying to manoeuvre it outside. Colin

showed his ID and gave him a hand. 'This door was shut earlier,' he said. 'What's through there?'

'It's the garage for the club,' said the guard. 'I had to let the van out.'

'What van?'

'One of ours. We use it to transport audiovisual equipment. The club nights have different set-ups. The venue's a dry hire so the DJs bring in their own decks and use our sound system.'

'How long ago did the van go out?' Colin asked.

'A couple of hours, maybe longer.'

'Do you know who took it?'

'No idea. They have their own keys.'

'Have you got him on camera?'

'Her. It's usually a girl. We cover the front, not the bay.'

'So someone just rocked up and drove your van off.'

'There was a gig last night. It's normal.'

'And it's normal for you to not bother signing them out?' asked Colin. 'Unbelievable. Give me the licence plate.'

46

HOSTAGE

It took them less than half an hour to find the van. Suddenly everything kicked into a higher gear. At the PCU, Dan Banbury turned from his laptop. 'The vehicle's a white electric Nissan. It went down through Farringdon on to Charterhouse Street. It's now parked beneath the canopy of the Poultry Hall at Smithfield Market.'

'Get everyone there,' said Raymond Land. 'What's the matter?' He looked from Banbury's blank face to Longbright's. 'Let me guess. My most senior detective is missing, nobody knows where he is, he's not answering his phone, he may be attending a séance or conducting alternative-dimension experiments with a doomsday cult. Well, you don't need him. I want everyone *else* there now.'

'What, even you?' asked Renfield.

'We're short-handed. I would feel bad if anything went wrong and I wasn't there.'

'You heard the man,' said John May, grabbing his coat. 'I'll drive.'

'John, you need to stay here,' said Land.

'Not going to happen,' May told him. 'If you want to suspend me you'll have to do it formally.'

The roads were unusually clear. They found the van in the arched tunnel of West Poultry Avenue, abandoned beneath the sweeping baroque ironwork that hemmed the market. Standing on the corner waiting for them was an elderly man leaning on his special Malacca walking cane, the one topped with the demon skull. Bimsley called it Bryant's 'arresting stick' because he always seemed to have it on him at the end of a case.

'I couldn't go in without you,' Bryant said, welcoming them. 'These shoes are a bit too slippy for a staircase in the dark.'

'How did you know we'd be here?' asked May incredulously.

'It's a long story. Can I have a word?' He led May to one side of the pavement. 'Listen to me, John. You can't be involved in this.'

'Not you as well,' said May. 'I've already had the same conversation with Raymond. The hostage is in there somewhere. We need everyone we can get.'

'John, you have to stay in the car. Margot Brandy says that if you come in for this part, the case will be thrown out.'

'Arthur, I swear I had no idea—' May began. Arthur had never barred him from an investigation. The idea was unthinkable.

'Jack, can you take care of this?' Bryant asked over his shoulder.

Renfield stepped in. 'You need to get back in the car, Mr May.'

'I'm sorry, this is the way it has to be,' said Bryant. 'We'll talk later. Just stay here. Renfield, you come with us.' He beckoned to the others and they headed for the entrance to the charnel house.

Bryant leaned back, holding on to his trilby, and looked up

at the sky beyond the roof. The rain had halted and moonlight outlined the concrete dome of the market hall. Long ripples of silver cloud were imperceptibly stealing towards him.

'A fascinating area, this,' he said as the group walked into the main hall. 'Most Londoners don't realize it's a public market. I sometimes send Alma up here for a nice bit of brisket—'

'I'm not your partner,' said Raymond Land. 'Zip it.'

'What are we going to do?' asked Bimsley. 'I mean realistically? We're not trained for this sort of thing. We're unarmed, for a start.'

'So is Sparrow Martin,' said Bryant.

The ground-floor butchers' bays had been emptied out. The market was closed until Monday morning at 2.00 a.m., but the stone walls exhaled the fleshy smell of marbled meat, bones, blood and fat. At the rear of the empty stalls a broad concrete staircase led to the labyrinth beneath them.

Renfield shone a torch down into the brownish gloom. 'Are we seriously going down there?'

'Do you have a better idea?' Bryant asked, easing him aside with his cane and leading the way.

It was cold to begin with, but as they descended the temperature fell sharply. Stalactites the colour of decayed teeth had accreted around the ornate pillars and in the corners of the low ceiling.

Mangeshkar found a panel of ancient Bakelite light switches. Cage lamps cast out the shadows and illuminated a vast stone space, divided off into sections that stretched away from them. In the larger alcoves the chilled bodies of skinned bulls hung like sacrifices in a temple dedicated to the Roman gods.

'It's like the Lupanar of Pompeii in here,' said Bryant, awed.

'While you're at it, try to remember there's a maniac waving a spear about in here as well,' Land reminded him.

Bryant had not heard. He shone his torch into the nearest dark tunnel and wandered off along it.

'We're not splitting up,' Mangeshkar called after him. 'I've seen enough horror films to know that's a really rubbish plan.'

'Then we stay bunched together,' said Colin, edging forward, 'but we're going to look pretty silly from a distance.'

The scent of blood hung in the air, even though the meat had been drained in abattoirs before reaching the market. It took five hours to empty the blood from a cow, so the dirty work was long past. An iron tang remained despite the daily bleach-washes that were sluiced across the concrete floors. Only rabbits and fowl were delivered with their skins intact. Some of them were staring at the officers as they passed.

Meera could see her breath forming in front of her. The group walked slowly and quietly, and stayed close. All sound was deadened by the frozen carcasses. Most of the alcoves contained skinned cattle, their split trunks ready to be unhooked and slung across the shoulders of porters.

Some of the tunnels were unlit, and revealed their contents under torchlight. One was filled with the mechanically severed heads of sheep and goats. Their eyeless sockets and gleaming teeth reminded Bryant of a Last Judgement mural in a medieval church. Each corridor branched to others, all filled with corpses or steel band saws that could slice a full-grown bull in half.

Longbright tried to see into the tunnels but gave up. 'They look like they go on for ever. We don't even know if he's down here.'

'Oh, we know,' said Bryant, pointing at something sparkling in the middle of the floor. 'I imagine that belongs to the young lady we're looking for.' He poked his walking stick at a rainbow pencil with 'Sparrow' embossed in gold on one side.

Above ground, John May stormed back and forth between the car and the market entrance, waiting for someone at the unit to pick up his call. Finally, one of the two Daves answered.

'They've all buggered off, mate,' he said. 'Even that living statue with the comb-over who never does any work.'

May knew exactly what had happened. When the unit was cleared of personnel it could be searched. This was how Darren Link operated. 'Have you let in anyone from outside?'

'It's a funny thing,' said Dave One. 'The bell went and there was no one there. Then Dave Two walked around the corner and there he was, that scary bloke with the funny eye, just standing in the dark.'

'You let Darren Link in?'

'I was nuts-deep in an immersion heater when he turned up so I could only talk to him through the grille. He made a phone call, said something about sending his officers to deal with your problem. I guess you know what that means?'

'I have a pretty good idea,' said May, ringing off.

A panicked flight of pigeons turned him around. A pair of white ARVs had swung into the tunnel with squealing tyres and were pulling up behind him, their doors already half open, black boots and weapons appearing. *SCO19*, he thought. *Link's crew. How they love making an entrance.*

'Wait!' He ran towards them, holding out his hands. 'This isn't a terrorist threat. You can't go in there with firearms.'

Darren Link slid out of the passenger seat and lumbered towards him. 'We're in charge now, Mr May. Why don't you head back to your unit? You'll be more use there.'

'You don't understand,' said May. 'Our staff have already gone inside. They're searching the cellars right now. You can't send an armed response team in there.'

'They know who they're after.' Link looked back as his officers checked Heckler & Koch carbines and prepared to invade the storage cells. May noted that they were also packing handguns, shotguns and tasers.

'This is excessive force,' May said helplessly as two of the women started unloading a portable projectile launcher.

'You've got a multiple killer in there with a hostage and you're worrying about us using force on him?' said Link. 'Sounds like your famous liberal agenda is still in place at the PCU. These are trained marksmen; they know what they're doing.' Behind him, someone dropped one end of a battering ram on the kerb and swore.

'Let me get the others out first,' May pleaded, then realized that they were not contactable beneath a floor of solid stone and permafrost.

'You need to stay here and calm down,' Link warned, raising a hand. 'We know everyone in your team, who they are and what they look like. These lads and lasses don't make mistakes. But so you understand, if that bastard has done anything to his hostage they'll take him out.'

'*You* don't understand. Arthur's down there. Meera, Janice, even Raymond. They – they don't really know what they're doing.' He instantly regretted the remark, and knew that Link would file it away for later use.

The squad set off, marching into the market with Link in the lead barking commands. May was left to follow helplessly behind.

They were now past the centre of the market, beyond the intermittent illumination of the strip lights. Bryant shone his torch along the wall and searched for another set of switches, but they evaded him. Pale carcasses could be discerned at the farthest end, stacked like corded lumber.

In one of the dark partitioned sections serried pairs of eyes glittered. Bryant raised his pencil beam and found a fleshy pyramid of pigs' heads, smiling and imbecilic, laid out on a long steel table. He thought of Damien Hirst's golden statue of St Bartholomew, flayed alive but still standing in the nearby church. The area was obsessed with corporeal cravings.

He saw the blinding torch beams of the others and silently begged them to switch off. They were turning themselves into targets. Hugo Blake was trained to act with stealth, and down here nobody would have a phone signal. Slipping further into the penumbral dank, he waved his walking stick before him like a blind man.

'Why has everyone else got a torch except me?' Land complained.

'You don't normally come out of your office,' Meera whispered. 'Here, I've got a spare.'

Land flicked it on and trailed the beam around his feet. 'What's that?' The light had picked up a sheen of fine wire. 'Everybody stop!'

They looked about themselves and found that they had been enclosed by a length of copper wire that ran between four of the main pillars, set about two feet from the ground.

'Don't come any nearer,' called a man's voice. 'I'll have to kill her if you do. Don't touch the wire or we all go.'

'Do as he says,' said Banbury.

'What do you want?' called Land.

'An answer.'

'What's he talking about?' Land whispered loudly.

'Do you have Sparrow Martin with you?' Longbright asked.

'She's here.'

'Let her speak.'

'She can't. You'll have to take my word that she hasn't been harmed.'

'We need to hear her.'

The chamber fell silent.

'Now what?' asked Land.

It was Longbright who first became aware that the SCO team had swarmed around them on both sides. Ahead of them ran a familiar stocky figure. 'Watch out for the wires!' she shouted.

'Renfield, get back here,' called Darren Link.

'Stay where you are, you bloody traitor,' said Colin Bimsley.

'What's going on?' Land tried to see. 'Renfield, where the hell do you think you're going?'

'He's working for the Missing Link,' Colin explained. 'He's been bribed to get the dirt on us. He switched sides to the SCD because he'd rather be their delivery boy.'

Land saw a shape in the darkness. Jack Renfield appeared in front of Colin and swung a fist into him that connected squarely, lifting him from the ground. A moment later Bimsley was back on his feet and running at Renfield, slamming him into a pillar. Although they were of roughly equal height and build, there was a deep ferocity in Renfield's anger. Jack took him down in a tackle that sent them both sliding across the wet floor.

Darren Link's team moved in to pull them apart. 'Leave them,' said Link, waving his team on. 'Concentrate on your target. Everyone else, stay where you are. We're in charge now.' The snipers obeyed and moved ahead.

Renfield was up first and dragged Colin with him. His nose was bloodied but he was barely out of breath. He effortlessly lifted Bimsley off the ground. 'Do you know how much I hated being sent back to the unit?' he asked. 'Listening to you lot rabbit on about old books and paintings. Shall I tell you what an embarrassment you are to real police officers?'

'Do you have to?' Colin asked. 'It's kind of boring.'

Renfield's next punch was a jackhammer, so fast and powerful that it put a crack in Bimsley's jaw and sent him tumbling towards the wires that were strung between the columns. He landed between split sides of beef in the murk of an alcove.

'You should have left me alone,' Renfield warned, heading

after him with fists clenched. 'You won't be coming back to work after this.'

From the darkness a vengeful pig soared at him. A great porcine head smashed into the side of Renfield's face and flipped him on to the floor. Renfield tried to lift himself up, then passed out.

Colin emerged from the darkness, holding the pig's head by one huge ear. He dropped it on to Renfield's chest and spat out a bloody tooth.

Limping over to Meera, he glanced back at the prone body. 'It seemed appropriate,' he said.

47

CHAT

Bryant turned away from the commotion at the far end of the chamber and stared into the darkness.

'I need to talk to you,' he said softly. 'I know you're there. I'm not with the others, and I'm unarmed. I'm an old man. I can't hurt you.' There was no response, but he heard a rustle of movement in the dark. 'There cannot be another four a.m.'

'I'll only kill her if she's the one.'

'Let me talk to you.'

No response.

'Please, Mr Blake.'

Silence.

'It's not Blake, though, is it? Names are unimportant. It's Tidiman. I went to your flat. I'm sorry, I had to break in. I found the name in your son's schoolbook.'

It took him a while to reply. 'It was always used against me in the army. Tidy Man. Because I cleared up after the dead. After I got out I changed it. Don't come any closer. The wires surrounding your officers are attached to grenades.'

The rest of the chamber had fallen silent now. Bryant

remained still. Considering he usually broke or fell over Banbury's cordons, he had managed to spot and avoid the glinting copper wire that crossed the floor.

'I know why you did what you did. You murdered three innocent people and nearly killed a fourth, so you can't expect a sympathetic ear from anyone. Not even if they know about your past.'

'I need an answer before I let her go,' he replied. 'I want to know who killed my son.'

Bryant sighed and looked for somewhere to sit. His legs were aching. 'If I tell you what I know, will you set Miss Martin free?'

'I don't know. It depends.'

He found a plastic crate filled with sheep haunches and seated himself on the lid. Behind him he sensed Link's team waiting beyond the wire perimeter. 'It's going to hurt if we talk honestly about this.'

'I've always been honest.'

'If we can reach an agreement, if you acknowledge what I tell you and release Miss Martin, I promise I will talk to my people and make sure you get a fair trial. I'll make sure they listen to the facts without prejudice.'

No response.

'But first I need proof that Miss Martin is alive and well.'

There came the sound of ripping gaffer tape and a gasp. 'I'm OK, I'm fine,' said Sparrow, 'please don't let—' He held her close to him and smothered her words.

'All right.' Bryant set his walking cane aside. 'Let me catch my breath for a minute. I'm tired. Are you tired? It's freezing down here. This is doing my chalfonts no good at all. I hope Miss Martin is dressed warmly enough.' He paused for a moment, half expecting a response, but heard nothing. 'I know what happened to you, Hugo. Who put the scrapbook together, your wife?'

'My son.'

'I know it was never properly finished, but perhaps I can complete the picture. It started when you returned from Syria after being deployed to launch a ground assault in Damascus. You escaped from ISIS militants when their HQ was hit by a missile. Your wife left you, and subsequently died of a prescription-drug overdose. After you were discharged, you insisted you weren't suffering from PTSD, but received psychiatric help. Your son Sebastian was by then fifteen and living with a grandparent. He'd changed dramatically since you'd last spent any time with him, and right from the start, when he came to meet you at the station, the pair of you didn't see eye to eye. Stop me if I go wrong anywhere.'

The lack of response felt like a good sign.

'You thought his schoolfriends were a bad influence, so you moved him to the flat. It was just the two of you again. But it didn't work, because every time you saw Sebastian you lost your temper. You loved him but you couldn't control him. It became a battle of wills, and the more you threatened him the more he defied you. At first he only dressed and behaved in a genderless fashion around the flat, but then one morning he went to school dressed as a girl.'

He waited, holding his breath. Nothing. He continued.

'You'd fought for your country. Some of the people you knew were either dead or so traumatized that they could no longer function in civilian life. Now you were expected to be mindful of non-specific gender pronouns, and had to apply them to your only child.

'With his hair tied back Sebastian looked naturally feminine, and that only made it worse. The teachers were supportive and suddenly *you* were the enemy. You were in the wrong for not understanding. He told you that he had never been comfortable in his own body and started to talk about making the transition to female. Soon "he" was behaving as "she" all the time, failing exams and staying out at night, and you were powerless to change anything.'

Tidiman's voice was thick with emotion. 'All this stuff in the press about deciding whether you're male or female. We had a fight. I wouldn't let him go out dressed as a girl. I was supposed to accept it but I couldn't. He said I was still his father, that I was the one who had to change. I couldn't understand.'

'A perfectly reasonable reaction,' said Bryant quietly. 'The boy was headstrong and independent, like you, and trying to discover his own identity. He had his own battles to fight.' Behind him he could sense Darren Link's army, fidgeting and anxious.

'Do you know how many cyclists died on London roads last year?'

'Actually I do know that,' said Bryant, caught by surprise. 'Sixty-seven pedestrian and cyclist KSIs in Central London alone. That's "Killed and Seriously Injured". About a third of all pedestrian deaths go unreported, and some of the victims are never identified. Six cyclists lost their lives in a two-week period, two females, four males.'

'You know your statistics.'

'Statistics I'm good with. People, not so much. How old was your boy?'

'He had just turned seventeen. He wanted to become a doctor, to specialize in cardiothoracic surgery. It's something I would have done. He never got to live out that dream.' He sounded close to breaking.

'What happened? I didn't have time to find any details. Is Miss Martin all right?'

'She's here. She's fine.'

'Your son,' he prompted.

'He was on a rental bike. A truck jumped the lights and he went under it. The driver's warning system didn't work when he turned. One of his side sensors was out. He just didn't see the bike down there. A thirty-two-ton lorry full of audio equipment. It all got smashed when the load shifted, not properly tethered. His company was fined over the lack of safety checks. A slap on the wrist. Their lawyer tried to get the driver off the hook because he indicated correctly before turning.'

'You say he *tried*.'

'Before the bloods came back. High alcohol content in my son's, amphetamines in the driver's. He'd been working triple shifts to try and make up time, popping pills to keep himself awake. The verdict was death by misadventure. The ambulance crew were with my lad when he died. He told them it was his own fault for not looking properly. *His fault.* That's the kind of kid he was. Dying, and he didn't want to get anyone in trouble. I kept the remains of his bike. It was crushed flat. The London Transport Police tried to charge me for it. They apologized, said it was a computer error. The investigation was full of procedural mistakes. There were questions unanswered, gaps in the timing, details that didn't add up.'

Bryant tried to process the fresh information. 'There's something I don't understand. The pair of you were living just across the road from the club. Why did he need to rent a bike?'

Tidiman lapsed into silence again.

'You'd had a fight. He wasn't coming home, was he?'

'I don't know. I'll never know.'

'You retraced his steps to the Keys club and found out who he was with that night. You heard how he crossed paths with two strangers who took a cab together. You felt sure there was one person who could give you more answers; the one who stayed silent and heard everything. You traced Jagan Cheema and got into his taxi. What you didn't know was that Dhruv, his brother, had taken his place.

'You set out to scare Cheema into telling you how Sebastian had died but he didn't have the answers to your questions, and the more he denied it the more you tried to frighten him until he started to scream and you went too far and he was dead.' Although it was icy in the chamber, Bryant found he needed to wipe his brow. 'You questioned the others and got nothing. You knew how to frighten them but they didn't help you. How did you find the girls?'

'He had my book,' cried Sparrow. 'My bat book.'

For half a minute there was no sound.

'Rory Caine is alive,' said Bryant. 'I promise I'll take you to him under my custody, on the condition that you release her.'

Link had been sensible enough to make his team stay back while Bryant talked. There was a shuffle in the darkness and a young woman with a tear-streaked face walked slowly and unsteadily into Bryant's torch beam.

He took her hand and led her to Longbright, then returned to the dark. 'Come on, Hugo, let's get you out of here,' he said. 'We'll go and talk to the only one who can help you.'

A figure emerged from the shadows. The tattoos on his thick neck and heavily muscled arms were taken from William Blake's 'Jerusalem'. They showed men and gods, in divine fire and earthly chains. Blake looked like a man who would punch a wall to punish himself.

'Keep your promise,' he said. 'Take me to him.'

Bryant started to lead him out of the cellar but before he'd advanced more than a few feet Link's team began shouting and swarmed in, throwing Tidiman to the ground and locking his wrists behind his back.

'You promised, you son of a bitch, you promised!' Tidiman shouted, and continued to roar until one of the men stepped forward and knocked him unconscious.

'Let that be a lesson to you, Mr Bryant,' said Link, giving him a sympathetic pat on the back. 'Don't make promises you can't keep.'

48

ARREST

'It's our investigation,' Bryant said. 'If you take it from us now there will be no closure to the case.'

'You don't need to close it,' Link told him as they headed back up to the street. 'We have all we need for a conviction so the SCD can take it over. I'm sure it'll be a weight off your mind. Take your team back to the PCU. We'll clean up here.'

'I had a deal with Tidiman,' Bryant pointed out with indignation.

'We don't make deals with murderers, old man, you should know that. You know how many years you've been bending the laws to get your investigations into prosecution? How many blind eyes have been turned to make sure that your cases get closed? It won't happen any more.'

'Tell me,' said Bryant, 'if you had a chance to save a soul and could do it by moving a couple of legal decimal points, would you do it? Would you honour the intention of the law and disregard its letter?'

'The fact that you can even ask a question like that says it all.' Link turned away. 'Go home, Bryant, you did well to find him but your work is done.'

'Don't you even want to know how I found him?' Bryant called.

'I only care about the result,' said Link, heading back into the market to join his team members.

And that might have been the end of that if Longbright hadn't dashed up just as Bryant was trying to work the remote for the Kia. 'Rory Caine's gone,' she said. 'He took a set of car keys from another patient's locker and left the hospital. He's still in a serious condition.'

'Call the others,' Bryant instructed, 'we're not going back to the PCU.'

May came running. 'What the hell happened?'

'Darren Link used Renfield to double-cross us. They've taken over the case. And Caine's done a runner.'

'What do you want to do?'

The question seemed absurd to Bryant. There was only one thing he could do. 'We go after him,' he replied. 'Janice, go back to the unit and don't let anyone in.'

'Just me?' said Longbright. 'What about back-up?'

'You *are* the back-up.'

It didn't take Dan Banbury long to locate the vehicle Caine had taken because it turned out to be a customized silver Mitsubishi Outlander, and it was currently heading right past them. 'Can I call in a chopper?' he asked optimistically.

'No you can't,' said Raymond Land. 'Do you know how much I'd get charged for an ASU? Helicopters don't grow on trees.' They swung out of the junction and on to the busy embankment road, amid warnings of roadworks.

Dan Banbury struggled to keep his laptop balanced on his knees. 'Why is he running?'

'I don't know about you,' said Bimsley, holding a hand over his damaged jaw, 'but if an ex-military bloke armed with a razor-sharp pastry cutter decided to take me out in a tactical operation I'd be bricking it.'

'Keep a lookout for the vehicle,' said Banbury. 'He should be just ahead on the left.'

They couldn't have missed the Outlander. It was trying to cut into the embankment's inside lane, pushing back the plastic barriers as it did so. A chaotic funnel of slowed traffic formed as the coned-off lanes narrowed.

'They're working on Blackfriars Bridge,' said May. 'He'll have to turn off.'

Meera appeared alongside them on her Kawasaki, waving a warning. Ahead was a carnivalesque maze of cones, tape, barriers, drainpipes and mounds of paving stones. Their flashing blue lights merely added to the surreal atmosphere.

Caine's vehicle suddenly lurched left, taking Queen Victoria Street. May spun the wheel, fighting for purchase on the rain-slick tarmac, then bumped over the kerb. Clenching his teeth, he urged the Kia forward, scraping it through a slim space between an Audi and a Mercedes, taking the paintwork off all three vehicles.

'You must be due for another driving test by now,' said Land unhelpfully.

Caine turned left up St Andrew's Hill, heading towards St Paul's Cathedral, but May kept the Kia close behind. On Ludgate Hill the Outlander found itself behind a queue of vehicles backed up from the traffic lights, so it crossed the central divide and dodged oncoming traffic.

The shocked driver of an Oddbins van coming from Mansion House slammed on his brakes when he saw the Outlander heading straight at him. His tyres air-pocketed and his vehicle slid through a forty-five-degree turn. Faced with a head-on collision, Rory Caine tried to swerve and lost control. Meera turned, putting her motorcycle between them. With its only escape route removed, the Outlander slammed up against a signpost, causing the post to snap off and land across the roof of the Kia. Everyone inside scrambled out on to the road. Colin Bimsley was ready to wrestle Caine into handcuffs, but it wasn't necessary. Caine's right leg was pinned by the car's stoved-in door, and he wasn't going anywhere.

An ambulance started to make its way through the backed-up traffic. Two small boys took selfies with the buckled Outlander.

Bryant rummaged in his pockets and made his way over to the car's shattered window. He peered in at Caine. 'It shouldn't take long for them to get you out. Are you all right?'

'I'm suing you,' said Caine.

'Oh good, we love being sued. You can come back to us for questioning first. Would you like a sherbet lemon?' He unstuck one from its bag. 'Excuse fingers.'

Caine shut his eyes in disgust and turned aside.

'As a matter of interest, why did you run?'

'There's a bleeding madman after me,' he yelled at Bryant. 'He already tried to kill me once.'

'As a matter of interest, where were you planning to go?'

Caine grimaced in pain. 'Victoria didn't come and visit me at the hospital. Nobody came. I could have died. You'd think somebody would care. I was going to go home, back to my flat. I just wanted to be somewhere safe.'

'And you don't think that's the first place he would have come looking for you? Incredible.' Bryant crunched his sherbet lemon. 'If you don't mind my saying so, you don't deserve visitors.'

Caine's panicked flight had used up the last of his energy, and he passed out.

At 11.00 a.m. the following day they reconvened at St Thomas'. Ellen Shaw, the ward sister, had been overruled in her attempt to keep visitors away from her patient because the presence of Link's team in Smithfield allowed interrogation under the Counter-Terrorism Act.

After losing his bout with Bimsley, Jack Renfield absented himself. While the Smithfield operation was being closed up, John May was quarantined in his office, leaving Bryant and Land to go to St Thomas' Hospital. They found Rory Caine sitting up in bed looking ready for a fight.

'Please forgive this unorthodox arrangement,' said Bryant as the others settled themselves. 'Mr Caine, I have your statement but I wanted you to answer questions in front of everyone. I see you've pulled quite a few stitches but I'm not allowing you painkillers just yet as we need you with a clear head. I'll try to keep it short. I brought you some grapes.' He dropped a wrinkled paper bag on to the bed. Caine shot him a filthy look.

'It's not our investigation any more so keep it brief,' Land instructed his detective.

'I know that, Raymondo, but don't you want the satisfaction of understanding what happened?'

'For God's sake get on with it.' Land folded his arms huffily.

Bryant loosened his scarf and brushed sherbet from his shirt in elaborate sweeps. He would not be hurried.

'Mr Caine, on October the twenty-seventh at the Keys club you met Sebastian Tidiman, who was at the time in female attire. He was delicate-featured and more convincing as a female than a male, and he knew it. He had explained to his father that he wanted to be considered for gender transition, and they argued about it. Sebastian required parental permission because he was not yet eighteen. He was anxious to start the process. On the night you met him, he proceeded to get drunk and flirt with you at the club. And you responded.'

'I bloody did not,' said Caine.

'We have witnesses who are prepared to testify that you

did,' Bryant continued. 'For the purposes of this conversation I'm referring to Sebastian as a man as he died before transitioning. Do tell me if I'm not being politically correct in my use of gender terms. My father was born during the reign of King Edward. I'm doing my best to adapt. Sebastian was pretty good with his phone. He took a selfie of you kissing him and then another of you taking drugs in the lavatories – did you know he uploaded them? We didn't, unfortunately. A bit of an age-gap problem there, I think. The young are always one step ahead. I can't imagine you were thrilled to discover that your adoring young acolyte was of the wrong biological persuasion. But by this time he was incredibly drunk and you couldn't get rid of him.'

He sat down opposite Caine. 'Tell you what, why don't you take over from here?'

'What do you want me to say?' Caine slumped back into his pillows. 'I already told you. Luke couldn't find an Uber so he booked through a taxi company who had flyers in the club. When the car turned up it was a pooler with two girls in it.'

'Sparrow Martin and Augusta Frost. Jagan Cheema was driving. Please go on.'

'We were about to leave when – what did you say his name was?'

'Sebastian, but you knew him as . . . ?'

'Vi. That's what she told me. She came running up to the car just as we were reversing, and we bumped her. She fell over because she was drunk, not because the car hit her. It was nothing, just a graze, but she made a big drama out of it and hobbled back to the club. I could see her sitting on the pavement around the corner from the entrance, sitting the way a man sits, but in a dress and leggings, with her head tilted back, smoking, the smoke drifting up through the lights.'

'At this point did you have any idea—?'

'No, none, I swear. I went back to make sure she was all right, and I think maybe that was what I was going to do, just check, you know? But when I got there I remembered the photos and put my hand inside her jacket to take the phone. That's when I realized she was a man. And I lost it. I took a swing at her – him. Just one sideswipe.'

'Where? I mean, where on his body?'

'I kicked him in the head,' said Caine, as if it was obvious.

'You kicked the person you had kissed earlier in the head, walked away and got back into the taxi.'

'I was angry. I didn't like being made a fool of.' Caine closed his eyes. 'Can you go now? I need some painkillers.'

Bryant ignored him. 'After you left in the taxi, your victim got back up and walked away. He couldn't have been thinking clearly, because he collected a hire cycle and headed in the opposite direction to where he lived. There's no indication that he set off with a destination in mind. He managed to get as far as Camden Road before he blacked out and came off – right in the path of an oncoming truck. When his father began digging into the official accident report he found anomalies – one of which was the failure to explain a bruise on the side of his son's head consistent with a kick. Tidiman suspected it was the kick that killed him, not the lorry. He started looking into his son's secret nightlife, and came to understand what Sebastian had been going through. His son had tried to play a normal male role in society and failed. We know now that he had taken advice from self-help groups and online forums. He tried everything he could think of to arrive at an answer, and he did it alone because he was convinced he could not ask for his father's help. We have this ingrained idea that we should be independent and self-sufficient. We're so stubborn. It damages us.' Bryant leaned forward and helped himself to some grapes. 'Tidiman was sure that the traffic police investigation was incompetent and incomplete. His son had sustained the injury to his head somewhere else, *before* he got on the bike. So he reverse-engineered the night's events, and arrived back at the club, where the incident with the taxi had occurred.

'But he didn't know which of the passengers had committed the assault because the most crucial pieces of information were impossible to come by. Nobody knew whether the girls had got out of the vehicle, so they remained under suspicion. But others were sure that the two lads and the driver had all got out. That made a total of five suspects. Nobody else outside this group knew anything about what had happened, which is why we had such trouble getting a lead. Tidiman behaved in the only way he knew how: he captured and interrogated them one by one. But as so often happens, it all got out of hand. Luke Dickinson blamed the driver because he knew who the real culprit was. He'd seen Rory here get out of the car and run off into the building's shadow, returning moments later, but he threw suspicion on the driver to protect his friend.'

'He wasn't my friend,' Caine muttered. 'In his mind maybe.'

'Wait, what about the photos on the trannie's phone?' asked Land.

'Nobody knew they were there except Mr Caine. Sebastian had used his female identity in a separate online account,' said Bryant.

'Then how on earth did you find them?' asked Banbury. 'You can't operate a toaster.'

'I had the idea when I saw the boy's bedroom,' Bryant explained. 'First there was a shoe. It was on the floor far under the bed, silver with a heel, like Cinderella's. Then on one of the walls was the photograph of a bust of a young Roman, identified as Sporus, a freedman. I knew a little about him, that the emperor Nero had ordered him castrated and had married him. I knew that Sporus had appeared in public in the wedding regalia of Nero's former wife, Poppaea, and that he had committed suicide before the age of twenty. Sebastian was seventeen when he died. It was an unlikely thing for a schoolboy to put on a bedroom wall. But then I realized that all of the posters had some kind of connection to gender and sexuality. And I saw the schoolbooks by his bed. He was studying *Twelfth Night* in his drama class. The play in which Sebastian becomes Viola. "One face, one voice, one habit, and two persons, A natural perspective, that is and is not." I began to think that the problem had started with the son. I tried to see how the events of the evening might have unfolded at the club if there had been an extra girl around – and of course there was.'

'Good luck proving that in court.' Caine raised a single finger to Bryant and gave a sour grin.

49

ENDING

'"Past and to come seems best; things present worst,"' said Arthur Bryant. 'The Archbishop of York says that in *Henry IV Part 2*. Nine words to sum up the world.'

It was, he decided later, the most miserable night of his life, and he'd had plenty of others with which to compare this one. John May sat at his desk, constricted and uncomfortable before his partner. They both looked exhausted. Rain battered their office window; water was pooling beneath the rotten frame and dripping on to the carpet tiles.

'You can see why I had to cut you from the investigation, John. Norah Haron was about to be arrested for fraud, obstruction of justice and withholding evidence. I was afraid you'd be subpoenaed for her trial, and I didn't know if there was anything more to come out. You must have known how risky it could be to get involved with her, yet you still went ahead.'

'I didn't think it through,' said May. 'We've always done things differently here. We've always ignored the rules.'

'But not like this. Now they have a perfectly valid reason

for closing us down. This time there's a trail leading right to our doorstep.'

'It's not right,' said May doggedly. 'Our intentions—'

'It doesn't matter what our *intentions* were. On top of everything else, you were consorting with a woman who was connected to a Russian felon currently under investigation. You know what they say, the wife of Caesar must be above suspicion.'

'I don't know anyone who says that,' said May, looking like a whipped dog. 'I don't know anyone who says anything you say.'

'John, listen to me. Darren Link is a ghastly human being but his moral rectitude is admirable. Ultimately his decision is right. Haron withheld information from you that put other lives in danger. All right, you weren't to know—'

May looked up at the open case files on his shelf that he was sure he would never be able to complete. 'I didn't want to know. Of course I realized she couldn't be trusted; I chose not to look. I stopped being suspicious because I didn't want to lose her.' He looked shamefacedly up at his partner. 'I've made a complete fool of myself. I failed you. I failed the unit. My career is over. Blaize Carter wants nothing more to do with me. What else could happen?'

'I hope your boiler breaks down,' said Bryant. 'You bloody stupid idiot. Land won't let you stay. He wants you off the premises tonight. If it was just up to me I'd find a way to put this behind us, but it's not. I can try and talk to Link. There's not much point in seeing Leslie Faraday, bearing in mind how much he hates us for getting the parks reopened and ruining his privatization scheme. I'll talk to Margot Brandy and find out what your chances are in court, but the unit will go. Did you know the *Hard News* website keeps a tote scoreboard on us? I've seen it. It's headed "Peculiar Crimes Unit – Monthly Survival Odds".'

May raised a hand. 'Arthur, don't, please. I'll take whatever they throw at me. I've ruined everything.' He looked down into his desk drawers. 'There's nothing I need to take with me. I have no personal items. It's all work.'

He stood and looked about himself. Collecting his elegant navy blue overcoat, he took a grey silk scarf from the sleeve and knotted it around his neck. 'I don't know what to say. It's probably the last time I'll ever see this place.'

'Stop being so melodramatic,' snapped Bryant, 'you're not Susan Hayward. You'll see me again when all this has blown over. I doubt we'll hold on to the building, though, so I may end up back in Battersea Park poisoning the pigeons.' He looked about the office. 'Did you know Faraday owns a property development company? Apparently it's identified this Victorian dosshouse as a prime site. King's Cross is becoming fashionable. Who would ever have thought it? I never imagined that the two Daves would outlast the unit. They'll probably be inherited by the next tenants like ghosts.'

May picked up a mug that read 'Keep Calm or I will use my Cop Voice', and dropped it into the bin. 'What will you do?'

Bryant adopted a look of hopeful cheer. 'There are *plenty* of things I can do. I'll finally have the time to attend library readings, hang around museums frightening children, visit art galleries and the theatre and – gosh you're right, what *am* I going to do? I could become a consulting detective like Sherlock Holmes. It's perfect; you can be Watson, Alma is Mrs Hudson and Raymondo will be Inspector Lestrade. We'd have plenty of Moriartys to choose from.'

He looked up and found Janice standing at the door with a look of devastation on her face. 'Oh, not you too. I'm trying to lighten the mood. If you're going to start leaving tissues full of snot and post-war lipstick all over the place—'

'Raymond says we've had the case taken away from us. I thought it was just the usual threat.'

'Not this time,' said Bryant. 'John's leaving.'

Longbright's face dropped even further. 'John, you can't go.'

'I can't stay, Janice. It's not up to Arthur.'

'But there's no unit without you. What will happen to the rest of us if you two don't stay together?'

'Oh, for God's sake.' Bryant had always been the enemy of sentiment. 'He can't be here, Janice. The investigation has to be handled by an impartial party now. The files have already been turned over. Our evidence can't be included in the case.'

'That's ridiculous,' said Longbright. '*You're* the one who always ignored the rules. John and I always had to find ways of justifying your methods. You've built entire investigations on inadmissible evidence, unsanctioned procedures, unreliable witnesses, crime scene contamination – and you've never filled in a form correctly in your life.'

'This is different. John has destroyed a trust.'

May was not used to hearing his partner like this, but was hardly in a position to argue.

'It sounds as if you agree with them,' said Longbright. 'John made a mistake but he's still the same person. We all still support him—'

'But *they* don't.' Bryant jabbed an index finger at the chain-of-command card pinned on their wall. 'He's played into their hands. They won't even pick up the phone to me.'

'Arthur, I didn't lie to you,' said May. 'If I'd known what Norah was prepared to do to protect her territory—'

'You *should* have known,' Bryant came back. 'You didn't see that she was exploiting your biggest weakness.'

'If you knew, why didn't you stop him?' Longbright asked. 'John has shielded you hundreds of times. Why didn't you do the same for him?'

'We don't need to discuss this any more,' said May, tightening the belt of his coat. 'It's OK, I'm leaving. They made the right choice, Arthur. But you could have stopped me from making the wrong one.'

He closed the door quietly, leaving Longbright staring furiously after him.

Raymond Land was not at all happy that his most senior detective had used his knowledge of Shakespeare and Roman sculpture to catch a murderer. It made a mockery of the entire law enforcement process. Darren Link was even more upset when he read the case details, but had the grace not to let it influence official proceedings. Despite his tough stance on law enforcement his judgements were based on evidence, not prejudice.

Land found himself in the uncomfortable position of having to side with Bryant. The case would now reach the Crown Prosecution Service via the Serious Crime Directorate, who had more chance of securing a conviction.

'Raymondo, you do understand that my hands were tied?' said Bryant, wandering into his office. 'If I had stayed silent, the investigation of Norah Haron would have continued anyway and she would have thrown John to the wolves. I was between Scylla and Charybdis.'

'I don't care if you were between Bond Street and Marble Arch, you've put seven people out of work and pushed Renfield to the opposite side. You wouldn't survive five minutes without the unit, and you know it. You're like those teachers who retire and promptly drop dead. The sheer boredom of being stuck in your flat with that landlady of yours singing hymns all day would send you mad. How is she?'

'They're letting her go home. She has to take it easy for a while.'

Land grunted. Bryant could see him struggling to think. 'Look, can't you pull off some kind of last-minute rescue?' he cried finally. 'You've done it enough times before.'

'In the past I had something to bargain with,' Bryant pointed out. 'I'd need to get the investigation back under our control, and the only way I'd be able to do that is if I could introduce new evidence. Unfortunately, they have everything they need now. I'm afraid it's too late, old sausage.' He dropped his hat on to his head. 'This is a sad day for all of us.'

John May did not leave immediately. He returned to the unit some time later and sat in his office armchair looking across at his partner's desk. Tilting his head, he examined the dog-eared books Bryant had carelessly stacked on his unused laptop: *Pioneers of Portuguese Waste Disposal*, *Wallpaper & Arsenic in the Victorian Home*, *Dismantling Belief Systems with Anthropological Witchcraft*, *A Guide to the Comparative Lengths of Airport Runways*, *Advances in Recreational Pharmaceuticals*, *Viennese Road Signs*, *The Forgotten Monarchs of Lithuania*, *Early Canadian Carpet Manufacture*, *Bats of the British Isles*. A slim volume sat on top filled with red and green sticky notes. It had small type along its edge that he could not read. He turned it around: *The Humanist Approach to Successful Working Partnerships*.

He was about to remove it from the pile and see which sections Bryant had marked when the door opened.

'I knew I'd find you here,' said Norah Haron. 'You're easy to predict.' She had her hair pinned up and was wearing a black business suit, perhaps subconsciously rehearsing for a court appearance. In her right hand was a modestly unobtrusive 9-mm Luger handgun.

May stared at the gun. The handle appeared to be engraved. 'Please tell me your Russian didn't get that personalized for you,' he said. 'How did you get in?'

'I've seen better security systems in nurseries,' she replied. 'I came by to tell you I'm leaving. It's all over.'

She fired twice.

The first bullet caught May in the chest and sent him out of his chair. She had decided that two bullets would be enough. He fell heavily, cracking his head against the bookcase. There was a sudden amount of blood, on the floorboards, on the wall.

After, she dropped the gun on to the floor and kicked it over to him. The unit was so incompetent that they would probably put it down as a suicide. Taking out her phone, she rang Bryant's number. Naturally he failed to answer, so she left a message.

Then she drew breath with as much dignity as she could muster and walked out of the unit just as the others came running.

50

NEXT

It had been bothering Bryant ever since he had managed to get hold of Sebastian Tidiman's medical report. On his way over to the Barbican he read through the notes again, and his puzzlement grew. The blow to the boy's head had left bruising and swelling, but the coroner and the EMT had disagreed about the cause of death.

Finding the right flat took longer than his tube journey from King's Cross; the housing complex inside the Barbican was notoriously impossible to navigate. He wanted to catch Sparrow Martin by surprise, which he certainly managed. When she saw him peering at her through the ground-floor window she screamed. She was in her bra and knickers.

'Sorry about that,' he said, gratefully accepting her offer of an armchair. 'I had trouble finding you.'

'Everybody does.' She smiled in apology, straightening her sweater. 'Barbican.'

'I wondered how you were doing?'

'OK, I suppose. I'm having trouble sleeping. I know he

killed people but I still feel something for him. I know it's wrong and I shouldn't. But losing his son like that . . .'

'Which rather brings me to why I'm here.' Bryant removed the medical documents from his tartan duffel bag. 'I found something in Sebastian Tidiman's autopsy report. Some confusion over how he died. Tell me, how is your brother doing?'

'My brother?' Sparrow looked surprised. She rarely told anyone about him. 'He can't work. He has panic attacks.'

'Is he here right now?'

'No, he's staying at a friend's in Crouch End. Frankly, I'm glad to have him out of the flat.'

Bryant put on his trifocals and peered over the top of them. 'Can you trust him?'

She thought for a moment. 'No. If you do that you end up being let down a lot. He's trying to get clean.'

'He has quite a history of substance abuse, doesn't he? I ran a check on him.'

'He's a good kid, he just has some serious problems he won't face,' said Sparrow. 'Why?'

Bryant folded his hands in his lap. 'Did you ever hear of a pharmaceutical called Liquid O?'

'No, I don't think so.'

'I fear I'm not making myself terribly clear. Let's go back to the night of the taxi ride. Would you mind?'

'Not if it will help.' Intrigued, she settled herself before him, her hands resting in her lap.

'If I've got the order right, Rory Caine remained behind and kicked Sebastian in the head for impugning his manhood, then you checked on him and went back to the car, and finally the driver, Cheema, went back and found him gone, yes?'

'It's hard to remember the exact order of things,' said Sparrow. 'We'd been drinking and it was late. There was no real reason for remembering the night at all.'

'I understand. Could you talk me through exactly what

happened when you went from the car to the club building to look at Sebastian?'

'We thought he was a girl.'

'I know that. Just tell me what passed between you.'

Sparrow shifted anxiously. 'Um, she – it makes me feel more comfortable saying "she" because he didn't look masculine – she was crying and holding her head. I thought she was making a bit of a fuss, to be honest – you know, playing the victim. She said something about not being able to see.'

'You didn't know that Mr Caine had just kicked her.'

'I assumed she was just seeing double, but I gave her my eye drops. I wear disposable contacts. It was the only way I could think of helping.'

'And what happened? Did you administer them or did she?'

'She did.'

'Then she gave them back to you?'

'Yes.'

'Had you used them that evening?'

'No.'

'Do you have them now?'

'I think so. I've been using another bottle.' She rose and went to her bedroom, returning with a small white plastic bottle. Bryant took it from her and examined it. He opened the top and touched it to his tongue.

'I'm afraid these aren't eye drops,' said Bryant. 'You picked up your brother's bottle by mistake. Liquid O is a form of tar heroin, and now there's a way of administering it suspended in a clear solution. Sebastian put heroin in his eyes. He was in a stupefied state from the excessive amount of alcohol he had consumed, and had been knocked over, then further concussed by Caine. His medical notes seemed to indicate the possibility of a heroin overdose, but a second test proved negative, probably because it was done a considerable length of time after the first.'

'My God. You're saying I was the one who killed him?' Sparrow looked horrified.

'It was a combination of misfortunes. Rory Caine became violent after discovering Sebastian's gender, you got out the eye drops because of the attack and Sebastian attempted to cycle off because he'd been drugged. A disastrous set of circumstances. It wasn't murder.'

'I remember grabbing the bottle before I went out. It was on the kitchen counter. This is awful. I would never hurt a fly.'

'You didn't do it deliberately but there may be consequences. You'll have to make a formal statement.'

'Of course.' Sparrow's hands were trembling with the shock.

As Bryant left the flat and searched for a way out of the complex, he felt confident that the new information would be enough to close the case. He also knew it would not restore the investigation to them. He was heading from the Barbican to University College Hospital when he picked up a message on the phone Dan Banbury had reluctantly lent him.

He listened to Norah Haron's hard-edged voice. 'Now you can say you were right about me all along, Mr Bryant. At four fifty-two this afternoon I shot your partner John May dead.'

He tried calling the unit but only got voicemail messages. Distracted, he boarded a Metropolitan Line tube and went one stop too far. Instead of going back, he alighted and slowly climbed the brass-edged station steps, unsure of where he was. Traffic, rain, hedges, trees; the next few minutes passed in a daze.

Arthur Bryant found himself standing in Regent's Park, near the fountain in the evergreen formal gardens, not sure where to go next or what to do. Time folded over itself. Was he here in the present or far back in the past?

Rain-worms ran across his spectacles and dripped from the brim of his hat. Rain ticked and pattered in the branches overhead. On either side of the lawn the serried bushes drooped in shame as if being punished. Scarlet cyclamen, lemon eranthis and winter jasmine shone wetly beneath the trees. There was no one to be seen in any direction. Perhaps he would just stay there, he thought, until the garden's lush green tendrils reached out and consumed him, mulching him into the brown clay soil of London.

He tried to make sense of it. Despite the fact that the unit was now a crime scene, the end would probably be a strangely undramatic affair.

A formal government notice hand-delivered from the Home Office, a private meeting between Raymond Land and Leslie Faraday, ugly conference rooms filled with strange new faces, registered letters mailed to all members of staff, formal notices, sequestered files, new locks on the front door of the PCU.

Rather than being blown up or burned to the ground, the unit would be quietly closed down and left to gather dust in silent disgrace. It was too much to bear. When next he walked through King's Cross he would be forced to avert his eyes as he passed the building.

But despite all this he was not broken. There was damage, and damage could be repaired. So long as there was hope he did not feel truly lost.

John May is alive. I have no doubt about that. Norah Haron lied. It's the only way she knows how to survive.

He repeated the mantra, over and over. *John May is alive, and this is how I know. For years we've been fed lies. We've been told there is no such thing as community, that we are all alone. But it's not true. We can overrule officials and governments and everyone whose purpose it suits to keep us all apart and powerless. We can defy convention and join together, John and Janice and Dan and Colin and Meera – even Raymond – because together we are stronger.*

John is not dead.

Concentrate on one thing at a time, he decided, forcing himself to break out of his reverie. Alma was due to be released, and would need help. *Do that first, take care of her,* he told himself, *then go on to the next thing. Why? Because it's what we do.*

We go on to the next thing.

And the next.

And the next.

Stamping his soaked boots on the path until he could feel his feet again, he began to walk. Fast, then faster, thrashing at weeds with his stick and picking up speed as he headed off through the glimmering avenue of elms and beeches, back to the people with whom he had shared so much of his life.

Bryant and May will return

ACKNOWLEDGEMENTS

This is probably the most fun I've had yet with a Bryant & May novel, but I couldn't do it alone. If there's such a thing as an amiable murder mystery, it's because my editor Simon Taylor keeps this intangible quality in the edit. Like a judge honouring the intention of the law rather than following its fine print, he brings a good-natured stability to my ravings. My agent James Wills supplies a further dose of bonhomie, doubtless inherited from our merry mentor Mandy Little. Rounding out the team are Kate Samano and Richenda Todd, who add a lightness of touch to the text. If you've read this far, I can admit it now: I have no idea what will happen next. I'll work it out. Trust me, I'm a writer. You can find me on Twitter @peculiar and on my website, christopherfowler.co.uk.

Christopher Fowler is the author of more than forty novels (including the universally adored Bryant and May mysteries) and short story collections. A winner of multiple awards, including the coveted CWA 'Dagger in the Library', Chris has also written screenplays, video games, graphic novels, audio plays and two acclaimed memoirs, *Paperboy* and *Film Freak*. His most recent non-fiction book is *The Book of Forgotten Authors*. Chris divides his time between London's King's Cross and Barcelona. You can find out more by visiting his website – www.christopherfowler.co.uk – and following him on Twitter @Peculiar.

For more information on Christopher Fowler and his books,
see his website at www.christopherfowler.co.uk
Twitter @Peculiar